TRAITOR

By E.A. STEWART

LEGENDS OF VALERÓS SERIES
Wheel and Serpent: 1
Traitor: 2
Hero: 3

ACCIDENTAL HERETICS SERIES
Book 1: *Bone-mend and Salt*
Book 2: *Trebuchets in the Garden*
Book 3: *Crux Lunata*
Book 4: *Song of Valerós*
The Mad Woman of La Catalane: A Novella
The Blue Door… and More Accidental Heretics Tales

Writing as Annie Pearson:
RESTORATION RULES SERIES
No One Dies
Reap Justice

RAIN CITY INCIDENTS SERIES
The Grrrl of Limberlost
Artemis in the Desert
Nine Volt Heart
The Pirate King

TRAITOR

LEGENDS OF VALEROS: 2

E.A. STEWART

Jūgum Press

For Jacyn, always.

"Of all the animals, the boy is the most unmanageable, inasmuch as he has the fountain of reason in him not yet regulated."
— Plato

Est-ce que personne ne me débarras de ce prêtre turbulent?"
("Will no one rid me of this turbulent priest?")
— Henry II of England (oral tradition)

TRAITOR

The Languedoc, 1214

BECAUSE OF THE EUROPEAN CRUSADES in the Outremer, the area that we now call the Languedoc in southern France became quite wealthy, first serving as one of the departure points for crusaders setting out to capture Jerusalem, and then benefiting from the trade and science the crusaders brought home, spawning an early renaissance.

In 1209, armies from the Pays de France invaded the Languedoc, an action called by Pope Innocent III to defeat a popular dualist heresy that is now often called Catharism. Carcassonne — still called Carcassona then — was the second city that came under siege during the first summer of the invasion. The prelate-soldier Arnau Amalric began the siege, but Carcassonne defeated itself with disease and hunger, unable either to keep itself clean or endure the siege. The conquering French forces expelled the former citizens, and then made sure the new inhabitants could walk freely and sleep peacefully.

From Pentecost to Michaelmas — the fighting season, May to September — French knights descended into the Languedoc as crusaders, and the ever-industrious Simon de Montfort rode among French forces in the field, too busy to visit Carcassonne often.

The king of Aragón, Pedro II, sought to establish peace for the Languedoc through a diplomatic relationship with Simon de Montfort, the French knight who had been made viscount of Carcassonne. Pedro promised his young son Jaume in marriage to Simon's infant daughter. Then, following royal customs, Pedro put Jaume under Simon's care for his son's education.

A Reconquista hero after the Battle of Las Navas de la Tolosa in Andalusia, Pedro came to the Languedoc in 1213 to support the southern lords in their resistance to Simon de Montfort's ongoing aggressions. But Pedro died in the first battle.

By 1214, the Languedoc rocked in chaos and fear.

1
Fiefs d'Argent

The Noble King pressed his fingers in prayer.
'You risked all for your lord and comrades.
I name you Knight of the Realm
With lands, knights, and a banner.
May the great martyr, St-Denis,
Bless all your doings, Sir Balthazar.'

Tuesday, 13 May 1214, Carcassona

AT SUNRISE, WHEN THE PRIME bell rang, Orlando the night-marshal ceased chanting the Song of Balthazar and finished walking widdershins along Carcassona's defensive wall, the fourth and last time for that night's duty, which only meant verifying that the *gardes du corps* at each tower were present and, perhaps, awake.

Orlando wanted more. He was owed more. Simon de Montfort, the lord to whom Orlando had sworn his loyalty, had returned to Carcassona the night before. On this day, at last, Simon would remember the promises he made to Orlando years past. And then Orlando could begin his true life.

"They say since Simon returned to Carcassona last night…"

Every rumor and wishful fantasy in Carcassona, whether among the French peacekeepers or the local workers, began with that same phrase, *They say*. If gossip were worth gold…they say every man would be rich as a king.

"They say we'll all get battle-duty pay."

3

Unlikely. Orlando knew what battle-duty meant—and the last battle fought here was a brush fire in the abbot's pasture at Michaelmas. Besides, who'd believe a rumor from a slovenly guard whose kit was filthy?

The indolent men of the *gardes du corps* were lured south by promises of booty for destroying heresy, but now they merely patrolled clean, peaceful streets in a strange land, bored and behaving badly. At the gates, guards did the morning task of searching dayworkers for weapons and contraband, while repeating rumors.

"They say Simon intends to wipe out the last of the heretics this season, now that the king of Aragón isn't around to stop him."

They said that last year, but voiced this time by a pudgy, rat-faced guard whom Orlando caught in an after-curfew dice game every week. Too many years on a foreign posting like Carcassona, you begin to hear the same rumors, the same way that the mistral wind can be counted on to blow each spring, leaving you feeling desultory and dirty rather than swept clean, ready for the next fighting season.

"They say Simon got the pope to issue a—what d'you call it?—an edict. Now the law says that women here with property cannot marry a local seigneur or knight."

Another guard voiced today's brilliant rumor, a man from the Paris suburbs who spoke at a shout, even if you stood right beside him.

"So each lovely must choose to ride a dragon who speaks God's own French or suffer in a lonely bed?"

"That's what they say."

The most ridiculous of rumors always began *They say Simon got the pope to—*

One guard held a young woman by her shoulders while his comrade groped, dipping his hand into the woman's bodice.

"Arrête!"

Orlando growled for the guards to stop, hoping his deep voice had an effect. The cold mistral blew over him as soon as he stepped away from the shelter of the wall. He advanced on the guards, who only grimaced, annoyed, when he approached.

"These women wash your hose and breeches," Orlando said. "Don't waste time searching people you know. Let them get to their chores."

He touched his night-marshal's badge, to draw their attention, though it was only slush-cast lead, with no more authority than a pilgrim's souvenir. He had no power to discipline any man on night patrol, only to set the duty rolls and report problems to the guards' commander—which felt like disloyal sniveling, far beneath his sense of honor.

The guard let the woman go, yet as soon as Orlando turned his back, he heard the guard spit on his shadow. Orlando's sense of honor couldn't do much to protect the dignity of the workers in line to be searched before their day's labor began. Yet several women hailed Orlando and waved at him in that open way women did in this part of the world.

"*Bonjour*, Captain Orlando!"

"*Bonjour, madames et mesdemoiselles. Bonjour*, Alice, Ermessen, Guillema." Orlando called out to his sergeant's wife, her sister, and the chateau's laundry women who lived in the tiny villages scattered around the foot of the tall, flat hill where Carcassona perched. "*Comment ça va*, Mme Estela? What brings you into the city?"

"The bishop begs a remedy for his gout, Monsieur Captain. Cat's claw herbs and sour cherries will make him right again."

When Orlando first arrived here, Mme Estela sent him bone-mend herbs for a poultice; wet leaves couldn't fix broken limbs, but unexpected kindness from a stranger helped. That morning she called to Orlando, "Do your poor bones ache with the mistral, Captain? Body and soul are well?"

"I'm well, madam. How long will it blow this year?"

"Six days. No more, monsieur. The wind will leave us by Pentecost, when we'll give thanks to the Good God. Pray that it doesn't drive men mad."

"Don't be saying such things to the bishop, mistress." He meant that peculiar turn of speech in the Pays d'Òc, calling on the Good God like heretics do.

Mme Estela laughed, the chimes of a young girl echoing from aged lips. "The bishop himself asked me how long the mistral might be this year, when he gave us the blessing on Easter Sunday at the basilica."

Mme Estela lay in the town square, knocked down with a soldier's lance, kicked by a circle of guards who cawed like crows, then rose up, flying away, leaving the old woman like a child's discarded tapestry doll, torn and lifeless. The smell of burning straw rose, like when farmers burn decrepit field huts.

The cold mistral wind tore at the scarf around Orlando's neck. He blinked, blinked again to destroy the kind of vision he'd been plagued with for too many years, seeing horrible dreams that, mercifully, only came true once, long ago. With every vision, a hideous burning smell flooded his senses, made his eyes water.

The mistral disturbed the women's skirts and veils, but the procession of women created an attractive scene against the stone walls of the city, where tarragon, asters, and bee balm bloomed, the young chestnut trees and rockrose bushes along the wall now as tall as these women. The land ravaged in the siege five years before had rapidly restored itself.

Leaving the gate, Orlando finished his ritual for the conclusion of each trip around the walls, turning the silver-handled dagger in his boot, tying a knot in his scarf, then trailing a finger along the walls of houses where people were waking up, safe as kittens, until he arrived at the duty-sergeant's desk at the bottom of the watchtower. He sat to write the night's report, secretly hoping this would be the last day of this duty.

All the convoluted turns in Orlando de Troyes's life had led to only two lowly fiefs *d'argent*: night-marshal and fight-master to other men's young sons. Twenty-five years old, with never enough silver to replace his lost horses and retainers; night patrols in every weather. He languished in Carcassona. The real battles were north with Philippe Augustus.

Orlando sighed, longing. The day's first headache pounded. A familiar rainbow-colored veil dropped over his eyes. His brother Etienne's ghost whispered in his ear.

Give thanks to God and St-Denis that you own a fief.

I hold a lowly pair of money fiefs with no power or glory. I've served. I've done as commanded. I am the knight upon whom God should shine His face.

You are blessed with the duty to keep the Peace of God. Many men have less.

Etienne served as his conscience, so Orlando complied, offering a swift prayer of thanksgiving, while also praying for more than he possessed. Every sound of his brother's voice came with a smell, like his visions, bringing Etienne close to him again; this time: the odor of clean mud like he and Etienne mucked in when it rained after spring plowing. He was grateful for the uncalled memory of life with his brother, but worried that he was keeping his brother from heaven rather than helping his soul.

One more prayer, then Orlando carefully cut a point on a quill and wrote a summary for that night's duty. They say Simon liked records for everything: the previous evening's gate check; the night's peacekeeping; the morning's inspection of workers.

Finished, waiting for the lamp-black ink to dry, Orlando undid the night's counting-knots in his scarf. Then he added the report to the collection in the cupboard, along with his night-marshal's badge of office. He'd concluded his night duty when the terce bell rang.

Now begins the day, which the Lord has made for us.

How do you know what the Lord intends if you aren't yet in heaven, brother? Is it a special day, as I hope? I need this dawn, this day to be mine. Simon has returned to the city.

You and I, as brothers, shall rejoice and be glad for the duty our Lord has given.

With the rainbow clouding his eyes and the pinching headache that came whenever Etienne spoke to him, along with the smell of warm pony from when his brother taught him to curry horses, Orlando began his daytime rituals. He whispered the next of the day's prayers for his brother's soul.

■

Orlando strode through the city to his duty as fight-master for a passel of feral boys whose knightly fathers had no brothers or cousins to entrust with their sons' training. He called a greeting and waved at the old woman who sat at her door every morning, waiting for her servants to bring home the day's bread. Then he turned the corner and walked up the street to the villa that housed his academy, unsure what he'd find this morning.

Dead birds fell from the sky above Carcassona yesterday.

The boys proclaimed an omen.

There'd been omens proclaimed often since Twelfth Night: A dead cat in the basilica, vermin crawling on its carcass. The ghost-voices of dogs in the city, when dogs hadn't been allowed in the gates since the siege. Ghost-faces in the *petit* well—that proved to be painted leather masks, another relic of Twelfth Night mummers.

And now, dead birds falling from the sky.

Except the birds fell after dawn's light by the refectory door and stacked themselves into a pyramid that toppled when Orlando's boot touched one bird, revealing that the doves had been hit with stones. The size you might use in a slingshot.

Which likely came from the boys' barracks on the upper floor. Or worse, from the villa's rooftop.

Captain Orlando wasn't generally inclined to believe in omens, since his own dark visions never came true; however, that omen of the doves indicated that the bored guards in the Church mill tower failed to notice boys running wild.

A new, foreboding omen manifested when Orlando rounded the villa's outer wall and entered the courtyard. The mistral blew fine dust in his eyes, but that wasn't the omen, only a reminder that seasons change.

"You have five new students today, Captain Orlando."

Mme Marguerite lingered on her portico, her embroidery tambour in hand, watching young boys scramble in her courtyard. A solemn and circumspect baron's widow, Marguerite rented her villa to serve as Orlando's academy. Her handsome face and soft brown eyes presented a warmth that contrasted with her precise yet delicate movements. Orlando, who'd likely never have a wife in this life, considered her the ideal woman, like in the best of poets' songs.

It was a comfort in his stalled life in Carcassona, to have her as a working companion and friend. "They came last night with Simon de Montfort."

"God's bones, madam. You should have sent for me."

Orlando, lurking in the shadows beside her, watched eleven little boys where yesterday there'd been six, which meant twice the work. Though he felt a familiar thrill at the challenge of shaping their lives, Marguerite would bear more of the burden.

"C'est bien, Captain." She spoke with a Paris accent, from the city not the suburbs. "We didn't want to bother you, since you had patrol until dawn. We doubled up the younger boys, so they share cots."

"This is too much to ask, having extra chores thrust upon you with no warning."

"Really, it's fine. But if you agree, Captain, we'll hire the mercenary who shepherded them from Fanjeau for Simon." Marguerite's silk-coated grey cat nuzzled around her legs, lifting the hem of her robe, so that her toes peeked out from light hempen sandals. "One more trustworthy man is likely enough."

"Yes, certainly." He resisted calculating whether the additional fees would pay for one more servant.

"Monsieur, I have a feeling in my bones that these boys need more from us than we've been called to do until now."

"Like an omen?" Orlando had learned the wisdom of omens on his grandmother's knee. But Marguerite preferred what she called pure reason.

"That mercenary, Karles, says…" She paused as if unsure, which wasn't like her. He'd never met a woman so certain of proper action and proper thought. "They say that Simon's youngest son is among the new boys."

Simon's son! Perhaps Simon did remember old promises.

And if not, this was an unheralded chance to prove his worth and loyalty. Orlando scratched that place behind his ear, considering the possibilities.

"What shall we do?" She prompted for an answer, because Orlando had fallen silent.

"The same as we would if we didn't know. Teach boys how to do their duty and how to behave with honor."

Embroidery tambour in hand, Marguerite prepared to return to her workroom. "Did you eat after patrol, Captain? We have a duck egg and those giant white beans you love, still warm in the kitchen."

"*Merci.* If you have a bit of bread, I would be grateful."

> *Mme Marguerite galloped astride an Arabian pony, her unbound hair streaming down her multicolored tapestry cloak, pursued in the heat of day by masked knights. Like a scene from crusaders' Outremer tales or from the poet of Troyes. Her face triumphant, like a queen. The smell of wet ashes and the steam of a doused hearth fire filled the air.*

He blinked, clearing his vision of Mme Marguerite, who claimed she'd never ridden a horse in her life. He remained in the shadows of the portico while he munched the bread and sheep's cheese her servant brought him, while she retreated into the deeper shadows of her workroom.

The boys hadn't noticed Orlando's arrival, so he could watch their play. It was play, not disciplined practice, because his sergeant Umbert had left them mostly to their own devices. The only rule that seemed to apply in the melee—led by his older boys—was "*Le vicomte dit,*" doing only what the vicomte Simon says. Just like life under Simon in the Pays d'Òc.

"*Le vicomte Simon, dit-il*...Shield foot at inner edge."

Only two of the new boys understood the command; the others had to glance about and then move like the older boys did.

"Sword foot at outer edge. *Arrête! Je nai pas dit 'Simon dit.'*"

The oldest of his boys chortled, gleeful at being able to shout the words: *I didn't say Simon says.* By the rule, the losers got two stinging finger flicks. But the first time, the older boys just demonstrated the punishment.

"*Le vicomte Simon, dit-il*...Slow work—defense!"

More scrambling among the new boys to imitate Orlando's trained students.

"*Le vicomte Simon, dit-il*...Step—swing."

They fell into pairs, swinging at each other without contact.

"Cross-block—sword hand!"

The new boys looked at each other, no idea of how to move. The older boys froze like stone pillars.

"*Très bien. Je nai pas dit 'Simon dit.'*"

Orlando wished more of the *gardes du corps* might be as well trained as his older students. But that wasn't his role in this city. No one but these boys were compelled to do as Orlando commanded. Yet, he had to endure the guards complaining about their captain's and sergeants' commands. Or outright arguing with their masters: *Is that what vicomte Simon says? We don't have to, if it's not Simon's command. Simon says…* And the only thing Orlando could do was to walk away, to keep from arguing when guards used "*Le vicomte Simon, dit-il…*" to speak their own desires.

"*Le vicomte Simon, dit-il…*Slow work—offense!"

Young boys imitated the older ones, as if they moved through the steps of a dance.

"Faster! *Arrête! Je nai pas dit 'Simon dit.'*"

"Yeow!" This time, five of the young boys suffered finger-flick punishment, shrieking at the sting.

"*Le vicomte Simon, dit-il…*Three-blow attack."

The resulting flurry of motion called for Orlando to intercede. "It's time."

"Captain?" Marguerite worked in silence, so her voice surprised him.

"It's time for the fight-master to meet the new boys. We shall praise God that you and I are given this chore."

Marguerite pursed her lips, as if in judgment. "It takes your presence, Captain, to quiet the chaos. Umbert doesn't have your way with the boys."

Orlando's own first observation was that Umbert shouldn't have allowed the new boys to take up the wooden practice swords without instruction. The older students, however, had been taught not to swing at each other and might be better guides than Umbert.

Proving Orlando's faith in them, an older boy admonished a smaller pair who'd just missed putting out each other's eyes. "Our captain says swords are not toys."

The biggest new boy scowled at the scolding, thrust out his chest and stood wide in challenge, hands on his hips. "My father says your captain's a cripple. A mangonel boulder fell on him at the siege of Minerve. It broke his winkle clean off."

Orlando let his shadow fall over them as he picked up the rude boy by the back of his jerkin.

"I have mine, *garçon*." He spoke low, knowing his deep voice affected the boys, especially when he whispered while correcting their ways. "Please tell your father that I appreciate his concern for my well-being."

The older boys shuffled, their eyes wide at the newcomer's impudence, startled by Orlando's reply. But the new boy hadn't yet surrendered his willfulness.

"My father is going north to fight alongside Philippe Augustus and drive out the demon king John."

Then this boy wasn't Simon's son. One down, four more to guess.

"Here I am," Orlando said, "fighting alongside Simon de Montfort for peace in the Pays d'Òc, while working to drive out the demons of ignorance from your father's son."

He raised one finger of his free hand. The older students whipped their wooden swords into their baldrics.

"Do as our captain commands," one hissed fiercely in a new boy's ear, "or we all suffer for it."

The younger boys imitated how the others came to full attention. Marguerite's servants had got them all into the academy's plain linsey-woolsey tunics and breeches, so at least he didn't have to begin by making them discard their childish finery. The only sounds drifted on the wind from a nearby yard where the older squires clashed in practice. Still holding the back of the rude boy's tunic, Orlando waited. The boys twitched for two heartbeats, worried about the penalty their captain would assign for misusing their swords.

While they twitched, Orlando studied the new boys, seeking the shape of Simon's face.

A flurry of color across the yard distracted him. A woman in saffron silk accepted bows and fingertip-kisses from three of the *gardes du corps*. Orlando glared, hoping to remind the guards that they earned their keep by protecting the city, not flirting with—

She faced him, golden eyes shining in the sun, locks of russet hair escaping her black veil. A widow then, with a son at her side, seeking to place him in Orlando's academy. She smiled. At Orlando. A smile to warm the courtyard better than the sun.

Orlando let go of the rude boy's jerkin, and the lad stumbled when his feet hit the ground. Orlando, who never raised his voice, never made threats that invited yet more challenges, had sublime control of these boys. Which the widow could witness.

"Here's a rule you know, or you'll learn quickly. As your fight-master, I am the same as your captain on the battlefield. All of you! What does that mean?"

"We obey!" The older boys shouted the answer and thrust their fists into the air; the new boys came in a beat behind, watching the others.

He clapped once, which announced the next command. "Five rounds with the chain caskets. Five rounds of the courtyard each time anyone misuses his weapon or questions his fight-master."

Half the boys had spent enough time under Orlando's tutelage to know this punishment, and it was a fine opportunity for the new boys to learn. The *gardes du corps* always left a dozen barrels in the yard for just such a purpose. Orlando pointed to his sergeant.

"Sergeant Umbert serves as your field commander while I am absent."

At the sound of his name, the diminutive Umbert stood straighter. Then crows cawed overhead, and he glanced up, ready to duck. Crows didn't like Umbert—his wife said he'd destroyed a nest near their house and no crow could forget his beaky nose. Any congregation of those black birds was sure to dive at him. Umbert had come with Orlando from Troyes as his *armiger*, the servant who manages a knight's armor. He came to Carcassona as the sole remainder of Orlando's knights and retainers.

"Master Umbert will supervise the important chore with which you *juvenes* are entrusted. Your work protects French knights in battle." Orlando maintained the pretense that these boys were old enough to be considered *juvenes*, young knights in service. Calling them *les enfants* would not instill the noble sense he wanted for each boy. Implying that anyone from this city might go to battle was a pretense Orlando maintained, along with his hopes that someday he'd have a knight's worthy quest.

And that he'd have horses and men enough for the quest.

2
Beau, Fidèle et Intrépide

WHEN ORLANDO CROSSED THE YARD to greet the woman who waited for him, he took care to hide his limp. The slush-and-clank of the chain caskets began, each barrel filled with oiled sand and chainmail, and just round enough to roll over swept sand and cobbles. Each boy's barrel sent a thump when turning under the covered breezeway. Umbert called after the boys not to cut corners when they rolled barrels through the turns. Orlando stiffly approached a handsome woman smiling in the southern sunshine as she held her veil in place against the force of the mistral wind, her other hand on the shoulder of a frail-looking boy.

"*Bonjour*, madam!"

Orlando bowed, greeting his visitor in French, though the manner in which the woman held her shawl, the cut and color of her robe, the direct way she examined him, all shouted that this was a southern senhóra, perhaps made a widow because of Simon de Montfort. No, that couldn't be — why would she come to live in the vicomte's city?

"*Oui*, it is a good day, monsieur. They say you are called Captain Orlando. And you're from Troyes. That's far north, isn't it?" She held out her hand. Before he could respond, she grasped his in the way a French knight would. It still surprised him, how people do things differently in the Pays d'Òc. When her hand wrapped around his, it happened the same way as always when a woman touched him: it burned, as if she pressed charcoal embers into his palm; yet she smiled, which lifted the corners of her gold-flecked eyes. "I am Taresa of Valeureaux. Though in truth, I still think of myself as Taresa of Girona, where I was born."

Orlando had an idea that Girona lay across the Pyrenees near Barcelona, but he didn't know the other place—the Pays d'Òc was littered with villages and hill-forts, and no one could recite all the names. But he pretended. "Valorous, indeed. Did they name the place for you? Or were you shaped by the virtues of your home city?"

"I married into it." The woman found his response amusing, which pleased him. The boy flinched, looked embarrassed, put his hand over his face. "I expected to find a gnarled crusader serving as fight-master here. Or did a djinni in the Outremer grant you perpetual youth?"

"You are kind, madam." And impudent. He bowed and touched her fingertips, finding her glove-free hand astonishingly warm for a chilly day. The sensation of a woman's skin pressed against his distracted his thoughts. And she smelled of sage, like a trail in the mountains; trees and rock outcroppings baked in the sun.

She sneezed.

"*Que dieu vous bénisse.*" He called for God to bless her, reviving a rusty set of Pays de France court manners. The boy wrinkled his nose, either distaining the sneeze or the blessing.

She sneezed again.

"*À vos amours.*" Blessing her lovers—it came out before he could restrain such impertinence, though he was quoting his grandmother, and so couldn't stop responding again when she sneezed a third time, asking that her lovers always last. "*Qu'elles durent toujours.*"

"You are kind." And then, as if she'd heard his thoughts, she said, "Such blessings always remind us of the teachings of our grandmothers, don't they?"

"Yes, of course, madam. I claim my own grandmother as among the best of teachers."

"But you were going to tell me why you are the best master for young boys." She put her arm around the sun-blond boy beside her. Slight bones, but perhaps tall for his age. The boy watched Orlando steadily, like a cat determining whether a stranger is friend or foe.

"I've spent ten years on crusade," Orlando said, "five of them here in the south with Simon de Montfort, who's the best model for all knights in this endeavor to bring the Peace of God to the Pays d'Òc."

"You believe that, Captain?"

"That we were called to come to this country to serve the Cross? I do." And he especially came to expiate the iniquities and evils of his first crusade, which went wildly wrong. Orlando finished offering his credentials. "And of course, I spent five years training under my own masters in Troyes. Time enough to know what must be taught our younger sons."

"They say your school can help young donzels shake off the stain of southern breeding. Do you feel that, Captain? That the ways of the Pays d'Òc are evil?"

"No, madam." Was she testing him? How would he know if he failed? "It's not the traditions of the south that we were sent to defeat. It's that some here rebel against the Church's authority."

"*Mercé*, Captain." She seemed to accept his answer. "The words people used to describe you…" She laid a finger aside her nose, pretending to find a memory. "*Beau, fidèle et intrépide.*"

Then she nodded, as if approving. She touched Orlando again, unnerving him, though it was just her hot hand briefly stroking his cold one. His hands were always cold. *Mains froides, coeur chaud.* As his grandmother claimed. But he wanted to forget his grandmother and enjoy the opportunity to banter with this handsome woman. And also, she smiled again.

"Just what I need. A man who is loyal and fearless."

The boy tugged her sleeve. "It is I who have the need."

"Of course, Henri."

She still held Orlando's hand. The gesture pulled at her sleeve, revealing a burn on her wrist, perfectly square. Almost like a tattoo. He endeavored to attend to the boy, but he couldn't keep his attention from drifting to her hands; cream lace dripped from her sleeves over large boney fingers. A gemstone and a flash of gold hung on a cord at her throat, seeming to generate heat like her too-strong hands.

A gust of strong spring wind blew over them, and he drew back, afraid he'd let loose the storm at the edge of his heart.

"Mistral?" she asked, withdrawing her hand when he shivered.

"It's as if it blows through one's body."

"Our hostess insists you get used to it if you live here long enough," she said. "Though I won't get used to sneezing at the odor of farm fields. It's embarrassing."

Shhuush, shhuush, clunk. Chainmail slushed in oiled sand, the rhythm unstopping. Orlando had remained where he could see his charges—or rather, they could see that he watched. However, he felt he'd been annealed in place by this woman's smile.

"You know what I mean when I say this." She leaned toward Orlando in the way court ladies play at seduction, her breath brushing his cheek. She lowered her voice, though the boy beside her could hear, even over the ringing of chainmail rattling in barrels. "Henri has been coddled by women too long. If he is to rule his lands as a good Catholic seigneur, he needs to learn what you teach, Captain Orlando."

"The sword and javelin?" Henri interjected an excited comment. He wiggled, impatient.

"Eventually," Orlando said. "Loyalty first. And honor."

"Exactly." Laughing, a warmer song than any bird in the Pays d'Òc sang, she tilted her head back, looking up at Orlando through gold-and-auburn lashes, like a woman in passion. Her saffron under-shift threatened to spill forth at the top of her robe, as if she contained a spirit that longed to run free. "Solidarity, loyalty, virtue. That's what they say you teach, Captain. Being true to your brothers. Serving God by protecting the weak."

The smile in her golden eyes burned into him, warming his insides, as if she were the incarnation of a queen in the Courts of Love. Incarnation? What heretical nonsense.

"It's as if you sing my own heart's song, madam. I do indeed teach knightly ideals of honor." He imitated a courtly bow, which must have been a wrong choice, because she frowned and then said the most surprising thing.

"I'm a stranger here." Her voice, as warm as the spring sun, didn't match her next words. "But it seems that it must be hard to hold on to honor while serving a lord who exceeds the wishes of his Church and king. Torturing and terrorizing people in God's name."

That was far different from an old woman casually speaking heresy as a mere turn of phrase. This was subversion.

"It's subversion when a man betrays his king," she said, as if hearing his thoughts—and scrambling them as a consequence. "Which is what Simon is doing."

He scratched at that place behind his ear, caught his own bad manners and stopped, and then said what he believed were the proper words. "Our work promotes the Peace of God where heresy formerly reigned. Our work serves the goals of Philippe Augustus and the pope."

She smiled, but her eyes seemed blank, as if Orlando had spoken in an unknown tongue. And she didn't answer.

Henri tugged at her sleeve. "No sermons, *se vos plai*." He might have wanted to sound haughty, yet he slipped from French into the local tongue. The boy glanced between the two adults, aware of the treacherous shoals his mother had entered. Orlando steered them all back to the morning's tasks.

"Madam, I do my best to shape boys' minds and bodies so that they grow to become worthy knights. You can trust this child to my academy."

"Truly?" She hugged her son, not seeming to know how inappropriate that was in front of the other boys; he squirmed, obviously past cuddling age. "Henri is my husband's cousin. He came into my care when my husband d—"

She covered her face with those warm, intriguing hands, the crystal at her throat catching the morning light.

"Your husband is dead," the boy Henri said. "You should learn to say it, *ma dòmna*. I'm the seigneur now. You're only the dowager and—"

"And your guardian. Who has her own lands in Girona," she said, not seeming affected by the boy's criticism, "where I shall return as soon as you find a worthy lord and mentor."

Orlando drew the boy away from her embrace, which caused Mme Taresa to touch Orlando again, sending odors of spice into the air around her. At each touch, he felt every mislaid hope pass through him again. His grandfather wouldn't surrender his father's land to him; he didn't have sufficient silver to buy a horse strong enough to ride north; he couldn't replace his stolen armor and horses and *aides de camp* to pursue a worthy quest that—four heartbeats, and then the rainbow veil blinded him and brought the smell of rain on dust after many hot days. Etienne's ghost whispered a warning.

> *Do not choose the foolish things of the world, which serve to confound the wise.*

It doesn't hurt to admire beauty. She wanted me to look. I kept lust from my heart.

> *There's no room for lust in your heart, for you know you can't have a woman like that.*

He blinked. When he could see again, he looked east, judging the sun's height. Would the sext bell ring soon? Was it time for the next prayer for his brother's soul?

"How many servants must I send with Henri?" she asked, bringing his attention back.

"The academy provides servants." French live-in servants, as Simon demanded; not locals performing daywork. "Do you know the fees, madam?"

"*C'est bien.* Henri can afford it." She pulled her cloak closely, hiding her hands in its folds. "Then your fees pay all their keep? You aren't growing rich off the backs of small boys?"

"No, madam." No, there remained scant chance he'd grow rich in this world, not off miniscule money fiefs like the academy and the night-marshal's duty.

"I'm rich." The boy Henri crowed this fact.

"Hush." She tapped the boy's ear with a knuckle. "Wealth doesn't measure goodness. Or mark one man as better than another. Bragging about it doesn't say who you are—except to declare that you are a braggart. Which no one likes."

Again, she sang Orlando's own song.

The boy wrinkled his nose at the upbraiding and looked up at Orlando. "Will we have sermonizing all day in your academy, Monsieur Captain?"

"No. You'll be too busy working."

The woman stirred in a way that told Orlando she'd finished her introduction. And Orlando needed to return to the boys, who'd made five tedious trips around the courtyard. Mostly he needed to draw away from this woman who spoke to his heart and his dreams. And murmured sedition.

"Adieu, Henri." She prepared to depart. "I'll see you at mass on Sundays. Don't lie, cheat, or steal. Treat your friends as if they were your brothers, and do whatever your captain commands."

"I don't know what brothers do," Henri called after her. "I have no brothers."

"Neither do I," she called back to him in the local tongue. "That's why you're going to school with Captain Orlando." She waved, then said in French, "Thank you for taking him, Captain."

Henri followed close by Orlando's side, turning shy the moment his mother disappeared, clasping his hands behind him, searching from one boy to the next in a way familiar to Orlando, because he'd forever been seeking a friend once he'd been exiled from his grandmother's care.

"*Jeune homme,* let's go meet the *juvenes* who will be your loyal comrades."

3

A Prince among Men

WHILE UMBERT REPORTED, ORLANDO CAUGHT the eyes of each of the older boys, all of whom resented the implication that they'd ever cheat. But then, Umbert didn't have a squire's training; likely every child in the courtyard knew more about the traditions of French knights and chivalry than Umbert did.

The whole mob gathered around Henri and Orlando. He counted heads, automatically, since young boys tended to wander off like cats.

"*Juvenes*, this is your new comrade." Orlando felt Henri quiver beside him. He glanced down at the lad: eyes wide, close to panic among the other boys, who pressed close. One boy fingered the carved bone buttons on Henri's jerkin. Orlando raised his hand, the sign that everyone was to listen. The older boys got the new boys into order in a circle around him. "Now, *juvenes*, you may each choose your fighting name for the coming season."

Before he could explain the rules for the new boys, one of his older *juvenes* asked, "May we keep the names we chose at Twelfth Night?"

"We begin anew," Orlando said.

"What if someone takes my old name?" The boy seemed only curious, worried, not challenging.

"You shall be too busy establishing your honor under a new name to worry about others." Orlando crossed his arms while he searched the reaction of his twelve students.

"Now, choose the name by which you shall be famous in this academy. Choose a name that shows your true character, as God sees your heart."

"Any name?" Three new boys cried out at once, enthused.

"Any name that won't offend God or a passing lady."

"Ywain, who rescued the lion," the oldest boy shouted, seizing the first choice.

"Can I be Galahad, the hero who last saw the Grail?"

The next boy, thin as a marsh reed and easily bent by a lesser wind than the mistral, crowed the name he wanted, dancing in place with excitement, his look of hope enough to break a bishop's heart. Orlando nodded, thinking that Galahad was likely to become a favorite for the sake of so much spirit in such miniscule form. And too dark, he assessed, to be Simon's son.

"Yes!" Galahad smashed his fists together, but startled at the pain and had to shake off the stinging in his hands.

So it went, through heroes from Homer's tales or from the songs about the ancient king Arthur by the celebrated poet from Orlando's home city. No one chose the name of a famed crusader, until a tall boy with blond curls shouted, "Hugues, the marquis de Beaurain!"

The sound of that name, of the marquis who'd been Orlando's general on the crusade to Constantinople, blinded him with rainbows and headache, flooded his nose with the smell of dogs returning to the kennel after a hunt. And roused his brother's ghost, shouting breathlessly.

He who wastes his father's glory is a son that causes shame.

Yes, brother, once I made a horrible, foolish mistake.

So much shame, more than you can bear. Fool, fool!

"You can't take the name of a living man." Orlando lifted his forefinger, the sign that they must be silent and listen. Yet Etienne's shadow flickered, ready to haunt his bones if Orlando didn't heed his brother's warnings. "It's like borrowing both his armor and his honor."

"You didn't tell us that rule. And the marquis de Beaurain died at Minerve," the boy argued. Was this one Simon's son?

"There's a new marquis." Once more a boy innocently dragged Orlando back to a humiliating past. "You must respect each living knight, like we respect the vicomte in this city. A man keeps his own name and honor while he lives."

"Just plain Hugues then." The boy sulked.

Orlando cast a cold glare on the boy and offered his favorite challenge to any boy's inclination to argue. "You'd prefer a life arguing in a bishop's court? Rather than to ride as a knight?"

The boy shrugged. "Percival, *s'il vous plaît*. The Grail Knight."

"Excellent choice." Orlando pointed to the next boy.

"Ricart *le Roi*." The new boy who asserted that name didn't shout, just stood, legs wide, arms crossed, obviously used to getting his own way at first request. A behavior that Orlando intended to stop before the next full moon. This boy, who wouldn't grow to be a beauty with that whopper of a nose and a thatch of ruddy hair, was half a head taller than his age-mates. Not handsome enough to be the son of Simon de Montfort.

"You are equals in this academy, the same way that Arthur seated his knights at a round table. Not one of you has yet earned his own honor. Choose a title that places you among your brothers-at-arms, not above them."

"Then I'm Hercules," the redheaded boy said, his arms not crossed now that he wasn't insisting on a king's name. "The hero who slayed the Gorgon."

"Perseus slayed the Gorgon. Hercules," the new boy Henri exaggerated the French pronunciation, "only slew the Hydra."

Not a good way to find new friends, Orlando thought, but it wasn't an appropriate moment to intercede.

The other boys selected their names. Orlando pointed at the most puppy-like of the lot of them. "Your choice?"

"Ajax, the hero at Troy."

Orlando approved and then asked the newcomer, "What name shall you choose, *jeune homme?*"

"I should like to be called Perseus," Henri said solemnly, "the son of Zeus and prince of Argos, who turned each of his enemies into stone."

Orlando nodded, agreeing to the name, even though he felt sure that Perseus had just singled himself out for an ass-kicking that would occur at a moment when Orlando couldn't intervene. He prepared to dismiss them, but the redheaded boy who'd chosen Hercules as his name waved his hand wildly.

"I've changed my mind," the boy said. "I shall be called Lancelot. The First Knight."

"Lancelot is a good name," Orlando said, though the knight in that tale betrayed his king. "A man of wisdom and valor to emulate. Now, Mme Marguerite's cook has rusks and hot milk in the refectory. Then you have the afternoon with your schoolmaster."

"*Merci, mon capitaine!* We obey." They shouted together, the new boys catching on quickly and joining in.

Mme Marguerite held the refectory door open, tapping each boy on the head as he passed by her, as if she too needed to count to keep track of so many new boys. Orlando relied on Marguerite and her servants to advance peace in this boys' kennel at night, to keep the boys fed and their cots clean, to deliver bread to the poor in the villages on feast days.

Orlando called to her. "The number is now twelve, madam!" at the same time another voice called his name.

"Captain Orlando! *Avant!*" Louis de Brienne, Orlando's own commander, hailed him. "Simon wants to see you. He asked for you by name."

Orlando crossed the training yard, quieting his wild hopes while wondering whether 'Simon asked for you by name' advanced his reputation with the new boys. That proud hope was interrupted by a bit of whiny grousing among the boys.

"We can't choose kings' names, but he lets the new boy call himself a prince."

When Orlando glanced back to see who spoke, Perseus fell to the ground and his hand was trod upon, but it wasn't possible to guess who'd pushed him. Umbert missed the transgression too while staring at crows landing on the city walls, only admonishing Perseus for lagging behind the others.

"Hurry, Orlando," Louis insisted. "You are summoned."

.

"Simon wants me?"

Orlando choked out the words, his throat clotted with hope.

"Yes. Here, I brought a clean shirt and jerkin from your barracks. You can't appear at court in such a well-used shirt."

"*Merci.*" Orlando stepped back into the shade of Mme Marguerite's portico to dress.

After the catastrophe in Minerve, instead of sending him home to Troyes, Simon had given Orlando two money-fiefs in Carcassona while also promising: "*When you're whole again, we'll find a place for you among knights with banners.*"

On the portico, Orlando dropped his dusty jerkin and tugged his well-used linen shirt over his head. It smelled of horse and his night's work, which Perseus's mother must have smelled while they spoke together.

"It's entirely possible," Louis teased, which you knew whenever he began with that phrase, his voice in a higher register, "that the great Simon de Montfort intends to reward you with a rich southern wife. We'll all retire to her estates."

"Live like princes." Orlando repeated the next line of what served as a private litany they shared.

"Drive her dependent cousins into honest work."

"Pay the Church tithe with silver from her city's oven rents."

"Bask in the glory of the southern Courts of Love."

That was their standard litany, though neither Louis nor Orlando had glimpsed the fabled courts of pleasure in Montpelhièr, Toulouse, or Narbonne.

Louis had classically handsome French looks, his blond hair in thick, shiny locks that his wife tended every morning, or so Orlando assumed, guessing what it might take for a man to be so presentable. A head shorter than Orlando, Louis made up for his small size by being faster and stronger than most people, even after he lost his hand in a mangonel accident outside Minerve. (Neither he nor Orlando had made friends of the siege machines there.) It was impossible to dislike the man, though Orlando quietly worried that Louis's excess kindnesses contributed to the bored complacency among the *gardes du corps*.

Orlando pulled the clean linen shirt over his head. It was as threadbare as the one he'd just discarded. He needed to scrape together enough silver for two new shirts. Perhaps if he washed his own shirts and breeches for the next month—

"Though it's far more likely the mistral shall blow us into the next county." Louis laughed at his own jest, like he always did. Orlando considered his friend's wit and quirks a blessing, similar to the sunshine and bitter wine of the Pays d'Òc. Who else, besides Mme Marguerite, could he claim as a friend? "Have women in the villages foretold how long the mistral will last this year?"

Orlando pulled his best jerkin in place and tied the linen strings of his shirt. "The herb woman says six days. All over by Pentecost."

When the mistral came each spring, the old women claimed it came in threes, that they'd have three, six, nine, or twelve days. Orlando believed their claim, but then again, the old women in his home village at Troyes claimed that eating fried bread makes your hair curl. Orlando ate plain bread for years, hoping to tame his wiry bush, since oiling and combing never kept a single lock in place. He brushed it back now with his hand, retying the leather string that bound it.

The sext bell rang. Orlando silently said the next prayers of the day. He dusted his boots with his discarded linen shirt, which would earn him a scolding among the laundry women, and then stashed his shirt and jerkin under a bench on the portico, to retrieve later. He couldn't afford a servant to carry his clothes to and from the chateau laundry.

"I have six new boys today, Louis. Five came to Carcassona with Simon last night."

"*Aiieee!* Much more work for Mme Marguerite's servants."

"Indeed. And," Orlando drew out the next news, because he didn't know how to think about it yet, "the rumor is that one of the boys is Simon's youngest son."

"*Bon Dieu!* That means—"

"Stop, Louis. I can't trust what it means. And I can't afford to hope."

Louis touched Orlando's shoulder. "When Simon arrived last night, I asked him to name you swordmaster for the squires. It's past time for you to be done with night-marshal duties and to give up training *les enfants*."

"*Merci*." He was grateful; he just longed for more.

"It would be disloyal of me to do otherwise," Louis said. "Now, besides Simon, which French knights blessed you with the care of their young sons?"

"I don't know yet. Except one sapling belongs to an unpardonably attractive woman. Not beautiful so much as captivating. Have you met Taresa of...did she say Girona? Though she came here from Toulouse."

"The charming widow who came on Friday with her cousin? Freckles and rusty hair? Didn't you see her in the basilica on Sunday? Everyone in the vicomte's chateau is buzzing around those two women like bees in lavender and balsam."

Of course, Orlando again was two horses short of a warrior's equipage. Other men must be on campaign well ahead of him.

"You're a worthy knight," Louis said. "Why not try for the handsome stranger? Simon would encourage it."

Louis, like several other knights, had married a local landed widow and took over her villa. Some guards, like Umbert, married women from the local villages and took possession of any property they owned. It's the way of the world and good business, Louis claimed, since it keeps whores from taking up business again.

"It's the carefree life for me," Orlando said, while in truth he didn't dare hope for a wife until he once more had a future as a knight. "No female tells me what to do. No female needs my attention. Except my horse."

"*Homme célibataire, eh?*" Louis answered absentmindedly. He straightened the linen ties above Orlando's jerkin. "You'll do fine for the vicomte's court. *Avant, mon ami.*"

Yes, *homme célibataire*, but not because he chose a path or a vocation, like a priest. Just like he didn't take a vow of poverty; celibacy and scarcity just came to him, uninvited.

They skirted the side of Marguerite's stone villa, where the refectory opened to the alleyway. A roof tile fell right beside Louis's boot. Both men looked up.

A boy balanced on the ridge-top tiles, putting one foot down to take a step. Another tile cascaded down the roof, landing near Orlando.

4

The Song of Balthazar

ORLANDO SPRINTED FOR THE VILLA'S south side, where trellises climbed all three stories of the whitewashed wall. He scrambled up the trellises, as if the stakes and dowels might hold his weight if he moved quickly. On the ridge of the roof top, he paused on one of the pallets that the roof-masons had left. Another pallet on the other side of the roof must be what the boy had used to climb up from a window to the roof.

"Captain Orlando!" Louis called. "Let your sergeant take care of this. Simon calls."

Orlando had no time to answer.

"Stay where you are, *garçon*." He commanded the boy's attention while seeking a way to get the boy out of jeopardy. He straddled the peak of the roof and slowly scooted toward the boy. It was the newest boy, Perseus, who recognized his peril. As Orlando inched ahead, Etienne whispered.

The Lord gives no power to the faint or the weak.

I don't have time to be blinded with rainbows.

Your strength is small. Beware! You shall fall. You'll kill yourself and the boy too.

In the bright sun, early heat rose from the tiles, even with the mistral blowing. Orlando shut his ears; he'd take Etienne's scolding later, though it meant hideous nightmares.

"Are we going to fall?" Perseus's voice quavered, having lost all the bravado from their first meeting.

"No. But don't look down." If Orlando looked down, the gravel lot of the courtyard on one side and the kitchen garden on the other seemed perilously far away. The trees and vineyards and villages and gardens in the rolling countryside seemed as far as the Outremer. When Orlando glanced down for one heartbeat, Louis gazed up from the gravel yard below.

> *A startled look crossed Louis's face as first one, then four crossbow bolts struck, piercing his chainmail. He still stared as his heart's blood burst forth, and he fell from his horse. Crows circled, attracted by the smell of burning meat.*

"Keep your eyes on me, *jeune homme.*" Orlando locked his eyes on Perseus; the bad, false vision of death disappeared, and the vast landscape behind the boy fell away from focus. Right then, Orlando saw only the frail-looking, straw-haired boy.

"Do you know the Song of Balthazar?" No one did, since Orlando made it up, but he wanted to distract the frightened boy. Although Orlando couldn't sing, his chanting voice mesmerized boys. "I'll tell you while we solve this problem."

"Will the roof break, Captain?"

"No. Listen to the story. I often test my *juvenes* to be sure they listen and detect the wisdom in the old tales of noble knights."

> Balthazar's comrades took the oath
> of the Order of the Wheel and Serpent,
> those preachers of brotherhood.
> They endured the night of trials,
> Each challenged to uncloak a false knight.

"If we fall, will we die?" Breathless, the boy hardly got the words out. He was looking down.

Orlando had reached the lad. He held out a hand.

"We won't fall. What was my command? Do not look down."

"*Òc, el meu capità.*" In his fright, the boy retreated into the local tongue.

"Grab my hand, Perseus. Harder. Now climb on my shoulders."

Once the boy balanced in place, Orlando inched back to the platform, the boy's damp hands scratching across Orlando's face and then grasping his hair. Orlando focused on his own black bush of hair being more useful than usual, while he gauged from the platform how to climb back down the trellis's lattice work.

More chanting, with no idea why he told a story he'd made up from his reckless errors in Constantinople.

> It came to Balthazar as if in a dream foretold
> how his sworn comrades proved false.
> And by listening to their pleas,
> Balthazar found in the darkness of his heart
> he'd betrayed a true and honorable knight.

First step down, while they were still high up, he had to fumble for position, accommodating his weaker leg. He adjusted the burden on his shoulders.

"Now tell me, Perseus, why choose to do this?" The older boys could be counted on to challenge newcomers, boys too young to recognize jeopardy and with insufficient strength or skill to rescue themselves. He didn't want names, only to understand what was happening in the boys' barracks.

As Orlando sought the next safe foothold, Perseus's voice whispered in his ear. "That boy Galahad drew the short straw. He's too young and afraid to tell the other boys no. So I stole his straw."

That was not what Orlando had guessed. "And yet you didn't say no to breaking the rules?"

"Once I held the straw, I had a duty to my family's honor. We believe in paratge. So I will take your punishment, Monsieur Captain. Will you tell my family what I've done?"

"No, what happens among your brothers stays only with your brothers. That is how you become united as comrades."

"But your song—Balthazar's comrades weren't faithful."

"That only happens when knights are badly trained. Here in my academy, you will learn better."

When they dropped to the ground, gravel scratching underfoot, Umbert waited for them, but hadn't moved to help Orlando down.

"Ah, the missing young gentleman." Umbert had Perseus by the elbow. "Monsieur Tutor found himself short one student." He led the boy away, toward the villa's main gate, calling back to Orlando. "The tutor hadn't expected so many boys today."

Umbert didn't repeat a claim he'd made more than once, that the tutor, a scholar from Paris who didn't want to be a priest, couldn't control the boys. Orlando motioned Umbert back, to have a word with him. It took three gestures before Umbert grasped that Orlando did not want Perseus to overhear.

"Don't punish that boy."

"But, Captain, it's one of your chief rules. The boys must stay together, where they are assigned. We can't allow them to wander off on pranks."

"That isn't what happened here," Orlando said. "I'll explain later. Put him back with his comrades and don't speak of it."

"That is surely a big mistake." Umbert shook his head. Orlando wanted badly to assert that arguing with his captain might be a mistake on Umbert's part. But Orlando bit his tongue; Umbert had remained loyal enough at Minerve to bring Orlando to Carcassona when Orlando's retainers stole his horses and deserted him.

He rejoined Louis, who was walking rapidly to the chateau. "I'll make worthy knights of them or die trying."

"The way you almost died just now?"

"It wasn't that much danger, for either of us. A broken bone was the worst the lad might have suffered."

"The rich widow whose son you rescued—she watched your heroics." Louis directed Orlando's attention with a twitch of his head, where one street emptied into the passage they crossed toward the chateau. "That'd be quite a fair catch for you."

You can't have that.

Two women in widows' veils watched the two captains crossing. Mme Taresa, tall and in saffron, had her arm around the waist of the smaller woman in crimson. The mistral blew southern grit into Orlando's eyes, but it seemed that Mme Taresa raised her hand and offered a wave with two fingers.

"Balthazar!"

A too-familiar voice called from the chateau gates.

Orlando blinked and turned away from the handsome, smiling woman to walk into the open arms of a dark angel who always unleashed nightmares.

.

"My dear brave cousin!"

Badoyn held his arms wide, grasped Orlando in the overly friendly way younger knights had adopted in Constantinople. A rust-colored greyhound at his side nuzzled Orlando, sniffing, shoving at Orlando's hand for affection. The midday sun burned down on their heads. Orlando froze at his cousin's touch, which was better than betraying the quiver that swept like the mistral into his heart.

"Dogs aren't allowed inside the city." The night-marshal inside Orlando came out first. He grasped Badoyn's shoulders, keeping him at arm's length.

"Simon gave me a pass." Badoyn escaped Orlando's grasp and slapped him on the shoulder. "It's lucky for us that Simon is our grandfather's old friend, eh, cousin?"

His beautiful dog, rust-colored save for its long black snout, still craved attention. Orlando would far rather welcome that tall, slim hound to the city than his cousin.

"I'm surprised to see you here. Who's helping Grand-père in Troyes?" Especially in the bright sun, they mirrored each other like brothers, except Badoyn was so blond and Orlando dark, his hair frizzing into a bush in the wind, while Badoyn's fell in long, well-tended curls, the extreme of Paris style. And Badoyn's broken nose, where Orlando punched him a decade earlier, remained bent, adding to his haughty expression. His scarlet silk coat shimmered in the sunshine, its tails tossed by the wind, leaving his expensive greyhound edgy. Orlando held out his hand to calm the dog.

"Last winter Simon asked me to take care of Giles's affairs," Badoyn said, with no regard for his dog, "and he now commands that I report what I found. And Grand-père begged me to bring you a message, my dear Balthazar."

"Giles de Nully?" The angel of dark dreams spread its wings, darkening Orlando's vision.

"He's dead, you know. Alas, poor Giles." Badoyn touched fingers to his lips, as if he were capable of feeling grief.

"Yes, we heard," Orlando said. "An accident with his horse."

"That's what his people say. I suspect heretics had a hand in it. You knew Giles. He was too good with animals to be killed by his own horse."

"Yes, I knew Giles."

His arm around Orlando's shoulders, Badoyn steered him through the chateau gates and across the courtyard to Simon's great hall. One hand dangled just in Orlando's vision, showing that disgusting tattoo they'd all gotten in Constantinople. His dog was sniffing at Orlando's hand, nuzzling, then licking. The rough slurp of the dog's tongue threatened to snap Orlando into a trap of memories, long days spent in the kennels years ago. It seemed improbable that Badoyn owned a friendly, beautiful dog, since he never used to care to spend time in the kennels, letting the master of the hounds manage them on a hunt.

Badoyn still chattered. "For Simon's sake, I spent the winter on Giles's estate, making sure the heretics and rebels see that Simon remains the Great Hope of the Pays d'Òc. *Bon Dieu*, Balthazar. You're brown as a summer stoat."

"We get more sun here in the south than in Troyes."

"Truly? I spent the winter and spring in Cahors, and I'm only burnt pink." Badoyn pretended to ponder a deep thought, though Orlando knew what came next. "It can't be as Grand-père says, that the devil in you will always out."

Orlando tried to withdraw, holding back to walk beside Louis. "Louis de Brienne, this is Badoyn de Troyes, my cousin. Louis is the master of the city's *gardes du corps*. I am night-marshal under him."

"*Bonjour!*" Louis held out his left hand. Badoyn returned a graceless greeting, awkwardly touching Louis's hand. "We met in Constantinople. But that's ten years ago."

"I'm pleased to meet you again!" Badoyn showed his teeth, a smile that flashed like silver in sunshine.

"Simon called us." Louis pointed to the inner courtyard doors and set off at a faster pace than Orlando could keep after his rooftop adventure.

"He sent me to greet you." Badoyn grabbed Orlando's elbow like he did in older days, leading his cousin into chaos. When they were halfway across the castle's inner courtyard, Badoyn huffed under his breath, "What a wreck of a chateau!"

"It is old," Louis said. "It's so old, my wife claims the famous Charlemagne slept here in ancient times."

"It's crumbling to pieces. Tiles falling. Plaster needs repair."

"There'll soon be time for repairs, when the heretics are defeated." Orlando impulsively defended the city. What Badoyn criticized was the result of a few years' neglect, since the city didn't have the funds or workers to undertake more than the repairs of the defensive walls. It had been a good chateau under the former vicomte. "It shall be a great city again, when Simon has time to attend to it."

"Perhaps." Badoyn wasn't really conceding. "After Philippe defeats the Angevin king, John, and sends sufficient army for Simon to tame the heretics and their rebel protectors."

Yes." Orlando intended to be agreeable. "Then people can get back to regular work."

"But you'll never guess what I found in your pathetic city." Badoyn slapped Orlando's shoulder. "The love of my life is here. I pursued the lady all winter, and I'll swear on any saints' bones that God brought us together here."

"Congratulations." Louis spoke, while Orlando waited until he knew what must be coming next.

"I have a plan for us both, Balthazar." Badoyn hung his arm over Orlando's shoulder again. "After Simon gives me Giles's estate, we'll find magnificent lands for you. What shall we do that's heroic? Find the greatest trove of heretics' treasure? Capture castles in Foix?"

Badoyn drew away, studying the upper gallery of the chateau as if he expected someone to appear there. His dog stayed with Orlando. Louis led the way to the great room, and Orlando hobbled behind. The dog licked Orlando's hand, leaving his side only when Badoyn whistled. Louis straightened Orlando's jerkin, brushing away dust from Mme Marguerite's roof.

"They say Simon has changed in the last year." Louis spoke close to Orlando's ear. "They caution not to argue with him. Question others, but not Simon."

"*Bien,*" Orlando said. "Simon is the hero of this crusade. We owe him respect."

"Yes, well…"

Louis tugged the huge door that opened onto the great room where Simon held court for judgment and strategy.

Behind them, Badoyn spoke to his dog. When Orlando looked back, his cousin was passing coins to the guard and then pointing to the dog, instructing it to sit and stay. Coming up behind Orlando, Badoyn said, "Grand-père Daniel sent Simon a message, too. To help you."

Orlando stopped himself from reaching for the small knife in his boot and attacking his perverse cousin. A headache started above his eye, squeezed his head. Rainbows danced before him and he inhaled the smell of grass from when the reapers set to work after Lammas.

The Lord put fire in his hand, and a knife; and the two brothers went both of them together into the wilderness.

No, you're repeating my bitterness; you were always kind and good.

Thou shalt burn thy enemy, and shall smite about him with this knife: and thou shalt scatter his bones in the wind.

Orlando glanced back through the archway to see where the sun stood. Not time for the next bell, yet he mouthed a prayer for his brother's soul.

5
The Mouths of Lions

"AH. HERE THEY ARE AT LAST." Simon's voice boomed from across the great room. "The dawdling captains of the *gardes du corps!*"

"*S'il vous plaît, pardonnez-nous.* An event near the basilica delayed us." Louis bowed in a way that Orlando had seen only when knights approached Philippe Auguste. Though surprised, Orlando imitated his commander.

Simon, his handsome face burned red from riding in the spring sun, sat in the center of the round court that had served the vicomtes of Carcassona for centuries. Simon's coat of arms, yellow lions on a blue field, decorated the wall behind him. Stacks of arrows and other arms crowded the other walls. Orlando couldn't help but notice that the vicomte had put on flesh since Michaelmas, which many French knights did over winter, outside the fighting season. But the strangest thing: Simon's hair was no longer streaked with grey, as you'd expect for a man his age. He'd colored it, so the streaks were now flower-gold, with the locks combed like the city knights from Paris. Like Badoyn's long, overly cultivated locks. Simon had always been a fighting man, and he still dressed the part, but in better silks now, blue like his shield, shot through with threads of gold, like the medallion on a chain that Simon held in his hand.

Because Orlando endeavored not to hear Badoyn's fawning bonjours, he was startled when Simon spoke to him.

"Orlando de Troyes, so happy you could join us. Louis has claimed for the past two seasons that you can do bigger things than keep Carcassona safe for our knights' wives and sons."

Simon did remember his promises! Orlando's modest wishes might come true! Perhaps no more night patrols? *Les enfants* left to another knight's care? The pause continued so long that Louis stirred beside him, causing Orlando to realize that Simon expected an answer.

"*Merci*, Monseigneur. It is humbling to have good men speak well of me. But I must again thank you for trusting me with work here in Carcassona."

"You are whole? That episode at Minerve with the mangonel didn't..." Simon's smile when he paused, pursed his lip, seemed to bespeak a desire to be discreet. Except rather than be discreet, he pointed at Orlando's loins.

"I am well." Orlando hadn't let a limp betray him when he crossed the great room. "And if you will allow, I must protest the rumors about my injuries at Minerve. I'm a whole man. With well-knitted bones."

Bones that ached in bad weather and while the cold mistral blew. But Simon was about to discuss Orlando's future, not his well-being.

"A letter from your grandfather Daniel asks me to find rich wives for you and your cousin." Simon and Badoyn laughed, nodding their heads as if this were a joke they'd shared earlier. Orlando pretended to see the humor, laughing when Badoyn did. Safer that way.

"Perhaps my cousin and I shall harvest wives from among the spare widows in the neighborhood." Orlando forced lightness into the words, though this wasn't like the private way he and Louis joked. He felt Louis beside him but couldn't turn to look, or worry that his commander took offense, since Louis had managed to marry a widow with a house in Carcassona.

"My old friend Daniel," Simon said, "also begs me to give you something big to do, Captain Orlando, for the greater glory of his house. Of course, I cannot deny my old comrade."

Blinking in the dim council room, Orlando rubbed his nose, overwhelmed by the imagined odor of a dog's rotten breath.

He has subdued kingdoms, wrought righteousness, obtained promises.

Simon made promises to *me*, years past.

He has stopped the mouths of lions.

"*Merci*, Monseigneur. It is an honor to be considered for new work." Orlando said what was required of him, but he wanted to ask if new work included horses and enough silver that he could leave the wretched life of the bachelor-knights' tower.

Simon waved away Orlando's thank-you, that medallion swinging from his fist. "So far, honor is due only to your father's departed soul. I haven't witnessed your prowess as a knight since Minerve."

"No, Monseigneur." Beyond his own discomfort, Orlando stared at Simon, trying to see if this was serious, not more jesting like moments before. He'd seen Simon be so…coldly imperious to others; but Orlando had never experienced it directed at him. What had he done to deserve that?

"Then will you allow me to set a challenge for you, Captain? To confirm your grandfather's plea, that you are worthy of new investment?"

As if Orlando or anyone in the room could refuse Simon anything. Or that Orlando could plead: *But you already promised.* Louis had warned him not to argue. "Whatever you ask, Monseigneur."

"What I have in mind, Captain Orlando, requires that you manage men efficiently, men who might not have the skills of knights trained the way we were in our homeland."

Orlando nodded, since he didn't have words. He scratched that place behind his ear, caught himself at it, stopped.

"For your challenge," Simon waved a hand, and a page gave him a piece of parchment, "I have this list of households that haven't paid tithes to the Church this year. In one day's work, how much can you bring from the villages to restore what's owed to the Church?"

Orlando nodded as if he agreed, which was a lie. The tithe lists contained no gaps; he'd ridden patrol, protecting the tithe collectors last September. They'd been thorough, down to the last groats of wheat and barley. He coughed dust from his throat, still smelling sick dog while hearing Etienne's voice.

> *The Lord is a jealous God and His anger has been kindled against thee.*

> But, brother, we are taught to pray to a forgiving God.

> *You can never win.*

He glanced at Louis to assess his judgment of Simon's senseless request. But Simon had all of Louis's attention. Simon leaned forward, close to Orlando, his marigold locks falling on his silk jerkin.

"Is today's challenge agreeable to you, Captain Orlando?"

Orlando brought his folded hands up to his chest. Just as Louis couldn't do anything but agree, neither could Orlando.

"Shall I begin today?" Orlando asked.

"Is there anything that begs you to wait?" Simon again spoke with biting, cruel wit, which Orlando had never seen before. "And take your cousin along so he can see how you keep the peace in this neighborhood."

Badoyn was praising this idea, but Simon seemed distracted. The bishop and three priests had appeared at the archway leading into the great room. Simon waved the visitors in, essentially waving Orlando off. "We'll invite our gentle ladies to salute you at a midnight supper, Captain. Any challenge improves if you can win the favors of a lady, don't you think, Captain Louis?"

"It's entirely possible," Louis said.

.

When Badoyn whistled in the courtyard, his rust-colored greyhound pounded to them, then walked at Orlando's side. Seemingly unaware of the fury boiling up inside Orlando, Badoyn had his arm around Orlando's shoulder as they strode to the knights' stables.

"Behold, Balthazar!" Badoyn rasped loudly in Orlando's ear. He jammed Orlando's jaw with a finger, forcing him to look down a nearby street. "Heaven shines its light on the south. My love walks here, and flowers spring under her step."

The woman who'd entrusted her son to Orlando stood at the top of the street. The charmingly seditious Mme Taresa of wherever she was from. The bright midday light shone around her like a halo, her saffron robe glowing as if from an inner light.

Badoyn hurried over.

And kissed the offered hand of the smaller figure in a crimson robe who stood at Mme Taresa's side.

There shone one tiny ray of sunshine in Orlando's day, that he didn't have to watch a woman he liked be ensnared by Badoyn.

Also, seen in the bright midday sun, Badoyn's intended was likely old enough to be Taresa's mother—at least a decade older than Badoyn. With those jewels and layers of embroidered crimson silk, she must come from a society a few places beyond that of the grandsons of Daniel of Troyes.

"Why does your cousin call you Balthazar?" Louis asked softly while they waited for Badoyn. "Oh, your birthday comes just after Twelfth Night. You share Balthazar's feast day?"

"Yes, among other things."

"Ah! You were born in the Outremer, like one of the Three Kings?"

"Yes." And Orlando hoped to return there some day. That would be a great quest, to pick up the Cross his father had carried until forced home with swamp fever, bringing with him Orlando, his half-orphaned son.

Badoyn kissed his would-be bride's hand, wished her farewell, and rejoined the captains while still singing the praises of the most beautiful woman in the world, his silk-clad arm again over Orlando's shoulder. Orlando needed to quiet the ghost that whispered in his ear and to stop considering why, here in this city, he was once more mired in a hell created by his disparaging grandfather and perpetually scheming cousin.

At the knights' stable, Louis sent his sergeant to summon the men he thought best suited for their days' work. Orlando offered his horse a wizened apple before saddling her, an aging chestnut roan called Midnight.

"Have you eaten today?" Louis asked Orlando.

"Thanks," Badoyn said. "I had a late breakfast with Simon."

Louis hung close by Orlando. "Did you get any sleep last night, *mon ami*? We're stealing your *migdiada* nap." He used the local word, since there wasn't such an idea in their homeland: a man sleeping in the afternoon. "You worked all night and all morning."

"I'm fine. Mme Marguerite fed me breakfast." Midnight gobbled the apple, her muzzle soft against Orlando's hand. At least his horse and his commander liked him. And Badoyn's faithless greyhound.

"Ah. My wife thinks Marguerite is more than fond of you. *Un béguin, certainement.*"

"*Un béguin?* Don't tease, Louis."

"It's entirely possible." Which Louis said when he was teasing. "Mme Marguerite would never be so foolish as to carry a tenderness for an impoverished knight, even if she weren't a baron's widow."

Louis stepped into the yard to explain the day's business to his guards. Orlando harnessed and saddled Midnight, double-checking his own cinching, like he would if his *armiger* prepared his mount for a journey. But no *armiger* for this knight; Orlando could barely afford to keep Umbert as his sergeant at the academy; perhaps he should let Umbert go to the *gardes du corps*. With what he saved out of the fief's silver, he could afford new harnesses for Midnight, and shirts and breeches and boots and—

Badoyn suddenly slammed Orlando's shoulder again.

"Hey, Balthazar! Don't you want to read Grand-père Daniel's letter? Simon didn't give me a chance to share it with you."

Badoyn laid the packet on Midnight's saddle, which his horse considered an impertinence; she shuffled away from his cousin. The beeswax-and-resin seal faced Orlando, the intaglio stamp obviously that of Daniel of Troyes. Just as obviously, the seal had been broken and then crudely reformed; Badoyn had already read its contents.

> 'I asked Simon to try again to make a man of you at last, before I resign all of my land to your worthy cousin.

> 'My challenge to you: are you loyal to your house and family? To your father's honor? Or are you content to be nothing but the minion of a man who comes from a lesser house than your own?'

Daniel surely didn't mean Simon had less prestige than a broke knight from Troyes. Was he insulting Louis?

"*Avant*, cousin." Badoyn wrapped an elbow around his neck, hugging Orlando close. "Don't let Grand-père get to you."

"When I wrote at Twelfth Night, I asked him once again to replace my stolen horses and lost armor." This new letter set a fire in Orlando's heart and burned the last of his hopes. "He didn't even answer my request."

"My dear cousin, our grand-père hasn't got more than a few dusty *deniers* to give either of us. He's still paying the mortgage for when your father ran off to the Outremer." Badoyn seemed bizarrely blithe. "Then Daniel gambled on us both to go to Constantinople, and you came home without a lord to serve or one *sou* worth of booty."

"How are you managing?" The two knights traveling with Badoyn were saddling horses, and they each had more than one horse to choose from. His cousin wore nice silks, and his horse was kitted out with a new, shiny harness and saddle.

"God grants me more luck than He does you. That's why you should hitch your future to my wagon. We can go places, cousin."

"Where can I go without horses and armor? With no retainers? Not one *sou* of silver?" Orlando rested his hand on Midnight's muzzle, a horse that deserved to spend its last days in a green pasture, not riding patrol on a dusty Pays d'Òc trail.

"Look, old Daniel's more than a bit skint."

"Skint?"

"Empty of pocket, though he's too proud to tell you."

"Why?"

"Because it was your dear departed father who mortgaged everything to go on crusade. Now it's up to you and me together to find our fortunes. And the best way is here in the south, where Simon is ripping the covers off troves of heretic wealth."

"Is he?" Orlando covered his temper, the way a cook covers a boiling kettle. "Then why are we sent out to beat tithes from villagers who can't possibly pay before the harvest—which is at Michaelmas, not Pentecost?"

Badoyn fell laughing on Orlando's shoulder, as if that were the day's best jest.

"*Bon Dieu*, Balthazar. We're here to help Simon succeed. When he's king here, you and I will be rich. It won't matter that your father cost all of Troyes more gold than he brought home. This is our chance to prove our loyalty to Simon. Isn't that your duty, Balthazar?"

"When Simon—what?"

"*Salut!*" Badoyn turned to greet the guards entering the stable. "What a day we shall have! *Devoir! Dieu! Fidélité!*"

As if duty, God, and fidelity ever mattered to Badoyn for one heartbeat.

6

Foxes in the Vineyards

His faithful lion at his side
Balthazar rode from the wilderness
On a horse called Midnight,
The lovely Laudine across his saddle,
His arms around her lithe form,
Chainmail jingling like tiny bells—

ORLANDO OF TROYES CHANTED ONLY loud enough to soothe Midnight, whose saddle never had a woman across it, lithe or otherwise. Out the gates and down to the villages.

Carcassona, like most every citadel Orlando knew, sat atop a hill, placed to protect the suburbs flanking it, not merely to shelter whatever vicomte currently ruled. Many of the Catholic citizens evicted after the siege returned the next year to resurrect the small villages below the hilltop city. Their village elders, eager to demonstrate their faith, named the small clutches of huts St-Mathieu, St-Marco, St-Luc, and St-Jean. To build shelter for people and their animals, the villagers combined older houses, shoveled up fallen siege rubble, and patched roofs. Whether on day patrol or night patrol, the *gardes du corps* rode around the villages, there being no direct passage through any of them. The villagers were unable to rebuild orderly streets, so each hastily reconstituted village included gaps between houses with paths to the wells and ovens, rather than any arrangement for people and animals to move through easily.

Louis, riding beside Orlando on the bone-dry trail, was coughing. Dust swirled like mist in the mistral.

"*Hé, commandant!* How long since you rode patrol, old man? Don't remember how to prepare?" Orlando handed over his scarlet-dyed linen scarf. "Tie it over your mouth and nose. Block the dust the mistral raises."

While Louis tied the loaned scarf, Orlando tugged at his coif to drag the under-linen over his face, hearing the thinning fabric tear. It wasn't as if they needed chainmail in this peaceful neighborhood, but their armor delivered a message—that they were on business, not out hunting with hawks. What he didn't look forward to was a summer season where chainmail chafed because he couldn't afford a new hauberk and coif.

It wasn't even full summer, yet here he was, leading a patrol to harass the same villages they'd been protecting every day since Orlando arrived—well, since healing from the Minerve catastrophe. What did Hugues de Beaurain call such missions? *Une course pour les imbéciles.*

Drat that little boy for putting Hugues in his thoughts. Do boys instinctively know how to call up the most humiliating moments in one's life?

In the village called St-Luc, Orlando knew the three men and four women who served as elders. One of the men poured a cup of wine to share while they sat under a large sweet-chestnut tree and discussed the problem Simon had presented. Others in the village found it a good time to tend their gardens, especially needing to weed along the hedge-row close to where Orlando chatted with the elders. Because it was Orlando who had been given this challenge, the guards, Louis, and Badoyn with his two knights remained on horseback along the trail, lingering at the edge of the village. Every few moments, Badoyn had to call his dog back, yet it barked no matter how Badoyn yelled at it.

Orlando stood before the elders and imitated a great commander he'd once served, years before, explaining a difficult order to surprised people. Exchanging bewildered glances, they asked him to repeat the request. The oldest woman, who was called Paulette and whose eyes were clouded with cataracts, knew where Orlando stood and stared at him with white eyes. "The vicomte wants us to pay this year's tithes early?"

"*Pas, senhórs e de madamas.*" Orlando forced out words he didn't believe, fumbling for words in the local tongue. "Simon, vicomte of Carcassona, insists these tithes were due at the last harvest."

This generated emotional denials and pleas—in the local tongue, so that Orlando had to concentrate hard to understand, continually interrupted by that unhappily barking dog.

"We paid at Michaelmas." This ancient man had come to the parley straight from his garden, his clogs and breeches dusty from spring planting.

"Before the rains came in October." This woman was so tiny, Orlando had thought at first a child sat among the elders. She also wheezed dreadfully, and could barely get her words out.

"The bishop's clerk wrote our names on the lists when we paid." This man, so old that his face had folded in on itself, shook his finger at Orlando, then stopped, tucking his hand behind his back.

What Orlando saw: people who were better neighbors to each other than he'd seen with his grandfather Daniel and their neighbors in Troyes. He knew these people had no ability to advance the next year's tithe before the harvest. Yet, doing his duty for the Church as the vicomte's official, Orlando could not officially agree with the elders' assertion. The dilemma burned in him, a humiliating fire.

"*Lo mieu aimat capitani, ajuda-nos!*" Paulette seemed near tears. *My dear captain, help us!* "We helped the French lords when they came. We know what's right."

He couldn't transgress his duty to Simon, though he knew what the elders said to be true.

The elder beside that woman grasped her hand, holding it to comfort her friend while he addressed Orlando. "We know the old vicomte failed us, letting seigneurs flaunt their contempt for the Church. Our old lords kept our tithes, which should have gone to Rome. Under Simon, we paid directly to the Churchmen."

If only the mistral, which had stirred dust around them throughout the conversation, forcing the women to hold onto their veils and skirts, would pick Orlando up and drop him in the Outremer. He'd leave Midnight behind, let his horse retire here with the distressed villagers.

"Let's meet tomorrow with the bishop's clerk." Orlando didn't know what other argument to make. He heard his cousin in the distance, once more calling his dog. "We'll review the list against his records from the last harvest tithes."

"You'll plead for us, won't you?" The elder's brown eyes brimmed with tears still. "You'll tell Simon he's mistaken?"

Another man said, "We won't have silver from trade until the merchant fairs begin, after Pentecost."

"*Atencion! Lo diable!*"

A voice shouted from the gardens, warning of the devil.

Overhead, a mass of crows darkened a patch of sky, their murderous caws ringing through the village as they hovered. People in their gardens stood up, waving their arms, their veils, their shirts. At the moment when the murder of crows mobbed the huge chestnut that shaded Orlando and the elders, a voice cried out in French.

"Bandits! *Arrêtez-les!*"

Orlando was running for his horse when the *gardes du corps* thundered past, riding into the village's passageways, which were too narrow for armored knights and horses. Midnight had shied away from the crows and didn't join the others. The greyhound bolted away, too. Orlando ran into the heart of the village.

Black smoke rose on the other side of the village. The mistral caught it and drove the dark spume to the south.

■

The murder of crows shrieked overhead, taking turns diving into the pastures and gardens, rising up and swerving away from the stream of smoke.

People ran past him, away from the core of the village. The guards had abandoned their horses and were kicking at doors, repeating the battle shouts from the year when Carcassona was seized and subdued.

"Montfort!"

"St-Denis!

And the ridiculous chant Simon taught men to cry the first year they'd come to the Pays d'Òc: "*Renards! Renards!* Foxes in the vineyards!" For whatever reason, his brother's voice chanted too.

Bring us the foxes, the wee little foxes!

Be still! There is no time!

Renards! Renards!

Orlando drew his sword, seeking to restore order among the rioting guards, who were ransacking the village, as if this were a clutch of heretics to be punished. Guards emerged through broken doorways with boxes in their hands. Orlando rammed the butt of his sword into one guard's kidneys, kicked at a guard carrying a lamb from a villager's backyard corral.

"*Arrête! Arrête!*" Orlando shouted at guards that he couldn't reach to physically stop them. Not one guard glanced his way.

It's too late! Bring us the foxes, the wee little foxes!

That cloud of smoke rose from a cottage at the far edge of the village—Estela's tiny hut, the herb woman who'd prayed that the mistral not drive men mad. Orlando ran toward the fire, fighting deep pain when his bad leg cramped, like an evil spirit wrapped around his leg to hinder his effort.

"*Bouge, fils de pute!*" Badoyn crudely admonished the guards to be sharp. "Be quick and be gone!"

Orlando didn't recognize the man who carried a body from the burning cottage and laid the person down, out of the way of the scrambling guards and fleeing villagers.

The body was Mme Estela, still as a broken tapestry doll.

Orlando sprinted for the cottage door, seeking anyone inside who needed help. The man who'd carried out Estela leaped ahead of Orlando, shoving him to the ground and then bounding into the cottage. In a heartbeat, that man carried out Louis and laid him down away from the smoke.

The man bent over Louis, sword in hand. Orlando stumbled to his feet, coughing in the black smoke.

"*Arrête!*" Orlando cried.

He charged ahead, forcing his legs to work, prepared to bring his sword down on Louis's attacker. The turbaned figure glanced up—a Saracen!—and stepped aside, arms outstretched, as if to embrace him. Or like the Savior on the cross. Yet still, Orlando's sword struck the man's middle in a death blow.

7
Bruixa

ORLANDO WOKE THINKING HE'D GONE blind, then saw the rainbow of colors that came with a scolding from Etienne.

Bring us the foxes, the wee little foxes! Renards! Renards!

Not blind, just lying in a dark room, nagged by his brother's ghost.

"You aren't dead." A man spoke in the tongue of the Catalan mountain people, both his voice and accent rough as the sand the mistral blew. Yet young. He stood over Orlando, a shadow in a turban. The Saracen from the village. "You've only been out for a worrisome long time. Are you well?"

"I killed you." Orlando felt the sensation again, his sword running through the man's middle.

"Not nearly." The man fumbled in the dark, then the sound of flint on steel rang. He lit a rush lamp, its flame flickering among the shadows in a derelict cottage. Broken roof tiles littered the stamped-earth floor where Orlando lay. The dancing lamplight glistened on blood that had dried above the Saracen's eyes. He wiped at his head carelessly with a kerchief. "See, only a rip in my surcoat. A nick on my forehead. Not as bad as the blows your comrade gave you."

His rescuer proved to be a heavily armed Saracen, sword at his side, one dagger in a baldric and another in his boot. A woad-blue turban covered his head, the tail of the cloth wrapped around his face. He wore a long saffron-dyed surcoat over chainmail, his loose linen trousers tucked into tall boots. As exotic as any man Orlando had met in the Pays d'Òc, even among *mestitz* mercenaries who

fought for the vicomte of Foix or worked as bodyguards on merchant trains.

"My comrade? You attacked us."

"No, your men ran through the village with blades drawn,
without provocation. And pillaged like pirates. The blond man who
ordered the guards struck your friend inside the cottage. And then
struck you just as you tried to stab me—though I'm sure you only
meant to rescue your friend. It was all a misunderstanding between
you and me, so I take no offense."

"No! They are my comrades. I don't believe you."

The Saracen shrugged, didn't argue. "In my opinion, a man who
clobbers your head isn't a worthy comrade. Anyway, the men you
call your comrades whistled for their horses and took your friend
along. Left you behind."

"They left me?" Even with worthless Badoyn driving the guards
to riot, this story made no sense.

"They might have looked for you, but I'd already saved you."

"Saved me?"

"I believe your so-called comrades intended to kill you."

"I abjure you in the name of God to speak truth."

"And I abjure you to lie still for a while longer." The Saracen
knelt by Orlando, resting a hand on his chest. Orlando started to
rise, but couldn't, as if his attacker held him in place with his fingertips. "A head wound like yours can be dangerous."

"Simon will exact revenge on your rabble." Orlando's head
throbbed. "Remember Bram?"

"When Simon cut the noses off the faces of a hundred men?"
The Saracen spat into the broken rubble on the floor. "How can you
serve such a man? Thinks he's the right hand of God, when he's the
devil's own toenail."

"Simon answered the pope's call for justice. We're here because
the Pays d'Òc has been mired in heresy."

"But this village? No. This village holds your bakers and laundrywomen and lads that muck your stables. You've inspected them
morning and night for years. Your comrades attacked Roman Christians and then betrayed you here, the same way Simon betrays the
Word of God and the king of France."

When Orlando blinked, and took too long to open his eyes again, he remembered smoke pouring from that cottage, Estela lying dead, like in his early-morning dark vision. And Louis, inert on the ground. "Louis is alive? You didn't kill him?"

"I didn't kill anyone, Captain. Your comrades, though, shoved that old woman too hard for her frail bones. God claimed her for His own before I could save her. I did come in time to carry your friend out of the fire. And to drag you out of reach of your murderous comrades."

"Who are you?"

"Call me Tarek. I'm a traveling knight who stopped to protect the weak and innocent. As required for my family's honor and as we are begged to do by our lord Jesus."

"A Saracen knight?"

"A Christian knight. The only Saracens around here since Charlemagne are merchants."

"But your clothes!" Orlando lifted a hand to point, but pain wrenched his shoulder, shot up to add to his headache.

"Hmmm. I wore these tatters in Andalusia to fight the wind and sun while we chased the caliph back across the Great Sea."

"Where's my horse?"

"I don't know. That cut above your brow is bleeding into your eye." Tarek handed Orlando the kerchief he'd used to wipe his own face. "I did what I could with the bump on your head, but you need to cut your hair to tend it properly. Now, how do we get you home?"

"I can take myself home." Orlando blinked again, still not sure he wasn't at least partly blind.

"Can you walk? Or are you too badly hurt?" He knelt beside Orlando, feeling for broken bones the way a field-surgeon once did, and then began swearing. "Judas's toe! How do you make it through the day? Those bones must plague you like a living devil. Did a shaytan burrow into you?"

"It's nothing." He wasn't sure what a shaytan was, and wouldn't ask. "Many men have taken worse."

"But most didn't live. A devil tore its way up your leg and through your middle to tromp around. Am I right?"

"It's nothing, I tell you."

"*Aiieee!* May the Holy Mother and her divine Son bless you. You need it more than most."

Orlando couldn't answer because he felt blood trickling into his eyes and heard Etienne's whispered warnings.

Thou shalt neither avenge nor bear grudges against thine own family for their transgressions.

I do not, brother. I take it all on my own soul.

Fool, fool!

Colors danced on the lids of his eyes. He smelled battlefield: offal and blood, human and horse shit. His head pounded like it did the first time, when his brother died, when his ghost came that night when Orlando claimed Etienne's silver dagger, the one their father gave him. The kind you give a small boy, not large enough for fighting, only to keep in your boot for emergencies.

He'd never believed in ghosts then, knew no spirits. He talked to a priest, a little man in the marquis's entourage, who said, oh yes, our loved ones can stay close, until our prayers carry them beyond this world. So Orlando spent every spare copper or silver penny buying intercessions for Etienne. All the prayers Orlando whispered, at each of the seven bells, were for the deliverance of his brother's soul. And he depended on Etienne's warnings.

Fool, fool!

"*Jhezu del tron.*" The Saracen called on the Savior in heaven, like a Christian would. "You're possessed."

"No, I'm my own man, body and soul."

"But your brother's ghost speaks to you. So you pray to God for intercession. Ever since Constantinople." Tarek wiped at Orlando's eyes. He blinked, trying to see.

"Are you a witch? A mage?" What did people call sorcerers here in the wild south? "*Bruixa? Masca?* Do you hear men's thoughts?"

"No, it's not magic, just second sight. We have to think about how to help you. This might take some time."

"I need to get back to the city. I have night duty. And a meeting with Simon. Please—"

A dog came snuffling into the broken hut.

"*Hola, gos!*" The Saracen—Tarek—greeted the dog in Catalan, then switched to French, as if dogs know languages. "*Qui est un bon garçon?*"

It came to sniff near Orlando, and now that he could see again, he recognized Badoyn's hound in the lamp light. What was its name? The dog lay beside him, as if it were as beaten down by the day as Orlando had been. The dog pushed his long snout up against Orlando's neck and sighed, its warm breath taking him back, to hiding in the kennels to escape his cousin, the tutor, his grandfather cursing him for hiding. That was after his father and then his grandmother died; Etienne had gone to Paris as a squire in the king's court.

Tarek lay on his other side, resting a hand over where Orlando's heart beat. It thumped harder at the man's touch, like when the widow touched him in the morning.

Alarmed, Orlando jerked away. The dog jumped up. When Orlando sat up, head throbbing, the dog padded back, laying its head in his lap.

"Monsieur Captain, you are possessed by a zaar."

"What's that?"

"A demiurge we've never met before. They all went to Egypt with the Sea People eons ago. Some went with Alexander to Sheba. That's what…people say." Tarek touched him like a field-surgeon again. "Burning pain in your middle? Nightmares?"

"Everyone has nightmares."

"Blackouts?" Tarek squatted beside him, silent, like a man listening to a friend or a commander. "A wind that blows through the hole the zaar carved in your heart?"

"My brother's soul watches over me, while I pray to get his soul on the road to heaven."

"It's not your brother's ghost," Tarek said. "It's an evil creature the Fire Lord discarded. It snatched a voice from your dreams and uses it to torture you. It eats the iron inside you."

"What? Why?"

"To be evil."

"No one is evil on purpose." Orlando believed that to be true. Except for one man. Who started the sequence of events which led to Etienne dying and Orlando cast out.

"Oh, you blessed innocent!" Tarek exclaimed. "You know for a certainty that Giles de Nully chose evil."

"Do you read my thoughts? How do you know him?"

"We met in Cahors." Tarek spoke casually. "If you knew Giles, you know he was evil. And if you believe in God…"

"Of course, I do," Orlando said. "It's why I came south with Simon. To serve God."

"And God lets us choose good or evil. Giles chose evil." Tarek scratched the dog between its ears. "Giles brought at least one spirit from the Fire Lord into this world. Did he call this zaar too?"

"He was a—a mage?"

"Giles? He was an evil fool. Do you want me to try to get this nasty thing out of you?"

"I don't…No. I need my brother to tell me…"

"This creature can't make its own sounds. It uses a voice you saved, and it feeds on secrets and guilt. If you won't let me take it away, perhaps you can starve it over time. If you can manage to let your secrets go."

Orlando said, "I've carried all my guilty deeds to our Savior. So my sins are forgiven."

"Forgiven by God, surely. But what about those you wronged? Don't let this zaar eat you. Let me remove it."

Orlando didn't answer. Tarek continued to argue about a possessing spirit, as if there were another man there to argue with.

"Hmm, one of eighty-eight emissaries? And we're supposed to dance and sing for three days? We don't have time for that. And we don't have goat blood to mix with butter. I'm sure this captain probably couldn't be coaxed to drink that."

With some stress, Orlando stood, grateful that the hound was so large that he could steady himself on its back. "I have to go back to Carcassona."

"When you get there, can you stop Simon from calling trouble down on people's heads? These villages don't deserve it." The man wiped at Orlando's eyes again with the kerchief. "*Jhezu del tron,* you serve a monster who wants to make himself king."

"I serve God. And the people of the city. And my own honor."

"Good for you."

"I'll go now. I can walk back to the city."

"If I can borrow one, will you ride a burro?" Tarek pronounced burro with a foreign-sounding buzz. "Maybe we can load you into the city with tomorrow's firewood. The bakers can be trusted to be silent. And the washerwomen who light their fires before dawn. Do you want to wait until dawn?"

While Tarek talked logistics, not seeming to expect an answer, Orlando felt his bones and contusions, finding the bump and cut on his head to be the worst, but also a long bruise down his forearm and another across his back.

"I don't need a burro," Orlando said. Nothing would relieve the ignominy of losing his horse and losing control of the guards on a simple patrol. "I'm expected at the chateau for a midnight supper."

"Come, then. You'll have to walk."

He set out, Badoyn's greyhound at his side.

In the village, walking through the narrow passages, Orlando noticed that more than half the houses remained burned out, scarcely livable. Along the edge of the village, old women and men tended gardens in the fading light. On foot he could see beyond hedges and fences that hid untaxed gardens from the trail. What he didn't see: small children; babies.

A few people were returning to the village from work. He knew most of them, but every single person refused to notice him. Doors were shut and windows shuttered. If he came upon any man or woman suddenly, they turned their backs on him and hurried along the road, as if Orlando were not just invisible but a repellant force. With only one afternoon spent outside the walled city, a handful of ill-disciplined *gardes du corps* had destroyed the peace everyone had enjoyed since the first season Orlando patrolled here.

While the hound snuffled for rabbits along the side of the trail, the walk back to the city gave Orlando moments alone to ponder how Tarek—Saracen, mage, or whatever—came to the hare-headed judgment that Orlando was possessed of a demon. He discarded that notion, along with Tarek's claim that Badoyn had struck him. The puzzle was that Simon hadn't already sent a force back to the village. Surely the guards all saw the turbaned bandit.

What he didn't hear on the walk was Etienne's ghost, only his own voice talking with the hound and chanting a song.

> With a courage-filled heart,
> Balthazar gallops
> to the castle of the cruel lord.
> His blood hot, he spurs his Saracen steed
> and cries 'All glory to God!'

Near the city walls, he found Midnight, as if his horse had chosen to take a holiday and dawdle where the grass was springtime sweet. With a grunt and a growl, the hound bolted from Orlando's side. It launched into the tumble of rocks long ago fallen from the walls or left by builders.

A cry rose from deep in the rocks, like a shrieking infant.

"*Viens, mon chien!* No rabbits in those rocks. Only wild cats! The rabbits live below the other side of the city. *Tiens, chien!*"

But the dog was quickly out of sight, not answering to calls. And Orlando the night-marshal was due in the city. Badoyn would have to hunt down his own dog.

8

A Stitch in Time

WHEN ORLANDO WALKED WITH MIDNIGHT up the incline to the city gates, noise rose from the walls. Men cheered, shouting his name, waving lances and crossbows. When he came close enough to be heard, Orlando called out, *"Bonsoir, messieurs. Comment ça va?"*

"We thought you were lost!" Umbert shouted from atop the wall. "Badoyn rescued Louis from the Saracen bandits."

"How is Captain Louis?"

Orlando tolerated the guards clapping his bruised back, having to ask several times before hearing that Louis had only a bad bump on the head.

"The bandits ran when you killed one of them!" Umbert exclaimed. "The guards chased the rest into the eastern hills. They thought you were dead. Or taken for ransom."

"Who'd ever ransom me?" Orlando said it aloud, when it should have been a private thought.

"Simon, of course. Your cousin told him how you saved Captain Louis. And how the guards found all the hidden booty."

Umbert likely embroidered what he'd heard, excited that his captain was hero. This story made a bit more sense than what the mage-knight told him. Tarek—what kind of name was that?

At sunset, when the vesper bell rang, Orlando walked across the city to confer at the watchtower with that night's duty-sergeant, who wanted to embrace him as a hero, and who had already assigned a guard to walk the night's duty in Orlando's place.

While the sergeant talked, Orlando wrestled with tension. Before seeing Simon, he wanted to know how Mme Marguerite fared with the new students, because from Umbert's tale of events, it was clear the sergeant had left the boys when Badoyn and the guards returned, and hadn't checked on the boys since. It wasn't a long walk across the quarter where the basilica stood, but as Orlando left the path along the wall, he still grappled with tension. He'd missed the mid-afternoon nones bell and his ritual prayer. He hadn't walked one circle of the city walls as part of his night-marshal routine.

Which wouldn't matter if he were pacifying a demon instead of praying for his brother's soul. That blasted mage-knight, if that's what he was, had disturbed the core of his life. Orlando couldn't find Etienne's voice, only the pain in his bones.

At the villa, Marguerite stitched at her needlework in her workroom, the door thrown wide to the night air. With light cast from rush-wick lamps, she bent over her tambour. A moth flickered close to the flame, then withdrew into the shadows.

"*Bonsoir*, madam."

"*Aiieee*, monsieur!" Startled, she jumped up and rushed to the portico. Her cat fell from her lap, scrambled up, and tripped her while scampering away. She clutched the shoulders of Orlando's shirt to catch herself. He steadied her, hands at her waist. She smelled of mint and roses, and trembled so much that the rings of his chainmail chimed. She straightened and stepped back.

"Your cousin said you were dead! That tomorrow the school would have a new master."

"Yet here I am, only a mite battered." A warmth returned to his veins because of her wild greeting. A friend. He had a friend.

"Well, no tears for you then." She sounded light-hearted, but only almost. "I have a bath waiting in the pantry, but you need it more than I do, Captain. We'll send your armor to the bachelors' barracks and fetch back clean clothes for you."

"You are kind. But Simon commands me to join his midnight supper. I only stopped to check that the new boys aren't plaguing you and—"

"The mercenary we hired, Karles, has taken the boys in hand. Please accept the bath, Captain. You can't offer such a frightful countenance at the chateau."

When Orlando emerged after washing, drawing on his soiled shirt, Marguerite was working again, but she ceased abruptly, rushing at Orlando with a linen strip she had near to hand.

"Monsieur, you need stitches."

Whatever the mage-knight in St-Luc had done to stop that cut above Orlando's eye, it'd washed away in the cool bath. He followed Marguerite to the kitchen, where more rush lamps were lit. She pointed to the stool where she wanted him to sit. "Only three," she murmured as she leaned over to inspect the cut. Her hair smelled like a garden in summer. "Do you need—"

"Nothing. I'm ready."

"Sit still and don't talk while I'm working."

He submitted to her needlework. Though she wouldn't let him talk, she chatted as she stitched.

"The older boys told the new ones that I'm Morgaine le Fey."

"The sorceress in Arthur songs? Oh, madam, I'm sorry."

"No harm. And don't talk while I'm stitching. Karles walked into the barracks when one boy was saying, 'If she stitches your image into her tapestry, she captures your soul.'"

"I shall stop that rumor tomorrow, madam, and I'll make sure they treat you with respect."

"Stop talking, *s'il vous plait.* And let the rumor continue. What's more respectable than a sorceress who steals souls? And stitches them into tapestries, to sell on market day."

Bring us the foxes, the wee little foxes!

Are you Etienne's ghost? Or a spirit that stole his voice? A demon?

Silky, silky foxes.

"*Ça va faire!* All done." Marguerite declared her own work to be good while snipping at the thread with tiny silver shears.

"*Merci*, madam." He wanted to be as lighthearted as she pretended. "Did you stitch my face into a heroic figure, like in your tapestries?"

"Do you want to be a hero? From the old tales, it seems to be painful work."

She returned to her workroom, fetching her embroidery tambour from a work-bag, and waited patiently while Orlando slowly followed. Her grey cat leaped from the shadows into her lap. She stroked it, to push it down in her lap so she could see her work. "Karles says the new boys need washing and barbering."

"As usual, you are one step ahead of me, madam." Orlando yearned for a return to mundane business. He'd sat still too long in the kitchen, and now needed to stand in her workroom. He didn't want his leg to stiffen up; he leaned against the door frame, so he wouldn't hover over Marguerite at her work. Then he decided he had no other friend to trust. It wouldn't do to approach Louis.

We want the foxes, the wee little foxes!

"I couldn't stop what happened on patrol today." This, perhaps, drove most of his tension. Simon had heard Orlando was a hero, but the opposite was true; he'd failed the challenge.

"The fire that the Saracen bandits set?"

"There were no Saracens." The fellow Tarek, the mage-knight, called himself a Christian. "The guards rioted. They're all ill-trained, bored ruffians with no honor, and...no, it's my fault."

"That French guards rioted? How is that your fault?"

"Simon wanted me to prove I could command men. If they went astray, it's on me. I was the knight in command."

"But your cousin is also a knight. Did he bear responsibility for those men, too? And Captain Louis?"

The mistral gusted, creaking the portico doors.

"There was at least that one stranger in the village, if not bandits. That stranger claimed my cousin Badoyn attacked Louis, then me. But I can't believe that."

"I am loath to admit it, but I took a dislike to your cousin from stories you've told." She glanced up from her work, her face soft in the lamplight. "Does he have any reason to harm you? For your family's wealth and title?"

"No, my grandfather will leave what little he has to Badoyn. There's no telling who struck me. It might have been an accident. It was chaos there, as if the mistral drove those men mad."

"Pentecost can't come soon enough," she said.

Orlando continued to declare the burdens he carried. "And Badoyn proposes that we team together, to help Simon succeed in the Pays d'Òc. He has some scheme to make us rich. Perhaps capturing treasure from heretics."

"Every knight hopes to find their treasure." Marguerite sounded disdainful. "All that gold hoarded by people who vowed poverty."

"Badoyn also wants Simon to give him Giles de Nully's castle in Cahors. Though it must belong to Philippe Augustus, to keep or give away. It's…disturbing, don't you think?"

"Yes, but if Simon plans to…" Marguerite's voice trailed off. She busily examined her embroidery stitches, leaning close to the rush lamp.

"To what?"

"Make himself king. God's chosen ruler in the south." She hurried into an explanation. "I'd never repeat such a rumor. Except you and I share God-given duties, so we should be united as the world changes around us."

He must be exhausted; although the idea of unity felt comforting, her first words stirred the trouble roiling within him. "I heard two different times today that Simon intends to be king."

"Does it make you wonder what the pope and King Philippe will say to that?" Marguerite spoke with a kind of hardness Orlando had never heard from her. "What will you do if Simon breaks his loyalty to Philippe?"

Instead of answering, he burst with all of the day's troubles. "Nothing is as I believed when the sun rose today. My family offers no future for me. Simon forgot the promises he made to me. My comrades ran riot in our own neighborhood." That mage-knight denied him the comfort of Etienne's voice. "My cousin—"

"Tried to kill you?"

"No, I don't believe that."

Then she said, "What do you want, *mon ami?* For yourself?"

Bring us the foxes, the wee little foxes!

You are not my good brother.

Silk, silky foxes.

He shivered, not knowing what voice he heard; his hands smelled as if licked by a dog, in spite of the bath. Tarek the mage-knight had broken something inside him. "I want horses and retainers again, like a bannered knight. Enough silver that I don't have to live in the bachelors' barracks."

"You are too modest. I believe you want more, captain."

"I want noble work. My father, my grandmother, they claimed I was destined to save the world. I've only saved the *gardes du corps* from serving double shifts. I didn't save the village today."

At just that moment, Marguerite's servant appeared, bearing Orlando's last clean shirt, which reminded him again that he needed to buy new shirts next market day.

"We sent your other shirt to the laundry women this morning." Marguerite didn't look up from her embroidery. "We'll send your ruined shirt also."

He stepped into an ante room to put on the shirt. The *gardes du corps* in the towers called the all-is-well signal to each other.

"You seem to be serving double shifts, Captain." Her voice carried from her workroom. "Even if the guards are not."

"And I'd best run to the chateau and do my principal duty."

"To serve Simon?"

"That seems to be the only choice." He retied the string that kept his hair back. "I cannot choose Badoyn's schemes."

"Wait!" She was at the archway that opened to the portico, Orlando's scarlet scarf in hand. "Captain Louis's wife sent this over when we feared you were lost. I washed it and—"

When he reached for the scarf, she grasped his hand. She was trembling again.

"Orlando, I believe you *are* destined to help make the world right. Your true comrades will find you."

"Madam—I—thank you." He didn't know what might be the right response. "May it all be as pleases God."

He was repeating Estela's words, that peculiar turn of speech one heard everywhere in the Pays d'Òc. Not words, however, that his brother ever heard spoken.

The mistral slammed him with a maddening gust, sand grinding into his face, which didn't serve as an answer.

9

A Host of Angels

BRANCHES OF CANDLES EVERYWHERE, THE great hall was brighter than it had been at midday (a lifetime ago!) when Orlando had come filled with hope. He stood at the doors near midnight filled with doubt. Halos from the candles glowed around the knights and their wives and visitors. The room buzzed with conversation. People had dressed up, shining under candlelight like a host of angels.

The chandler's men offered mugs of wine among the milling crowd that waited for supper. Of the twenty or so women from the city, a dozen stood with their husband-knights, and the others clung together, many linking arms like sisters. Mme Taresa linked elbows with her smaller companion. They turned each other loose when Badoyn offered a toast to Simon in the manner Orlando knew from Pays de France courts. Badoyn hung near his lover's side. When he spotted Orlando, he called across the room.

"Here's the day's hero! Captain Orlando brings all glory to the county of Troyes!"

People clapped; several called out *Orlando! Orlando!*

Startled, Orlando bowed modestly and stepped close to his cousin, far too aware that Mme Taresa inspected him, her lips pursed in judgment. "*Qu'est-ce que c'est*, cousin?"

"I told Simon how you earned the day for God and France."

"*C'est quoi ça?* What did I earn? I was knocked out and you abandoned me."

"Peace, Balthazar. For our plan to work, we must be united. I'm happy to make you a hero in Simon's eyes with this victory!"

"Victory?" His insides boiled up, remembering the disaster in the village and smelling the ruinous fire again.

Aged women become not holy, become false accusers, given to much wine.

Estela was innocent. She died exactly as in my vision. She died because I failed.

Let your women keep silence; it is not permitted for them to speak.

Badoyn had turned his attention back to the woman he'd designated his true love.

"It's the local wine, isn't it?" The woman wrinkled her nose at first sip. "We should create better markets between the Rhône and Carcassona." She tapped Badoyn's hand to emphasize her point. "People seem ready to live a civilized life here, but the vineyards haven't recovered. That quandary is an opportunity for the right man. There's gold to be made in Rhône wine."

Badoyn seized her hand and kissed it. "Mme Hélène, may I present my cousin, Orlando de Troyes?"

"A knight from Troyes, like *mon cher* Badoyn?" Hélène held out her hand to Orlando. "Or are you a poet?"

"Men from Troyes are all poets." Orlando performed the court rituals, holding her hand in his, kissing it lightly; her long nails dangled from black net fingerless gloves.

"Your hand is so cold!" Hélène exclaimed.

"*Mains froides, coeur chaud.*" Orlando played at court manners while noticing that the ruby Hélène wore at her throat would outfit three knights for a year. He said what he was supposed to say, playing by rules of court life. "Your hands are so soft, madam."

"Yet I have claws." Hélène dragged her nail down the center of his palm, sending an outlandish shiver up his arm. She was certainly beautiful—dark hair caught up in a gold net, a turned-up nose, lips as red as the ruby at her throat but more luscious—and she'd worked harder at it than God did for her in the beginning.

Badoyn was not subtle about turning her attention back to him. "Hélène, do you want to greet the vicomte, as I promised?"

Taresa said, "*Ma dòmna,* your friend's cousin is the famous Captain Orlando, who's responsible for Henri now."

Hélène was being led away by Badoyn, but she said over her shoulder, "Thank God someone took the brat off our hands. And thank God you're alive, Captain. We thought poor Badoyn would be forced to take over your school."

Hélène followed Badoyn to where Simon was surrounded by his traveling knights and their wives. The milling crowd bumped Mme Taresa, thrusting her close to Orlando.

> *She stood boldly, arms outstretched like Our Savior on the cross, wind blowing her russet hair, and the soldier's lance pierced her side. Deep. Run through as if on the battlefield. The smell of singed flesh everywhere, as if a firebrand burned marks on the spring foals.*

Poulains. Branding the *poulains.*

Mme Taresa stared into his eyes, as provocative as she'd been at their first meeting.

"Are you quite well, Captain? You've had a hard day."

"*Oui*
, *s'il vous plait.*" He answered mechanically, then considered that only she and Mme Marguerite asked after his well-being. His eyes drawn repeatedly to Simon, who hadn't acknowledged him, Orlando fumbled to recover his court manners. "Welcome to Carcassona, madam. We usually entertain only wives and sisters of our knights. Tell me what brings you to the city."

Taresa smiled at him, which he found all too pleasant. "From what the servants say, Carcassona hears the news as rapidly as the sun moves over the city. You must know."

"I'm usually the last to hear news, madam, unless it happens after curfew."

"Yet people who see me sipping wine beside the day's hero will endeavor to know our secrets before their bread is baked at dawn. Alas, there's so little to tell."

Was she flirting? Or toying with him? "Tell me what brings you to Carcassona."

"Hélène's aunt needed help, and we wished to find shelter in a safe city. Chaos swirls around Toulouse like crows in the chestnut trees at sunset."

Crows. Crows. A murder of crows, blackening the skies like smoke. Fire! Fire!

I cannot believe your nonsense. Or the visions and odors.

Crows of the valley shall pick out its eyes.
Eagles shall eat it.

"How'd you gain permission to live in the city? Simon isn't free with passes for any but knights' families."

"My mentor Hélène is the dowager marquesa de Beaurain. She asked the new marquis to intercede with Simon. So here we are now, three widows in a sad villa."

She touched his wrist, the heat and the Beaurain name sending a stream of unwanted memories through him. On the day Minerve surrendered, ending the siege, Orlando had been abandoned in a hospital tent, in full view of the pyre, the smoke and stink wafting over him while the crowd drank the health of Simon and Jean-Luc de Chartrain, now the marquis de Beaurain.

"Do you know the new marquis? The hero who convinced the city of Minerve to surrender?" Taresa sipped her wine. The heat from her fingers lingered. "The new marquis is as avid as a camp-priest, preaching loyalty and fidelity. Isn't that what you teach in your academy, Captain?"

Her seditious remarks echoed from earlier that day. *Torturing and terrorizing people in God's name.*

No, no! The foxes, the dirty filthy foxes in the vineyards!

He blinked, fighting headache and rainbows and the smell of burning bodies, which stayed with him after the surrender at Minerve. He needed to recite a creed. "A knight must be loyal to his king and Church if he is to have any personal honor."

"Yet loyalty can be turned to serve evil ends." Instead of all that touching and teasing in their morning conversation, she harangued him. Softly. In whispers. "A leader who follows true principles doesn't need to invoke loyalty. It comes on its own, because it's deserved."

"That's why a knight also owes loyalty to those beneath him, and to his comrades." Was he repeating lessons, like a fight-master?

"Even to comrades who desert you in the field?" While she asked, her eyes drifted away from him, as if his list of loyalties lost her interest. The lady seemed touched by a provoking lesser angel, the kind who incite annoying quirks in a woman, the way old wives claim house-imps curdle milk. "Simon is motioning to you. I believe you are wanted."

Then Louis was at his elbow, dragging him away from the widow. "*Bon Dieu!* You're alive! Those bandits spared you!"

"*Et vous, mon ami?*" Relieved to be parted from that provoking woman, Orlando hugged his commander, as if they'd been apart for years, not half a day. "You are well?"

"A bump on my head." Louis touched the back of his head, any injury perfectly hidden by French curls. "Never saw the bastards coming. But let's go. Simon wants to hear your story."

10
A Quest

"HAIL THE HERO FROM TROYES!"

Simon was in an expansive mood, like when the archbishop anointed him as vicomte. One hand on his hip, grinning broadly, Simon stood by the head table. The bishop and a clutch of his knights hung at his elbow.

"Hardly a hero," Orlando said. *Don't argue.* He felt Louis at his side, tugging the back of his jerkin. He blinked, blinked again, refusing the blinding colors and the odor of sunbaked dust, his brother fishing beside him on a hot morning long ago.

You lust, and have not.

You are not my brother's ghost.

You desire, and cannot obtain.

"Playing at humility, eh, Captain Orlando? O noble knight!" Simon lifted his wine cup, halfway to a toast. "You proved today to be worth the investment I'm asked to make in you."

"You are kind to say so, Monseigneur." Except Orlando hadn't proved he could manage men; he failed to stop mayhem. Badoyn stepped close by his side, the man's heat kindling a dread inside Orlando.

"I have a new challenge for you, Captain." Simon pushed at his nose, folded his arms, and spread his legs, gestures Orlando recognized from earlier years working close to Simon: the vicomte had made up his mind about something.

"I shall do my best to help your work here succeed."

"Simon is giving us a quest, cousin." Badoyn held his hands clenched over his loins, as if they stood before the king rather than a lord who'd gained his title when the previous vicomte died of camp-sickness in his own dungeon.

"A quest? Tests of loyalty? Saving ladies from dragons?" Simon grabbed onto this idea with glee. He fiddled with the medallion in his hand, running its chain between his fingers. "Shall you be like knights of chivalry out of a tale from the poet of Troyes? Just what I need—and think of the glory that might come to your house."

"*Merci.* I am grateful." Orlando intended to go along with Simon's mood. "I am like Alexander, who 'did not dare request what he really desired.'" Clearly Simon didn't recognize the poetry. Too late, Orlando added, "A line from the lays of King Arthur, promising loyalty to a king."

"'God grant that chivalry be cherished here, and may the honor we've given refuge never depart from France.'" Badoyn chanted the words, having found a better line of poetry than Orlando did, though he mangled it in delivery.

"If I remember back to those years," Simon seemed on the verge of laughing again, "when we set out on crusade to the Outremer, you and your cousin always performed best when your captains set a competition between you. I seem to remember a magnificent foot-race before we departed from Zara."

Orlando risked a glance at his cousin, who seemed spell-bound by Simon. In fact, as he glanced around the great room, every man in the room rendered Simon rapt attention. The vicomte surely wasn't about to propose a footrace.

"Your noble quest, my loyal knights," Simon's lips twitched, suppressing delight, "is to cleanse the neighborhood of filth and to collect the remaining unpaid tithes owed the Church. Rid the villages and seigneurs' farms here of rebels and heretics."

"Yes, Monseigneur." Badoyn had turned solemn. "We shall."

When Orlando tried to ask a question, Simon held up his hand. "Let me finish, so you understand. At great cost to knights and lords of the Pays de France, and our own counties at home, we did as the pope asked, to rid this land of the smut of heresy." Simon paced, three to the left, then back again, the way he did when haranguing troops before an assault. "The pope's letters promise that he has sent a prelate, his favorite lawyer, to judge how well we've done our duty. Many seigneurs still rebel against the Church. They allow their heretic cousins to return from their hovels and hideouts in the hills."

Simon, pacing, stopped in mid-motion. He pointed an accusing finger at Louis and then at Orlando.

"The workmen are carrying stones out from our walls to rebuild their villages. Grain goes out the gate, defeating the efforts of the abbot and my chandler to ensure this city can withstand months of siege. Even for a year like the Cid did in Valencia."

Simon seemed to wait, wanting Louis to answer, but Louis remained silent, his head bowed, his hands folded over his loins like Badoyn. In Constantinople, Orlando saw what happened when men were falsely accused. He had to speak.

"Respectfully, Monseigneur, all our inquiries find deceptions in supplies coming *into* the city rather than theft from the stores." Orlando felt heat coming off Louis, as if he shouted in battle: *Arrêter! Arrêter! Arrêter!* Yet Orlando couldn't let the injustice stand. "We banished five guards for taking bribes, sent them back north. And we ceased purchasing from local seigneurs who sold us false weights. There's a writ before the bishop's court—"

"Ah, the bishop's court of judgment!" Simon lowered his voice, almost to a whisper. The famous technique that Orlando used with little boys, to force them to listen. A threat, then. "We enforce the judgment when the bishops offer justice. We cannot always wait for the Church's courts of law. But now, we're waiting for a prelate who will come judge us."

Simon paused in his pacing again, this time staring at Orlando, who knew an answer was required. Simon tapped a foot, which must show impatience, while he clutched that medallion in his hand, its chain swinging from his fist.

"No, Monseigneur." Orlando bent his head the way Badoyn and Louis had, folding his hands over his loins, conscious now that it was a gesture of protection.

"And the quarried stones missing from the effort to mend the city's wall? Those *paysans*—" Simon spat the word "—are building hovels with stones from the city walls."

People had re-used old stones since long before Charlemagne slept here. Orlando walked every day beside the stone works along the length of the old wall that ran from the chateau to the basilica. The piles of stones, recovered from fields below or newly quarried, had increased since the previous season. As night-marshal, he'd supervised the evening inspections when workers left the city. No stones could be carried away. *Don't argue,* Louis had said. Or was it Etienne?

"And you, Monsieur Louis," Simon turned his attention, "it's time to prove your *gardes du corps* has full control of the city and its neighborhoods."

"We are prepared to undertake your quest, Monseigneur." Badoyn brought his clasped hands up to his breast. God's bones! His cousin was prepared to crawl up the vicomte's backside.

"Let's make it interesting." Simon mused. "What did the poet of Troyes say about how knights of old proved their worth?"

"They went in search of the Grail," Orlando said.

"Well, you won't find a sodding grail in a damned heretic's hovel, will you?" Simon said it to amuse himself. Badoyn laughed. "A contest, then. Better than today."

"Like jousting in the lists at home?" Badoyn asked—but he couldn't be proposing that, since Orlando always beat him on horseback; a bad leg didn't affect his ability to ride or bear a lance.

"No, let's do more. I like the idea of a bounty. The bishop's clerk can be your scorekeeper. Franciscus?" He pointed to the portly clerk hovering near the bishop. "Two points for each heretic or rebel you hang. One point for each heretic's lair you burn, plus whatever booty you win by driving them into the hills. You'll pledge your very life on this quest, and we'll judge the score at Pentecost."

Simon shook his fist, having decided; his medallion chain swung, wrapping around his forearm. For the first time, Orlando saw the figures on the medallion.

Pledging your very life. Simon carried a Wheel and Serpent medallion, from the confraternity Giles de Nully invented in Constantinople. Where Giles's craven schemes got Etienne killed and Orlando humiliated.

Simon picked up his sword from beside his chair, an old-style iron war blade, its new hilt worked with gold. "Let's do like the old-time knights did. You can kneel and swear on your honor."

Badoyn had his arm linked with Orlando's and dragged his cousin down with him when he knelt. Like he had when Giles played a trick on them in Constantinople.

The mistral whistled through slots in the great room's walls, rushing back through the archways into the courtyard. Badoyn had revealed years before what he was capable of if riches were promised. Orlando couldn't compete; he couldn't hunt people to score points. He could say no—and thus surrender the night-marshal and academy fiefs. He lost track of Simon's words for a heartbeat, but his cousin was repeating them.

"I, Badoyn of Troyes," he repeated his father's and mother's lineage, "of my own free will do undertake this quest for the glory of God in service to the vicomte of Carcassona, for the salvation of the Pays d'Òc."

Simon held his sword for Orlando to place his hand on the hilt. The medallion dangling from his hand banged into Orlando's fingers. The Wheel and Serpent cast in gold, burnished to shine. A chill crawled up his scalp. No, it must be just the mistral.

You lust, and have not; you kill, and lose the battle; you desire, and cannot obtain.

I was promised!

You fight, and lose the war. Because you cannot have what you want. Fool, fool!

"I, Orlando of T–Troyes," for the sake of all that's holy, he would not add his father's name, "grandson of Daniel of Troyes, undertake this quest for the glory of God, who is merciful, and pledge my honor and my salvation in service to the Church's crusade for men's souls."

"How poetic!" Simon snatched back his sword. A knight behind him took the blade to stash it by Simon's chair. "Upon your honor and your salvation—and so pledging your very life, like knights of old!"

"Do we begin immediately?" Badoyn asked, his head, neck, and shoulders up the vicomte's arse.

"I'm not a tyrant sending you out the castle doors to fight dragons. You've done enough for today." Simon twirled that chain. "Make arrangements with your men tomorrow. Write the duty rolls so you don't leave the inside of Carcassona at the mercy of evil while you're…on quest. Oh how I like that! A quest."

"*Merci*, Monseigneur." Badoyn murmured.

"Now for our supper!" Simon exclaimed, not acknowledging Badoyn's sniveling.

Orlando stepped forward instead of back to the trestle tables, a question burning. "Who will take charge of the boys and squires in training while we undertake this quest?"

"Surely you, Captain Orlando, can do one thing in the morning and another in the afternoon." Simon's attention had already drifted elsewhere. He beckoned to one of the knights with him, speaking to Orlando over his shoulder. "Everyone says you're the best guide for young boys, which is why I sent my son to you today. I finally shook him loose from his mother's care. Why would I settle for less than the best for my son?"

> Simon raised his sword, commanding a charge while siege engines thundered all around, stones falling like hail. At a cry too near his ear, he looked up to see the boulder that would carry his soul away. The sizzling odor of torch-arrows filled the air, singeing all around him.

"Which of my charges is your son?" Orlando blinked away the evil vision; it surely came from a sinful corner of his heart.

"Better that I not say." Simon pressed his lips together as if he were protecting a secret. "Every boy deserves your full devotion to his training. And needs your protection for his wellbeing. I believe you'll risk everything for your charges as well as for your quest."

"*Oui*, Monseigneur."

At this point, Simon turned to Louis. "Now, can we eat?"

11
Gentlemen

AS VICOMTE SIMON CLEARLY EXPECTED, Orlando stepped back. But it wasn't Louis lurking behind him; it was Mme Taresa, arms akimbo.

"He put your life at stake with that oath, Captain." Taresa stood close in the crowded room, heat coming from her body in waves, whispering for only him. Her eyes shone in the candlelight. "What does Simon get from that?"

"I—he wants tithes for the Church. He wants peace in the neighborhood before the pope's prelate comes."

"He wants more. Simon wants fear in the villages. But why you? Why did he make you stake your life on doing evil for him?"

She might as well have kicked him in the gut. His thoughts couldn't find where to rest when Simon turned away from him, churning on the knowledge that he'd soon lose everything. When he already had nothing.

"Of course, you can't answer." Her eyes flashed, glancing at someone behind him. "You need to find better comrades. Perhaps you could be Hélène's *cavaller de la casa* until we find a better place for you."

She mixed Catalan among her words so Orlando had to consider what she meant. "House-knight? Serf with a sword?"

"Balthazar!" Badoyn had Orlando by the elbow again. "Come sit with my lady. And the lovely Mme Taresa." He towed Orlando and Taresa over to where Hélène sat, a few seats down from where Simon was dining with the bishop. Orlando sat between those two ladies, catching a wave from Louis, who was taking his place farther back in the room, entertaining the sergeants of the *gardes du corps*.

The woman who just proposed that he abandon his sworn lord put her hand on his thigh under the table. "It will all be as it pleases God. We'll make it be so, you and I."

His already spinning thoughts tilted, then flew about the room. He removed her hand.

The chandler's men placed platters and truncheons of food before the guests. A bread bowl for each, filled with river salmon creamed in a sauce of ground almonds and a good deal of saffron.

"But no ginger," Hélène sniffed.

Taresa fingered that charm she wore, still studying Orlando. She replied as if she habitually settled Hélène's complaints, "Ginger won't return to anyone's table until late in the summer."

The food might as well be stones on a dusty trail. Broken tiles in a hollowed-out cottage.

"What's this?" Hélène picked at a dish of tiny carrots, parsley root, and turnips.

"I believe," Taresa said, "it's pickled from the spring's early harvest. The radishes and fennel make it—"

"Spicy! It's almost as if we're in a civilized city. And look, a clafoutis. How clever." Hélène's voice rose as bowls of cherry clafoutis appeared, its roasted red fruit immersed in custard.

"It is," Taresa said. "How amazing that the cooks could produce a feast within a day of the vicomte arriving."

Hélène munched on mushroom pie spiced with black pepper. "True. Simon gave no warning about coming here."

"It's been rumored since Easter." Orlando finally made his voice work again.

"That didn't leave the kitchens any better prepared to create a feast in one day." Taresa licked delicately at the corner of her mouth. "You aren't eating, Captain. You need food to recover from this day's travails."

Before Orlando could answer—a stone sat in his belly—Simon demanded everyone's attention.

"For my beloved knights, and especially for their ladies, I brought rare entertainment. From the pontiff's court in Rome."

A tall *trouvère* stood where Orlando had recently sworn away his soul. Strumming an odd instrument, he sang crusader hymns and *chansons d'amour*. The afternoon's tragedy left Orlando wide open to songs of grief over loss of comrades and lovers. He studied the man, trying to hold out against emotion that boiled within him. Betray his lord by deserting? Or betray his honor by doing as his lord commanded?

> *Whatsoever thine eyes desire shall be kept from you, your heart withheld from all joy.*

No, you are not Etienne. He didn't even know scripture.

> *This is your portion for all of thy labor.*

Orlando refused to listen or argue with that ghost-voice. No rainbows. Only powerful pain throbbing behind his eye, in his bad leg. The smell of wildfire racing across dryland pasture.

"That singer is the same sort of *papillon* as Pedro of Aragón." Badoyn's sniping whisper carried to Orlando, though it was intended only for Mme Hélène. "As fey as that dead bastard king."

"Ah, *mon petit bricon*, you knew that king?" Hélène purred. She called Badoyn her little scoundrel.

Taller than any man in the room, the singer was also willow-switch thin, perhaps broad enough in the shoulders to support chainmail, but not so broad as Orlando. His long hair, white from sun, had been pulled into a braid that hung to his waist, rather less civilized than the French court style, more like a savage Brabant or, more likely, a wild Celt. He might be called handsome, with a long face and narrow jaw, a romantically broken nose, piercing blue eyes. But he smiled all the time, in a way which Orlando interpreted as a cynical grimace.

Beside Orlando, Mme Taresa persisted in chatting while picking at her food, apparently no more interested than he was in morose songs.

"The jongleur outdoes knights from Paris. Such long locks."

"You disapprove, madam?" He guessed from the critical tone in her voice.

"Summer is coming. Pays de France styles aren't the best for this country." Taresa speared a carrot with her slim eating knife but only studied it, didn't take a bite.

After six songs from the *trouvère*, Simon motioned the singer to his table and called for everyone's attention. "Let me introduce these two men."

Then the singer's friend stood, one hand on the wild Celt's shoulder, gazing out on the great room. Orlando endured the strangest sensation, that the man stared at him. Smaller than his Celt friend—a head-and-a-half shorter—he had the compact build of a *mestitz* fighter from the Pyrenees, with skin that seemed stained by dried walnuts. If Orlando worried that his own hair might escape its tieback-and-oil taming, this man didn't care; his wiry hair spun out like a halo, with wide streaks of white shot through it and through his well-tended beard. Judging from his immaculate fustian jerkin and silk shirt, the man must be vain.

Except his face had been carved into a puzzle and then stitched back together. A long slice dissected his eyebrow, ending at the corner of one dark eye. Another ran the length of the man's face. And the unkindest cut of all split the man's upper lip, creating a permanent twist of distain.

Rather than inspect these unusual creatures, Mme Taresa seemed interested only in her creamed river salmon. She hadn't glanced up while Simon introduced them, and Orlando didn't hear their names, because Taresa laid her fingers across his wrist.

"You deserve a quest better than Simon's. You should be protecting God's anointed kings, not serving that imposter."

"Madam!"

She held his wrist tight, her hot hand setting his blood on fire. "Simon trapped you with that oath. He's forced you to do whatever he wants on his way to being king."

"God's bones, madam! You cannot say such things."

Orlando whispered low, deep, in the way that his boys would take as a warning, while he shut out the false ghost's voice and the memories it tugged into his thoughts.

You trapped yourself here, because you failed.

"By my sainted grandmother, Captain, why may I not speak my mind? My husband's…Henri's *domus* pays its taxes and takes care of the poor. We're faithful Catholics. Simon can't set me on fire or shoot me with an arrow just because I noticed that he's an ambitious tyrant. He's using the Church to perpetrate cruelty, and he means to be the crowned ruler here."

"Madam, you are speaking treachery while sitting at Simon's table. You can't say—"

"Leaping goats! Will you swear on the altar of the basilica that you don't see it? To make himself king, Simon trapped you into terrorizing the villages."

"You're repeating servants' gossip and rumors. I must beg you to stop." He'd found her handsome in the sunlight; but in the candlelight, Mme Taresa was provoking rather than provocative.

"Why? Are you so loyal that you'll turn me over to Simon for speaking heresy?" Under the cover of the table, Taresa squeezed his thigh. "Or will you shoot me yourself?"

Watch out! Fool, fool!

Simon's voice rose again, pitched to reach the other side of the buzzing great room. "Captain Louis, these gentlemen came to me from the papal guard in Rome."

"*Gentlemen?*" Hélène hissed the word like a malediction.

Simon didn't hear. "These two trained the pope's own men, and have been training my guard since Easter. You may borrow them until midsummer, Captain Louis, to train your squires and any worthy soldiers you'd like to promote."

Louis stood when his name was mentioned. "You are generous. *Merci*, Monseigneur."

Simon laughed. "I'm not wealthy enough to be generous. You can pay them out of the *gardes du corps* silver until Captain Orlando and his cousin collect the missing tithes."

This is your portion for all of thy labor.

Hélène's voice rose just above a whisper. "That's enough for me for the night, *mon cher*. Will you walk me to my villa?"

Badoyn murmured an answer. Hélène laughed—a practiced laughter, to make men strive to elicit that music. "But I'm a defenseless woman who needs the services of a questing knight for her protection."

.

That was how Orlando ended up on the city streets at a time of night when he should only be walking the city walls and checking on the guards. He asked the guards at the door for lanterns, when it appeared that Badoyn had intended to stumble into dark streets he didn't know. Orlando walked beside Taresa, while Hélène and Badoyn walked ahead, hand in hand.

"Where do you live, madam?" And why didn't he know, since the night-marshal should know every inhabitant in his city?

Taresa said, "We're camped with Hélène's aunt, Agnes de Leuc, who lives by—"

"I know her villa!" He passed the widow's open door every morning, returning her shy wave as the old woman sat waiting for her servant. "Everyone knows Mme Agnes's story."

"It's so sad." Taresa touched his wrist again. He glanced down, wondering if the heat from her hand would leave a mark…and why he'd ever let her behave so intimately with him. "Her husband was killed at Béziers, supporting the French. Yet she starved in the siege of Carcassona like everyone else."

"Mme Agnes is under Simon's protection, because of her husband's loyalty." Orlando had missed the Béziers and Carcassona sieges, having been sent elsewhere by Simon, not returning until after the booty of Carcassona had been divided among other knights. "He let Mme Agnes remain in the city when the citizens were forced out."

"Òc, such a reward. She hasn't left her house since. She relives the terrors of the siege in her nightmares." Mme Taresa slipped into the local tongue. She tugged at the cord that held the charm she wore around her neck. "And Mme Agnes cannot seem to get on the list for the stone masons to come make repairs. Her roof still has a hole from the siege machines." Her probing glance was too bold, disconcerting. The gold flecks in her eyes shone more like the reflection on a steel blade. A thin white scar danced above her eyebrow, which he hadn't noticed before, but now it reflected like silver in the lantern light. "If Simon truly honored faithful knights, Mme Agnes wouldn't be living in a battle scene, too timid to venture into her garden. Which is filled with siege rubble."

At the *petit* well—Hélène and Badoyn having led them on a long arc from the chateau to the other side of the city—Hélène insisted on making a wish, tossing in a coin.

"That's a gold morabatin!" Badoyn exclaimed.

"I have significant wishes." Hélène clasped his hand to her breast.

Taresa hung back with Orlando, neither of them wanting to be in the midst of that courtship. She stood so close he could feel her heat, even in the chill of the mistral. He said, "*Et vous*, madam? Do you have significant wishes?"

"In such a time as this," Taresa's eyes locked on his, "God asks action of us, not mere wishes."

"Action? There is only duty. To God. And king. And—"

"Which king?" She spoke quietly, but so furiously that it felt as if he'd raised a cat's hackles. "Tell me what loyalty means to you. Will you let a false ruler like Simon play with your life? Or would you prefer to risk your life for a real king?"

"Balthazar!"

His cousin's shout kept him from answering the treason this woman spoke. Badoyn grabbed Orlando's elbow once more. "Can I kip with you in your widow's villa?"

"I don't sleep at the academy."

"I'm amazed. Your landlady wept when I told her you were lost. And that *madam* inherited the nicest villa in Carcassona."

"Which is filled with boys and servants." Orlando was too tired to ask why Badoyn called Marguerite *madam* in that way. "Sleep in the bachelors' tower at the chateau. I'll give you my bunk for the night."

"Balthazar, you rogue! You surely don't sleep with your sergeants and guards?" His cousin sounded horrified.

"They aren't my men. We serve the same commander."

The two women went silent, looked up from their conversation. Taresa played with the cord of her necklace. The marquesa arched her fingers as if at prayer. Impatient prayer.

"Thank you for your escort," Taresa said. "And your excellent company."

"*Bonsoir, messieurs*," Mme Hélène said. "May all your dreams come true."

"But the night is young!" Badoyn protested. He turned to Orlando. "They say there's gaming at the Roman tower. Come with me?"

"I still have duties tonight." While Orlando looked past Badoyn, Taresa was disappearing into the door of her villa, pausing to wave two fingers at him, like she had when he'd hauled Perseus off the roof. Hélène pushed playfully at her friend's shoulder, and they both disappeared behind the door. "But I need to ask you something first."

"To begin making our plans?" Badoyn seemed eager.

"No. Why are you out to destroy the peace here? Your attack in the village poisoned the Peace of God that we've maintained in this neighborhood."

"*Appelez-moi un diable?*" Badoyn swore. *You're calling me a devil?* "We came upon bandits who'd set on the village."

"We haven't seen bandits since Muret. And if there were roaming bands, why would any choose to attack where Simon is quartered? Where an armed patrol is gathered?"

"Are you saying I'm a liar?"

"You lied to Simon. I did nothing heroic, only failed to stop you from robbing that village."

"We were doing what Simon asked. Looking for heretics—"

"Simon is wrong. There are no heretics robbing city stores."

"You and I, Balthazar," Badoyn dropped his voice to a whisper, "need to be united. Simon means to end the struggles and rule the south. We must gain a place with him together. If he wants rebels and heretics, that's what we give him."

"I'm not robbing poor villagers. Or burning old women in their houses."

"Those people attacked us," Badoyn said. "That story about the Saracens? We agreed to say that to keep Simon from sending a force down on the village and burning it to the ground, hanging every man and woman. So, you see, I saved you. And your dirty little village. You wound me, calling me a liar." Badoyn shook Orlando, as if this were all a jest. Orlando pushed him away. "Come, Balthazar. Be reasonable."

But then his hound appeared, alone, licking Orlando's hand first, sitting beside him as if awaiting instruction.

"You can't keep a dog in the bachelors' tower," Orlando said. "You'll have to beg a bed from Simon."

Badoyn started back toward the chateau, having to snap his fingers twice to get his dog to follow. "Surely, cousin, a good night's sleep will put you in a reasonable mood. Let's plan together tomorrow. Meet me at *petit déjeuner.*"

"I have duties tonight and with the academy in the morning."

"Then invite me to observe your work as fight-master," Badoyn said. "Perhaps you can teach me your methods."

The gates of heaven have closed.

You aren't my brother. Leave me.

There will be no more angels.

Badoyn, once he got his dog in motion, couldn't get a response from Orlando, and so left him to his rainbow-colored headache and the odor of burning brands, as if in an army camp.

Orlando considered that the mage-knight's advice, to deny his ghost, might be the best guidance he'd had since an ancient itinerant swordmaster had corrected his stance while fighting with a steel war sword. Though he'd never had a chance to use that skill in an actual fight.

12
Poulain

ORLANDO'S WRIST STILL BURNED WHERE Taresa had touched him while she asked him to betray his lord. However, Taresa was bound to leave him alone when she discovered how deeply impoverished Orlando was; women always did.

Juggling the many stories Badoyn had told, deciding which to believe, Orlando walked the path near the wall, as he usually did at night, to verify that the night patrol was awake. When the matins bell rang, he'd completed one circle, and tied one knot in his scarf, whispering a prayer for the dead while the voice of monks singing psalms echoed softly from the basilica. When he walked on, voices rose from the yard below the Roman tower.

"W—why should we care what a black Moor and a fey *trouvère* think?" A Paris accent. One of the guards from the riot in St-Luc village.

"What we think?" The Celt sounded friendly, but that didn't match his words. "We think you're celebrating that evil escapade in the village. Not a respectable party. Not one we care to join."

"We're heroes. You're—"

"Heroes?" The Moor spoke French, as oddly accented as the Catalan that Orlando heard him speak earlier. "You killed an old lady and stole a sheep."

"And faithlessly left your comrade behind." The Celt spoke with great gaiety.

"Left him bleeding," the Moor said. "The stitches on his head prove that you're—"

"Stop, brother! Don't say it!" The Celt sounded suddenly serious. "Don't use the word *baquelar*. Don't call sad *peccadors* vomit-eating dogs. You weren't there. You don't know what might cause worthless donkey-cocks to betray a comrade."

"It was Saracens." The man who protested slurred his words.

"Does your mother know you lie?" The Moor couldn't match the Celt's gaiety. "Does she pay priests to say special prayers for your half-rotted soul?"

The unmistakable sound of steel drawn. Boots tramping.

By the time Orlando reached the Roman tower, four men lay in the yard. The Moor stomped one guard's hand as he tried to rise and then kicked the guard's sword away, so that it spun across the yard, stopping near Orlando.

The tall Celt had the point of a dagger at the back of another guard's neck, his knee on the small of his back. "Come on, man, say it. Say, 'Please, God, forgive me. I'm a liar who deserted my captain.'"

"Gentlemen!" Orlando projected his deepest, most masterly voice. "It's past curfew. You aren't on duty."

"*Oui*, Captain Orlando." The man getting up answered for the other three.

"Please retire to your barracks. We shall discuss this incident with Captain Louis in the morning."

They stumbled off, rather more like nocturnal vermin than respectful soldiers. But then, Orlando didn't know if there were any worthy men among the bored and slovenly *gardes du corps*.

"*Bonsoir, messieurs*." Orlando called a greeting to the two strangers, intending to go on to the duty-room at the foot of the watchtower. "It's long past curfew and a long time until dawn."

"*Hola, poulain!*" The Moor called after him. The word—unless the man spoke another language than French—was an insult Orlando had heard ancient crusaders sling in Constantinople. A nastier form of *métis*. Half-breed. Mongrel.

"His name is Or–*lan*–do." The tall Celt was as drunk as the men he'd just laid out on the streets. "He's Simon's hero."

"No. He's pure *poulain* like us. A brother."

"Not every man you call *poulain*—" the Celt spoke a weird mush of Catalan, an accent Orlando couldn't identify "—wants to call you *frère*." He sang lines of a *chanson de geste* about brothers in arms.

"Or–*lan*–do," the Moor imitated his friend's careful enunciation, "come have a drink with us. We have dice."

"I promise they are honest dice," the Celt said. "Upon my honor."

"No, *merci*. I have two days of work behind me and two more come morning." Orlando strove for a knightly response, checking the resentment welling within. And the guilt: he couldn't control those guards; he'd failed to control their bad behavior twice that day. "Can I help you find the bachelors' tower? Or has Simon placed you in his quarters?" Which would be as offensive as giving these reckless knights Louis's income from the squires' school.

"The night is young," the Moor said.

"And we know our way. We always know our way." The too-tall Celt caught his boot on a cobble, tripped, then leaned on the edge of a wall, suddenly overcome with laughter.

▪

Defended in the streets of his own city by decadent Catalan knights. Total strangers to him. How could men like that have come from the papal court? More likely to be itinerant mercenaries, serving any despicable seigneur who might hire such sword-trash.

Begged to commit treason, or at least abject disloyalty, by a woman who, uninvited, put her hand on his thigh.

And trapped into dishonorable acts by a liege lord who had forgotten promises made under oath years before.

Orlando visited the night-duty sergeant and left instructions to double the guard in the quarter near the academy and the basilica, making sure the men patrolled close to Mme Marguerite's villa throughout the night. And, asserting that he carried a message from Louis (a falsehood he'd repair later), Orlando left a list of which men should report at midday to begin "a stronger peace patrol," though stories of "the Quest" had already raced through the city.

"Don't assign anyone from yesterday's adventure." Orlando recited those men's names. "They need to guard the stone masons' work yard until Pentecost. Both the morning shift and afternoon. Then evening shifts at the door to the Church mill tower."

"Captain Louis is letting them rest up after the heroics, eh?"

"You might say."

Rather than finish his walk around the city, Orlando cut into the streets across from the basilica, intending to fetch his shirt and jerkin from Mme Marguerite's villa, to carry them to the laundry women.

·

Orlando struck flint and steel to light a rush lamp on the portico and then passed through the villa's empty kitchen, where he found a boy in the shadows, where no boy had a reason to be lurking, either for chores or to prowl for more food, the cupboards all being locked immediately after the boys' supper. When Orlando spied the lurker, the boy retreated further into the shadows, so Orlando had to guess who it might be.

"*Ça va, jeune homme?*"

"*Ça va bien, Monsieur Capitaine.*"

"Yet you aren't in bed, *garçon.*"

Orlando ached in every bone and wanted no more duties that night solving others' sorrows. Yet as soon as Orlando spoke, the boy moved again, and Orlando's heart caught in his throat.

"It's Galahad, isn't it?" Orlando spoke as softly as he would to calm a spooked horse.

"*Oui,* monsieur."

"It seems perhaps you fell—from your cot?" A significant cut brimmed crimson along the boy's right brow. Orlando's cut throbbed in sympathy. A bruised eye was swelling, and the boy had wiped at his forehead with a torn tunic sleeve that glimmered rusty in the lamplight. Not a tumble from his cot. "I believe you need a bit of soldier's field aid."

"Perhaps, Captain."

Suspecting he wouldn't get more out of the boy, he dragged a three-legged stool to the stone cistern where the servants stored water for kitchen use. Instead of groping in the dim light for a towel, Orlando untied the scarf around his neck, the one he'd loaned to Louis to defeat dust raised by the mistral. "Come, *garçon*. Every knight learns to let a surgeon care for his wounds."

As gently as he could, Orlando drew the boy into his lap, which was like holding a boney bird, the boy so thin and his heart beating so fast. Orlando wet his kerchief in the cistern and wiped away the worst of the blood that had flowed from the cut on the boy's head. The cut was minor and didn't need stitches, but a head cut will bleed like the devil. Talking the whole time, because it seemed the right thing, Orlando rinsed the rag and had Galahad hold the cold, wet cloth over his eye.

"You wouldn't know it to see me now, *garçon*, because I've become such a handsome knight, but my cousin called me an ugly duckling when I was—oh, surely about your age."

"But ducklings aren't ugly, Captain. They can be so clever."

"It's from an old tale, about an odd duck who finds himself in the wrong nest."

"At Fanjeau, a goose kept the ducklings when..." Galahad's voice trailed off. "The duck mother died."

"I lost mine, too." That didn't seem too much to share. Orlando kept talking, hoping to soothe the child. "My cousin told me that the real son of our household had been stolen as a babe, and I'd been left by fairies. When I asked my grandmother—"

"Fairies, monsieur? What are fairies?"

"Tiny creatures that live in rocks and streams, but only in grandmothers' stories. Remember your grandmother's tales?"

"I don't have a grandmother." The boy trembled in his arms. Marguerite's grey cat nuzzled at Orlando's feet.

"That's a tragedy. Tell me, Galahad..." He felt the boy stiffen. "I shall never ask a boy in the academy to betray his comrades, so I'm not going to ask who hurt you. But I want you to tell me what you quarreled about."

"I never quarrel, Monsieur Captain. The priests say we are to maintain the Peace of God in our own lives."

"What were the boys talking about?"

A long silence. Orlando scooped up the cat. It wiggled into the boy's lap, so Orlando cradled them both. Galahad hesitated for only a moment, then began petting the cat with long, slow strokes.

"Lance...One boy said we must tell who our fathers are. Most of the boys refused, because it's your rule. Is it your rule?"

"Yes."

"Therefore, I was going to refuse, but then that new boy from Toulouse, Perseus, he—Perseus told me at supper that I should do like he does, because he knows how to keep the devil from the door. What does that mean?"

"He knows how to keep out of trouble." Though Orlando couldn't swear to that, after Perseus's walk on the roof ridge. The cat, however, begun purring while Galahad petted it.

"Oh yes, Captain. Perseus is brilliant. And he promised to be my friend. So now I have two friends, because Ajax also—"

"Galahad, what did Perseus say about his father?"

"He insisted he didn't know who his father was, and it didn't matter, because in the Pays d'Òc, every man is his own man, and he'd already become seigneur of his family's estate. Is that true?"

"It's true," Orlando said, "as I understand the ways here. Even women can inherit land. What did you say?"

"Just like Perseus did. I said I didn't know my father. And then Lance...one boy said that meant I was a bastard, and my father is a heretic because only heretic bastards make new bastards, so I was a double bastard and when Simon is king, he will kill all the heretics and all the bastards, like he killed the bastard king of Aragón. And so I..."

The boy fell apart then, his thin body shaking with sobs.

It had been a hard day, and Orlando had been on his feet or shepherding boys or watching the guards attack a village since this time the night before. His own tears traced along his cheeks while he waited for the boy to finish weeping. Orlando swiped at his cheeks and forced his thoughts elsewhere. The boy's matted hair was too long and hadn't been washed in some time. Marguerite was right; they needed to barber and wash every boy in the barracks.

"Galahad, what happened?"

"I bit him."

O God's bones.

"Then he cried and yelled that I'd poisoned him with bastard heretic's spit, and Perseus called him a monkey's winkle, so he tried to punch Perseus, but he missed and hit me. And then, I fell over Ajax, which made him cry and…" Back to sobbing.

Orlando had no words of wisdom that a fight-master might offer, so he just rocked the boy and chanted the first song that occurred to him, expurgating the tale of a lesser-known hero.

> Small, but with a courage-filled heart,
> The young knight gallops to the castle of the cruel lord.
> His blood hot, he spurs his Saracen steed
> and cries 'All glory to God!'

This boy was too young to be here. Orlando didn't need a ghost to tell him. But also, he couldn't send the child back, telling Simon: Keep this one with his nurses another year.

> Freed from bondage through his courage,
> the young knight strikes his enemy
> with such strength he breaks his lance.

Orlando kept chanting, hoping to give Galahad a story to tell himself, and he kept his eyes on the grey cat, because if he closed his eyes, he saw his sword slide into the mage-knight. It had to have killed the man. Or there were two of them. And if so, the village would have to bury the man he'd killed along with Estela, who'd died in the village, who had been so kind to him…

Seeing the images in the village again, he drew a breath, which startled both the cat and the boy. The cat kneaded Orlando's leg with its paws, and Galahad's sobs began again, though quieter.

> The lord of the mystery castle bowed to the knight.
> 'I see you are too young, and if I defeat you
> I gain no fame or praise. I only win myself shame.
> Let us no longer fight, but join arms as comrades.'

Orlando hadn't killed a man in close quarters before. The old Marquis de Beaurain had declared him too young for combat in Constantinople. The first summer he came south in Simon's retinue, whenever they rode into heretics' villages, they found the towns deserted, save for old women who knelt in surrender, chanting their creed while his French contingent rode by, lances in one hand, swords in another.

Galahad had ceased sobbing and wilted in Orlando's lap, ready to nod off.

"*Jeune homme*, Galahad, are you sharing your cot with Perseus?"

"*Oui*, monsieur."

"I think you can go to bed now. I promise you, this night's troubles have ended."

"*Merci*, Captain."

"Wait." He held out that red linen scarf, which had dried while he chanted the story of the knight and the mystery castle. "This trophy was given to me by a great lady from Paris." Mme Marguerite, in fact. "It brought me protection and great luck in battle. That lady would surely be proud if you wore her token."

He tied it loosely around the boy's neck. "Your neck, your arm, your boot. It doesn't matter where you tie it. Luck and courage will flow through every limb."

He walked with the boy to the narrow stone steps that curved up to the boys' barracks. "*Bonsoir, garçon*. Say your prayers the way your gr—the priests taught you."

The cat padded softly up the stairs behind the boy.

He wiped his cheeks again, smelling unwashed boy on his sleeve.

Not bothering to check whether Badoyn had taken up the offer of a loaned bunk in the bachelors' tower, Orlando climbed the watchtower and told the men stationed there to join the patrol around the academy villa, that he'd take their shift in the tower.

Not for the first time: it was the only place in the city where Orlando could be alone.

He leaned on the worn stone wall, the mistral buffeting him while he looked out over the surrounding neighborhood. No lamp light leaked from any shutter or door. No moon. Only stars shone in the wind-worried sky. Even if rebels and heretics prepared to attack the city, it'd be impossible to see enemies approaching in the moonless night.

But no enemies were attacking—rebel, heretic, or Saracen. This city was the safest in all of the Pays d'Òc. Orlando stripped and laid down on the tower's wood floor, folded his last clean shirt for a pillow, and recited his prayers, hoping to sleep. The bump on his scalp ached; he should cut his hair to make sure his head wasn't broken. The stitches above his eye throbbed. He shifted, to avoid the bruise across his back and the one along one arm. He pulled a length of canvas over to block the wind, canvas that had been laid there to protect bundles of arrows. Arrows were useless in this tower, which served only for sentry work, not armed protection. But Simon had turned every spare space into an armory.

You should be protecting God's anointed kings, not serving that imposter. Not his ghost speaking; his ghost never voiced that much faith in him. Words from that traitorous Catalan widow. But the first part echoed what Orlando's father used to repeat over prayers every night: *You'll serve the king; he promised me that for you.* "The king" meant Philippe; not the trumped-up zealot who held Orlando in thrall.

Forget the past years' longing for horses and retainers. All he needed was an honorable lord to serve.

Surely, God would never anoint that vain, cruel man as king.

13
Siege Rubble

ORLANDO WOKE, STIFF AS THE oak floor he lay on, with a clear idea for the morning. The best next lessons for the boys would be to perform real work in unison and to instill charity in their hearts. He made the last quick check on the night patrol, certain he knew how to bring the new boys into the routines in which his older charges were trained.

When Orlando passed Mme Agnes's house in the dawn light, the tiny old woman sat in her chair at the door, like every single day since he'd begun passing that way. Instead of bowing to her respectfully and returning her shy wave like he always did, Orlando stopped, hearing again what Mme Taresa had said. *If Simon truly honored faithful knights, Mme Agnes wouldn't be living in a battle scene.*

This presented a good opportunity for the boys—and he'd let himself confess later that he wanted to argue with Mme Taresa through deeds, not words.

"*Bonjour*, Mme Agnes."

Her chin trembled, perhaps from her famous shyness. At last she spoke. In the local tongue. "*Bon dia*, Monsieur Captain. May the Good God bless you and bring you to a good end."

"*Merci*." Orlando couldn't produce more words for a moment, shocked that the widow of a Béziers martyr offered a heretic's greeting. The mistral caught her shawl, lifting its edges to wave at him. "Madam, your cousins tell me that your villa hasn't yet been repaired by the masons."

Her eyes drifted, she tipped her head, either considering his words or listening for voices he couldn't hear. "My villa?"

"Your roof hasn't been repaired."

"I cannot take more guests, even one as handsome as you. You may not know…" She began to describe how she'd taken in home-less cousins and their dozens of servants and children—she hadn't expected children—and they filled every corner of her villa with their chests and boxes, so that if she wanted to take another guest, like the handsome captain, she wouldn't have room for her own servants, and she needed them, because an old woman can't be left alone at night, not in the middle of a war when Saracen invaders are destroying houses and enslaving children.

So: the roof of her villa was broken, and her spirit and mind, bruised in the siege of Carcassona, had not recovered.

"Thank you for your concern, Mme Agnes. I don't need a room. Rather, I propose to arrange repairs for your villa. If you will allow it."

"It is no problem, Captain. We are sheltered by God. The Good God who promises us a good end, if we live a pure life."

A woman came up the street then, her basket filled with bread. As soon as she recognized Orlando, she frowned. Her pace picked up. "*Bonjour*, Monsieur Captain. Is there a problem?"

This was the first villager he'd encountered who had heard what happened in St-Luc village the day before, and who consequently couldn't mask her fear and trepidation.

He explained his intention to make sure that Mme Agnes's roof was repaired. As they spoke, he learned that the woman's name was Joaneta; she made household decisions, and her chief con-cern was the cost.

"No, I'm not going to hire workers," Orlando said. "If you'll trust me to handle it."

Joaneta said, "It would be a blessing if it happens before the rains come again. We've stopped up the worst of it to keep the mistral from blowing us to the Great Sea."

"May I take a look at the damage?"

"Use the servants' stairs. It's the only passable way to the upper story. But be careful!"

.

The stairs were steep, more like a stone ladder, and so narrow that Orlando could use the walls as a brace when he needed to skip one or more rubble-filled steps.

At the top, he found a wreck in what had been the upper floor: a massive hole in the roof, crudely covered with waxed canvas; mounds of broken roof tiles, topped by whole tiles that had tumbled in; broken floor boards, shattered into slivers in places. In the middle lay an actual boulder, too similar to the one he'd encountered intimately in Minerve.

His idea—or impulse—was to bring the boys to begin the work, since they hadn't done service since Easter. If they removed the rubble, he might dicker with the masons' master to spend time— maybe half a shift each week—to come to the aid of a martyr's aged widow. He stood on the boulder and tugged aside the canvas covering, boosting himself on the remaining timber to see how badly the damage appeared from the outside.

Suspended there, the mistral blowing his hair free, he was looking toward the city gates, where a cloud of dust rose, caught in the wind. Voices cried out. Harnesses chimed. The cloud of dust grew, trailing down the road out of the city.

He let himself down, sitting on the siege boulder.

Simon had left Carcassona.

"Jove's pissing monkey! What gravel-brain scheme brought you here?"

Orlando jerked, surprised at the voice, turning to look, before he realized a man spoke in the room below, out of sight through the gap in the broken floor.

"I'd forgotten that you're a master of invective." It was Taresa's voice, answering in Catalan. "*Bon dia*, Tomás. I'm fine, thank you for asking. And you? You too, Chrétien. I trust you are both well."

Below the gap in the floor, Hélène appeared, yawning, stretching daintily, clutching a silk shawl around her linen shift. She said, "So every goat in town died? That's why you two are in my salon?"

"Isn't it your great-aunt's salon?" That tall Celt called Chrétien answered. "*Bon dia, ma dòmna.*"

"What are you two doing here?" Tomás the Moor sounded dis-tempered. Perhaps Hélène affected his mood in a negative way, like she did Orlando.

"Grabbing his son." Hélène spoke in the local tongue—at the same time that Taresa said in Catalan, "Taking his son."

"Are you using the captain to find the boy?" Chrétien asked.

"*El capità mestís.*" Tomás called Orlando a mongrel. The worst plague of an eavesdropper, hearing yourself discussed; if you're slinking where you shouldn't be, you can't argue for personal justice.

"You'd know." Hélène yawned again. "They breed them in the Outremer, right?"

"Indeed," Tomás said. "But he doesn't know who he is."

"He's a good man who knows he should serve a better lord than Simon." Mme Taresa defended Orlando, which would please him if this overheard conversation weren't utterly confusing.

"Are you two playing luscious widows with the captain and his cousin?" Chrétien said. "Don't make that nice man fall in love with you. It's unkind."

"By 'nice man,'" Hélène said, "you mean the captain. His cousin is already in love. *Avec moi.*"

"I disagree with Hélène," Taresa said, "about employing seduc-tion as a tool of war. Though that's how we learned Simon was mov-ing the boy to Carcassona. I believe that you either pay your army or engage their hearts as warriors."

Tomás said, "Is that your plan, *xicheta?* To use the captain to get to his son."

"No," Hélène said. "I am using his cousin. Taresa is too pure of heart to use men to get what she wants. Which makes everything take longer than it needs to."

Taresa, whom Orlando could not see, said, "He isn't with the squires. The youngest boys study with Captain Orlando. Whatever plan you two hatched with the pope, you didn't know how to find him, did you?"

"The pope?" Hélène's voice dripped disdain. She lifted her hand, waving a dismissal with those long nails. "If you came from Rome, why didn't the pope send a prelate with you?"

"And where's Sebastián?" Taresa asked, her voice coming from farther away than it had been at first.

"We haven't heard," Tomás said quietly.

"Is Rome such a great city that you didn't see him?"

The room below was silent for several heartbeats.

"It's like that?" Hélène laughed, clutching at her shawl. "You've never been to Rome in your life."

"The captain knows he's protecting Simon's son. But he doesn't know which boy is which," Taresa said. "When we find the right boy, we'll get him out of the city."

"*Per l'amor de Déu,* how?" Tomás still sounded angry. "Hiding in a market basket? Hauled out with the night soil?"

"Don't tell them!" Hélène warned.

Taresa said, "I'll share my methods if you get your hands on his son before Hélène and I do."

Hélène said, "We came here with an extensive, well-considered plan, rather than a hunch or gambling with fate. Different from how you proceed, Don Tomás."

"*Ma dòmna,* however you managed to talk Taresa and Henri into this dangerous masque—"

"I talked Hélène into helping," Taresa said, "And Henri has no idea of our plans. We put him in school for his own safety."

"While you," Hélène—the only speaker Orlando could see through the broken floorboards—pointed an accusing finger, presumably at the Moor, "left Henri with a goodman heretic who won't touch a supper knife to defend himself. Who vows he'll never fight again. No, wait. He can't vow anything because he's a damned heretic who can't swear an oath for fear of offending the delicate feelings of the Good God and being reincarnated as a dog."

Tomás said, coldly, "Senhóra Hélène, I must insist that you keep out of my family's business."

"Henri is *my* Montcava cousin." Hélène sounded like a chipper songbird when she argued. "Taresa of Girona is my cousin's wife."

Someone sneezed.

"*Beneeixi,* Taresa," Chrétien said.

"You don't govern either of us, Don Tomás." Taresa answered when she'd stopped sneezing.

"You certainly don't govern me," Hélène had her hand over her breast, her shawl slipping away. "I swore an oath to his mother. You—you swear some kind of made-up oath to your—what do you call it? Your *bon amic?*"

"I'm the only one here with a real boyfriend," Chrétien said. "You mean, perhaps, our oaths as *bonfraires.*"

"And I'm here at the king's command," Taresa said. "Besides, we arrived first. When we fought in Andalusia, being the first army on the field meant something."

"We are also here out of loyalty to the king." Tomás sounded more than sullen. Orlando wanted badly to see expressions on these people's faces while they quarreled.

"Therefore," Taresa said, "I'm calling on you as *bonfraires* to do what's best under God's heaven. We have a plan. You have only hopes. And your swords."

"*Qui s'ho creu?*" Chrétien repeated it three times: *Who knew?*

"Come have some warm bread and hot milk with us," Taresa said. "We encourage Mme Agnes to sit with us in the garden each morning."

Their voices drifted away, then Chrétien's echoed back. "But your garden is a battlefield."

Tomás's voice trailed behind: "That *pech baquelar* from Troyes told you Simon was bringing his son here? How did he know?"

"A pet dog…"

The rest of Hélène's answer was lost in the garden.

After a few moments, pondering what he'd just heard, Orlando came down the stairs, both hands trailing the wall, skipping two steps wherever he could, trying to make sense of what he'd heard. These strangers, though new to the city, weren't new to each other. And they were plotting to kidnap Simon's son.

Simon had commanded Orlando to protect his son. With his life.

At the door to the street, Orlando promised the housekeeper that he'd ensure Mme Agnes's roof was repaired. He was turning the corner into the next street, when he heard Mme Agnes's door bang open. When he glanced back, the not-from-Rome Moor stood at the door and a woman kissed him, though Orlando couldn't see who she was. Likely *not* the waspish Hélène.

Ruin Louis's income.

Fight with the gardes du corps.

Plot against Simon.

Ruin perfectly nice women.

He wanted to blame the deplorable litany running through his thoughts on the false ghost, but only the parts about Louis's income and the plot against Simon were true. Those drunken guards deserved their beating last night. The women in that household, Taresa and Hélène, were…too mysterious to comprehend.

"*Hola, poulain!*"

The Moor and his Celt friend ambled up behind Orlando, though it didn't seem they walked fast enough to catch up.

"My brother Chrétien nags me that we didn't properly introduce ourselves last night." The Moor held out his hand for Orlando to shake, and there was no way to avoid it. "I'm Tomás of Cyprus." He pointed to his friend. "My brother and I, we're the sons of Miquel of Morella. Pèire Leteric was our mentor."

The names meant nothing to Orlando, and his face must have shown it, because the two men glanced at each other when Orlando responded.

"I'm called Orlando." Not *poulain*. "My grandfather is Daniel of Troyes." He wasn't about to share his father's name with these interlopers.

"Shall we trade teaching stories?" Chrétien asked. "Perhaps over breakfast? We don't want to be embarrassed, trying to teach these squires lessons they already learned in your school."

"After mass on Pentecost, perhaps." Orlando delayed. "Simon has me deeply employed until then."

He walked on, and they didn't hail him again. After listening to the strangers' plot, Orlando wasn't in the mood for pleasantries. *I'm here at the king's command.* That's what Mme Taresa said, but how could that be? How had Philippe come to command a woman to plot against Simon?

The foxes, the foxes, the pretty pretty foxes.

Starving, mostly sleepless, Orlando was deeply undecided. He felt confident about protecting the boys in the academy, perhaps more possible if he determined which boy was Simon's son. He couldn't otherwise act—to condemn these plotters to Louis, for example—until he understood what was planned. It seemed he'd have to confront these strangers to know what they intended.

Carcassona had become a mare's nest of waking terror dreams.

14
Un Béguin

ORLANDO SLIPPED INTO THE ACADEMY'S kitchen to beg for breakfast, receiving with gratitude a cold boiled egg and a warm loaf of bread, which he gobbled as if it were trail food.

A man's voice drifted from Mme Marguerite's workroom as Orlando approached. Another Catalan accent. "He's too handsome for the world's own good. It's too bad for me he's taken."

Orlando called *bonjour* as he came to her workroom. A man stood in the archway that led to the portico.

"*Bonjour*, Captain." Marguerite jumped from her chair to approach him, but only to verify the health of his stitches, her feather-like touch exploring his brow. "*Ça va?*"

"*Ça va bien*. No fever." Yet he enjoyed her cool touch too much.

"Captain Orlando, this is Karles, the mercenary we hired to help with the boys."

"*Bon dia*, Captain. *Bonjour*." The man greeted him in Catalan, then switched to French. Taller than other craggy Catalan men Orlando had met, Karles moved like a long-time warrior, the kind who'd left his cradle to be a soldier.

A servant called Mme Marguerite away, which left Orlando free to examine Karles, one man talking to another.

"You shepherded the boys in Fanjeau, Master Karles?" Orlando repeated what Marguerite said about the man, while worrying about the many strangers he had to track in Carcassona.

"On the journey here, not when they lived in Fanjeau." Karles spoke French with an accent rather like Mme Taresa's, so indeed, a

Catalan from the Pyrenees. "I was in Philippe's court last winter as bodyguard for a lord's children there. I traveled south with his family, where Simon's marshal hired me for this journey."

"Then you're not their tutor? We need a new schoolmaster."

"No, I'm only a bodyguard. These children never had a tutor before now. In Fanjeau, they still slept in their mothers' houses, tended by nurses. You can see that they're daunted by this sudden change. The journey was rather like shepherding baby lambs."

"We have one or more black sheep." Orlando repeated the story he'd heard from Galahad.

"*Je suis désolé.* I slept outside the barracks door last night. I won't make that mistake again." Karles flushed darkly, apologizing, embarrassed. "Please do not think I'm derelict. I know what boys are capable of. I promise to protect them—even from each other."

Orlando held up his hand, then tucked it behind, not meaning to present the same commanding signs he used with the boys. "We need to make sure someone is close by until we sort out the savages. If you need to be away—"

"Summon me," Marguerite said, returning to her workroom at that moment. "I'm prepared to help with whatever is needed."

"Except," Karles said, "these boys need to quit running to their nurses for help. No offense intended, madam, but they are here to learn how to be knights."

Orlando said, "If you whistle, Master Karles, one or more of our *gardes du corps* will appear. Or shout for them."

Karles said, "Trust me, Captain. We are comrades in this work, righting the world's wrong. I'll sleep in the boys' barracks and eat my meals at their table."

With a modest bow, Karles was gone.

"'Righting the world's wrong?'" Orlando echoed the man's words after he departed.

"We heard about the quest Simon gave you," Marguerite said. Of course: the chandler's servants had told the story of Simon's supper at the wells and the bakers' ovens. "And they say it's true, that Simon's son is here!"

"It doesn't change anything, knowing the rumor is true."

"Except, I noticed more guards patrolling the streets in this quarter." She motioned for him to take a seat on the bench in her workroom. "I prepared a tisane for you, Captain. All your bruises from yesterday's adventures can't have healed so quickly."

When he accepted a tin mug of tea, her fingers lingered—or did he imagine that? She looked at him with that frank, open expression which made him appreciate her calm, gentle presence even more, along with the momentary peace that he felt when alone with Marguerite in her workroom.

"*Merci beaucoup*, madam. You are kind."

"*De rien*. You carry too much on your shoulders. If only we could relieve more of your burden."

She spoke these unexpected words so passionately that he had to look away, as if the boys in the yard drew his attention. He sipped the tea, to swallow the same feelings that threatened to overwhelm him while he'd comforted Galahad in the kitchen. She laid a hand on his shoulder—but certainly she didn't mean to press on yesterday's bruise, so it didn't really hurt. Then she retreated to her work, picking up her tambour, finding her needle, choosing a new silk thread. When she glanced up, he saw her as he always did: the ideal woman; strong, noble, capable.

She's not in love with you.

I know I can't have a woman like that. Or any woman. And you aren't my brother.

Fool, fool.

No headache. No rainbows. Only the odor of scorched porridge where the cook's early-morning fires burned hot. He forced his thoughts back to the duty he owed the academy.

"Marguerite, are you certain of your servants' loyalty?"

"Is another villa out to filch French serving men?" She began lightly teasing, but being quick witted, she next said, "You're worried about how safe Simon's son is here."

"Yes. But I had such a day yesterday..." and such a morning already "...that I'm likely to jump at my own shadow."

"Mme Hélène came yesterday to buy scarves and tapestries. She asked where to find good servants. I'll whisper the word among my people, and we shall see who goes out to hear the marquesa's offer."

The idea, so ludicrous, led him to laugh aloud.

"Captain, we haven't heard you laugh since the boys dressed up as mummers at Twelfth Night."

"The world hasn't been as upside down as it is now."

While he finished the tea, Orlando watched the boys in the yard. Four servants had boys on stools, enduring severe barbering. Umbert and Karles had the other boys running relay drills while they waited their turn for barbering.

As he observed the boys' barbering, Taresa's disparagement of French styles nagged him. *Pays de France styles aren't the best for this country.* However, Mme Taresa's opinion didn't matter—about anything. He now knew her to be planning a crime against Simon de Montfort.

"Mme Marguerite, may I beg you to cut my hair?"

"This moment? Why?"

"To find any more injury from yesterday," he said. He'd worried about his scalp since the mage-knight told him to cut his hair. "And summer is coming."

Marguerite stepped into another room, from which Orlando heard the music of her voice, but not her words. She returned with scissors and a razor. "How short, monsieur?"

"Down to the skull. Use the razor."

She shook out a square of linen from her work table to wrap around him.

"Don't soil your beautiful cloth. I'll take off my shirt." He pulled his tunic over his head so rapidly that it took decency a moment to catch up. When had Marguerite became such an intimate friend that he forgot himself? She, however, stared.

"So many bruises, monsieur! All from fighting yesterday?"

Orlando faltered, his shirt half on, half off.

"Tell me that Captain Louis is punishing them, monsieur."

"No. He believes my cousin's tale about bandits. Are you ready?"

He sat on the portico just outside her workroom. The razor's scratch across his skull felt comforting, a reminder of when he'd been shaved before being sent on crusade. Her grey cat jumped onto the nearby table, wagging its head, watching Marguerite work, and then batting a paw, trying to catch his locks as they fell away.

"I'm taking the boys off to do a good deed." He wanted to hear his idea aloud. "It would be best for them to be working instead of..."

"Making up gruesome stories about what happened in the village yesterday? They've already begun."

"But I want them to learn..." What? That he'd never attack a village for no good reason? "That loyalty to king and God must mean more than..."

"Collecting tithes in already broken villages?" She spoke low, words that shouldn't drift away as freely as his shorn locks. "You need a better lord. You are worth more than the quest Simon gave you."

"Thank you for saying so." Scratch, scratch. The wind was rising again, chilling his skull, driving his black locks across the portico flagstones. "Simon wants this work done by Pentecost, so by next Sunday..."

"You'll be free to choose a better quest?"

"Perhaps."

"Or choose another lord?"

"Choose..."

"Monsieur, I still know people in Paris and the Pays de France. People who matter. We can find a place for you, better than the filthy task Simon gave you." She whispered, her breath warm on his ear. "Especially since Simon is surely cheating Philippe in order to make himself king."

"Madam!" He was surrounded by women speaking treason.

"You are the kind of man who can correct the world's wrongs. If you are serving an anointed king and not a—Sancta Maria!" She swore softly, the way a local woman might, her fingers behind his ear, just above Orlando's hairline.

He'd forgotten that tattoo. "It's a souvenir of a squires' gang in Constantinople." He felt her finger tracing it, which caused him to shiver. "Which led me into shameful acts. If you knew, you wouldn't think me the kind of man who..."

"Captain Orlando, I wish you would trust me. As I trust you."

"Madam! I do trust you. Why would I not?"

"I—if you knew me, you'd have doubts."

"That's not possible, madam. I—I shall tell you my secret, because I trust you. In Constantinople, my cousin talked me into playing a boy's prank. It ruined a man's life. And caused me to be sent home to Troyes in disgrace."

He waited for that ghost-voice to scold him, but heard only Marguerite's soft breath. Her hand rested on his bare shoulder, distracting him from the pain of confession.

"Whatever you did as a boy, you saved me here, Captain. Your academy allows me to keep this villa." She finished the razor work on the scarred side of his skull. "You won my respect, because you are an honorable man. I can't claim that for my story."

"I refuse to believe that." He didn't believe any story could be worse than what he'd heard, and overheard, since the day before. The mage-knight, whom he thought he'd killed, claimed an evil spirit pretended to be his brother's ghost. His cousin's lover and her protégé plotted crimes. Simon's pet swordmasters from Rome were in fact from—Cyprus? A dark angel's underworld?

"I came here with Simon's army." Marguerite's breath swept softly over his newly-bared skull.

"So did I."

"But you rode as a knight. You'd never have noticed me. After the first week's travel, my dear baron took me out of the *putes'* camp and made me his mistress." She brushed a strip of linen cloth over his head. "After the siege, he married me. And left me this villa when he died. But I had no income, since the *gardes du corps* bar working women in the city. So you saved me, paying to house your academy here."

A gust stirred the cloud of Orlando's clipped hair on her portico. She bent to scoop it with the towel in her hand, her skirts and veil rustled by the wind.

"Mme Marguerite, your story…" Touched him. This woman had always taken care of herself; she was the most practical and self-possessed woman he knew; yet she considered Orlando her savior. It was nothing like learning that those Catalan strangers planned to kidnap Simon's son.

"Appalls you?"

"Touches me. That you have struggled so."

"Then you aren't surprised? I suppose everyone in the bachelors' tower tells the story of the baron's mistress."

"Life in Carcassona, living in a strange land, holds too many surprises, beyond ancient stories of how people came here." He hadn't heard her story in the barrack's gossip, but now he understood why Badoyn said *your madam.* "We came with the same army. Everyone had their work to do, yours perhaps as important as mine. And you continue to work with honor, given what you do here every day."

"But, Captain, you must believe—"

"I believe that our Savior forgave the Magdalene. And once forgiven, always forgotten." Unlike his perpetual secret, living as a Judas, carrying a transgression for which there is no forgiveness. "We've done good work here, together. We have more to do."

"But now—will Simon take away all your fiefs if you fail on this...quest?"

"I don't know. Since we are confessing, I have decided to let my cousin win the contest. I won't participate in massacres, or even theft. I don't know what I'll lose. But I hope to keep my soul."

"What will become of your school if you fail Simon's quest?"

"It will most likely go to Louis, who will take care of you. You can't be so unlucky that Simon gives it to those vagabond sword-masters who claim they're from Rome."

A servant waved for attention. All the boys were now also cropped close. Marguerite whisked the towel across Orlando's shoulders, sending one more shiver down his spine.

"Go. Teach the boys to do good deeds. You have only a bump and scratch on your skull. Nothing as bad as the cut we stitched."

15
The Song of Roland

ORLANDO LED THE BOYS, WITH Umbert and Karles keeping them in orderly ranks, to the stone-mason works near the Roman tower. The masons' master listened, and then agreed to bring barrows and baskets to try Orlando's idea for a day.

At the villa, Mme Agnes had forgotten their earlier conversation. She once more greeted him with giggling shyness, appreciating his attention. Joaneta the housekeeper did remember, expressing shock that the roof might indeed be repaired.

He set the boys into a brigade, passing baskets of rubble, with the smallest boys inside the upper room filling baskets, and the other boys passing baskets down the stairs.

While the boys worked loading and passing baskets of broken tiles, Orlando told a story in the way he usually did when teaching. He gave them a choice, and they begged for the Lay of Roland.

> A knight suffers for his seigneur,
> Endures freezing cold and scalding sun
> And loses blood and flesh.
>
> Roland lifts the ivory horn to his lips.
> In the high hills, the voice of the horn blares.
> It echoes over thirty leagues.

Orlando finished the story, and then whistled with his two fingers, indicating time for a rest break. In the tile-free attic, the boys gathered around, all dusty from sorting and hauling tiles.

"Let's talk about Roland and what his tale tells us about being a knight. How did he arm himself and his brothers?"

He accepted their recitation, each of them shouting another detail for kitting out and making ready. "And what did Roland and his comrades do when they were unhorsed?"

"Band together!" Three-quarters of the boys had the answer, and the older boys took it as a signal to jump up and move into formation, back to back, ready to strike out at imaginary foes.

Orlando signaled his approval, then waved them back into the teaching circle.

"Now, tell me what you learned, *juvenes*. We all know it was too late when Roland blew the horn. The man who should be Roland's comrade, Ganelon, is off betraying him, keeping the Franks from responding."

The new boys jumped around, squirming against each other, crying *I know, I know!* The oldest of the boys, Ywain, raised a hand to be chosen. The others immediately copied him, a forest of hands waving, stirring the dust even more than the mistral did. Orlando pointed to Ywain, who stood to recite. Ywain enjoyed knowing the rules, the stories, the rituals.

"Ganelon the betrayer is Judas's child. He betrays the men who were his brothers, and worse, he does it for gold and glory."

"*Bien.*" Orlando nodded. "Continue. Why do we especially remember Roland?"

Ywain hesitated, then decided he did indeed know the answer. "Roland died, but his warning—when he blew his horn—saved hundreds, including the king, who found the betrayer and punished him."

Orlando had the next question ready. "What do we know from Judas about the punishment of a betrayer? Of a traitor?" He pointed to Perseus, the boy from Toulouse, though that boy hadn't raised his hand like the others.

"He's cast out—" Perseus began to speak from where he sat, but Ywain prodded him to stand while speaking. Perseus did a good imitation of how Orlando observed southern seigneurs speaking in court, as if addressing higher angels. That is, arrogant. "He's cast out of the brotherhood of men. When he dies, his body is tossed onto the potter's field. His heart is eaten by vultures. His eyes are pecked out and carried away by scorpions."

The details were embroidered, from Orlando's knowledge of the story. He asked the next question. "What happened to Ganelon the betrayer?" He pointed to the ruddy-haired boy, Lancelot, to answer.

"He was tied to four horses and pulled to pieces." Lancelot gestured the pulling, his hand knocking into Galahad, seated near him, toppling the boy. Which let loose a moment of riot, with boys shouting.

"His guts spilled on the road!"

"His arms went east and west!"

"His head stood up and begged for mercy, blood coming out of his mouth."

"Out of his ears!"

"Out of his eyes!"

Orlando whistled again. When everyone was seated once more, he said, "We are in a gentlewoman's home to help her. Let's leave her in peace. Shall we go to dinner?"

When the boys came down from the attic to return to the academy, Mme Taresa stood at the bottom of the stairs, handing a dried date to each boy as he passed. Umbert hurried the boys up the street to the academy. Karles murmured *bon dia, ma dòmna* to Taresa and followed the boys.

.

While Orlando was thanking Joaneta the housekeeper for her patience, the masons' master appeared with four of his men, seeking the borrowed carts and baskets. The master professed joy at the broken tiles the boys had piled for him. "It's as if the Good God answers prayer! We need rubble to fill the wall we are repairing."

He clapped Orlando's shoulder, insisting that they'd finish the job here, since broken tiles were better than gold for his purposes. The master sent his men on with the carts and followed them, but then turned back, motioning Orlando to him.

"Monsieur Captain, we know what you tried to do in St-Luc village yesterday. That you meant to do what the Good God would wish for us."

"I didn't intend—"

"Senhóra Estela was my great aunt. I am grateful that you tried to save her."

"I'm sorry for your loss.

"The elders of St-Luc and St-Jean asked me to tell you. We have gathered payment for the Church, which you can collect today. At Mas-de-Cours. You know that place?"

"Yes. Of course." A derelict collection of shepherds' shacks, in the hills south and east of Carcassona.

"We pray for your good end. And hope your goodness will soften the vicomte's—"

The villa door banged open. The mason straightened, bowed, and headed toward the stone works by the wall.

Likely Mme Taresa had heard this exchange, but Orlando found he didn't care for either her approval or critique. Or whether a stonemason uttered heresy while protecting his village. Taresa joined him in the street, speaking softly.

"Roland in the song isn't a hero. It's a cautionary tale, not a romance."

"What caution?"

"Ensure you know who to trust," she said. "Blow the horn as soon as you suspect danger. Don't wait."

"You are a scholar of battle, madam? Or of heroes' songs?"

"I am your friend, I hope." She grasped his hand, looking into his eyes. "Remember, we are brothers in arms who share beliefs."

No. You have no friends.

While arguing with his false ghost, Orlando had trouble removing his cold hand from her smoldering hot one. Before he could answer either Mme Taresa or his ghost, she spoke again.

"Don't fall in love with me."

She spoke loudly enough that everyone in the villa might have heard, while repeating what that Celt jongleur said to her early in the morning.

Orlando extracted his hand, though she'd been holding it hard enough to crush it. "As a courtly knight, I shall always endeavor to do as you command. However—"

"Alas, there's no 'however.' You yearn to be in love, and I just crossed into your sight." She laid her fingers across the back of his hand, and again it felt as if she were setting him on fire. "My heart belongs to my husband. I cannot return your affection. But I admire your courage. And your commitment to honor."

"How can any man decline to be in love with you…" he tipped his hand over and grasped hers "…when you read a man's thoughts like a hedge-witch at the village fair?" He imitated that smirk Badoyn used while saying the opposite of what he meant.

She laughed, as if he offered a jest. "Then you and I understand each other."

"To a degree," he said. "However, when you next consult Mme Agnes's housekeeper—if she has a free moment while attempting to steal Mme Marguerite's servants—you'll learn I was in your house today. While you entertained guests and discussed one of the boys I am protecting with my life."

"Balthazar!" Badoyn appeared from the villa's doorway. "Ready to ride on quest for today?"

You'd think she'd show shame. Fear. Guilt. But her wide mouth broke into a smile. Her eyes shone. "Then you'll help us? I knew it!" She threw her arms around him, jumping up to kiss him on the mouth, her lips burning his like hot coals.

"Come, cousin!" Badoyn called.

Orlando braced for another too-friendly bashing of his shoulder.

.

Before the day's ride, the *gardes du corps* and their captains had to be blessed by the bishop. Orlando, Captain Louis, and Badoyn stood among the knights who assembled in the courtyard.

Orlando always felt he could use any blessing that might be made available to him, even when it meant enduring cold waves of the mistral. But then Badoyn stepped between Louis and Orlando, draping an arm over Louis's shoulder before the bishop began, as if he and Louis were bosom companions.

Gall welled up from Orlando's middle. Would his cousin take everything, including the sole friendship Orlando enjoyed in this foreign town?

A tall, irascible man, the bishop had come south with Simon and remained the vicomte's close associate. Due to some misfortune in the distribution of blessings from God, the bishop's thin voice wasn't up to admonishing a crowd, sounding too much like an angry starling, his words drifting away when the mistral gusted, blowing his words to heaven.

"In your work, you shall recall the admonition of the prophet." The bishop's voice rose suddenly to a shriek. "'Take us the foxes, the little foxes, that spoil the vines: for our vines have tender grapes.' Every man here recalls our battle cries from our first year fighting heresy in the south."

Renards! Renards! Foxes in the vineyards!

Yes, that was the battle cry. Leave it be—we are no longer battling the people here.

Bring us the foxes, the wee little foxes!

The bishop recaptured his normal, hectoring voice. "You ride out to defeat villains who revile the sacrament of the Eucharist, saying that it cannot contain the body of Christ. They say that if it were so, Christians would have consumed the Savior's entire body by now, even if our Lord's body had been as giant as the largest mountain."

Badoyn muttered. "This is as bad as sitting through nagging sermons on Twelfth Night, when all we want is the feast."

The bishop, however, loved the sound of his own words. "They cry that Mary Magdalene was a concubine of Jesus. That the host is merely common bread, that we must also worship every thorn and every lance if we worship the tortures of the Christ. They live shamelessly, mired in sin, but believe a single laying on of hands will save them."

"While nothing will save us from this," Badoyn sighed.

Louis leaned past Badoyn, catching Orlando's eye, then seemed unsure whether he had the power to upbraid Badoyn.

"You'll ride with me, won't you, Captain Louis?" Badoyn whispered, turning the same sheep's eyes on Orlando's commander as he had on his lady-love the night before. "I don't know the territory. Please show mercy and be my guide."

If it were possible to convince Simon that no heretics gathered here or stole from city stores, it would not be Louis who'd attempt it. Louis was too loyal an officer to voice his doubt. Unlike Mme Taresa. Or Marguerite. Neither of those ladies had to deal with the path Orlando and Louis had been forced down. But, as he taught his boys: When your captain commands, you must obey. Simon gave them a command. How to help Simon understand that he had bad information?

The bishop was building to his final words. "This is how you will know them. If you find no meat or eggs or cheese in their houses, you must ask them to swear their faith in the one true God. If a man or woman refuses to swear, you shall know them for a heretic."

The bishop, ancient beyond telling, lay on a narrow bed, a coverlet pulled to his chin. Cistercian monks crowded the cell, chanting a benediction. One reached to restore the bishop's hands into a prayerful clasp. Another dipped a strip of linen in a dish of water and wiped the spit running to the bishop's ear. He folded the linen and scrubbed the waxy shimmer on forehead, cheeks, chin, tending to a man who'd slept for days, might sleep for days more, but who'd never wake. Incense burned in a brazier, bringing tears to all eyes.

Orlando blinked away the vision, guilty that he dreamed the bishop's death only because they'd all die on their feet, awaiting the end of the bishop's sermon.

"You must go forth into the fields," the bishop chirped, "as the prophet says, and as the archbishop exhorts us. 'Catch the foxes, the little foxes, that spoil the vines.'"

Bring us the foxes, the wee little foxes!

He's repeating God's word! If you are a demon, you cannot speak so.

Renards! Renards!

Rainbows blinded him, but Orlando kept his head bowed through the benediction, refusing to let that ghost harangue him, hoping the smell of fresh-cut grass was blown into the city by the mistral.

Orlando's internal turmoil continued because of what those ladies and even Badoyn said, that Simon wanted to be king. Yet the ultimate commander Orlando served was Philippe Augustus. That loyalty wasn't helping him here in the south. Orlando had calculated too many times—virtually every time he spotted the North Star in the night sky—that he couldn't strike out for Troyes or Paris with no silver in his pockets and only poor aged Midnight to carry him.

"*Benedicamus Domino*." The bishop chirped his final words. A crow on the roof of the basilica cawed back.

"*Deo gratias*." Orlando repeated the response along with all the men gathered in the basilica square.

"Thanks be to God!" Badoyn slapped Louis's shoulder. "We can ride now, right?"

Outside the stable, Louis divided up the guards, counting them off to send them into Badoyn's squad or Orlando's. His cousin also had the two French knights he'd brought with him. Orlando had whoever Louis assigned him, none of whom were men he trusted well enough to believe he could command them. Louis, swayed by Badoyn's imprecations, chose to lead Badoyn north toward the village of St-Matthieu. Louis undoubtedly recognized the worthlessness of this quest, since St-Matthieu was filled with infantry and baggage tramps from the Pays de France who had seized deserted houses and gardens and farms when the locals were evicted.

As much as Orlando tried to avoid it, Badoyn cornered him, backing him into the harness-menders' corner, then flipping a coin to the two young men there and pointing to the stable door. When they were alone, he moved too close, so Orlando could smell woman's perfume in his hair, which was not yet bound up for the ride.

"Is that a battlefield haircut?" Badoyn brushed his hand over the tattoo above Orlando's ear. "Girding your loins?"

"Preparing for the next Saracen bandit attack."

"I was going to give you one of Giles's coins," he flipped a piece of gold in his hand, "in case you lost yours. But I see you're showing your Wheel and Serpent souvenir. Too bad Simon didn't see it at supper. He's one of us."

"I noticed."

"Listen, Balthazar. We have to make a plan. Now, before Simon returns at Pentecost. How many times last winter did he tell the story of the Angevine king Henry and Thomas Beckett? 'Will no one rid me of this turbulent pest?' My plan requires Simon to be gone, and it cannot work without you."

"Then you cannot do it. I'm not betraying my king."

"That's a bit grandiose, Balthazar. No one will call us traitors. Because no one will know. Except Simon, who will reward us."

"Stop calling me that. I'm Orlando of Troyes. We are equal, under the law and under God's eyes."

"*Si chaud, mon frère?*" Badoyn called him hotheaded. "When did I ever cause you harm? Who else but my cousin, almost my brother, would I share such an opportunity with?"

"I'm not undertaking any scheme with you."

"But my marquesa claims your own sweet widow says you are with us. I saw you kissing her."

Two miscommunications, and the sun was only mid-sky. Still, the more Orlando knew about these miscreants' plans, the better prepared he'd be to protect the boys. "Fine. Do you want to take Simon's son hostage? Hold him for ransom? Because then you'd need me to tell you which boy belongs to Simon."

"You are brilliant, Balthazar—oops, Orlando!" He slammed Orlando's shoulder. "A fantastic idea. We take him, make sure he doesn't know any of us. Then we save him in a dramatic rescue. We'll look like heroes. No one will ever figure it out."

"The mistral must have already driven you mad," Orlando said. "It's a terrible, reckless idea."

"But you had the genius idea! Me, my luck works only when I am reckless."

"Is this truly the best way to get Simon's attention?"

"I don't need attention. I want Simon to know he owes me when he's king." He wrapped his arm around Orlando's neck. "Can you get *les enfants* beyond the city walls tomorrow? We want to grab the boy without fifty guards jumping on us."

"I won't let any of the boys be hurt."

"You and I aren't in the business of hurting boys." Badoyn was walking him away from the harness-menders' work bench. "We'll return to the city acclaimed as heroes by sunset tomorrow. You are smart like a fox."

Bring us the foxes, the wee little foxes!

In Troyes, I hunted foxes. They're not smart. Just quick. And kits eat their own dead littermates.

Silky, silky foxes.

Orlando sniffed, thinking he smelled smoke, but it must be his own smothered anger. He'd just learned enough to stop what Badoyn intended. Then he couldn't cease thinking of Badoyn as anything but a fox kit out to devour his littermates.

16
Bona, Senhór

AFTER WAITING UNTIL BADOYN AND Louis left the city, Orlando requested packhorses from the stablemaster, plus pack harnesses.

"*Sommetiers,* Captain? Expect to win big today?" the stablemaster asked. Ansel was a large Norman from Courcy, with big hands, a drooping nose, and a kind voice, as capable of whispering peace among men as among his horses. "The bets are running in your favor, because you were a hero yesterday."

"And me with no pennies to bet on myself."

The stablemaster roared with laughter, congratulated Orlando for being a fine fellow.

The eight guards assigned to ride with Orlando quietly grumbled all the way down the hill from the walled city.

"We aren't merchants."

"These packhorses slow us down."

Orlando, who led one of the extra horses, called back, "How do you know how slow you're going when you don't know the destination?"

That didn't help, so Orlando made what he could of the ride, it being useless to decry the indolence of the *gardes du corps.*

They followed the Narbonne road east. Just past the turn to St-Marco village, the trail narrowed where it cut through a hill that had served the ancients as a limestone quarry. After that passage, Orlando led his party onto another trail that went south into the forest hills, seeking a certain wide place in the trail called Mas-de-Cours. The three standing "cottages" there were shepherds' dry-stone shelters, spaced well away from each other, as if those who'd lived here didn't love their neighbors in the same way that other villages prefer to huddle together for protection. Or perhaps the wolves never came to the door here.

If any rebels had returned to the area, as Simon insisted, the empty shell of a hamlet might be a hiding place. Orlando led the guards to circle around what could only be called a hamlet. Deserted. He sat on Midnight on a rise above the shelters, while his band of *gardes du corps* hobbled their horses and paused in the shade of a beech grove to gulp their trail food. He was reasonably certain that they shared a leather flask, though he didn't see it whenever he looked.

The horses stirred first, so Orlando was up on his feet when eight sheep ran into the clearing, a ragged blond mastiff nosing them into a huddle. A boy followed, calling encouragement to the dog. He was dressed in last year's linsey-woolsey tunic and breeches, frayed at every edge, a hole over one knee. His hair was bound up in a knot on top of his head, straggling locks falling on the collar of his brown tunic. He was dirty, as you'd expect of a boy living as a shepherd, and browned deep from the sun.

The guards were calling to him, "*Bonjour, garçon métis.*" But the boy didn't understand French, looked bewildered. He addressed Orlando in the local tongue.

"*Bon jorn, senhór.* Here is the tithe for the Church."

"*Mercés, gojat.*" Orlando did his best with the local tongue, none of the guards volunteering to help out. The dog was the same size as the child; it wore the spiked collar of a dog that fought wolves. It moseyed up between Orlando and the boy, sniffing. "What is your dog's name?"

"Lop."

Orlando liked it when the Pays d'Òc and Pays de France words matched easily enough. "Why would you call a dog Wolf?"

"Because it's his name, *senhór.*" The urchin pretended patience, but betrayed his dismay at the stupidity of the French captain.

"*Comment vous appelez-vous?*" When the boy didn't answer, Orlando switched to the local tongue. "*Quin es lo sieu nom?*"

Even then, the boy repeated *Qué? Qué?* twice, because he didn't understand the captain's accent.

Robi ("*Just Robi, that's all*") said the villagers had sent him with these sheep, and the sheep obeyed only Lop. In fact, Lop believed these to be his sheep and insisted that his sheep must be handled gently, and that Robi and Lop didn't know what might become of these sheep when they were forced to eat French grass.

"Do your mother and father think it best that you bring these sheep to the Church with us?"

"They have gone to their good end, so it's only me to decide what they might think best. Unless, who can tell, one might be so lucky to be born among Lop's sheep."

So the boy was an orphan and, if not hereticated, too thick-headed to not talk about incarnation of souls with a French patrol that served Simon de Montfort. Lucky for the boy, none of the indolent guards had learned enough of the local tongue to do more than bargain at a Thursday market.

"You'll have to say your creed to the bishop."

"My mama's granny Estela taught me well how to say it."

The guards complained about being treated as baggage boys while hobbling sheep and tying them as cargo on the packhorses. The youngest guard complained about carrying the shepherd boy on his horse. The dog ("*Lop is worried about his sheep having to eat and sleep in French pastures*") followed when the guards set off, keeping near the boy without harassing the horses.

Orlando considered the whole affair a success, since he'd convinced eight men to do as he commanded.

"I'm going to scout to the west, for any sign of heretics' hide-aways," Orlando said, getting little response from the guards once they'd resigned themselves to the afternoon's chore. "I'll catch up with you on the road home."

·

After circling Mas-de-Cours again, he found no sign that anyone lived there, or had even waited for Orlando to come fetch the tithed sheep. The dry-stone shelters hadn't been inhabited since early spring, judging from the cold fire pits. He studied the path leading west over the rise, believing the best that might be gained in that direction would be water for his horse.

He did find a paradise for Midnight. Untouched grass, a pooling stream with clear water, with damselflies as the only distraction. He hobbled his horse, letting her rest more before returning to the city, and ambled further up into the hills.

The chateau-sized groves of beech trees broke occasionally where meadows were filled with poppies and foxglove. A chestnut tree amid rocks was surrounded with broom and blackberries ready to break into full bloom. Along the narrow trail, suitable only for sheep, he found scat from deer and—ah, foxes! A green lizard ran off the trail ahead of him. He smelled mint and the other spicy undergrowth that grew here, everything that he'd admired when he first came to this country. Overhead, a golden eagle screamed, winging above to hunt during a moment of calm in the mistral.

And a moment alone to enjoy it. He could find solitude in the city only by retreating into a deserted tower, likely to be interrupted by the next patrol of guards. Out here, far enough from the city, he didn't hear the nones bell, though it must be that late. He said the ritual prayer. And even though he must be late with his prayers, he remained unbothered by that usurping ghost.

An oak and a beech tree grew together near the top of a rise, their branches intertwined. Orlando stood below, admiring the majesty of trees that seemed so old, they must have been here when the apostles first came. In a childlike impulse, he began to climb, quickly lost in the dense branches, concentrating on finding the next handhold, the next foothold. When it seemed like he'd reached the last branches that would hold his weight, he peered out, seeing Midnight far, far below, enjoying the kind of paradise where his old pony should be allowed to retire.

He turned the other way, the boughs swaying at his step. Perhaps he'd overestimated how high he could safely climb.

An animal moved in the next vale over, as far away as he'd wandered from Midnight. Not just an animal, a horse.

Followed by a dozen more, ambling down to a stream.

When he concentrated, straining to see into the distance, he finally recognized that the rocks in the clearing were men. Armed men in conversation. He counted. Twenty. No, twenty-five. They rose, moving into close formation, and then faced him. They didn't wear any lord's colors, but he knew enough about armies to see they were a fighting unit.

They faced the direction where Orlando hung in the tree because another man appeared and addressed them. A tall, red-haired fellow in chainmail and long leather boots, motioning with his hands while he spoke.

Not Saracens.

Not French.

These men were dressed more like mercenary units he'd seen move to the south after the battle at Muret. Catalan warriors, perhaps. Like the rage-monsters from stories of the *reconquista* in Andalusia. Savage mountain killers.

He climbed down, not shaking branches, and then returned to Midnight, not ambling, not enjoying solitude. By the time he'd unhobbled his horse and prepared to saddle her, the tall redhead galloped up on a black Arabian, stopping within sword's reach. Though Orlando had no inclination to draw a weapon.

"Are you Orlando of Troyes?" The stranger spoke in rapid Catalan. Orlando struggled to answer in that tongue.

"*Si.*" He wanted to say more, to feel less vulnerable. "The night-marshal of Carcassona."

"*Hola, mon ami!* They said you would help us."

"They—who?"

"Not the marquesa, obviously. She's after the other fellow. I'm the marshal of the Valeureaux knights." Up close, the man was no older than Orlando, but not a man anyone wanted to encounter in close combat.

"*Comment allez-vous?*" Then Orlando managed the Catalan greeting. "*Estàs bé?*" The man must mean Taresa, but Orlando had spoken to her only moments before leaving the city. How could a misunderstanding between them have spread into the wilderness so rapidly?

"It's good to meet you, Captain. Will we take the boy tomorrow? We saw Simon leave the city. Which means it's far more dangerous now."

"It's certainly dangerous." What was he supposed to say? Or do? Orlando might as well be naked out here, facing wild mountain warriors.

"*Bona, senhór!* It's a pleasure to meet you. We shall see you tomorrow. On the battlefield, so to speak." He laughed at a jest Orlando couldn't perceive. "*Adéu,* Captain Orlando. May it all be as it pleases God."

Midnight nudged him, ready to travel.

·

Orlando and his band of indolent guards returned to Carcassona before the refectory bell rang for supper at the bachelors' tower. They came through the gates bearing eight sheep and an orphaned shepherd boy called Robi who apparently was part of the tithed flock. Rather, his dog Lop's flock.

Only Orlando carried knowledge of a small army of Catalan warriors encamped just over the horizon. Enough men to destroy any French patrol that left the protection of Carcassona's walls.

And an explanation, at last, for the Catalan-speaking mage-knight he'd met during the guards' riot in St-Luc village the day before.

Inside the city, Orlando left Midnight with Ansel the stable-master, stashed his armor in the bachelors' barracks, and went to the basilica to quarrel with the bishop's clerk about how the Church was to manage both the sheep and the orphan boy.

"Tithes are paid with silver." Franciscus the clerk kept rolling his quill-knife between two palms.

"Tithes are paid with whatever people have. At this time of year, that's sheep."

"We can't keep sheep in the city."

"Tomorrow morning we'll move them to the abbot's pastures. It's too late in the day to do that now."

"Do you expect the Church to feed and clothe this boy, too?"

"He can eat with the servants in the academy kitchen."

"The fees from your school are for the care of pages learning to be knights."

"He's learning to be a soldier of the Cross, practicing in the way our Lord did, as a good shepherd. Where's Captain Louis? Has he returned?"

"Long before now, Captain." Franciscus wanted Orlando to see that he was annoyed, displeased. "With a bucket of silver and a man the bishop says is one of those black-robed teachers. They lodged the heretic in the prison tower. Worth many more points than eight sheep and a *métis* orphan."

"Where is he?"

"Captain Louis? He's home, entertaining your cousin and his two knights from Paris. His wife prepared a feast, they say."

17
The Tower

ORLANDO MADE SURE ROBI THE shepherd had supper and a place to sleep, and knew to keep his wolf-collared dog off the city streets. Robi declined a bed at the academy in favor of a shed by the abbot's corral, because his sheep tended to be homesick whenever they were forced to change pastures.

Foregoing his own supper, Orlando set out to take up his duties as night-marshal. However, the nighttime duty-sergeant was not yet at his post, since the sun had not set and the bell had not rung. That left time to check on his boys. But when Orlando started out from the watchtower to cross to the basilica, he found a crowd of boys in the yard below the squires' tower, *la tor de l'escòla*.

Karles said, "Your boys drove the tutor from the villa in tears. So I brought them here to watch the squires practice. The new fight-masters suggested we pair them with the squires to learn how to hold their blades."

"*Merci.*" Orlando could get out only one word, taken aback by this intrusion on his authority, coupled with Karles's friendly enthusiasm for the interlopers' suggestion. Could Orlando control nothing that belonged to him?

"Your older boys insist they always wrap their blades, even their wooden pells," Karles said. "So I judged it to be as safe as having them run drills around the academy courtyard."

"Do you think so?" Orlando wasn't feeling that this day was better than the one before, even though he hadn't been knocked on the head.

"What I think," Karles said, "is that you need a new tutor who can manage little boys. I shall do what I can to keep these boys busy, but I'm no tutor."

The squires' new fight-masters joined them, hands out in that too-friendly way people in the south liked to greet each other.

"Your older boys are model students, Captain. Our only complication this afternoon," Chrétien said, "is that your boys insist their captain is a better hand-to-hand fighter than Don Tomás."

"And the claims escalated until the squires joined them," Tomás said. "So now I cannot escape the challenge."

Orlando's boys—and the squires who had formerly been his students—stomped and shouted, waving their pells overhead.

"*Orlando! Captain!*"

Tomás held up his hands, as if surrendering to heaven, as if helpless to intercede, which of course he was, having taken over the squires only that day.

"My idea," Chrétien said, "is that my brother and I will offer a display of fight styles from where we've taught. We were just about to commence that demonstration."

"*Bien.*" Orlando had no more inclination to draw his sword here than he had out in the wilderness. "It's been a long day."

Karles stood beside Orlando, both of them watching the boys, while the mismatched brothers, one tall and the other compact, attacked each other, calling out the schools or battles where they'd learned different strikes and defenses.

"From our Saracen masters in Cairo!"

"From crusader knights on Cyprus!"

"The long-sword style of Normans from Sicily!"

To Orlando's way of thinking, and from his training, a sword was only for close work, when a knight lost his lance or was unseated from his horse; or when riding over infantry, striking hard. The two brothers—if that's what they were—had some idea that swords were for more than hacking at an enemy who came close enough to strike. The Celt, Chrétien, whirled away as if dancing in retreat but then returned in an attack stance that the Moor, Tomás, had to parry. How could these two be brothers? But then, they seemed to read each other's planned movements as they attacked and parried.

The canvas wrapping flew off Chrétien's blade after one ferocious parry by Tomás. The Moor held up his hand, crying, "A draw! A draw! Is it not, Captain?"

Not waiting for Orlando's answer, the two brothers linked arms and bowed to the array of boys in the audience. Rather than this display ending the earlier excitement, the boys stomped and shouted and waved their enthusiasm again.

"Orlando! Captain!"

Orlando folded his arms and shook his head. He raised one hand in the sign that the boys were to be quiet and listen.

Instead, the older boys from his school and the squires began chanting one of the tales he'd made up for them.

> With a courage-filled heart,
> The young knight gallops
> to the castle of the cruel lord.
> His blood hot, he spurs his Saracen steed
> and cries 'All glory to God!'

"Orlando! Orlando!"

"My own father never cheered for me the way your students do." Tomás imitated Orlando's stance, arms folded, but he also wagged a finger as if chiding the squires—which Orlando knew would only provoke resentment among older boys who don't want to be treated as children. "It seems we'll have to give them a demonstration."

"O God's bones!"

Orlando couldn't produce other words. He'd just seen a display that he couldn't match for five heartbeats.

You never could. Even if you could walk like a whole man.

You are not my brother, who was always kind.

Even if you could put on the whole armor of God.

Why had he ever decided that Etienne's ghost spoke to him? Yet his vision clouded with color for a moment.

"Don't worry." Chrétien murmured in Orlando's ear. "He won't defeat you in front of your boys. My brother is a bit of a *punxor*, but he's never a merciless bastard. Or hardly ever."

"*Orlando! Captain!*"

Tomás took off his shirt and discarded the other multitude of weapons he carried. When Tomás deposited his knives by his brother, his turned his bare back to Orlando and the squires, who gasped. The man's back was a hashed landscape of wide welted scars from the kind of beating a man doesn't usually survive. The boys in Orlando's school didn't get this view, and they chanted for their hero.

"*Orlando! Captain!*"

To at least stop the shouting, Orlando yanked off his jerkin, and then pulled his shirt over his head. That movement contained too much of his anger and frustration, for he heard the thin linen tearing as it passed his shoulders. The first sight as he tossed off his shirt was three women under a portico at the edge of the yard. Mme Marguerite with Taresa and Hélène. Taresa lifted a scarf and waved, like a lady does when her favored knight enters the lists to joust. The colors shone in the late afternoon light. It was a piece of Mme Marguerite's embroidery.

Behind him, the sound of steel exiting its scabbard rang in the practice yard. Orlando said, "My armor and kit are in the barracks. I don't think—"

"*Orlando! Captain!*"

Chrétien was at his side, a war sword and shield in his hand. "We're only demonstrating. So here, use my kit."

He began buckling his belt and sword around Orlando, who was too surprised to shrug it off or step away.

"How's that feel?" Chrétien pressed Orlando's hand to the unfamiliar sword hilt, encouraging him to pull the sword from its scabbard. Which was much longer than anything Orlando was accustomed to. "No use adjusting the scabbard so it hangs right. Better idea, let's do away with it."

Chrétien unbuckled and tossed aside his loaned scabbard, and snatched up the shield. He was dressing Orlando like you do a child, wrapping Orlando's arm through the shield straps in an odd, unfamiliar way that pulled the shield close.

"I don't think—"

"*Avant!*" Tomás cried. "That's how they say it in French. Am I right?" He was circling around Orlando, studying him while Orlando moved into the stance his last swordmaster taught.

"*Aiieee*, Captain! Did a snake bite your head?" Tomás circled his sword in a way that Orlando felt as menacing. "Are you truly Wheel and Serpent? Like Simon?"

"No."

"They carved their sign on your head."

"Years ago. They caused—never mind. I can't cut it off."

"Attack now, Orlando de Troyes, and you shall defeat me."

Tomás stepped off at an angle, so that his next move could not strike decently at Orlando, opening him for a strike from Orlando that would disarm him.

Orlando raised to strike, but a motion drew his eyes upward. He dropped his sword and threw off the shield, running for the half-ruined Roman tower.

·

Two boys perched halfway up the external stairs on the ruined tower. Lancelot, the boy leading, argued that he wanted to climb down. The other boy below froze, clinging to Lancelot's boot, afraid to move. It was the smallest of all the new boys, the one who wanted to be called Ajax.

A red scarf on his wrist wagged in the wind.

No. Not Ajax, Galahad.

"Stay there. I'm coming to you!" Orlando commanded as firmly as possible, keeping judgment out of his voice. *Trust me.*

Yet Lancelot defended himself. "The squires pushed us back so we couldn't see. Sergeant Umbert said we could climb to see better."

The boys were many steps beyond merely a better view. Higher than the villa rooftops.

"Let go!" Lancelot shouted to Galahad. "I can't move."

"We'll fall." Galahad said it so softly that Orlando only heard the words because he expected to.

"Wait for me," Orlando commanded. "And don't look down."

Was this his new calling? Getting boys off high places?

The Romans or whatever ancients built these exterior stairs wore smaller boots than Orlando. It'd be years before masons got to this chore, repairing broken tower steps.

He leaned into the tower, preparing to grab the boy, steadying his legs to catch Galahad's weight. "I'm going to count to three. When I say 'three,' let go and I'll have you."

"We'll fall."

"I won't let you. One. Two—"

"Let go of me!" Lancelot shouted. He kicked.

And Galahad was falling.

With the help of the blessed angels, Orlando caught the boy. Then caught his own balance.

One boy in his arms. Safe.

"What about me?" Lancelot pleaded, having just nearly murdered his younger comrade.

"Hold on. You're on a sturdy step. I'll be back."

Climbing down with boy-weight in his arms meant sliding against the stone wall. The mistral gusted, but he didn't have time right then to be driven mad.

Karles waited below and took Galahad so that Orlando could come the rest of the way down without scraping off the other half of his bare skin.

"I'll fetch the other lad." Chrétien didn't wait for an answer, scrambling up the tower with far greater dexterity than Orlando. "*Ça va bien*, brave boy? I only count to two and you come down. Be ready, because—One!"

He didn't wait for Lancelot to move, just grabbed him around his thighs and pulled him into his arms. Since Chrétien had put his shirt on while Orlando and Tomás pretended to fight, he climbed down with greater grace than Orlando. He set Lancelot on the ground, giving him a shove into the crowd of his waiting comrades.

"No wonder your boys love you," Chrétien said. "I never once had a master who'd risk his life for me. You must have inherited the heart of a lion from your father."

Like a lion with eagle's wings, it was lifted up from the earth, and man's heart was fed to it.

No, no! My father was a lion, and this man honors him.

The young lions lack courage, and suffer hunger.

"M—*merci*, monsieur."

"You'll need it." Chrétien stalked away, calling for the squires to come to order and return to their tower.

With everyone back on the ground and the mistral blowing away all his sweat, but none of the residual fear, Orlando called for his academy to return to their own practice yard, walking behind the boys as Umbert and Karles herded them to the villa.

"We're in for it now!" Whichever boy whispered, his voice trembled.

His boys hung close to each other, not because of the foolish risk their comrades had just taken, but dreading the consequences, knowing Orlando typically assigned any punishment to the entire band. He held up his finger, the sign the boys were to listen with full attention. Ten boys went completely still, then squirmed to admit Lancelot and Galahad. The two boys beside Lancelot stepped close to him, so Lancelot couldn't move. Ywain reached over and pinched him.

Just as Orlando began to declaim their punishment, he suddenly saw that he'd gotten everything all wrong. He wanted the boys to cease childish bullying, but he'd been punishing all the boys, forcing them to bully each other into correct behavior.

Too similar to how Simon wanted the villages punished, to teach unknown rebels to fear what might come their way.

"Who does a knight serve?" Was using his deep voice another intimidation, a kind of bullying?

"The king!"

"His lord!"

"His retainers!"

"His comrades!"

"His father's honor!"

"The people who stay home and work the land!"

Orlando wasn't quick enough to see who shouted the last long response. "Indeed, among all his other duties, a knight must serve his household."

A motion in the corner of his eye caught his attention: The women on the portico still watched. And he stood in the practice yard filthy from climbing, his breeches torn. Half-naked from that ridiculous sword display. Trying to scare little boys into right action.

Orlando pulled on his shirt and jerkin, determined not to care what any of those three women thought about his malformed body, or how he loomed over little boys. He raised his voice only enough to keep their attention.

"As comrades, you are called upon to protect your brothers, even at your own peril." Though one of his little boys just tried to kick another off the tower. "Your brothers are called in the same way, so you must live in truth with your brothers."

"Sergeant Umbert said we could climb." Lancelot muttered under his breath, yet Orlando and everyone else heard.

"If your brothers listen with open hearts, but believe you are lying, then how can they trust you? How can they be called to protect you, if they suspect you cannot be trusted?"

He had their attention, and it was time to do the unexpected.

"Mme Marguerite complains of smoke in her workroom. I believe her hearth needs raking. The villa's jakes need lime. The kitchen firewood needs splitting. It's not work for gentlemen, and yet, a woman in distress needs to be rescued by courtly knights. What *juvenes* will volunteer?"

"Me, Captain Orlando! I shall!"

"*Je vais le faire!*"

"*Moi aussi!*"

The two boys beside Lancelot shoved at his hands, forcing his arms up. While looking the other direction, Orlando said, "I want volunteers. Do not raise your hand if you don't truly see your duty."

When Ywain tried again to force Lancelot's arm, Lancelot stepped behind two younger boys. Pushed at his nose. Folded his arms. Spread his legs to shove those two boys away from him.

Orlando discovered, then, which of his charges was the son of Simon de Montfort, vicomte of Carcassona.

18
Curfew, Monsieur

"MASTER KARLES, A WORD."

Orlando hailed the Catalan bodyguard, delaying his entry into the academy refectory behind the boys. Was Karles a member of the Catalan force camping in the valley? No, he'd come to the city with Simon, and from Paris before that; he couldn't be.

"*Si, senhór?*" Yet the man slipped into Catalan easier than French.

"Don't let the boys out of your sight. Find a pair of servants you trust, and take turns keeping watch all night."

"Of course." Karles dropped his voice. "Do you think an attempt will be made against the boy tonight? Because Simon left the city?"

The boy. Not the *boys*. Then Karles *was* one of them.

"We're all worried." Karles didn't wait for Orlando to answer. "Mme Marguerite and I are sure of all the servants now. She had to let one go. So Mme Hélène lent us two of her *footmen*." A smirk. "We are prepared."

"*Bien.*" Loaned footmen? When Hélène had been seeking servants earlier? Did he dare ask?

The bell rang, signaling the beginning of his night-marshal duties. "I'll check in through the night. You know my whistle."

"*Si. Adèu!*" Karles called after him. "It shall all be as pleases God, Captain."

Orlando headed for the *petit* well, as the closest path to the city gates, counting doors on his way like he did when crossing the city at night. One blue door, with rosemary as large as a tree by the steps, sheltered the wife and new baby of a knight from St-Germain who'd traveled south with Orlando and now rode on all of Simon's forays, while his family stayed safe in Carcassona. The iron-red door, where a knight from Brienne (Louis's distant cousin) had nailed a shield with his family arms on the door; a knight who paid his sergeant to take his required place on the duty rolls. At the next villa, the steps and outer yard were swept cleaner than other villas on the row. Behind its yellow door—the carpenter's master charged more for this color than his other three choices—a knight from Orleans led an austere life under the rule of his rich wife, a Pays d'Òc native.

Mme Taresa stood beside the *petit* well, alone on the street, arms akimbo, waiting, as if she expected him.

"Do you know which boy it is?" she asked, not bothering with any friendly greeting.

"Yes. And your brother-at-arms Karles is staying awake tonight to help you, it seems." He walked on, intending to keep space between them, to prevent the kind of intimacy where she held his hand and pretended to read his heart.

"Karles? He's not from Valeureaux. He belongs to the king." She walked beside him, tucking her arm into the crook of his elbow. "We must trust each other, Captain. Because we both know Simon is dangerous to kings in Christendom."

"I can't break my own vows—"

"Come serve as a Valeureaux knight. Keep better vows."

"I do not know which heretics' hamlet is called Valeureaux. However—"

"You're saying it wrong. It's Valerós. Castell-de-Valerós is south, in the Pyrenees. And not hereticated. At least in the castle. Of course, every farmer, baker, and weaver from Lyon to the Great Sea is hereticated, to Simon's way of thinking."

"My vows begin with Philippe Augustus and he—"

"And he, like Simon, has left you without horses and retainers. Let us restore you to the warrior's life you should be living."

"You don't know my secrets, madam."

"I know you languish in Carcassona. You cannot deny it."

"And you are in Carcassona plotting secrets."

"You said you'd help, Captain."

"Actually, I didn't say any such thing. Further, I met your army in the hills today."

"Oh good. I thought you might. But please, don't tell—"

"Don't tell the commander of the *gardes du corps* that a hostile force is camped outside the city?"

"No, of course you won't do that. I mean, don't tell Don Tomás and Chrétien. It will make them overconfident. Reckless. No use involving them as more than couriers."

"As night-marshal, I'm betraying my duty, not telling my commander that the city is filled with Catalan traitors who—"

"Who owe nothing to either Simon or Philippe, and therefore can't be traitors. What does every Catalan baron say? 'Not our wolves, not our lambs, not our fight.'"

"You don't believe in the Church's project to bring the Peace of God among heretics?"

"No, but that scarcely matters for the work that you and I must do. And you know in your heart that Simon's terror in the villages does not serve God here on earth."

"It's my duty to tell my commander what's happening."

"Your cousin has made your commander his great friend. He's at Louis's house right now, beguiling him. Captain Louis won't help you protect that boy. Though perhaps he doesn't know what your cousin intends."

"God's bones!"

"Trust us." She persisted, however rapidly he set the pace. "Valerós isn't a threat to Carcassona. Or to Philippe Augustus. We keep faith and pay our knights with gold and loyalty. And we do not betray our kings or lords, because our lords never betray us."

She touched Orlando's arm at that moment, trying to get him to slow down while they talked, but her hot touch filled his thoughts with images of the night before, standing in front of Simon, who didn't remember his past promises to Orlando. Both before and after that siege-boulder crushed his leg.

"Come live an honorable life, Captain Orlando. Which you cannot do as long as you serve Simon."

"My final vow to Simon, which I am keeping, is to protect these boys with my life. All of them." They'd arrived at the city gates. He stopped, folding his arms, wanting her to leave him alone.

"That will be good enough. That's what we want, too."

She kissed him again, right in the city street, but only on the cheek this time. She grasped his arms, like a soldier does, peering into his eyes, her own glittering in the guards' torchlight. She rested a hand on his chest. "I know you aren't capable of evil."

Then she curtsied, like ladies do at court, and hurried back through the darkening streets toward the *petit* well.

At the gate, Orlando stood behind the guards who searched workers as they departed the city, folding his arms again, to look authoritative. Though the guards had stopped their lazy searches to watch the night-marshal be assaulted, body and soul, by the handsome and rich senhóra who'd come to Carcassona to help Mme Agnes, widow of the martyr of Béziers.

.

Near the City Mill tower, on his second turn around the walls, the bakers were lighting the ovens, their servants having laid wood for the early-morning fires before going home to their own villages.

Guards answered lazily at the fourth tower over. The Vicomte's Mill tower was currently an armory and storehouse, not a working mill. Would the fields offer a rich harvest this summer, requiring another working mill?

It will all be as it pleases God.

Where did that thought come from? He'd heard it several times, from villagers and from the gaggle of Catalans swarming this town. Heresy? Even if it was some heretics' turn of phrase, like Mme Estela's calling for a blessing from the Good God—well, who could argue with the thought? Except it wasn't something he'd think to say; he'd definitely argue the idea with his false ghost. He'd have to give up all he believed, about honor and redemption if he thought God was pleased with his crushed leg and lost fortunes.

At the Carpenters' tower, Orlando called twice before the guards responded. Just like every turn around the walls, every night.

He passed the towers around the chateau, where knights who lived in the city either escaped their wives to gamble privately, or paid other guards to take their place on the required duty rolls, watching for intruders in the chateau itself. These were slowest to respond whenever Orlando called for a report: The Chapel tower, the bachelors' barracks (hard to tell if any guard took seriously the protection of the bachelor-knights' residence), St-Paul's tower.

The watchtower, Orlando's favorite hiding place, had no defensive purpose, and these guards also likely slept as much as they traded their silver with each other in dice games. Beyond the tower stood the bricked-up river gate. If Simon ever decided to restore this entrance to the city, guards would be serving there again.

At the decaying Roman tower, the guards always answered quickly when Orlando hailed them. Because until the matins bell rang, guards gambled there, whatever the weather.

All was quiet in the young squires' barracks, not even lights visible in windows and arrow slits. Then mumbled answers came from the towers behind the Basilica St-Nazaire, at the Church mill tower, and the next two towers.

Orlando stopped, gazing up at the prison tower. *Le Mur.* Usually empty for the past year, it now held whatever poor soul Badoyn grabbed in St-Mathieu village and declared a heretic.

On to the towers near the *petit* well. He called twice before hearing the guards report. Then at the battered tower, which took as much damage in the siege as the city gates did. Repairs had been done on the out-facing sides the first year Simon ruled the city, as had the next towers, which had also taken heavy hits from the siege machines. Trebuchet boulders still littered the ground inside the city, roughly stacked, waiting to be ammunition in a future siege.

And back to the gate that opened to the road to Narbonne. Guards drowsed at the opening level and in the towers above. If an army invaded, like the French had, who'd be awake in the city to hear? Orlando shrugged over that concern. Carcassona now was overstocked with what it needed to withstand a long siege: food, water, crossbow bolts. And who would attack? Not twenty-five Catalan wild men. Not any Pays d'Òc seigneurs, who couldn't keep loyal house-knights, couldn't come speedily to the side of the king of Aragón, the only king who'd offered to protect them.

That night's duties were no different from any other night he'd spent in the past years. Making sure the streets remained empty after curfew. When he cut across from the City Mill tower to the grand well, he passed one dark figure scurrying along, the mistral sending the tails of his cloak flying.

"Curfew, monsieur." Orlando used his deepest voice, but not loud enough to disturb anyone in nearby villas.

"*Mais oui*, Captain. But I had to be gone before her husband comes home from his own tryst. He's likely the next transgressor you'll see."

With the chateau as his destination, Orlando did not encounter the husband. He needed to find food and rest, having endured more that day than any man could be expected to when not in actual battle. Except the battle continued in his thoughts, between the voice that wasn't his brother and the lingering provocations of the golden senhóra of — what was it called? — Valerós.

Orlando had knotted his scarf three times, having walked widdershins from gate to watchtower and back to the gate, counting steps, calling softly to the guards in each tower, making sure they were awake, in order to earn a handful of silver pennies from Simon.

In the bachelors' barracks, Orlando found bread and cheese in the refectory, and then asked the night-porter whether the bath waters had fallen cold yet. Assured he could still warm his bones, he descended into the bath wearing only his breeches, carrying a rushlight to find his way in what had probably been a laundry a hundred years ago. He held onto his last remaining hope for the day — no, it was already tomorrow — that he could soak away pain from the day's travails. Besides his aching bones, his back still stung, rubbed raw while bringing Galahad down from that tower.

However, he pushed open the heavy iron-and-oak door to find two men in the small pool. They'd lit half a dozen rush lamps so the cavernlike room glowed, apparently so they could see the backgammon game they played while soaking in the pool.

19

A Song of the Outremer

ONE MAN GLANCED UP WHEN Orlando entered, while at the same time the other cried, "I win again!"

"*Hola, poulain!*" The darker of the two called to Orlando. The bath had been claimed by the two mercenaries from Cyprus who'd stolen the fief fees for the squires' training.

Orlando stripped, since he hadn't fetched other clothes, and slipped into the end of the small pool. The rocking water proved those two were also naked. "I'm called Orlando. Captain Orlando."

"Tomás isn't insulting you." Chrétien scratched at a pile of coins on the floor by the bath, extracting some and dragging them to a pile near him. His long hair was bound in a braid that hung in the water. "It's a term of affection that our father's knights called us."

"Both your fathers?"

"We are brothers," Tomás said. "Some badly behaved knights in the Outremer use *poulain* to disparage *mestitz* children. Men in my father's camp claimed otherwise."

"Though our mother is a Kurd," Chrétien said. "My adopted mother, that is. She was related to Saladin himself. But then, don't most Outremer *mestitz* sons claim to be children of princesses from Cairo or Damascus? Except you actually are."

"What?" The water splashed; Orlando wasn't sure he'd heard. "I don't claim any such thing."

Chrétien didn't seem to hear Orlando's protests. "Of course, they called our father Miquel a bastard Moor in every country he visited. Though we know for a fact his parents were married."

"And he was Christian," Tomás said. "Else why would Miquel be a crusader, eh?"

"He was a crusader because he liked to fight. And it paid well," Chrétien said. "Same as Orlando's father. Why do you fight, Captain Orlando? To earn your way to heaven faster?"

"You have me at a loss, gentlemen." As in the sham sword fight earlier, Orlando felt he'd come at a disadvantage. What made these vagabonds feel free to intrude in his life? "You don't know me to speak of my mother. Or my father."

"You're Orlando of Troyes, right? Fabien, your father, fought with ours in the Outremer."

"My father fought under Philippe Auguste, not..."

"A bastard Moor?" Tomás found this funny. "I meant to say, Fabien of Troyes fought side by side with Don Miquel of Morella, our father."

"Along with Hugues de Beaurain and Pèire Leteric of Valerós," Chrétien said. "When Philippe went home because he was ill—"

"Because he wanted possession of Flanders," Tomás said.

"Not relevant." Chrétien brushed aside the comment. "After your mother died, Miquel begged Fabien to come to Cyprus with him. But Fabien wanted his son—that's you—to live among his people in Troyes. So he went home with Philippe."

Like a lion with eagle's wings, it was lifted up from the earth.

You lie! This seems true. If unbelievable.

A man's heart was fed to the eagle.

This story struck at Orlando's heart in the same way as when that mage-knight in the village declared an evil spirit possessed him. Only that evil ghost could quarrel with the story Chrétien and Tomás were telling.

"This isn't the story I heard in my childhood."

"Is there another Fabien of Troyes?" Tomás asked.

"Besides the one our father described as a man of impeccable honor?" Chrétien sounded casual while saying things that overwhelmed Orlando. "Is that possible?"

Orlando's heart, that unreliable organ, swelled and warmed the blood in his veins, the throbbing in his ears like when you're underwater and everything sounds far, far away.

"How can you know my story?" Orlando coughed, trying not to betray the clot of emotion in his throat. "I have never heard it."

"Truly?" Chrétien sobered. "You aren't having us on? You sincerely don't know?"

"No," Orlando said. "And I beg you by all the saints—"

"You don't have to beg," Tomás said. "I swear on St-Denis and St-Georges, and all the dancing saints you can name, that we speak only truth."

"Our father Miquel witnessed the charter when Philippe promised to buy Fabien's debts," Chrétien said, "which paid off what Fabien had mortgaged to go on crusade."

"And made Fabien richer than all his comrades," Tomás said. "Though Miquel swore he wasn't jealous."

Richer than...Orlando struggled to rise above the waves of emotion and confusion that swept over him. Did he hear what they said, or dream it?

"And we didn't call you *poulain* as an insult to your mother," Tomás said.

"It's such a romantic story," Chrétien said, "how Fabien rescued a wealthy Egyptian woman that Angevin crusaders were holding hostage. The old knights on Cyprus turned it into a song a decade ago."

"They knew my mother? You knew her?"

"We were wild to be squires then, and weren't home if we could help it," Tomás said. "But I do remember another woman, as beautiful as our mother."

"She sang," Chrétien said. "She taught me two of her songs."

"Our mother, Numa, was with her when she died. She offered to take you, to be your nurse," Tomas said.

"Like Numa did for me," Chrétien said. "But Fabien wouldn't part with you."

"This is—" Orlando couldn't form words.

"You were about this high when we said adieu, *fraire pichon*." Tomás measured a small space of the water, calling Orlando 'little brother' in the local tongue. "We have every reason to call you our little brother, and no reason to quarrel, for the sake of our fathers' honor."

Young lions lack courage, and suffer hunger.

He refused any ghostly imprecations. Orlando's heart had swelled so that he struggled to breath, to get air past the wave of warm feeling.

"Now, tell us your story," Chrétien said. "Perhaps we can make a song. Tales of Orlando, a hero lost in the Pays de France, escaping the heretic brotherhood of the Wheel and Serpent, longing for —

"*Arrête!*"

The two men did stop, silent for long moments while Orlando considered whether the mistral or that evil ghost had driven him mad. He'd entered a strange world three times now: with the mage-knight at St-Luc; in the hills above Mas-de-Cours; in the cellar of an ancient chateau with two rogues who praised his father to the heavens.

"Perhaps," he hesitated, "I don't understand your French."

"Perhaps I could sing it as a song," Chrétien said.

"Don't tease him anymore," Tomás said. "Why didn't Fabien tell you? A hero like that must want his son to know."

"He died a year after we came home," Orlando said. "Swamp fever. I was five. Almost."

"*Je suis désolé.*" Chrétien repeated it, in several languages, seeming to mean it.

"We had our father with us until a few years ago." Tomás seemed thoughtful. "I'm sorry you didn't have that."

"This is…" Orlando tried to start, but couldn't form words.

"I'm a good storyteller," Chrétien said, "but if I ask the right questions, will you tell a story worthy of a song? What happened after your father died?"

"We lived in my grandfather's house," Orlando said. "He's a stern man, but my grandmother was good. Taught me to read and cipher. When she died, I was sent to a fight-master. My older brother was sent to Paris as a squire."

"And your fight-master taught you the poetry of Troyes but not the heroics of Fabien of Troyes?" Tomás was deep in thought.

"He never mentioned my father, had never been to the Outremer himself. He taught fighting and chivalry, mostly using the birch-stake method."

"You mean learning with wooden pells, like your little boys?"

"No, I mean birch stake applied across my hide." Orlando remained good at not thinking much of those years.

Chrétien swore, at least that's what Orlando assumed, though he didn't know what language it was.

"The bath is growing cold," Tomás said. "Shall we walk? Do you have a room in your academy where we can talk? We should hear more of your story."

"We can claim the watchtower."

.

They dressed in silence. Orlando observed the niceties, his eyes on a flickering lamp wick, not taking that chance to stare again at the hash that had been made of Tomás's back, at the patches of stitched scars along Chrétien's arms. Then they walked in silence across the chateau courtyard and entered the watchtower. Above, Orlando once again relieved the two guards of duty, fairly certain they'd only just awakened, hearing boots on the stairs.

Protected from the mistral by the tower's walls, Chrétien shed his cloak, unbuckled his sword, and leaned on a window ledge beside Tomás to study a view too familiar to Orlando. After they'd exclaimed how high above the world they were, and how bright the stars, with only a fingernail's worth of moon, Tomás began again.

"Why didn't Philippe tell you that your papa was a hero? He's walking around now, pretty much the greatest king in Christendom, only because Fabien risked his life for him."

"I don't think Philippe has ever heard of me."

"You didn't train in Philippe's court? But you said your brother went to Paris."

"When I was twelve, Grand-père Daniel sent me with my brother and cousin to serve in Simon de Montfort's retinue. We were supposed to go on crusade to the Outremer, but when Simon left that crusade, we found a new lord. And ended up in Constantinople."

"*Aiieee!*" Tomas exclaimed. "We left that fiasco at Zara. It took a year to earn back what we lost on that endeavor."

"It did teach us how to know whether a master is worth serving," Chrétien said. They described their own experience, traveling as mercenaries, not *juvenes.*

The telling of their story averted any cause to tell more about Constantinople, except the greatest catastrophe of all.

"My brother Etienne died there." Orlando stopped to describe his noble older brother, who'd been born in Troyes four months after their father went to the Outremer, and so knew Fabien even fewer years than Orlando had. "The only Saracens I saw on crusade were mercenaries in Christian armies. I returned to Troyes. Later, Grand-père Daniel sent me off with Simon de Montfort again, to reclaim the Pays d'Òc for the Church."

"An endeavor of peace," Chrétien said, in his wry, sardonic voice, "to restore the true teachings of Jesus and the prophets."

"Mmm. Grand-père said it was my best opportunity to bring glory to my father's name."

"Why?" Tomás cried. "Your father's name is hung with glory in roses and gold!"

These asides—all glory to his father's name—filled up chinks in Orlando's heart, like masons repairing a broken wall.

"I—I don't..."

"We've overwhelmed you," Chrétien said quietly. "I'm sorry."

"Your grandfather is..." Tomás fell back into Catalan, reciting a litany that castigated Grand-père Daniel. Orlando understood a few of the words: *baquelar, mustela, peccador, punxor.* Others were strange to him, and spoken too quickly for guesses. "You must despise him."

"Daniel? No, I feel beholden to him. My grandfather gave me horses and hired knights so I could travel with Simon under my house's banner. When I was injured in Minerve..." The two men interrupted Orlando's story as he told it, wanting to know details that only fighting men would ask, so it took many moments to get to the end of the Minerve tale. "While I was being nursed by monks, my knights deserted, taking my horses and armor with them. My grandfather can't afford to replace them. So here I am, the night-marshal in Carcassona."

"I'd have wished for you," Tomás said, "that your father had lived to see you right in the world, as our father did for us. Did he say nothing to you when you were a wee *fadrin?*"

Orlando didn't know that word. But he heard his father's voice, rocking him to sleep. *You'll serve the king; he promised me that for you.*

"It's not like I'd ever pry into your family business." Chrétien held up his hand when Orlando tried to object to more prying. "But is it possible your family cheated you? That your cousin made his luck at your expense? That your grandfather took your father's wealth and left you in the wind?"

"No," Tomás said. "The wind would take better care of you. Even that foul cold wind that blows here."

"It's called the mistral." His thoughts racing, Orlando responded with trivia. "It'll be over by Pentecost."

"I have a good idea that your cousin wants you dead," Tomás said. "Before Pentecost. That in Constantinople he intended you go to heaven along with your brother. To be crushed in Minerve. Perhaps he's tried other times."

"Like yesterday in St-Luc village?" Chrétien said. Which the mage-knight who'd rescued Orlando had claimed. "You have amazing luck, little brother."

Orlando didn't feel that, but he felt gratitude and friendship for these men. He no longer wanted to quarrel with them.

"Your cousin is Simon's agent," Chrétien said.

"And he has made your commander his great friend," Tomás said, with firm conviction.

"Do you know that for certain?" Orlando pleaded. "Badoyn wants Simon's attention—"

"And will do anything to keep the attention he's already won," Chrétien said. "We watched them become fast friends this spring in Fanjeau."

Tomás stared out at the stars, which were gradually fading as dawn approached. "You must wonder how we came to be in Fanjeau."

Orlando didn't respond, but Chrétien lazily told a story of their winter's attempts to get close to Simon, finally settling on forged letters of introduction from the commander of the pope's bodyguards, with testimonials from a French marquis.

"Everyone in Fanjeau is either Simon's true believer or sufficiently bribed that we could never get close to the boy," Tomás said. "We were lucky enough to get invited along when Simon moved to Carcassona this week."

"But we're finding the same problems here," Chrétien said. "Though loyalty in Carcassona seems to be purchased, rather than being a city filled with crusading true believers."

"The games are filled with silver tonight," Tomás said. "Ten times what was gambled at dice or backgammon in the Roman tower last night. Someone is pouring silver out to the guards."

"And Simon left this morning," Chrétien said. "Which means Badoyn is buying the guards' loyalty—as far as loyalty might go at a perverse posting like Carcassona."

The matins bell rang. The monks' voices drifted on the wind, chanting the twelve psalms.

Time to pray.

A headache started over his eye, but Orlando listened to the psalms, and didn't repeat the prayers the false ghost always made him say in the predawn hours.

Tomás spoke when the psalms ended. "Look, we don't have time, *mon ami*. We need to do our work and be gone before Pentecost. They say that's when Simon will return."

"Our work will go better and faster if you help," Chrétien said. "We want to call you brother. That you'll trust us, and we'll trust you, and we'll work together."

Orlando shook his head, unhappy that the long night's tales led here. "My cousin Badoyn has the precise same idea, to kidnap Simon's son."

"Simon's son?" Chrétien wrinkled his nose in distain. "Whatever would anyone want with the vicomte's brat?"

"Badoyn will pretend to kidnap him, and then pretend to rescue the boy. So Simon will reward him." Orlando offered the same empty hands he'd offered to Mme Taresa. "But I won't break my oath. Simon made me swear to protect his son with my life."

"No, we heard what he demanded," Tomás said. "Simon implied your life was forfeit if anything happened to his son. That's different."

"Not a difference I know how to measure. I will not help Badoyn. I cannot help you either, for the same reason. My oath is my bond."

"Your oath," Chrétien said, "is to Philippe, who will not want Simon usurping him in the south."

"If you are so loyal," Tomás said, "look upward, to what your king needs. Like your father did."

"It's unfair of you to call on my father's name."

"No, it is fair," Chrétien said. "We know that Fabien would look down on any lord who breaks faith with Philippe."

"I will have no part in stealing his child." Orlando didn't want to discuss it more.

"Too much risk if we fail?" Tomás asked.

"Simon did threaten our little brother's life," Chrétien said.

"No," Orlando said. "It's wrong to use children as markers in a backgammon game."

"But that's why we must remove the child from Simon's clutches," Tomás said. "Simon broke faith—and his own oaths—holding that boy as a pawn."

"Simon's son?" Their pestering left Orlando confused.

"No, we want the other boy," Tomás said. "To restore him to his people."

"And we want to keep Simon from making himself king in the south," Chrétien said.

Tomás leaned toward Orlando, earnest. "Help us. Your father would."

"Which other boy?" Confused *and* frustrated.

"Jaume, the king of Aragón." Tomás said it slowly, as if Orlando were dim-witted.

Chrétien said, "We can rescue him by vespers tonight if you will please tell us which is the right boy."

20
Lo Mieu Aimat Capitani

Orlando saw why, now.

Why the forest was filled with Catalan warriors.

Why little boys had a warrior bodyguard.

Why Badoyn nagged and plotted ruthlessly.

"Your friend Taresa of Valerós wants the same help from me."
Orlando saw how he'd misunderstood what she'd asked. "I overheard you with her at Mme Agnes's yesterday."

"With Hélène, the devil's adulterous sister!" Tomás cried. "The gravel-brain marquesa put crickets in that girl's head."

"No, brother." Chrétien whapped at Tomás's hand. "Taresa makes up her own mind. And then gods and angels must watch out for themselves."

"The marquesa seems to accept my cousin's advances." Orlando now saw that in a different way. "Though I overheard Mme Hélène say she was using him."

"That won't be to your cousin's advantage. Hélène," Tomás spit her name as he moved close to Orlando, "watched while my face was rearranged. Whatever those women have proposed to you—

"I misunderstood when Mme Taresa asked for my help. I understand now that it's not about stealing Simon's son." Orlando repeated what he'd avowed earlier. "What I intend to do is let my cousin win Simon's quest. Meanwhile, I'll do whatever I can to keep these boys safe. But I can't do more if it means placing those boys in danger."

"No," Tomás said. "You have to do more. Tell us which boy is Jaume. So we can take him away from Simon."

"I don't know. I didn't know until now that we sheltered a king." Did Marguerite know? She'd been an instant confidante of Karles, the bodyguard. Worse, he began to wonder if he'd chastised the king of Aragón. Let him volunteer to slake lime in the jakes?

"Is Karles your comrade?"

"We all served Pedro," Tomás said. "Karles was one of his body-guards. We endured Andalusia for Pedro's sake."

"I met a stranger in St-Luc, a Catalan knight. Is he one of your comrades? He hates Simon. He was in Andalusia, too."

"Perhaps," Chrétien said, "he's one of the relay riders that Karles enlisted. There's a dozen in the countryside, waiting to help deliver the king to his countrymen."

Relay riders? That must be what Orlando had met in the hills, and mistakenly considered them to be Taresa's army. He didn't seek confirmation from these two, because she'd asked him not to mention them.

"Captain, can you suborn the guards who inspect people departing the city?" Chrétien asked.

"No." Must he confess that he had no power or respect in this city, except for twelve little boys?

"No," Tomás said. "Because Badoyn is spreading too much silver about town. We can't trust any of them."

"By now, Karles must know which boy is Jaume," Chrétien said. "He's had weeks to find out."

"I'm very uncomfortable to find my academy penetrated by schemers." Orlando spoke his unease as mildly as he could, given the storm raging within him. How could he agree?

"I'm sorry if it feels as if we'd planned a cruel trick. Like your cousin's tricks." Tomás sounded warmly sympathetic. Then he said, "Except, we three want the same things. We carry the same kind of honor. We swore oaths to a king."

"Tell me how I can help—while keeping my oath to Philippe and while protecting my boys."

"First," Tomás said, "go along with what Badoyn proposes. So we know where and when he intends to launch his scheme."

Orlando nodded, agreeing so quickly he surprised himself. "He wants me to bring the boys out of the city, so he can snatch Simon's son. Then he'll use another disguise to pretend to rescue the boy. He must have the same plan for...the other boy."

"No, *mon ami.*" Chrétien was more serious than he'd been all night. "Your cousin isn't going to hold Jaume for ransom."

"Your cousin means to kill the king of Aragón," Tomás said. "And he needs to do it before Simon returns at Pentecost."

"Kill the—"

No use repeating the horror: of course that's what Badoyn intended. Orlando couldn't argue; it was just the kind of chance his cousin would take to gain glory in Simon's eyes.

Bring us the foxes!

Chrétien said, "He seeks to rid Simon of his problem while leaving Simon's hands clean."

Yet another misunderstanding—what Badoyn meant when he repeated the tale of the Angevin king Henry. *Will no one rid me of this turbulent pest?*

"We need a worthy plan," Chrétien said. "And we need to get enough sleep to take action before today's sunset."

Orlando had a thousand doubts. "I don't see how we get him out of the city without great risk. I can protect him here in the city with Karles's help. And yours."

Tomás said, "That works until Simon returns and demands you hand him over. Then Jaume is in more danger than ever. We have to get him out of Carcassona and away from Simon."

"Can we run a feint today without the boy?" Orlando didn't like plans without practice. "Draw Badoyn into showing what he plans?"

"Then you're joining us, little brother?" Tomás asked.

"Of course he is." Chrétien gathered his cloak and sword.

Tomás said, "Excellent. But we need to remove Jaume today. There's no time for practice."

"How do we take advantage of your heretic-hunting quest this afternoon?" Chrétien asked. "How do we save a king and return him to his countrymen?"

Tomás drew his sword half from his scabbard and then rammed it in again, the sound ringing in the stairwell. "The same way Fabien of Troyes saved Philippe. With brute force. And daring."

.

Only two days earlier, Orlando had insisted that the mage-knight in St-Luc village was wrong; it couldn't be true that Badoyn attacked him.

He'd refused Taresa's invitation to become a knight of Valerós.

Why believe two vagabonds with rude manners, odd Cypriot accents, and more scar tissue than flesh?

Beyond merely believing them, he'd agreed to a reckless plan created in the watchtower's stairwell—because they'd acclaimed all honor to his father; knew his father's name; knew his mother, whose name was never mentioned in Troyes.

However, they'd also asked brief, pointed questions.

"How well do you ride?"

Better than most.

"We scarcely saw you hold a sword. How are you at close arms?"

The best among comrades ten years ago. Haven't practiced since Minerve.

"Javelin?"

Great, last season, but no practice since then.

"Quarterstaff? Pike?"

No, never served as an infantryman.

"Other weapons? Flail or mace? Morning star?"

No.

"Fast footwork in armor? No, don't answer, little brother."

Those questions left Orlando feeling that he'd inadequately trained as a warrior. The two men whispered adieu when Orlando set out to finish his night's duty, supervising the guards who searched workers entering the city, made more complicated because it was Thursday, market day, so nearly every worker pushed a barrow that had to be unloaded, examined, reloaded. Merchants with two wagons sought entry—men who'd been part of the original army that came with Simon, but now traipsed regularly from Narbonne to Toulouse and back, trading along the way. Checking their wagons took until the terce bell, because the two wagons were full and the guards bargained for their own purchases. So Orlando had to make sure they weren't shaking down the merchants for extra silver or special bargains as the price of entry to the city.

At last, Orlando went to the duty room at the bottom of the watchtower, where he greeted the departing duty-sergeant, wrote his report, and laid his night-marshal badge in the cupboard.

Likely for the last time.

It finally struck Orlando, hearing the badge clatter, that if he helped his new friends, he could never return to Carcassona. Simon would consider him a traitor. His life would be forfeit.

He passed Mme Agnes's house on his way to the academy. It wasn't the closest route, but he needed to make a kind of farewell. Mme Agnes sat in her doorway, waiting for her servants to return with the day's bread.

"*Bonjour*, madam."

"*Bon jorn, lo mieu aimat capitani.*" She smiled as if delighted, and slipped into the local tongue, calling him her dear captain. "You are so kind and good. May it all be as it pleases the Good God, today and forever."

Orlando wasn't good; he had plenty of evidence that showed otherwise. But he said, "That's a lovely shawl, madam."

"Isn't it? My niece gave it to me. It's embroidered with flowers and a valiant knight. I think it's my husband. He's so handsome."

He slowly extricated himself from the newly talkative lady; bone-tired, he sleepwalked to the academy.

Mme Marguerite greeted him from her workroom, made him sit on the padded bench she kept for guests, and forced him to eat what must have been her own breakfast.

"Karles asked me to tell you." Marguerite hesitated. "Galahad. That's who Karles came here to protect."

"How does he know?"

"Perseus whispered to Karles at breakfast."

"They knew each other?" Orlando remembered Taresa at Mme Agnes's house, telling the two brothers from Cyprus that the boy Henri—Perseus—had no part in their plot. Well, at this point, did friendly deceit matter among comrades? "Madam, are you part of this plot?"

"Plot, Captain? Karles brought me a letter from an old friend who begged me to help protect the tiny king."

"Yet you didn't trust me to share your secret. We shared other secrets yesterday, while I—I learned about the king from strangers." Who claimed him as their little brother.

"In these strange times." Marguerite hesitated again. Then she sat beside him on the bench. "I've pleaded for you to be included, since I've seen you struggle with the arduous burden of your oath to Simon. Now Mme Taresa claims she convinced you to help."

He held her hand. "*Merci*, madam. You and I remain the two who care more for these boys than does anyone else." Beside him, she felt more withdrawn and stiffer than usual. "It...it shall all be as pleases God. That's what they say, isn't it?"

"You will help protect him?" Her voice trembled. "Not just because he's in our villa?"

"*Oui*, Don Tomás and Chrétien the jongleur convinced me."

"Those mercenary swordmasters?"

"They are like Karles, knights of Aragón in service to the king."

A voice called Marguerite to the boys' refectory.

She turned her head, listening, but didn't respond. Instead, she said, "Monsieur, are you in love with her?"

"What?" Only a knock on the head with a stave could have gotten his attention faster.

"Mme Taresa. She's charming. And brave. Rich and—"

"And duplicitous and infuriating. No, I'm not in love with her, madam. Even if I did find her charming, which I don't, I cannot afford to play in the Courts of Love."

The servant called again. Marguerite started for the refectory. "Excuse me, Captain. I'll be just a moment, and then we'll make a plan for the day."

Did he, after four years of working together, have to say to Marguerite what Taresa said to him? *Don't fall in love with me.* No, saying anything like that would insult her. Marguerite was too sensible. Practical. Kind. Perpetually looking out for his well-being, as well as for the boys.

He rubbed at his eyes, sandy from the mistral wind. And closed them just for a moment.

21
Un Can Francés

A BARKING DOG WOKE HIM. A big dog. He'd fallen asleep in the kennels again while hiding and now would have to face his grandfather's wrath.

"Monsieur! Captain! *Réveil!* Wake up!" Mme Marguerite called to Orlando from far, far away.

Soft hands shook him. "The sheep got into the monks' garden."

A voice, warm as the southern sun. "They say two monks tried to chastise the shepherd boy. Captain, wake up."

A deep breath, nose full of sleeping dog. A hand jostling his jaw. "Come now. Before they kill the dog."

He that kills a beast, he shall be put to death.

Grand-père killed my dog when it chased the chickens.

They might see. They themselves are beasts.

Fighting off that demon voice, Orlando finally roused. "God's bones! What?"

He'd slept in his jerkin. His shirt stuck to him. His face pressed against the bare boards of the bench, its cushions cast to the floor.

Marguerite urged him, anxious. "His dog chased the monks into the Church mill tower. Come, Captain. The guards want to shoot the dog with arrows."

That woke him like cold water. Orlando was on his feet. He had his boots, his jerkin, his sword. The dog barked madly.

Orlando ran behind the basilica, following the noise of barking dog and shouting men. In the first open-air landing at the Church mill tower, two monks held Robi, shouting down at the barking dog. Lop leaped and lunged, repeatedly barking. Any fool with two eyes could see that Lop wanted to rescue Robi, not attack the monks, who held the boy, smothering his ability to calm his dog.

Orlando stepped between the guards and the dog. "Put down your bows. We can fix this without hurting the dog."

To the two monks, who'd been treed like foxes, Orlando called for them to unhand the boy, to let him call his dog.

"Let's be reasonable. We need the dog to round up the sheep." Orlando appealed to the guards and monks at the same time, which called for raising his voice so they all heard. "And honorable men don't shoot dogs for barking."

"They're priests," one guard said.

"Then they can check the scripture for what it says about tender mercies and protecting the animals God puts in our care."

At that moment, Badoyn's greyhound appeared and was distracting the two guards, who now couldn't turn their backs on either dog to have time to pull and cock a crossbow.

"Robi!" Orlando called in the local tongue to the sadly distressed boy, hoping he had the right words, the right accent. "Call Lop. Tell him to get his sheep back into the corral."

At Robi's call, Lop took off after the sheep, the greyhound trailing behind, not exactly useful, but not in Lop's way. Robi and the monks climbed down the inner stairs and out the gate of the tower.

Orlando sent the guards back to their patrol. Robi ran after Lop and shut the corral gate once all the sheep were inside. Orlando comforted the monks, promising to move the sheep to the outer pasture that morning. He walked with them to inspect the damage done. The sheep had spent most of their freedom browsing grass in the shade of the city walls. They'd only just discovered the patches of greens for ordinary porry—saltbush, spinach, red-veined silverbeet, garden cress—when the monks scared the woolly beasts back into the grass. Untouched in the monks' garden: parsnips and leeks and the red roots that people here called *carròtas*. The cucumbers and gourds on trellises were intact, the gourds now at the young and tender stage for the best soup, or so said Mme Marguerite's cook.

Orlando joined Robi, checking that the gate was securely latched. "Robi, *mon ami,* you claimed that Lop would take care of his sheep."

"It wasn't Lop's fault. He was asleep with me when someone opened the gate. Who could want to lead sheep into sin and trespass? They are pure in God's eyes and—"

"Did you have breakfast, Robi? Did you save sausages from last night's supper like I told you?"

"*Òc, capitani,* but I shared with Lop and his friend Renard because they both looked so sad. Renard was crying, he was so hungry."

"Renard?" Orlando puzzled—Robi used a French word for fox, not a word in his own tongue.

"Your hound, *capitani mèstre.* It's not my place to say, but your dog ate my breakfast because you didn't feed him."

"He's not my dog. Why do you call him Renard?"

"Because that's his name."

"Don't you say *guèine* in your tongue, not *renard?*" He wasn't going to ask why a rust-colored greyhound was called Fox.

"*Mas es un can francés, capitani mèstre.*" Robi was once more astounded at Captain Orlando's stupidity. *But he's a French dog.* "It's how he says his name."

"Let's get you some breakfast, and then we'll take the sheep to the abbot's pasture."

Breakfast meant begging at the bachelors' tower refectory, and then taking cold leftovers, since it was closer to dinner than second breakfast. Orlando needed food, too, but enjoyed watching Robi eat, then stopped him from shoving food under his shirt to bring the dogs.

"We'll ask the cook for scraps. You don't want your dog to get used to sharing your meal."

"But, Captain, he always does. How else will he eat?"

After Orlando begged the cook again, this time for scraps for two dogs, Robi went off to feed them, while Orlando went to retrieve his leather riding jerkin, and to saddle Midnight for another ride with sheep.

He needed to deliver the recalcitrant sheep to the abbot's pasture as quickly as possible, and then return to finish the day's plan with Tomás and Chrétien.

.

Herding sheep was a better task than wielding nets and brooms the time two cats got into the abbot's chickens behind the basilica. That happened right at matins, about as far from any villa as possible in the city, and yet the racket managed to wake half the city. Orlando, as night-marshal, regretted having to report the incident of the rampaging chickens, like he'd regret having to report the marauding sheep. He had taken on night-marshal duties believing he was defending the city. But instead he chased cats and chickens, admonished adulterous knights after curfew, and woke guards who drowsed at their posts.

Ah, but after today, he'd no longer be night-marshal. He'd no longer write reports about the dull transgressions Carcassona committed in the dark of night.

He dressed in riding boots and his padded jerkin, and fetched his horse from the knights' stable. No guards as company and no armor—they'd be in sight of the guards on the walls for most of the journey to the pasture. Robi believed that you must walk when herding, but Orlando needed to return faster. They set out down the trail that circled the city's hill. The two dogs, who didn't like being separated, darted back and forth between the sheep and Robi, with the greyhound—that called itself Renard and spoke French—coming beside Orlando every few moments, until Orlando spoke.

"Qui est un bon chien?"

After accepting Orlando's praise, the hound bounded away to walk by Robi again.

That morning, the mistral behaved like a gentlewoman, fluffing Midnight's mane, and the sun this close to midday woke the bees. Crickets that had been hiding from the cold mistral called to their mates, or whatever it was crickets sang about.

They traveled half way around the hill to where the walls stood tallest, the hill steepest, and piles of rubble prevented any access to the city from attackers. During the siege, this side of the walled city received little attention, because it was so difficult to bring the engines close, and because of the scaling challenge. The piles of rubble were ancient, as old as the Romans who'd erected the tower above and the invaders who'd taken their place. Wild olives and blooming greenweed grew in the rubble, which cascaded down to the abbot's large pasture. More sheep—cousins of Lop's flock—and a few milch cows grazed. Five goats were busy browsing in the broom and blackberries that sprouted at the edge of the rockfall. When the two dogs appeared, rabbits munching in the sorrel and lilies dashed for the rockfall, which must hold their warren.

Unlike the crotchety scribe the day before, the abbot's master shepherd was happy to greet Lop, his sheep, and Robi. A small man, as old as Orlando's grandfather, Drogos had an easy smile and the thickened, baggy face of someone who'd lived sixty decades under the Pays d'Òc sun. Drogos expressed surprise only at how late in the morning the flock arrived.

"They say—" Drogos began, and then repeated all the gossip that had drifted out of the city since Orlando brought home the bleating sheep-tithe the day before.

Orlando introduced Robi and tried to follow their efforts to learn in detail how they were related. Robi's father's second-degree cousin Anfos was married to Ermessenda. Anfos often grazed his sheep in the hills west and south of St-Jean, and it was during summer grazing in the higher hills that he'd met Ermessenda, a grand-niece of Drogos's cousin Pons. Pons kept burros and rented them as pack animals for people who wanted to cross the Pyrenees on the road to Urgell.

While Orlando sat on the dry-stone wall that served as a corral for the sheep at night, Renard's head in his lap, he listened to the shepherds' conversation while bees browsed in the borage that grew along the wall. If he let his thoughts drift, watching the sheep make themselves at home in the fescue and vetch, Renard nosed him for attention.

The two shepherds' discussion drifted to where in the Aude valley these sheep were used to grazing. But the names of places were all in the local tongue, which Orlando didn't recognize. Too comfortable, sipping cold goat milk that Drogos shared, Orlando forced his thoughts to the afternoon's plan, to be undertaken with men who called him brother! But a plan with more holes than his grandmother's lace shawl.

Orlando would depart on his day's quest close to vespers rather than the mid-afternoon nones bell. He'd announce his intention to examine the outer hamlets and to camp in the countryside.

He didn't believe that more than three guards would be willing to join the expedition: little chance for glory, and every chance to sleep on a pile of rocks. There was the first hole: what if more volunteered? No, Badoyn had been bribing the *gardes du corps*, who knew how impoverished Orlando was. No, Orlando would not have volunteers.

Tomás and Chrétien would volunteer, interested in seeing the countryside. They'd also set Karles to convince Mme Hélène's house-knights to join them, because by then they'd have possession of the king. They'd wait until Badoyn departed for his own quest. Orlando had to ensure that the guards on duty in the watchtower would not call attention when he and his companions traveled east instead of west toward St-Jean.

Orlando was to fetch Galahad from the academy, wrapped and ready to travel, packed onto Orlando's horse in a way the guards wouldn't question. There was the largest hole in their plan. It relied on the guards' usual lack of diligence and how their attention would be taken up inspecting workers and tradespeople departing the city after market day.

Then they'd ride down the Narbonne road to the relay, where fresh horses and fresh men would travel through the night. They'd be armed to address the main flaws in the plan: what if Galahad was found to be missing? What if they were pursued too soon after leaving the city?

Orlando waved away a fat bee that came too near. He ran his hand over his bare head. He considered again: this was his last day in Carcassona if he collaborated as he'd agreed. While this plan might be what Philippe Augustus would prefer—as Chrétien claimed—surely Simon would see Orlando's participation only as treachery.

Would he be forced to accept the provoking Mme Taresa's offer, to be a house-knight in the wilds of the Pyrenees? Or should he seek sanctuary with the Church, who hire their own mercenaries and so might accept him? Ride to Toulouse or Narbonne and find a southern seigneur who needs a French-speaking mercenary?

That seemed the only possible outcome: life as a mercenary. No banner. No retainers. No service to the king of France. He had to find a lord who'd feed him and his horse in return for Orlando's hired sword. Become a vagabond mercenary like Tomás and Chrétien.

While Orlando's thoughts wandered, the two shepherds had figured out all their relatives and had agreed upon which were the best pastures in the Pays d'Òc.

"Your girls will be happy here. Let's see what kind of bed we have for you." Drogos had a gentle hand on Robi's shoulder, leading the boy to the dry-stone shack that was the shepherd's home, sheltered under the twining branches of two huge oaks.

"I haven't told Lop that the Church claimed his sheep," Robi said. "Lop thinks the sheep belong to him."

"And well he might, because he's a very good dog. I'm pleased to welcome you, *fadrin*. The abbot has promised to send me help since Michaelmas, and at last, here you are. I'd never hoped that it'd be my own kinsman. With the best dog in the Aude valley."

Lop and Robi bounded ahead of Drogos, both happy in their new home. Robi waved when Orlando called adieu. Drogos said adieu to Orlando, then paused. "At St-Luc, they say you're a good man. You've done good things for the people here, and for this boy."

"*De rien.*" Orlando shook the man's hand, a huge, weathered paw.

He led Midnight back to the ring trail. The old girl wasn't happy about it, seeming to find the grass here better than what she enjoyed when spending days in the knights' pasture.

Orlando, however, let his spirits soar. *They say you're a good man. You've done good things for the people here.* He let Midnight go at her own pace, while giving himself a few moments' respite from too much worry. He repeated the compliment to himself. *You've done good things...for this boy.* Out of that wretched week, Orlando had at last managed one good outcome. Though only by luck. What had Badoyn said? That he was merely luckier than Orlando?

Except Chrétien claimed that Badoyn made his luck at his cousin Orlando's expense.

22
A Feint

WHERE THE TRAIL CURVED AROUND the hill just across from St-Jean village, Orlando kicked Midnight, to speed his return to the city and his duties. At this curve, the canopy of trees covered the trail, so it was lost to the sight of the guards atop the city walls. But no Catalan insurgents lurked here; only foxes and rabbits and cats. The feral cats skittered for shelter in the rockfall above the trail. Renard the greyhound raced ahead, barking. The dog might speak French, but it didn't obey commands in its native language.

"*Viens, mon chien!* It's a cat. Even more of a ninny than you, *maudit chien.*"

Another horse came toward Orlando under the canopy of oaks and sweet chestnuts, surprising Renard, which ran at the horse, dodging its hooves, barking as though it attacked St-Georges's dragon. The horse reared.

"Renard, *arrêter!*"

The dog lunged at the horse's exposed flank. The horse stumbled.

The riders—two boys—tumbled into the rocks. And then the horse fell into the rocks, missing the boys by a hand's breadth.

Orlando left Midnight, dropped the reins, and ran for the boys. A red scarf fluttered in the morning wind where one boy was scrambling to get to his feet. The other boy writhed, shrieking.

The horse screamed, thrashing in pain.

Renard barked and danced close to Orlando, as if urging him to act, yet getting in the way.

"Galahad! Lancelot!"

Orlando lifted the big boy, Lancelot, trying not to jostle what must be a broken arm. Orlando looked, but didn't see blood or other signs the boy needed immediate attention. He laid the boy in the mat of verbena, mint, and thyme at the edge of the trail.

"Galahad! You can walk? Come! Sit by Lancelot."

Galahad—God's bones! The king of Aragón!—only nodded, frightened, but not witless. He had a black eye from the other night, but didn't seem to have new cuts or obvious bruises. Galahad circled around to Orlando and Lancelot, keeping his distance from the screaming horse. Midnight, wanting nothing to do with the other horse, trotted away toward the city road, stopping as far away as she could while still in sight, tossing her head, another creature pleading for Orlando to come rescue her.

Galahad approached Orlando with caution. Orlando hated seeing a boy cringe. "You aren't in trouble, *garçon*. You need to be brave and sit by Lancelot while I help your horse."

The boy nodded, sank to his knees, and put his small hand on Lancelot's brow, which he must have seen a nurse do. Lancelot threw off that comfort. Renard, the source of all this trouble, lay down beside Galahad, sticking his long nose in the smaller boy's lap.

"Galahad, say a *pater noster*. Try to get Lancelot to say it with you." Orlando began the prayer, urged the boys twice to pray, then began murmuring comforts to the fallen horse.

Lancelot cried, pleading for help. "Help me! Not a damnable horse. It's me you must help."

Twelve men stalked him on the battlefield. He was hemmed in, then stabbed with a lance. Blood poured from the wound in his neck. The man who'd thrust the spear stood over him. 'You heard it as a child. Both you and your father will meet your deaths in the name of justice and truth.' The acrid burning and death-stink of the battlefield overwhelmed other senses.

Orlando blinked away the vision. These evil visions never came true. Except for Mme Estela. In Orlando's memory, rather than vision of death, Simon appeared to say that if anything happened to his son, Orlando's life was forfeit.

Now Lancelot, Simon's son, lay moaning alongside the trail. Even if Orlando did nothing more to help Chrétien and Tomás, he needed to be gone from Carcassona that night.

Galahad called, "Monsieur, what do I do?"

"Repeat your *pater noster* until I come to you."

A thin voice stammered a prayer, accompanied by the rise-and-fall of Lancelot's moans and sobs, while Orlando attended to the wretched horse.

It had ceased thrashing because the reins had caught on a tree limb. After the fright of the fall, it seemed gradually to sense that it would choke if it kept thrashing. Orlando drew up everything he knew about calming a horse. Whispering. Blowing on its nose.

When he had the horse calm enough to let him touch its nose, Orlando continued to murmur sweet words while checking its bones. Bruised, perhaps. Scratches from tree branches along its nose and neck bled, but the cuts didn't seem deep. No sign of broken bones. The challenge was to sweet-talk the beast until he could free the reins from the tree branches. The better solution seemed to begin with the tree, which Orlando climbed and then edged out on a limb he didn't believe would hold him, reaching until his muscles hurt, until he finally flicked the reins free.

Back down the tree, his hands rubbed raw, Orlando coaxed the horse to its feet, still murmuring. *C'est bien. Ça va bien. Doux cheval. Bon cheval.*

On its feet, the horse shook its head, splattering more of its blood on Orlando.

Down the trail, Midnight called.

But this horse was having none of either Orlando's or Midnight's friendship. It backed away from Orlando, then started down the trail toward the abbot's pasture.

"*Hé, cheval. Non!*"

But the horse moved from a walk to a trot to get away.

A righteous man regards the life of his beasts, knowing tender mercies are cruel.

God's bones! By all that is holy, depart from me, devil.

When God manifests, you shall see that you are a beast.

At least now he could tend the boys. Wiping his eyes with his scarf, Orlando found that his jerkin and face were splattered with the horse's blood. Lancelot screamed, seeing him. Galahad only trembled. The greyhound burrowed deeper into Galahad's lap, demanding attention, taking the boy's eyes off Orlando.

"*Bien*, Captain?"

"Yes. I'm sorry you're frightened. But the horse will be fine. Now, Lancelot. Close your eyes. Take a breath. I need to tend to your arm. Then we'll return to the city."

Orlando tossed his jerkin aside, took off his shirt, and tore the sleeves free. Not readily finding what might serve as a temporary splint, he took Etienne's knife from his boot, the one that never keeps its edge. First, he wrapped the boy's arm loosely with his now filthy scarf, then laid the blade where it could do the most good and the least harm. And wrapped it with the sleeves torn from his sweat-drenched and blood-stained shirt, all the while admonishing the whimpering boy to sing a song if a *pater noster* wouldn't do.

Beside him, Galahad watched closely, still embracing the long-nosed hound.

Since he couldn't coax a song or a prayer from either boy, Orlando tried to get Lancelot talking, to divert his attention.

"How did you come to be on this road?" He spoke lightly, neither in the mood to scold nor thinking it useful. "It's divine providence that we met when we did."

"No," Lancelot moaned "Your dog attacked our horse. We were fine until you came."

"It's not my dog." Orlando said it instinctively, but otherwise, he couldn't reject the accusation.

"We're going to find the Grail." Galahad volunteered an answer. "They say it's buried in St-Jean village."

"Shut up! Shut up!" Lancelot cried. *La ferme! La ferme!* "It's a secret."

"If it's a secret, how could we know?" Galahad argued.

Orlando finished tying the rude splint in place. "That's the best I can do, *garçon*. We'll return to the city in a heartbeat. A Grail quest is a noble thing, but you'll have to seek the Grail another day, *jeune chevaliers*."

He pulled on what was left of his shirt and shrugged on his jerkin, which should probably be burned instead of washed. Midnight would not come when called, so Orlando had to carry Lancelot while encouraging Galahad to keep his hand on Renard's back while they stumbled down the trail to where Midnight waited, dancing nervously. Orlando explained how they had to cooperate with him so that all three might ride the horse.

Lancelot pushed at his nose and spread his legs. "I shall ride and you two shall walk. Only I suffered hurt."

It seemed that a great deal was not yet clear. Were these only errant boys like any others? Or was this Lancelot's second attempt to do away with the king of Aragón? Orlando's response would have to serve for either case.

"Ah, *garçon*. When the surgeon has given you a poppy tonic and properly set your arm, when you next drift to sleep, you'll recall that your captain is the same as your field-commander in battle. You do as I command. We'll ride together."

"I am the son of a mighty lord."

"I am the son of Fabien of Troyes, a mighty lord who saved Philippe Augustus at the Siege of Acre." That was delightful to say, especially pitched in his lowest, most commanding voice. "You can brag that you were rescued by the son of a king-saver."

"You shall be punished for this." Lancelot stomped, then winced because he'd jostled and hurt himself.

"We must do as our captain commands." One hand still on the hound for assurance, Galahad spoke up, glancing at Orlando for approval, then decided to give himself approval. "We made this tempest. Now we must obey."

"*Bien dit, garçon!*" Orlando mounted Midnight. He held out his hand and lifted the slight Galahad up, then steadied him while the boy climbed behind. "Now, hold tight."

Still belligerent, but hurting too much to put up a fight, Lancelot followed instructions, using Orlando's boot as a mounting block, and letting his captain take his weight until he was seated in front of Orlando. Then they were under way, with most of Orlando's words to calm and encourage Midnight, hoping the words worked on little boys, too.

.

They'd emerged from the canopy of trees that shielded the ring trail from view of guards in any of the towers. Orlando shouted, but the mistral picked up then and blew his words out over the Aude valley.

"*Aide! Aide!*"

Just when Orlando gave up believing anyone would see and come to their assistance before he reached the gates, Badoyn and his two knights rode toward him on the trail.

"Balthazar! What a coincidence!" Badoyn and his companions reined in their prancing horses.

"*Bonjour, mon ami.* We've had a bit of trouble." Orlando watched Badoyn, not believing for a single heartbeat that his appearance on the ring trail was a coincidence. If Tomás was right, that Badoyn intended to murder the king of Aragón, this was a fair opportunity. Orlando couldn't draw his sword or kick his horse to outrun these knights. "The boys' horse threw them. But we're fine now."

As if Orlando didn't have two boys across his horse, Badoyn began with his usual smooth way. "We looked for you in the city, cousin, hoping you'd enjoy a peaceful morning hunt."

They had swords and bows, but no hawks and no huntsmen to guide them in unfamiliar woods and fields. And Orlando had his cousin's hunting dog.

"Will you forgive me for not tarrying, gentlemen? One of my boys needs a surgeon."

"Balthazar! Our plan!"

Badoyn's eyes darted, following his thoughts; one hand hovered over his sword, the other half raised as if to give a command. His knights watched Badoyn, as if awaiting a signal. Badoyn's own blessed greyhound watched his master, a growl rising in its throat. Even the man's dog distrusted him.

Orlando pointed, encouraging the other three riders to look up at the walls that loomed over the ring trail. "Behold! Carcassona watches us."

He kicked his horse, encouraging Midnight to carry them to the city gates. Badoyn followed, his knights behind him. Orlando's back and neck prickled with dread, a whining burden squirmed in his arms, and a featherweight king floated behind him, shifting and hiccupping, with no protection at all. Orlando worried with every heartbeat that Galahad might let loose of Orlando's jerkin and be lost. Or that Badoyn might decide he was free to attack even with guards in the towers watching.

Six more knights rounded the next bend in the ring trail, riding toward him. Orlando strained to see, until finally he made out Karles and Chrétien, the tallest of the lot. Then Tomás. The three other men in chainmail wore Mme Hélène's house colors. They carried javelins, shields, and swords. Not a hunting party, either.

"*Hola, poulain!*" Tomás called.

That pejorative never before offered such comfort.

"We thought you'd departed on your quest for today," Chrétien called. "And we longed to join you. For *practice.*"

"I'm not departing on quest until closer to vespers," Orlando said. "The mistral seems kinder near sunset."

"Brilliant idea," Tomás said. "And the sun is hot today. Too hot to *practice.*"

Chrétien played out his friendly self, introducing everyone, reminding Badoyn and his knights how they'd met in Fanjeau, and that one night after Easter Tomás had won silver off them at dice. The way Chrétien told the story, everyone had to laugh.

Orlando endured the stories, whispering to the simpering Lancelot and prompting Galahad frequently: "*Ça va, garçon?* Only a few moments more, *garçons courageux.*"

A lifetime later, the guards on the wall above the gate hailed them. As soon as the gates opened, and Midnight ambled through, Karles dismounted and came to Orlando's side, taking Lancelot from Orlando's arms.

"He broke his arm," Orlando said. "Who's the best field surgeon in the city?"

"I am," Karles said. "I've set dozens of broken bones."

"No," Lancelot cried. "No filthy servant shall touch me."

Chrétien took Lancelot from Karles, dangling the boy under one arm like when he descended from the tower. "We shall carry you to the monk-healers to see if they know what to do when a merlin breaks its wing."

Tomás held his arms out for Galahad. "Come, *fadrin.*"

"I want to stay with Captain Orlando."

"As you shall, *fadrin.* But your captain can't come down from his saddle with you attached like a burr on a wolf."

Rather than waiting, Tomás reached for him. Renard jumped between the knight and the boy.

Orlando called to the dog. "*Viens, mon chien!*" But Galahad was already talking to the dog.

"*Ça va, chien. Ça va, bien.*"

When Orlando could finally dismount, he was squeezed between two men with the same and yet opposite demands on his attention. Tomás planted Galahad beside Renard, one hand on the boy's head. "Let's get a drink for your dog and my horse, *fadrin.*"

"He's not my dog."

"Are you sure?" Tomás led horse, dog, and boy to the trough near the grand well. "He might have a different opinion."

Karles and the marquesa's house-knights took their horses to the common stable. Badoyn's knights headed for the knights' stable, leading Badoyn's horse.

Badoyn scarcely acknowledged his departing knights, the same way he offered no attention to his dog. He tugged Orlando close, then noticed how filthy Orlando's jerkin was and rubbed his hand on his surcoat.

"We need to talk, Balthazar."

"Yes, cousin. You told me you had big plans—which I thought meant a better idea than a rash morning ride, out in view of God and every man in the city."

"We expected to be past St-Jean village by now." Badoyn spoke with the kind of hostility Orlando had been used to, years before in Troyes. "You interfered."

"Interfered? I didn't hear of a plan that involved Simon's son breaking his arm on a hare-minded ride in the country. Can you inform me before the next *plan?*" Orlando spat the word.

Badoyn nodded, one brow arched. Suspicious. "We are together in this, then?"

"I am fully committed." Orlando spoke the words, hand on his heart, not describing the world-changing act he'd committed to.

"When I ride out on quest later today, I'll cross the Aude river. Perhaps if you depart before me, you'll have a more productive hunt than this morning."

"You'll have the boys again?" Badoyn whispered, though no one stood close enough to them on the walk to the stable to hear.

"Only the one boy that matters. There's nothing to be gained by involving Simon's son again."

"*Mon cher cousin!* I knew you'd accept this challenge." Badoyn embraced him, which Orlando found repugnant. His own blood, his cousin, wanted to murder a child.

At the stable, Badoyn's knights tossed their reins to the horse-squires. Badoyn stalked off with them, claiming an engagement with his beloved. Galahad left Tomás's side and once more moved as close as possible to Orlando. Renard trotted on the other side of the boy. Tomás lingered.

"So then. We've survived a feint." Tomás spoke in Catalan, slowly enough that Orlando could translate. "Tonight is it."

"How did you know to come down the ring trail to find us?" Orlando attempted to answer in Catalan, likely ruining half the words with his bad accent.

"We saw your cousin leave. Then Karles found that two boys had escaped the schoolmaster."

"Lancelot and I were on a quest." Galahad understood some of what passed above him.

Orlando said in French, "*Garçon,* did you meet Don Tomás of Morella yesterday when he showed us how to fight?"

"*Bonjour,* monsieur."

Tomás asked in French, "Are you the *beau juvene* they call Galahad?"

"*Oui,* monsieur."

Renard kept muscling his way between Tomás and the boy.

"Sir Galahad, please tell your dog that I'm a friend, as loyal and honorable as any man can be."

"Why do you say he's my dog, monsieur?"

"Because dogs and horses can see into your heart. They know when true loyalty is due." Tomás then spoke to Orlando. "I'd like to come along on your quest tonight, Captain. Do you need our help until then?"

"No." He recognized the real question: Did Orlando need help protecting the boy? But he'd already directed Badoyn's attention elsewhere. "If you come along, Don Tomás, be prepared to camp in the wild. I don't expect to return to the city tonight."

In truth, Orlando couldn't return to Carcassona. This night's action would cut all his ties to Simon and this city.

Orlando took Galahad with him into the knights' stable, to talk while they rubbed down Midnight. Renard the greyhound followed close. The mistral swept through the street then, tossing grit and gravel, dusting his ruined jerkin. Galahad shaded his eyes against the wind and the midday sun, then winced when his hand brushed that black eye and cut on his head.

"Monsieur Ansel," Orlando called to the stablemaster, "there's a horse from the common stable out on the ring trail. It was injured in a fall, though not so badly as to keep it from running away. Can you send word to the common-master?"

Ansel the stablemaster caught it all in a glance: the blood splashed over Orlando's boots, breeches, shirt, hands; the quivering boy beside him. Ansel offered Orlando a tight smile of sympathy, shaking his head.

"Je suis désolé, Captain. We'll send men out to find the horse. I've already heard that you did well in dire straits."

Those kind words were hard to endure. Orlando kept his own chin from quivering for the sake of the boy at his side, while describing where to find the horse that ran away in the middle of a foolish escapade.

Or in a crude attempt at regicide.

23
Curry Bells

"As I promised back on the trail, you won't be punished, *garçon*. You made a mistake, and then you witnessed the consequences. There's no good that can come from chastising you."

"Monsieur Captain, it's my fault the horse suffered."

"Was it your idea to ride outside the city? Or Lancelot's?" Orlando spoke low, so his big voice wouldn't frighten the boy.

The boy didn't answer, busy scratching the greyhound's ears, dipping his head to hide that he was crying.

"My horse is called Midnight. Here's her favorite currycomb, *garçon*. Do you know how to comb and comfort a horse after it's worked hard for you?"

"Yes, Captain."

"She's a sensitive horse. Be slow and gentle while you work. Here, before you start, make Midnight your friend." Orlando gave Galahad a wizened apple to feed the horse, because nothing is so comforting as the soft muzzle of a grateful animal.

"Start at the top. Work with the horse's hair, not against it. Do you see? We curry in gentle circles. Not like scrubbing when you're in your bath."

Galahad murmured his assent. They combed and cosseted Midnight for a while, mostly in silence except for Orlando's quiet praises for Midnight, for working so hard, being so brave, until the horse relaxed, her ears turned out to the side. The greyhound, having caused enough turmoil for the day, turned around twice and lay down in the straw near Galahad. After long moments of only curry bells and horse sighs, Orlando judged that both he and the boy were calm enough to talk.

"You know it's against the rules to ride outside the city, *garçon*. Not my rules, but Simon's rules."

"Yes."

"You let Lancelot lead you into trouble for a second time. No, a third time. After he tried to hit you, and after we had to rescue you from the tower only yesterday. Why let him lead you into transgression once again?"

No answer.

"Didn't Perseus advise you to follow the rules? Didn't you and I agree that Perseus was a good friend to you?"

"Perseus was gone when we left. He didn't know about—" Those few words, then Galahad lapsed into silence again.

"Galahad, I know who you are. I'm sworn to protect you." He said it softly, which commands greater attention. "I won't call you by your true name. No one else needs to know right now."

Galahad mumbled, "Yes, Captain?"

"Perseus knows and is also sworn to protect you. So is Master Karles, who was your father's knight. Several of us in Carcassona want you to be safe."

"*Merci*, Captain. Perseus gave his promise to me this morning."

"So you know Perseus is your friend. Other friends here claim you need more than our protection. Your father's knights will take you to the archbishop, who will help you return to your country."

Curry bells rang. Then: "I didn't know all of this. Until Perseus told me."

"How did Lancelot talk you into this jaunt in the countryside?"

"He said—he said—" Only jingling of the currycomb.

"Let me guess. He dared you to show your courage, while he repeated those taunts, about your father being a bastard."

"And me. That I'm not a lord. Only a—" Weeping added to the jingling of the comb.

"Peace, *garçon*. Let's not repeat others' lies. You are the true son of a true king. Do you believe me? I'm your captain."

"*Oui*, monsieur." A whisper.

"Lancelot's taunts—is that why you went on a Grail quest?"

It touched too closely to Orlando's morning dreams, hiding in the kennels, taunted by his cousin. A grown man would know better, but those taunts were like pouring Greek fire over a little boy's wounded soul.

"Yes. Lancelot said the Grail quest is the bravest thing a knight can do. It proves to God you have a pure soul."

"How did you escape the villa? How did you persuade the stablemaster to give you a horse?"

"We climbed on the roof and down the trellis. At the common stable—not the knights' stables—there was a horse saddled. Lancelot said it was his."

"How did you get the guards to let you through the gates?"

"The guards only waved at us. No one stopped us."

It was, therefore, as Chrétien claimed: Badoyn had suborned the *gardes du corps*.

"Captain? Lancelot wants to be a knight of the Grail, and he said we'd find it, because we're pure of heart. But is it true? Is the Grail hidden in St-Jean village?"

The nones bell rang, though it felt like many days since Orlando sat on Marguerite's bench at the terce bell. He wasn't prepared to tell a boy that Lancelot was more like Ganelon, betraying Roland and his comrades. "If the Grail were near, the bishop would know. He'd go and get it before breakfast on Pentecost. Now, are you ready for dinner?"

"You truly won't chastise me, Captain?"

"Truly I shall not. You have already suffered every penalty for your mistake today."

"Whenever I tried to join other boys in their games, when we lived in Fanjeau, the nurses chastised me."

Who beats a king? Who gives nurses permission to chastise a king? For that matter, who beats young, timid boys?

"Let's go eat, *garçon*. When we return to the academy, I want you to stay with Karles. You have to go to the jakes, Karles should be there. You go to bed, you go to eat, you go into the courtyard. Karles must be there. This is a command from your captain."

"I will obey, Captain." Galahad hung the currycomb on its hook, imitating what he'd seen Orlando do. "Master Karles is my second favorite knight, after you."

The greyhound nuzzled against the boy when they started out across the city, which knocked the boy close to Orlando, who put his hand on the boy's head.

"You were very brave today, *garçon*. Don't let anyone say otherwise. No one on the road was as brave as you."

.

Orlando crossed the city with Galahad, thinking that it was Thursday, market day. He needed to spend his silver on a shirt, or else he'd be leaving Carcassona threadless.

When he arrived at the academy, Marguerite excused herself for only a second, not showing surprise or disgust for Orlando's wretched condition. But then, she likely knew about the adventure because Karles had already returned from accompanying Chrétien to the infirmary with Lancelot. Karles took possession of Galahad, insisting he needed a bath and hot milk. Renard followed them.

When Marguerite returned, having once more foreseen his needs, she offered Orlando breeches, linen, and a shirt. A new scarf, scarlet like the one he'd given to Galahad. She called a servant and sent Orlando's boots off to be cleaned.

"These were the baron's." Her fingers lingered when she handed him the folded clothes. "They won't fit you well. But I hope they'll do for the moment. I've reused most of his linen for my needlework, but I still have these in a cupboard and..."

She trailed off, both of them aware that Mme Marguerite never indulged in nervous chatter.

"I'm happy you are safe, Captain." She folded her hands, then grasped them behind her back. "You are very good at rescuing naughty boys."

"Perhaps Simon might consider bestowing a new fief, especially for my peculiar talents."

They laughed, both nervous, both momentarily relieved.

"And I have to dismiss the schoolmaster, don't I?"

Marguerite agreed. "From the sept bell until we called the boys to dinner, he taught basic *mathematica* while not noticing he was missing two boys."

"I think he was paid not to notice."

She looked startled, like one does when discovering suddenly that you can't trust the person next to you. Then she finished the morning's story. "Karles sat in front of the schoolroom door, armed like a bandit, while two boys went out a window."

"Why didn't Perseus say anything?"

"He was with me, discussing how we can best protect Galahad. He's very upset about this." She folded her hands in front of her again, kneading her apron. "This was my fault."

"No, it was the schoolmaster's fault. And Lancelot's. Let's leave him in the monks' infirmary until Pentecost."

"A fine idea."

"Can you send a servant to attend Lancelot in the infirmary?" While she was nodding in assent, Orlando added, "The man you send should be someone who came from the Pays de France. Best it be a man with the patience of the ancient prophet. The prophet who endured boils and plagues."

Then Orlando explained that she needed to shelter Renard.

"Your cousin's dog? But dogs are forbidden in the city."

"My cousin has a pass from Simon for his dog. Badoyn hasn't noticed that his dog transferred his affections to Galahad."

"Are you riding out on your quest today? Even after this morning's adventure?"

"Yes. We're using Simon's challenge as cover to get the king out of the city."

She stepped back from him. "But it's our job to protect him. You and I together."

"The only protection is to get him away from Simon."

The pinched lines in her brow, the bitten lip. She was severely distressed. "It's your cousin who wants to steal him. That's what happened today, isn't it?"

"No, my cousin wants to do away with the child-king, to please Simon. Didn't Karles and your Catalan friends explain why we have to protect the boy?"

"*Aiieee,* Orlando!" She embraced him, buried her face in the shirt she gave him. And wept. He felt her shake, her shoulders seeming fragile under his hands, though he always considered her strong, a woman capable of carrying any burden the world shifted onto her.

"Marguerite, I—"

"How many times until it's the last time?" She pushed away from his embrace, wiping at her face with her apron. "It's bad enough that you don't eat, you don't sleep. You can never please Simon or leave him. But my rooftop. The village riot. The tower wall. Today's accident on the trail. It's always an accident. Except it isn't, because God seems to want you in heaven so badly. Is tonight when I finally lose you? Because of a little boy that no one can keep track of?"

Karles called from the outer hall. "Mme Marguerite?"

"One is never alone in this city, living elbow to elbow. And certainly never in this villa." She wiped her face again, and went to answer. Orlando stopped her.

"Marguerite, I can't return after tonight. If the boy is taken away— whether I help or not—I've forfeited my life. Simon declared that before he left Carcassona. After I leave tonight, I don't know when I'll see you again."

He touched her shoulder, embraced her. Kissed her. He meant to kiss her like you kiss young cousins goodbye. Then found he couldn't stop. She responded, unlike any kiss he'd ever known, both of them holding their breath. She tasted and smelled of mint. And salty tears.

> *Do not choose the foolish things of the world. You can't have a woman like that.*

By St-Denis and St-Georges, leave me.

> *That woman. You can't have that woman.*

"Where will you go?" she whispered.

"I don't know. Narbonne, for now. That's where they plan to take the boy, to shelter him with the archbishop."

"Mme Marguerite?" The Catalan knight's deep voice called her, urgent. "*Avant!*"

24
May-fair

THE MARKET IN THE CHATEAU'S outer yard drew most people in the city by midafternoon. Modest flags flew from all the wooden barrows and from the two merchants' wagons, each flag dyed the brightest colors people could buy or harvest in their own gardens. With the mistral blowing, the flags flew high or bounced on the cords that held them.

The flags alone, twisting in the wind under the sunshine, elicited a pang of homesickness, which Orlando usually conquered because the tiny market in Carcassona compared to May-fair in Troyes the way a kitten compares to a warhorse. At Troyes, May-fair meant a month of booths and wagons and vendors stretched across the entire county, with money markets and galas to suit everyone, from barons to peasants to jugglers and whores, everyone seeking a bargain.

French peacekeepers held this city and patrolled the Pays d'Òc. Ever since the French forces came, the Italian cloth merchants chose to travel only from midsummer to Lammas. On this day, in mid-May, women sold out of their barrows the linen and linsey-woolsey clothes they'd spun and woven over winter. The shirt, stockings, and under-linen Orlando needed to buy that day had to be sturdy, but not as white or soft as he'd find at a summer fair. That didn't matter.

He bought the two shirts he needed but couldn't afford. One from a woman who lived in St-Luc village. She accepted his silver, saying *mercés* but didn't look him in the eye. However, she added a pair of wool stockings, and whispered, "We know you tried," in the local tongue. He purchased a second, softer shirt from an older woman who was from St-Jean village. She didn't say *mercés* but rather murmured *Have mercy* in the local tongue.

He glanced around, wishing he'd convinced Mme Marguerite to accompany him to the market. What he expected: the wild joy of bargains argued and struck, people greeting each other with the effusive embraces common in the Pays d'Òc. What he saw: subdued bargaining, people shaking hands like they do at a funeral. That one afternoon of rioting guards in St-Luc, plus Badoyn's raid on St-Mathieu, had precisely the effect Simon wanted: these people were frightened, more by what might happen next than what had already occurred. They'd been evicted from Carcassona that first summer, forced out of the city with only the clothes they wore. Now, five years later, their nervous and false cries of *bon jorn* added to the whistle of the mistral as it swept the city. He saw the question in each villager's eyes: were they about to lose everything again?

Orlando fingered a second pair of stockings at a barrow that belonged to a woman from St-Jean village who had a stern, hatchet face, and cold, sharp eyes. Yet she whispered, "Thank you for what you did for Robi. We've asked the Church to take him for a year now. But you persuaded them. *Gràcies, capità.*"

He accepted the thank-you, not with humility but complete humiliation. He didn't deserve a thank-you. He'd participated for years in the pretense of keeping the Peace of God—while depriving people of their homes. And this week: he'd done nothing. He'd failed the people of St-Luc. He'd been sent to fetch sheep, not an orphan boy. He'd participated in a colossal accident, a series of star-struck coincidences. What he'd promised to do that night was no more heroic than all the accidents and happenstances that plagued him since...since his father died.

"Balthazar! Welcome to the fair!" Badoyn's voice dripped sarcasm.

"It's just market day," Orlando said, though he had no reason to defend Carcassona from his cousin's contempt.

"Why, it's just like May-fair in Troyes!" His cousin linked an arm in Orlando's elbow. Mme Hélène caught Orlando's other arm, hugging him to her, making it awkward to hold his new shirts. Hélène wanted spices from the spice-merchant's wagon. While she dickered for cinnamon, dates, and sugar cane, Orlando surveyed the rough hemp for ropes, lengths of linen, sinews for bowstrings. Nothing for which he had a penny to spare.

Orlando stepped to the next wagon, where the merchant was a thin, dark man who looked more like a fox than Renard did. He dealt in iron and copper; the pans and pots hung on a sturdy rope danced in the wind, chiming as loudly as the St-Nazaire bell. He perched on a stool behind a narrow trestle table that displayed kitchen and stable tools for all purposes, implements in varying degrees of decay from when they'd first been cast or smelted. Behind him, the worn wooden sides of the wagon displayed an array of weapons. Badoyn crowded Orlando's shoulder, having dragged Hélène away from the spice merchant.

"No man wants to put a bucket of rust on their head." Though he spoke right by Orlando's ear, Badoyn's mocking voice rang out, louder than the clash of copper pots banging in the wind.

The merchant was indignant, of course. "This armor belonged to the great crusader Henri of Champagne and Jerusalem, who wore it at the Siege of Acre."

"His sainted toenail is worth more than this rusted relic." Could any French knight be more arrogant than Badoyn? "And from the dents, Sir Henri must have worn it at Acre when he fell out the window and died."

The iron-merchant was French, too, and not to be outdone by Badoyn. "Any honorable man would be lucky to have this souvenir of the Outremer hanging in his great hall. Henri girded himself and fought the Saracen in this kit."

Hélène wiggled between Orlando and Badoyn and then cuddled up close to her would-be lover. Or victim, if you'd heard how Tomás described the marquesa. "I've fallen in love with this cunning dagger, *mon petit bricon*. Bargain for me. He'll cheat a woman."

The fox-faced merchant folded his arms and seemed to just barely restrain himself from baring his teeth. The marquesa didn't care that she'd insulted him, and Badoyn seemed unaware of the insult his lady had offered.

"You don't want that," Badoyn said to Hélène. "It's too big for a dinner knife."

"I don't need it for bread and butter. Did you not hear me say just now that I want it?"

Badoyn didn't seem to hear the warning in her voice any more than he'd detected the insult she offered the merchant. "A woman doesn't need a weapon like that."

"*Lo mieu pichon pecador.*" She called Badoyn her little sinner in the local tongue, then switched to French. "One thing my sainted husband knew was to never tell a woman what she needs, or doesn't need. Nor deny a woman what she wants. Surely you can perform as well."

"Leaping lizards!" A woman cried out. Orlando startled at the voice, having not noticed Mme Teresa at his side. "That's my sword. I must have it back."

> *She stood boldly, arms outstretched like Our Savior on the cross, wind blowing her russet hair. The soldier's lance pierced her side. Deep. Run through as if on the battlefield, the smell of singed flesh everywhere.*

Orlando shook off the vision, this time of the senhóra speared like a warrior.

The merchant tilted his fox nose to see where Taresa pointed in his rusty collection of weapons. He named a price.

"It's not worth half that." Taresa stepped closer, as near as she could come to the merchant where he perched on his tall stool behind his trestle table. "It doesn't keep an edge. It's too short for any man taller than a ten-year-old. The boy who stole it last summer chipped the blade. The wrap on the grip is frayed to shreds."

The merchant repeated his price. "You said you must have it."

Tomás stood at Taresa's other side. "Come, senhóra. The blade is wrecked. You'll have to pay a smith the same amount of silver to get it right again." He seemed to be ignoring the bright angry roses blooming under Taresa's freckles.

"I myself do not have to have that sad ruin of a sword," Chrétien said. He was on Tomás's other side. "However, I'll offer what you ask." The merchant brightened. He lifted it down from the narrow shelf on the side of his wagon, ready to present it to Chrétien, who then said, "If you'll add that cunning little dagger."

The merchant agreed, apparently only to spite Mme Hélène and Badoyn, both of whom scowled. Tomás smirked.

Orlando was squeezed between his new friends and his traitorous cousin, who in the past three days had tipped the equilibrium of his life, so that Orlando was falling into...he didn't know. Orlando clutched his shirts close and turned to wiggle out of the market crowd. He didn't escape, however, before seeing Chrétien make a present of the dagger to Mme Hélène, apparently for no other purpose than to peeve Badoyn.

■

When Orlando reached the edge of the market crowd, Tomás, Chrétien, and Taresa surrounded him, so close that you'd think they'd followed him. Taresa had her hand on Chrétien's wrist, the same way she'd handled Orlando with her too-warm fingers.

"Will you sell it to me?"

"No, it's mine." Chrétien removed her hand. With his other hand, he held the sword she wanted out of her reach. "But I'll give it to you, if you confess what you're up to."

"Confess? That's what you do for your sins." She touched his hand again. "I am pure of heart."

Pure of heart...with a small army camped two valleys over. Why did these people keep secrets from each other?

"A pure heart doesn't need a worthless sword." Chrétien held it overhead. Since he was so tall, Taresa had no hope of reaching it.

"How about a wager?" Taresa fingered the charm she wore around her neck. "I bet that before the terce bell tomorrow, my strategy is successful. If I win the bet, you give me that blade."

"And if you lose?"

"It will be because your plan was more effective than mine. And you'll be so happy with *that* prize, you'll want to give me the blade in celebration."

"You have no idea how to gamble," Chrétien said.

"You don't want to take a risk?"

"He'll take the bet," Tomás said. "Just because it's a bet."

Taresa clapped her hands, just once, as if in victory. Then she had her hand on Chrétien's again. "Swear on it?"

"I accept the wager," Chrétien said. "But, senhóra, please unhand me. Tomás will hold the blade until the terce bell rings."

"Oh no," Taresa said. "We need an innocent to hold the blade and judge the winner. Captain Orlando, is that you?"

"I have duties…" If he had a vision of the future, it was a barren and foreign landscape. "…that make it impossible for me to participate."

"Who's the most trustworthy man in Carcassona?"

Orlando considered. "Ansel the stablemaster."

"Then he shall hold it. I'll carry it to him right now." Chrétien seemed gleeful.

"Fine." Taresa grasped the corners of her shawl, which the wind had whipped up. "You have until tomorrow's terce bell to enjoy being a prize *punxor*."

Tomás said, "That particular state is likely to continue beyond the morning bells. Chrétien can't help it. He was born that way."

"How can you be so lighthearted?" Orlando's pent up frustration burst forth. He'd aligned his honor and his future with these strangers—and they loitered in the marketplace for no purpose but to tease each other.

"Surely you must remember what it's like before a battle, little brother?" Tomás asked.

"No. I was too young at Constantinople. Here, I've only participated in sieges and peace patrols."

Chrétien said, "Then, *mon ami*, you've missed all the piss and *punxor* jokes told just before the drums beat."

"I haven't missed it." Taresa pulled her shawl tight around her shoulders. "I'll leave you valiant knights to beat your drums. Or what have you."

She glanced around, then joined Mme Hélène, who'd returned to the spice-merchant's wagon, an impatient Badoyn beside her.

.

"I need to fetch my kit from the bachelors' barracks." Orlando spoke low, though he was alone with Tomás and Chrétien in the empty chateau courtyard. Everyone who wasn't on day-patrol duty was at the market. "Then I'll prepare."

"For night patrol?" Tomás asked.

"For a permanent exit. After Badoyn's attempt this morning, we cannot wait." Orlando was sure of this.

Tomás said, "Are we better prepared than your cousin was this morning?"

Orlando repeated the elements he understood: Wait for Badoyn to depart, who believed Orlando planned to ride north to join him. Orlando would take the boy out of the city, wrapped up like part of the night-patrol gear.

"Badoyn has bribed the guards to let me pass unmolested." Orlando felt certain of this portion of the plan. "I'll have you in my patrol. I've also assigned three of the most worthless men in the *gardes du corps* for our night patrol."

"We'll have Karles with us," Tomás said. "Mme Hélène's mercenaries will join us, since they all served with Pedro before…" His voice trailed off.

"Before?" Orlando longed for more history, since he'd committed to join at least a portion of his future to theirs.

"Before Muret," Chrétien said. "We all promised…"

His voice trailed off, too. Orlando had heard their stories the night before in the tower, but he hadn't grasped the depth of their…what? Grief. It was nine months since the king of Aragón had been killed in battle. These two hadn't recovered. Was that true for Karles? Mme Taresa, too? That gulf—Orlando knew what grief felt like, and how long it lasts—must be the source of rifts and secrets among them.

"We send the three guards to scout the trail to St-Jean that I told Badoyn I intend to take." Orlando brought them back to the night's plan. "And then what?"

"We ride down the Narbonne road faster than Badoyn and his purchased knights can follow." Chrétien spoke lightly, but Orlando had come to know that was his way.

"Fast enough to stay out of arrow range? And yet pass through the countryside undetected?"

"*Òc,*" Chrétien said. "That usually works for us."

"We'll meet other knights of Aragón," Tomás said, "who are waiting to ride relay to Narbonne. The boy will be with the archbishop in time for Sunday mass."

Orlando had to ask. "Will Mme Hélène's house-knights truly join you? I don't understand your rivalry with those two ladies."

"Yes, they'll join us, because they were Pedro's knights," Tomás said. "The only question is whether they can escape the city without Taresa noticing."

"One wrong word," Chrétien said, "and she'll be out on the road to Narbonne in chainmail, with a sword at her side and a dagger in her teeth."

Orlando laughed, the image as comical as his boys dressing as mummers at Twelfth Night.

"Let's go now," Tomás said, "while the ladies remain amused at the market."

25
At Twilight

"OUT ALL NIGHT, CAPTAIN?"

"Yes, Master Ansel. It's asking too much of the horses to ride beyond St-Jean village and then back tonight." Orlando breathed in the scent of this familiar, comfortable stable. One more adieu.

"*C'est vrai.*" Ansel helped Orlando saddle his horse and strap his gear in place. "Especially since your Midnight had an adventure this morning. But no packhorses this time?"

"No. The villagers don't have more tithes the size of sheep."

"What do you expect to find?"

"They say," Orlando repeated the phrase that launched all gossip in the Pays d'Òc, "the Grail is hidden in St-Jean village. I have a pure heart, so I have high hopes for tonight."

Ansel slapped Orlando's back, laughing with him.

Orlando led Midnight through the streets to Mme Marguerite's villa, where Karles met him.

"The boy heard the entire plan from me. He knows we are his father's knights and agrees with the plan," Karles said. "Mme Marguerite insists you take trail food. She's certain you haven't eaten, so she's waiting for you in the kitchen."

Orlando had slipped on all his courage when he put on both of his new shirts and new socks. After the morning's calamity, he'd leaned on Marguerite to quell his fears. He needed to quell similar unease before he took charge of Galahad, but he couldn't achieve that if he said another goodbye to Marguerite. He could be brave for the sake of Galahad; however cowardly it seemed, he couldn't say adieu to Marguerite.

"Please fetch the food, Master Karles. I'm…checking the boys." He glanced around for anyone else that might hear.

"Fine. She insisted the boy stay in bed after this morning's ruckus. You'll find him in the barracks."

He did indeed find Galahad in the barracks, along with all the other boys. And Renard. As a consequence of the morning's adventure, Galahad had all the attention any boy could want, and he was using it to tell a fanciful version of a Grail quest. Galahad, who didn't see Orlando come in, said, "But Gawain was the best of knights, more loyal to the king than any other. Like Captain Orlando."

"*Juvenes.*" Orlando called out as if he hadn't overheard Galahad's tale. "Mme Marguerite commands you all to supper. I believe there is a pudding tonight."

The boys scrambled past him, shouting, "*Merci,* Captain." They always shouted when excited. Galahad started to rise from his cot.

"Not you, *garçon.* Mme Marguerite says you're to remain in the barracks. A servant will bring your supper."

He thought every boy had scrambled out, but when Orlando closed the door, Perseus stood beside Galahad.

"I want to come, too, Captain."

"*S'il vous plaît, Capitaine.*" Galahad pleaded. "He's my only true friend. Besides Ajax. And Renard, your dog."

"*Je suis desolé.*" Orlando offered sincere sympathy. "But it simply is not possible."

Galahad bit at his lip. "If I'm the king, don't you have to do what I say?"

"When you're anointed by the Church, then all knights who swear an oath to you must obey. Right now, you're my *juvene* and I'm your captain. Neither Perseus nor Renard can come."

After Perseus left, shepherding out the greyhound, Orlando sat on the opposite cot.

Galahad pulled his coverlet closer instead of rising from his cot. He looked small—and battered, with that black eye, which had only begun to fade. "Captain? Will I be a good king?"

"Yes, *garçon*. As soon as you have faithful teachers and advisors to guide you. You proved this morning that you have a true heart and uncommon sense. Did Master Karles explain tonight's plan?"

He watched Galahad's silent nod. The boy seemed subdued, perhaps because of the morning's failed Grail quest. But then, the lingering bruise from the first tussle in the barracks made it hard to read the boy's expression.

"You understand that our plan is dangerous?"

"Yes, Captain. I'm ready. But I thought Master Karles would rescue me tonight. I'm surprised it's you, Captain."

"Why? I promised to protect you, didn't I?"

"Because you're Simon's man. If you do this, won't you be a traitor to him?"

Why did little boys always know how to pick on a man's open wounds? "I'm sworn to Philippe Augustus. He's your kinsman."

"I thought it would be Master Karles." Galahad seemed unsure, not merely subdued. "Perseus said it would be Karles. Sergeant Umbert said—"

"What's wrong, *garçon*?"

"When he told Lancelot we could climb the tower, Sergeant Umbert said we didn't have to obey your rules, because you're a traitor. He whispered it to me again today, when he brought me hot milk. When Master Karles wasn't here."

"God's bones!" Orlando was inclined to curse Badoyn, who of course had easily subverted Umbert. After all, it was Grand-père Daniel who'd first hired the man. "I'm a knight, sworn to uphold my own father's honor. Do you believe a sworn knight or a faithless... *bricon*." He couldn't think of another word than scoundrel. An unfamiliar desire to punish his sergeant washed through him. Though it couldn't matter: he'd never see the fellow again, since Orlando was about to leave Carcassona forever.

"That's what I told Perseus. Because you saved us this morning, and then didn't punish me for going on a Grail quest."

"We're leaving on a quest that's just as great as seeking the Grail." He sought to instill excitement in the boy, and not dwell on being betrayed by his sergeant. "If you can seek the Grail, you can endure this new adventure."

Galahad threw off the covers and rose from his cot. He was dressed for travel, his red scarf tied around his wrist.

Orlando said, "Are those your warmest clothes? The mistral is cold tonight."

"I have a cloak, too. But I have to wee first."

"Fine. Then we go. Tomorrow you meet your countrymen."

.

The thickly cloaked king of Aragón left the academy in bundles of travel gear and food packs. On the portico, Karles and Orlando helped each other into chainmail and surcoats. Tomás and Chrétien appeared, leading three horses. Orlando mounted Midnight, and Karles passed the floppiest travel bundle up to him. One hand emerged to wave, the red scarf on his wrist, when Mme Marguerite called farewell.

At the city gate, all six of Hélène's house-knights were mounted and ready to ride, their horses also laden with gear for a night on the trail. But only two of the *gardes du corps* assigned to the patrol waited, carrying excuses that the third man had been struck sick in the gut from a meat tart he ate in the market.

One less French guard to be rid of later, leaving only two of the most worthless and disliked of the *gardes du corps*. Those two he sent to ride as advance scouts, up the road to St-Jean village.

Orlando's quest-patrol passed through the gate with only grudging calls of *bonne nuit* from guards who considered themselves grievously overworked, having to check every barrow and cart departing the city at the end of market day.

"*Ça va, garçon?*" Orlando murmured the question on the ride down to the main road. The answer hummed inside the thick cloak. Orlando could scarcely hear his own thoughts. To quiet his anxious heartbeat, he relied on Midnight's steady pace.

And the Lord shall do unto them as he did unto the old king.

You aren't my brother. You only lie. Be gone.

And unto those from his land, whom he destroyed.

The only burning he smelled was the comforting odor of village cook fires on the evening air. The road to Narbonne unfolded in front of them in the twilight.

The vesper bell rang, echoing from the castle across the valley.

The plan to restore the young king to Aragón was succeeding.

.

Their escape slowed and the mistral wind rose when they reached the narrow gap in the road that ran between tall, decaying humps of the ancients' limestone quarry. A farmer's heavy wagon with a broken wheel was stranded sideways, nearly blocking passage, where a rockfall crowded the edge of the road, too steep for a horse to traverse, especially in the fading light. An ox, still yoked, moaned plaintively. The farmer was nowhere to be seen, likely having gone to St-Marco village in search of help.

"We can't waste time clearing it," Tomás said. "Let's go around."

"Is it a trap?" Orlando felt his heart beating again.

"No one knows we're on this road," Chrétien said. "It must just be a farmer's accident."

Karles and Chrétien unharnessed the ox and led it to the sweet grass further up the trail. Karles returned to fetch his own horse, then again to take Orlando's burden, carrying the boy past the narrow gap between rockfall and wagon.

While Orlando awaited his turn to lead Midnight past the overturned wagon, he felt it, perhaps in his feet, rather than hearing it. Horses pounding down the road from Carcassona.

A cloaked knight jostled him. "Help me move the cart. It's not enough to stop them yet."

What the knight intended: upending the cart, ensuring it totally blocked the trail. An impossible task.

"We can't—"

"You win! Go with God!" The knight beside him shouted to the loyal knights as they mounted their horses on the other side of the wagon. It was Tarek, the mage-knight. Aventail over his face, swathed in a turban. "It's up to you and me together. Let's turn this wagon into a barricade."

No use in arguing. The mage-knight was already pushing the wagon, so Orlando joined him. He put his shoulder against the wagon and concentrated all his strength. The long muscles in his thighs ached. His calves seized. He stopped for one breath and to get firm purchase with his boots on the trail, forgetting that it was impossible to move the wagon.

Forgetting that he and his horse were on the wrong side of the barricade.

"Shove hard! Now!" Tarek shouted in Catalan.

Orlando gave it everything, sure that the cart was caught, that they weren't strong enough, that God wasn't on their side. But then the heavy wooden beast moved. A hair's breadth first. Then it finally tipped over, twisted across the trail so no horse could pass.

Tarek punched Orlando's arm in a brief salute to their mutual success. "Lances now, Captain! Then swords."

"Get on your horse!" Orlando urged. "They'll cut us down if we're not mounted." He was on Midnight with more speed than he'd managed in half a decade, lance in hand. Renard skittered away into the undergrowth.

Tarek tapped his weapons, checking that each was in place. Slowly, it seemed to Orlando. The mage-knight moved so slowly, while horses thundered down the road from the city, growing ever closer. The sound of horses on the other side of the wagon grew fainter with each heartbeat, until he couldn't hear an echo of what might be happening up and away along the darkening road to Narbonne.

"I don't have a horse." Tarek stood beside the overturned wagon, hands on his hips, a tilt of his turbaned head, like a curious raven in an olive tree. He spread his feet for a sturdy stand, a war sword in one hand, a dagger in the other. "But we won't let them pass, *mon ami*. You and I shall stand together."

"They are too many for us. We don't have a prayer."

"It's too late to pray," Tarek said. "Even though we have pure hearts. We'll have to lie our faces off. I hope you're good at it."

"I shall handle my cousin." He'd done fine, earlier, lying to Badoyn.

"Because, Captain, we can't allow them further down this road. If words don't suffice, we'll have to kill them."

The wind gusted over them, strong and cold, and then died down just as quickly.

"I killed men at Las Navas de la Tolosa in Andalusia," Tarek said, a wavering note in his voice. "But that was only mercy blows after battle. Still, I think I can do this. Can you, Captain?"

A thundering mass of crows descended into nearby oak trees, clung to broom, strutted on the road, calling to each other, as if they too guarded the trail. Orlando's thoughts, empty of poems and aberrant prayers, darted to whimsy, wondering if the crows awaited his sergeant Umbert.

The crows fluttered into the upper reaches of the trees, their wings as loud as the mistral, which rose again.

Then the rumble of approaching horses ceased, and Badoyn was in front of him, with Louis and Umbert beside him. All eight men were armed and in chainmail, but none wore helmets. Half hadn't laced up their aventails. Why were they so badly kitted out? Did they think they'd find only Orlando and a pair of ill-trained *gardes du corps*?

"You have our treasure?" Badoyn growled, impatient.

"Gone. Those new swordmasters stole the treasure from me." Astride Midnight in the twilight, Orlando shielded the unhorsed Tarek from the others' view. So far, the lie cleaved close to truth.

"You let other men steal our—" Badoyn, furious, spluttered for words, then glanced at Captain Louis "—treasure?"

"The swordmasters from Rome aren't what Simon claimed they were. They're Catalan knights in league with soldiers of Aragón." Orlando admired his response, since it wasn't a lie.

"You didn't fight? Did you participate in this treason?" Louis, challenged him, seeming convinced that Orlando had committed a crime. Orlando heard that censure with dismay, but there was no time to persuade Louis that he'd been led astray.

"Alone? Against eight knights?" Orlando held Midnight in tight control, the horse nervous in spite of her age, wanting to sidle away from this confrontation. "Bless you for thinking me so capable."

"Playing holy fool, Balthazar?" Badoyn's anger felt familiar, from years past. The greatest danger on the trail. "Are you as lunatic as your father in his final hours, claiming Philippe was his friend? Step aside. We need to pursue the Catalan thieves."

"Come, cousin." Orlando held hope that he might get through this alive, yet he could not let them pass. "I'm not a traitor. We cannot involve Simon in the murder of a king."

"That's our quest, fool." Badoyn kept his voice cold, but he was as angry as Orlando had ever seen. "I promised to remove barriers for Simon. He'll happily crawl for forgiveness in a hair shirt as long as he becomes king thereafter."

"Murder of a king?" Louis seemed as startled as a man encountering an unexpected monster. His shudder sent his horse prancing sideways. "We came to stop Orlando from stealing tithes. Didn't you say—"

Louis turned to Badoyn, his aventail falling open, his hand on his sword.

Not four crossbow bolts, as in Orlando's vision.

No bolts piercing chainmail.

Instead, his betraying cousin stabbed a javelin into Louis's exposed throat. As in the vision, Louis's blood sprayed forth. He fell from his horse, which screamed and danced sideways, prancing away.

Midnight wanted to follow. Orlando fought his horse while fighting revulsion, not wanting to look at Louis lying dead on the trail.

"Anyone else?" Badoyn shouted at the men with him. Six now, including his own two knights and Umbert. "You are with me? Else, you are traitors to Simon himself."

"You stand with the man who murdered your commander?" Orlando raised his voice so the guards heard. "Are you all murderers? Traitors to your oaths?"

> And it shall came to pass, you shalt drink of the river of death; and I shall command the ravens to feed upon thee.

You aren't my brother. He is surely in heaven now.

> Their feeding upon your flesh shall render the ravens an abomination.

Midnight tried to take herself away. Before Orlando could rein in his horse, the mage-knight was exposed to the attackers.

Tarek leaped up on the wagon side, feet spread wide, holding a javelin in battle position. He pulled back and released his javelin with force, striking down one of Badoyn's knights, the one closest to his master. The dead man's horse whinnied and tossed off his burden, which distracted the other men. Tarek drew a long dagger and hurled it, smashing the face of Badoyn's other knight.

Umbert backed his horse out of the milling horsemen. Orlando guessed his sergeant wanted to get away, since Umbert never liked either work or danger. But Orlando misestimated: Umbert rode straight for him, his lance out.

No shield and now no lance, Orlando danced Midnight out of the way just as Umbert came in range. Orlando felt the lance pierce his thigh, but had no time to attend to pain. His sergeant had always been a clumsy horseman and couldn't react quickly when Orlando swung his sword, sending Umbert to the ground, if not dead, then on his way there.

"Desperta, Ferro!"

Tarek screamed into the wind. Feet still planted firmly atop the wagon, the mage-knight stretched out his arms, as if embracing certain fate, like a saint to be martyred. Except Tarek held his war sword high. Wind blew his surcoat, the saffron color glowing even though scarcely any daylight remained. Badoyn rode for him, but Tarek brought down his sword when Badoyn came close, striking for where his cousin's chainmail hung open.

Badoyn tumbled from his horse, which reared and ran away.

Still holding Midnight in firm check, Orlando rode at one guard, slashing with his sword, intending maximum damage. Riding past, unable to see how much harm he'd managed, Orlando pulled Midnight back hard, and then returned, slashing at a second guard, who struck back, his sword tearing at Orlando's thigh. Orlando struck again, disarming the man. That guard's horse shied, not liking the smell of blood. The second guard fell, and his horse trampled him.

The remaining guard rode hard at Tarek, his lance piercing the mage-knight's side. Deep. Knocking Tarek to the ground.

Tarek, run through on the battlefield, just as in one of Orlando's useless visons.

Yet, a noble way to die.

Orlando spurred Midnight to ride at the guard, who hadn't yet released his lance. Orlando struck with his war sword again, bringing full force down on Tarek's murderer, the last of their attackers.

Then Orlando calmed Midnight and dismounted as quickly as possible, given pain and chainmail. He went to Tarek, praying that the mage-knight had a chance, all sense telling him it wasn't possible. He knelt, ready to seek Tarek's heartbeat and whether he could staunch blood loss.

Tarek opened his eyes, staring up at him. Open aventail. Turban askew. And not a man: Orlando was gazing at a handsome, freckled woman with a smile and a gold-flecked eyes that caught the last of the twilight.

Then Taresa shrieked in Catalan. *"Vés amb compte!"*

Orlando turned his head, facing his cousin, like in nightmares, and then his world collapsed, his shoulders and head smashed, as if crushed again by a boulder from a mangonel.

26
Your Mother's Luck

A SCRATCHING NEAR HIS EAR. Close by. A peck, like a pinch. He couldn't move to turn away.

"*Lluny, corb!*" A wild waving over him. Like a blanket or a surcoat. A mad flutter of wings and complaining croaks. "Away, crow. You can't have this one."

A woman's voice, talking to crows in Catalan.

"Taresa?" He tried to speak, but his throat produced only pain.

"Ah ho! You're back with us, Captain." A hand across his head, closing his eyes. "You aren't blind. It's very dark. I need you to think about one thing, Captain. Quiet your heart. Be very still, and think about saving your blood. The ground here is drenched enough."

A hand on his thigh. Wrenching.

"We peeled your hauberk off just now. We did our best to stop the blood, but we can't do more out here in the open, Captain. Guards are likely to come from the city. And I'm not sure everyone we struck down is dead. Now, aren't you happy that I'm here? You'd have been valiant without me, but perhaps you'd also be dead."

Jostling. Pain. He strained again to cry out.

"Don't try to talk. You took a sword bash to your throat. Your coif and chainmail kept your head attached, but we'll have to do some hard work to fix the damage. But first, we have to tend that slash from your groin down your thigh first. Your sergeant got a good piece of you with his lance."

More rustling, then a jolting rest on rocks.

"I'll take you to shelter, but let's stash our armor and weapons here, so I can carry you. We'll both remember the spot. See: a clutch of cistus shrubs with a young chestnut growing out. A scraggly caper bush in front. And broom on each side. Stay here while I hide our gear. I'm putting my surcoat over you to keep you warm."

He couldn't see, only darker shadows. He closed his eyes for the throbbing in his head. The rustling in the bushes scraped near where he lay. He fought against the sense that an animal might jump on him. His heart still beat as though he needed to fight. What did the mage-knight say? *Quiet your heart.*

A sneeze. Another sneeze.

The mage-knight returned to his side.

Not a knight. Mme Taresa of Girona.

"I think it's the broom that makes me sneeze. Mostly when I sneeze, there's a blur of visions that my brother Yusuf calls *déjà vu*. That means 'already seen' in your tongue, doesn't it? But ever since we came to this city, I'm sneezing with no glimpse of the past or the future. The broom must be to blame. And I don't even have clean linen to wipe my nose."

More pain. From manhood to knee. Then heat coursing through his limbs, as if hot water replaced his blood.

"I'm not touching you there for my pleasure. And I'm not talking to amuse myself. You need to stay with me, Captain. Listen to my words. Don't let ghost voices drag you away. In Andalusia, I saw men on the battlefield go into a fog and die, even when a good surgeon tended their wounds. A man's own spirit tries to find the hurt but gets lost. Then shivers start, and the stricken man wants to go to sleep, because that's easier than the work it takes to stay alive."

More pain than—he couldn't find a memory of pain that seared so deeply. Was this what it felt like when the blacksmith closed a wound with a hot iron?

"You can't go to sleep, Captain. So I'll keep talking, and you must listen to me and not that fawning devil that wants to lead you astray."

Bring us the foxes, the wee little foxes!

Leave me!

Silky, silky foxes.

"*Aiieee.* Amastri, my companion, says we must remove your zaar now. We can't heal you while that thing chews a hole in your heart. You know now that it's not your brother's ghost? Still, I wish you'd agree first. Maybe you can blink to tell me yes?"

Companion? There wasn't a third person near them. Orlando blinked, trying to see who else might be there, but only Taresa bent over him.

"That means yes? Now, listen. Don't let sleep steal you away, because I don't know if we can bring you back."

She touched him.

Pain tore through him. Pushed invisibly by a force as strong as the mistral. Blood left his heart.

"Oh! There are two things here."

Orlando tried to scream but choked instead. It felt as though Taresa had thrust a hand inside his belly.

"*Shhh.* Amastri says it's a charm not a daemon."

Inside his belly. Groping. Touching, then withdrawing.

"It's your life's luck, Captain."

So much shame, more than you can bear.

"Your mother set a charm so you'll never die at your enemy's hand. Her charm kept Badoyn from killing you and stopped the zaar from eating your heart."

Taresa spoke in a language he didn't know, but he must have heard it before. In swaddling clothes. In his mother's womb.

"We'll leave it right where she placed it," Taresa whispered. Then she spoke in the local tongue.

"*En nom de Jesucrist, el nostre Salvador.*"

Or maybe it was Catalan. Orlando understood only the name of God. Her hands moved from his heart down, over the hard edge of Orlando's breast bone.

"We order you to return to the Fire Lord. To be judged."

More words. If it was Catalan or the local tongue, Orlando didn't understand, until Taresa said in Catalan, "What do we say or do next, Amastri? It's not nearly as strong as the last time we touched it. Captain Orlando must have been starving it."

Or he imagined all of it. Orlando still couldn't make out a third person in the shadows. Taresa stammered, pausing as if to get words right in a language Orlando had never heard. The pain that racked his body wrenched away his attention at the same time Taresa began to sing, louder than the sound of his heart pounding.

Long before this, Orlando had mastered ignoring pain. He now wandered as if lost in a labyrinth, the one they'd found in Constantinople. When he reached the center, he walked through the gate to the place he most feared, where wind tore across the plain and into the abyss of his heart. There at the brink, teetering on the edge, was his brother Etienne, who cried out in French. *It was never your fault.*

Orlando reached out, to grab his brother, to stop him from falling. Falling again. The dream that never ceased.

Then Giles de Nully stood at the brink, holding out his arms to embrace Orlando, whispering about the loyalty of brothers.

Cling to me. Be faithful.

But the roar of the wind turned into a song, and Giles became a lizard that shed its skin, his face peeled bare, fangs instead of teeth, black holes instead of a nose. He…it…opened its fanged mouth, hissing *fidèle fidèle fidèle* until the song was too loud to hear the Giles-creature's words.

Home. You want to be home.
The Fire Lord calls you home.

The lizard-creature lay prostrate, its hands…claws over its skull as if pleading.

Time to go. This eagle will carry you home.

A flutter of wings, like ravens on a battlefield. Then a song drowned the sound of the flight and hoarse scream of the eagle.

·

Wild cats howled in the night.

"Are you with me, Captain? We're waiting for Amastri. She's escorting the zaar to another creature. From the yowls, I think she found a cat."

The core of his pain was gone. Oh, the wound along his thigh throbbed. His head ached. His throat felt wrecked. But the pain that consumed him, that he fought most of every day and every night, it was gone.

A miracle.

Taresa held his hand. "Not a miracle, Captain. Rather, God works more slowly than you'd wish. We just caught up with the work your mother began."

Orlando opened his eyes. To black space.

He tried to remember what he'd last seen and heard.

Cling to me. Be faithful.

Taresa still held his hand. "You saw Giles again, didn't you? Calling you. It was a dream. He'll never call you again."

Guilty. So guilty. Etienne died.

"Guilty, Captain?" While Taresa held his hand, it was as if she heard Orlando's thoughts. "We need two different words. One, for when you've taken action and feel awful about the consequences that have fallen on others. Except what happened to your brother wasn't your fault. It was Giles de Nully. That's why we need another word altogether for when a man like Giles does what he knows is wrong and strives to avoid the consequences. Until he dies."

Giles is dead. Orlando called back all the relief he'd felt when he first heard that news.

"Yes, Giles is dead." Taresa whispered. "Giles enthralled men, then destroyed them if they didn't obey. That's what happened to your brother, isn't it? And you, too? It was Giles who gave you that zaar. But now you're free."

Taresa gripped his hand, hard.

"I was like you when I ran away to follow the army. Alone. My father died, then my uncle. No friends. But that changed on the baggage train, traveling into Andalusia, where I learned who to trust and how to be trustworthy. And then I left the baggage train to join with Valerós."

Trust. He trusted—

"Did you decide before you rode out tonight whether you'd come to Valerós, Captain? Is there anywhere else in God's earth you can go, except to join us? Badoyn says your grandfather promises never to give you so much as shelter again. Can it really be, as Badoyn said, that your grandfather can't abide how your father polluted the family by bringing in Saracen blood? I don't even know what to say. But it seems that your grandfather is a sinner of grand proportions. How could a good man like you deserve exile from his own family?"

Taresa fell silent while they waited, listening to night sounds. Howling wild cats. Barking dogs far off in the countryside.

"No riders have come from the city yet. Do you agree that our friends are far enough down the road that no one can catch them now? They must have made it to the first relay station. That makes us happy, doesn't it, Captain? We succeeded. Fresh horses, fresh riders, taking that boy to Narbonne."

She shook him.

"Let's go, Captain. Amastri is back. Your zaar is gone. But you'll still have to take care of whatever guilt it fed on all those years. Maybe you can tell me that story one day."

•

A dozen years ago, Orlando, Etienne, and Badoyn went off on crusade as *juvenes* under Simon de Montfort. For boys—Orlando was twelve when they left Troyes—the journey itself was perpetual excitement, even if the *juvenes* performed entirely mundane tasks. Orlando loved caring for the horses, took seriously the job of oiling his knights' harnesses and chainmail, and sat as close as he could to the knights' fires at night, listening to their stories and songs. It was, certainly, the most exciting time in Orlando's life, which he'd shared joyfully with Etienne. The distance of their ages and Etienne's service in Paris had separated them previously, but on that journey, Etienne and Orlando became close friends and learned what it meant to be brothers.

At Zara, Simon quarreled with the Norman leaders' decision to serve the Venetian doge by attacking Constantinople. It was a commercial exchange—if the French crusaders restored the Venetians' favored ruler in Constantinople, then the doge promised to provide ships and supplies for the crusaders to continue to the Holy Land. Simon departed from the main force, and the *juvenes* from Troyes were left behind under another lord. Why? Orlando still didn't understand that part of the story, but he'd accepted it at the time.

The three of them then served the marquis de Beaurain—Hugues, the last marquis, Mme Hélène's husband. Even if they were no longer on their way directly to the Outremer, their new position seemed glorious, *juvenes* in service to a famous crusader, a hero from when the kings Philippe and Ricart the Angevine strove to take Jerusalem.

When Etienne, Badoyn, and Orlando joined the marquis's entourage, they worked under the direction of a young bachelor-knight—a knight without a banner—who regaled them with tales of his own adventures as a *juvene* in the Outremer, teaching them songs he'd learned in the camps of Templars, Catalan mercenaries, and French lords who held titles and land in the Outremer from the crusade sixty years earlier.

As *juvenes*, they weren't allowed on the ships that carried the warriors who breached the walls of Constantinople. But a day later, the boys were inside that magnificent city, assisting the comfort of the knights who worked to tame the chaos of a conquered city. They brought the knights water and food, tended the knights' doss sites, and repaired weapons and armor when they weren't stumbling through the city's burning streets.

And they followed their leader, the bachelor-knight, into jeopardy. He'd let them do things other *juvenes* weren't allowed to partake in—drinking wine at the older squires' rowdy campfires, carrying messages and loitering where the knight and his friends entertained women. And he'd let them play pranks on other *juvenes*: disappearing bedrolls, late-night false drills, hunting fabled questing beasts. Therefore, it didn't strike any of them as out of the ordinary—except Etienne refused—when their leader sent them to play an enormous joke on a bannered French knight, hiding booty in his doss kit.

All those years since, besides being plagued by what Taresa insisted was an evil spirit, Orlando burned with the guilt of that foolish prank Giles had spurred them to commit. It had caused Hugues de Beaurain to send Orlando home, shamed. The French knight who found stolen war booty in his doss kit? He was stripped of his banner and exiled, barely escaping being hanged for stealing booty from the Church.

That same night was when their leader Giles transformed, as if into another creature altogether. He and Etienne fought, and Etienne fell from the precipice into the Great Sea and was lost.

Only now did Orlando understand that their leader, Giles de Nully, had sent a devil's imp after Orlando.

Even without a demon nesting in his heart, it didn't seem likely that Orlando could ever forgive himself, much less find the courage to ask that exiled knight to forgive him.

27
Out of Sight

"*Aiieee!* Captain, stay awake, so I can keep you alive! Shall I tell you a story to keep you awake?"

A hand on his head. Lifting his shoulders.

"We need to go now, Captain. I'm not sure how fast I can move, carrying you. But we don't have another choice. The knights' horses all ran away. They'll return to the city. Sooner or later other guards will seek Badoyn and his knights."

A long wrenching pain down his middle. *Quiet your heart.* Not the voice of his ghost. No, it was Mme Taresa who had transformed, as if by magic, from the dead mage-knight.

"This must hurt you, *mon ami.* I'm sorry. Move your thoughts away from pain. Listen to my voice."

Taresa lifted Orlando, shifted, then had Orlando over her shoulder. The impact knocked him breathless again. She seemed to sense this, shifted Orlando so his belly lay across her sharp shoulder. She proceeded down the trail, back toward the city, first trying to jog, then settling into a hard stride. Orlando rocked, dizzy. Not able to speak. Only sensing the bushes and trees they passed. He smelled sage. And his own blood.

"Can you conceive how much planning and hard work this took? Of course you can. You've been on crusade. But this did take the entire autumn and winter to plan. We had to find good men for each element: procure horses, engage loyal riders, and move supplies. We put a dozen messengers in place just to track Simon."

He tried to make his throat work. A thousand questions needed to be answered.

"Don't try to talk. Just stay awake. What were we discussing? Oh yes, how we had to find good people in every town and village where Simon might take up residence. It cost half of Hélène's fortune, and I had to borrow from Sebastián's estates. Of course, Sebastián would do the same if he were here. But I'd prefer to draw on my own fortune."

The riot of crows cawed. In the distance now.

Taresa paused, turning in a circle as if seeking something, then set out again. Orlando lost her voice, pondering where he'd heard the name Sebastián before.

"However, if I'm to regain my land in Girona and the dowry that Pedro gave me, then I need the king of Aragón, or at least the Count of Barcelona, to render judgments and keep promises. I'm not complaining, of course. The entire county of Barcelona and all of Aragón endure far deeper grief than I do. It's my common sin of pride, that I seek to claim my own worth in the world."

Orlando reached for a memory, his thoughts falling into a dark cloud, but then he only wanted sleep.

"*Aiieee*, Captain. You're slipping away. Come back. Stay here and listen to me chatter. I'll tell you more about provisioning our expedition. Since that's all I've thought about since Michaelmas."

She stopped again, shifting Orlando to her other shoulder. If not her voice, then the jostling of new pain awakened him.

"We knew from the beginning that it'd be like planning the army's journey into Andalusia. Except we didn't have five years to arrange things. Though I confess, however sure I felt about the plan by Easter, we didn't believe we could rescue the Aragón king before midsummer. Until we met you."

Taresa stumbled in the dark, then righted herself and set out again, picking up her pace.

"Awake, Captain? *Bon homme!* You might be wondering why I'd take on this work. After all, I'm Catalan, and we don't care about kings. We strive to avoid them, unless we need protection from another enemy. Pedro did that, but because he was count of Barcelona, not because he was king of Aragón. Unlike you, I didn't grow up believing that God anoints kings. But we swore oaths to him, more like brothers to brothers than knights to a king. Pedro was good to me. Which is why my blood boils, seeing an evil man holding Pedro's son, stealing justice from Aragón and from the Pays d'Òc. That's why I'm not resting until we stop Simon and save Pedro's son."

Boots crunched on the hard-packed trail, the sound trapped among the bushes that lined the way.

"What we hadn't calculated was your damnable cousin convincing Simon to suddenly move the boy to Carcassona. We thought that made it harder to reach the boy and easier for Badoyn to advance his evil idea. It thrust us into a flurry of new tasks. We had to get ourselves into the city and quickly find new allies. We've been trusting only Pedro's true allies, men who'd sworn a personal oath to him, who needed to take action after failing him at Muret. Hélène wanted to buy people's loyalty in Carcassona, because that's what she usually does. But our work can't be done by bribing people. We need people who will act to uphold their own honor."

A dog barked in the distance. They must be close to a village, because another dog answered, and then another, dogs' voices echoing around the valley.

"Simon filled Fanjeau with true believers, noble knights from the Pays de France, which made that city hard to penetrate. But here in Carcassona, it seems Simon has stashed away men he couldn't rely on. We weren't interested in failed and lazy soldiers, though. That left only you, Captain."

Quiet your heart. Quiet your soul. Not the voice of his ghost. It was Taresa's command. What was he supposed to do? Stop the pain, which started in his head, burned in his nose.

Taresa continued to talk, on her quest to keep him awake. "Hélène teased me today, that I'd failed to convince you. That it took Miguel's sons to show you the path of righteousness. But, don't you agree, it would betray my soul and yours, too, to do what Hélène does? And not just because I'm ardent about waiting for Sebastián to return. Yes, Hélène did excellent work, using Badoyn to learn Simon's secrets and plans. But, leaping lizards! Can you imagine letting Wheel and Serpent slime touch you?"

He wanted to sleep. To find a place to lie down, to not answer a bell. To forget duty.

"Oh, no offense, Captain. After all, you and I agreed, the first day we met, that Giles de Nully was indeed a viper. It must be as it pleases God that he's dead, but I felt no joy, watching him die."

He woke, jolted. Taresa saw Giles de Nully die?

"Here we are, Captain. This will do for the night. I hope it doesn't take us longer than that to fix you. Now I'm going to have to drag you into this shelter. It might hurt. I'm sorry."

She shoved this way and that, finally tucking her arms under his and then dragging him over broken rocks. It did indeed hurt. No chainmail. Only his jerkin and shirts to protect his flesh from sharp rocks. His earlier injuries stressed and banged on the rocks.

"Here, sit on this rock for a moment. I don't fear spiders, but I don't like scorpions and snakes. Let me shake the blanket and kick a few rocks before you lie down."

He slumped, guessing at sounds in the dark. What was he supposed to do? *Quiet your heart. Quiet your soul.* Not his brother. Not a ghost. That voice is gone.

"With my surcoat over the opening, we can light a lamp. I planned to stock this space better. But I delayed when Badoyn and Simon dreamed up that ridiculous quest. By Pentecost! Well, Simon's impatience didn't do him one spit-cup of good. So we're stuck here with just a blanket, a lamp, and one flagon of water."

Orlando wanted light. He wanted to know what dark place he'd come to. Taresa embraced him again, dragging him onto a blanket.

"We're going to start now. We want to be gentle, but this is going to hurt far more than stitching up a sword cut, though you'd probably say you've felt worse if you could talk. Once we start, we can't stop, however much it hurts. And until we fix your broken throat, you can't even scream. Here, take the strap of my baldric between your teeth. It's nice soft leather. You can bite hard when you need to."

Taresa moved away from his side. Flint and steel struck, ringing against the walls of where they huddled. She coaxed light from a rush wick. Shadows flickered. They were in a small cave or a shepherd's stone shack. Two of them. No sign of her companion.

Orlando fought to keep his eyes open, but his lids drooped, however much he struggled, like a child falling asleep in his father's arms, wanting to hear the stories, wanting to see...

"Don't go, *el meu capità*. Stay with me." Arms around his shoulders, Taresa embraced Orlando like a lover; no, like when his father stayed by his side, comforting him after a nightmare. So long ago. And so warm, so comfortable, rocking in his father's arms, who'd keep him safe from the entire world.

"Open your eyes, Captain. It's not time for heaven yet, not for you. Come back, Monsieur Captain." A hand joggled his face. He opened his eyes. "Now, let's keep you from bleeding to death."

He looked where Taresa laid her hand on his thigh, which glistened with gore.

"It never hurts me when Amastri repairs wounds." Her voice came to him like waves against the side of a boat. "But we haven't tried this for others. We'll see. Just breathe until..."

■

"Welcome back from the arms of Morpheus, Captain. Is that the right story? I hope you were sleeping, not lured away by sirens like Odysseus."

"Are you a witch, Madam?" The words scraped his throat.

"Ah, he speaks! We've been worrying about your poor throat. And please call me Taresa. After the battle we fought together, aren't we the same as brother and sister?"

"You're possessed of a devil!"

"No, I'm friends with one of God's creatures. She's my companion, helping you."

"There's only you and me here."

"We seldom see our protective angels. Amastri isn't like the zaar that gnawed at your core. She's baptized and strives to live a proper life, just like you and me."

"Your spirit-creature is Catholic?"

"I suppose. Save your breath, *si us plau*. I need to go out for a bit, to find a way to deliver you to friends."

"Don't leave me here!" His voice broke.

"You'll be fine. But you need water and food. We discussed it while you slept. Amastri will stay with you until I return." She touched his hand.

The invisible companion? A spirit?

"One of God's creatures. I can't explain."

"Do you hear my thoughts?"

"No, it's just a kind of second sight I was born with. When I touch people, I see dim memories. Often as not, memories aren't true. Rest now. I'll be back."

Orlando protested, but his throat burned, like when he'd had a vicious fever, that year his father died. Taresa tipped water to his lips, placed the mostly depleted flagon beside him, and pulled back the covering she'd hung over the door.

Predawn light colored the rocks and trees in shades of grey.

"I'm going to leave the shelter open," Taresa said. "If someone finds you, it'll save me the chore of carrying you home. Claim a miracle. Now, close your eyes and sleep, Captain."

When Taresa was gone, he didn't close his eyes. He studied the cave walls and found it was no cave at all, but a dry-stone shelter some-one had created in the rockfall below Carcassona hill. He listened to early-morning sounds in the nearby trees and bushes: larks sang. He heard the fluttering of birds in the branches, but could only see a shouter bird that perched and seemed to stare at Orlando. What did Louis call them? Cuckoo bird.

Louis was dead. He and Taresa had survived the massacre his cousin intended, but Louis had died. *Aiieee,* his poor wife. How was Orlando to explain? That Louis had been duped, and then murdered?

His didn't realize he was weeping until he felt tears flowing down to his ears.

And Umbert and Badoyn were dead. And those knights. He'd killed men. Was it in faithful battle? True to what the Church teaches? *Justice dans la guerre?* He tried to remember those men's faces—most slept in the bachelors' tower, where he did. He tried to pray, the prayers he'd repeated for his brother for years, asking God to admit them to heaven. He shivered. Would he spend a dozen years hearing their voices? Accusing him of the unforgiveable?

You shall be well, Captain. Just give thanks to the Good God.

He turned his head, seeking the voice that spoke in the local tongue, an accent like Mme Estela's. An animal scratched near his head, so he opened his eyes, worried that the crows had found him again. A creature settled on his chest, kneading like a cat does and peering into his eyes like a curious dog. Except it had the face of a woman. A beautiful woman with dusky eyes and long lashes. Full lips. His thoughts darted, not believing what he saw.

You may call me Amastri.

The creature was hairless, white bands on its grey flesh, like layers of clouds. Ears like a bat, flicking forward to listen. He'd been touched by the moon. That's what had happened to him. The only thing that made sense. But nothing made sense.

That thin slice emerging from the dark new moon? The crescent moon can't turn men into lunatics.

He'd seen a lance run through the mage-knight, a death stroke for any man.

Steel can't harm her if I'm there. Like your mother's charm protects you from your enemies.

He'd taken a blow to his head after every other man lay dead on the ground. Mme Taresa could not possibly carry him on her shoulders for five breaths, must less for the league from the ancient quarry back to Carcassona hill.

Your mother had a beautiful voice. What was that song she sang to you? Il rêve à la lune, car toujours si bonne. No, that's how your father sang it. It was different in your mother's tongue.

The mistral. It drives men mad. Mme Estela and all the old women claim it's so.

Old wives tell tales. Often true tales. But you aren't mad.

The creature kneaded his chest with her paws again. Purred.

Sleep. I need to finish helping you. Don't your eyes feel so heavy?

Yes. They did. He struggled to keep them open. This felt too much like when the monks drowned him in poppy syrup after the catastrophe at Minerve. But he didn't want to enter the country of sleep, because his dreams all led to nightmares, nagged on by an evil ghost, an imp that lived in the hole in his heart. He pressed his nails into his palm, checking that he was awake and not dreaming.

Your zaar is gone. You're a free man. Who shall carry his mother's protection until—

The creature startled, like a wary cat, looking all around and then skittering into the rocks that made the wall.

"*Jhezu del tron!*" The childish voice spoke in the local tongue. So hard to follow in a dream. "Are you dead, senhór?"

"He's covered in blood!"

Three boys knelt on the rocks beside him. Robi?

No, Orlando was in a fever dream. His eyes burned. His throat was too dry for him to call out. Little hands patted him.

"I think he's alive. He's burning up."

"Let's take him to the village."

"That's too far. He needs water."

"We don't have any."

"Then we'll take him to water."

"Why is he here, do you think?"

"The Good God might know, but I don't."

"Here, drag the blanket. He's too heavy for us."

"We should sing a song. This is going to be a chore."

Jostled over rocks, hitting his head, Orlando listened to a choir of boys singing songs from his dreams.

> Small, but with a courage-filled heart,
> The young knight gallops
> To the castle of the cruel lord.
> His blood hot, he spurs his Saracen steed
> And cries 'All glory to God!'

That creature sat on his chest, still kneading like a cat, purring. Admonishing him in accented French.

Sleep. I'm still helping you.

28

A Tapestry

"Monsieur, forgive me, but I have to cut away your shirt and breeches. The dried blood sticks them to you."

Marguerite knelt beside where Orlando lay on a pallet in her kitchen, the morning fire burning in the hearth behind her, the light like a halo around her. Her hair, free of its veil, streamed down her shoulders. Why had he never seen her luminous beauty?

She whispered close to his ear. "Is the boy safe?"

"Yes. Please don't worry. How did I come here, madam?" The words scraped through his throat like the rasp of a mason setting a stone in mortar.

"Villagers found you at the edge of the river and brought you to the gate." Marguerite received a kitchen knife from the servant, who placed a pottery bowl and pitcher at her side. "Mme Hélène saw the guards carrying you and had them bring you here instead of the monks' infirmary."

She sawed at Orlando's two new ruined shirts, pausing to pour warm water where the crusted cloth clung to his skin. Then she cut away more of his clothes, beginning on his breeches once his chest was bared. "Your hands are so warm. I'm used to feeling them as always cold." She held her hand on his head for a long moment. "But no fever. The Holy Mother and all the saints must be looking after you."

"Midnight! My horse!"

"Your horse came to the stable on her own."

"My mail! My sword!" St-Balthazar, one of the three magus-kings of the Nativity, might know how he'd ever afford new armor and weapons; Orlando surely did not. No, the mage-knight hid them. Marked by cistus shrubs. A young chestnut sapling.

Not a mage-knight. Taresa of Girona.

"Peace, monsieur. Perhaps your mail and weapons are in the pile of armor that the guards brought back from that massacre."

"How—"

"How did you travel a league back to the ring trail with half your heart's blood gone? The saints may know, but I don't. Were you attacked where Captain Louis was massacred on the Narbonne road?"

"Yes. My cousin Badoyn attacked us. The others in our party escaped. They took the boy. He's safe."

Marguerite scraped away his clothes, except for a scrap of breeches close to his loins. She swabbed his thighs with linen that she wet repeatedly in the pottery bowl. As if surprised, she leaned back from where she'd been kneeling.

"Captain, is this another man's blood? Or are your wounds where I haven't yet touched?"

Orlando felt where his thigh had been sliced open by—who? Umbert and his lance. Yet now he felt only a long, thin weal, like an ancient scar long healed.

More awake than perhaps he'd ever been in his life, Orlando bounded from the cot, tearing away the final remains of his breeches to feel himself.

Intact.

"Monsieur." Marguerite turned her head away, handing him linen toweling.

Too shaken to be embarrassed, he wrapped the linen around his loins and paced in front of the fire, energy flowing through him like before a battle. He rubbed his hands together, finding that his hands were warm. The perpetual chill gone, along with the pain and the ghost-imp. The entire fantastic story must be true, that the mage-knight Taresa saved him. She'd ripped out his demon, so his heart no longer had a hole.

"It was…it was…" He began twice, trying to find the words to tell Marguerite, who glowed like an angel in the kitchen's firelight. So beautiful!

And who seemed both embarrassed and nervous. She said, "I sent a servant to fetch clothes for you from your barracks."

"I have nothing left in the barracks. What happened here?"

"When horses returned without their riders, a dozen guards went looking for their missing riders. They brought back Badoyn. He's in the monks' infirmary, though no one thinks he will live. The rest of the guards died. Including Captain Louis and your sergeant Umbert."

"Badoyn lived?" How? The mage-knight—Taresa—dispatched him. Twice. "He forced his knights to attack us. That *bricon* killed Louis."

"Will you seek justice for that?"

Still thrilled by the life running through his own veins, Orlando quickly discarded any idea of justice. Or revenge. "I have to be gone from here before Simon returns. I can't waste time on Badoyn. And he can't do more harm. What's the gossip in the city about what happened to me?"

"Mme Hélène insists that you and her house-knights must have been attacked by the same bandits that massacred Badoyn. She begged that men ride beyond St-Jean village, to recover her house-knights who'd been with you."

"But no one has gone looking?"

"With Louis found dead, and Simon absent, the guards are quarreling about who's in charge. And about what kind of bandits attacked Badoyn."

"Then I should be able to claim my horse and leave the city." He pondered the tasks for that. "Can you give me food? A couple of days for the trail?"

"Yes. I'll find more of the baron's clothes for you. And leave you to your bath," Marguerite said. But instead of leaving, she stared at him, her eyes shimmering. "How did you end up by the river, instead of going to Narbonne? Is the boy truly safe?"

"Yes, he's safe. Village boys found me and dragged me to the river." They'd chanted a song from the poet of Troyes. Which seemed improbable. He'd dreamed that part. "Madam, I don't know what happened after we fought Badoyn."

"But you are well?"

"I'm fine," he said. "More than fine." No ghost. No limp. *Did you see? I didn't limp.*

"Orlando—" she never spoke his Christian name "—you left without saying goodbye. Then, when the horses returned at midnight, I thought you'd died. And lost the boy, too."

He walked to her, not to show that he didn't limp, but to hold her. "I'm so sorry that you worried. Especially since I was a coward and didn't want to say goodbye." From the small shakes of her shoulders, she was weeping. "And here I am, back in your villa. Where I have to say goodbye again this morning."

He tipped her head up and kissed her, deeper than when they'd fumbled before. She tasted like life. Or his own life bubbled up so that they shared kisses that tasted like wine. With her hair free of its veil, he let his fingers comb through it, locks falling over his hands in waves.

She shivered, then seemed to recollect that she stood in the kitchen embracing a naked man. With her usual severe posture, she bowed—in the manner of ladies in the Pays de France—and left him to wash.

Orlando again touched that scar, a lengthy line of white along his darker skin, as if light glimmered underneath.

•

After Orlando washed in the pantry, he tugged on the linen and breeches a servant had left for him. The baron's clothes fit him badly, except for the clean stockings. Now, where were his boots? He walked, stocking footed, to Mme Marguerite's workroom, hoping she had them.

Marguerite wasn't there, but Mme Taresa and Mme Hélène intently examined needlework scarves and shawls, Hélène seated on an upholstered stool and Taresa on the bench where Orlando had slept—was it only the previous morning?

"*Bonjour, mesdames.*" He took Mme Hélène's lazily offered hand and kissed it in the style of courts in the Pays de France.

"*Bon dia, capità.*" Taresa spoke in Catalan, so rapidly that he didn't catch all the words. She offered her hand, then seized his when he clasped hers. Heat rushed through his veins again, and then Taresa's hand was excessively hot. "I trust you are well."

Orlando sat on the bench beside her, not sure he could remain standing. Marguerite's grey cat jumped onto his lap, turned in a circle, then nestled down, purring like that creature he'd dreamed of in the stone cave. "*Merci*, madam. I'm grateful that you loaned me your…companion. Unless I've gone mad."

"They say the mistral can have that effect."

"We did it." His voice had returned, but he whispered, claiming their victory.

"And survived." Taresa released his hand.

"And now we leave town as quickly as possible," Hélène said, "since Badoyn remains alive."

"The *baquelar* is alive only because you claimed his fate should be yours to judge, *ma dòmna*," Taresa said.

"I'll return to home to Arles," Hélène said, not answering Taresa. "Captain, you are welcome in my household. And you, Taresa."

"*Mercé, ma dòmna*, but I'm going to Narbonne. I want to see how the rest of the story goes."

Marguerite joined them, carrying more needlework for the two women to inspect, her veil once more in place.

"We are determining what to do next," Orlando said. "I need to depart as soon as possible. And I'm hoping you can give me a few days' worth of trail food."

"*Bien sûr*," Marguerite said. "I'm sorry to say goodbye, Captain. We pulled you into our plan, and now you're in jeopardy because of us."

"Let's settle the captain's fate," Hélène said, "for the summer at least. Do you think he should come to service in my house or Mme Taresa's?" Hélène laid a piece of needlework across her lap, inspecting it closely.

"Or should we help him return to the Pays de France?" Taresa said. "Orlando has family there. We must help with whatever he decides, since he risked so much to help us."

"Indeed," Hélène said. "You were bold, Captain. Diverting your cousin Badoyn's attention. Taking that boy out of the city."

Marguerite rubbed her hands, as if anxious. "But I'm still worried for his safety."

"For the captain? He'll find his way to safety," Hélène said. "We'll take care of him."

"No, for that poor boy." Marguerite was ringing her hands.

"We took great care." Orlando wanted to reassure her, yet the colorful needlework in Hélène's lap kept snatching at his attention. "Believe me, I too worried for the boy, with every heartbeat."

"But our plan worked," Taresa said. "Escape, diversion, relay. Safe as sheep in a pasture. Thanks to our careful planning—and Captain Orlando's great risks. Will you leave this morning, Captain?"

Taresa seemed to be waiting for an answer, but he'd gotten caught up with that needlework. Marguerite had indeed stitched a knight's face into her flowery tapestry. His face. Taresa prodded him. "Captain, we can promise Marguerite that the boy was never at risk, can't we? Surrounded by Catalan and Aragónese warriors."

"Yes, safe and snug." He glanced at Marguerite. Did she see that he'd recognized his face in her needlework? "The king of Aragón is on the way to Narbonne. Perhaps he's there by now, meeting the archbishop."

"But you took Ajax." Marguerite jumped as if startled, still wringing her hands. "As a foil."

"No," Taresa said. "The captain took Galahad."

Marguerite shook her head. "Galahad was sharing his cot with Perseus when we woke the boys this morning. Isn't that why you asked for food, so you can take him out of the city?"

29
Balthazar in the Wilderness

"NOT GALAHAD?"

Orlando's throat worked now. His thoughts raced while the world once more turned upside down.

"When will Tomás and Chrétien discover the mistake?" Taresa seemed calm, though perhaps Orlando didn't know her well enough to guess. Orlando's heart beat so hard, he felt grateful again that it no longer had a hole.

He said, "As soon as Karles sees the boy in daylight."

"What next then?" Hélène said.

"Likely they're asking the same thing right now," Taresa said. "While cursing my name."

"No, they're casting my name to the devil," Orlando said. "I'm the one who carried the wrong boy out of the villa."

"Tomás will blame me. I bragged that I had the better plan."

"There's no priest here," Hélène said. "So no need to exaggerate your sins. Or to worry about Tomás."

Taresa said, "I'm not worried about Tomás. Only jittery."

"We can surely trust that Karles will keep Ajax safe." Orlando's thoughts rattled like a stone in a tin cup.

Marguerite said, "How will you protect Galahad?"

The note in her voice—masking terror—struck at Orlando, for how much he'd worried over his own fate, while Marguerite had risked all for Galahad. She still worried for these boys, while he'd been thinking about how to run. *Fool, fool!*

"Who's watching Galahad now?" His voice croaked, like it had when he first could speak again

"One of Mme Hélène's house-knights," Marguerite said. "One we borrowed yesterday. He and Perseus have been with Galahad since breakfast. In the barracks."

Taresa said, "We have to get Galahad out of the city right now. Before Simon returns."

"Before Badoyn has a chance to bribe any of the guards to do something dirty," Hélène added.

"Badoyn thinks that Pedro's son is on his way to the archbishop." Orlando said it as fact, while trying to remember what words had been exchanged before the battle began.

"Our relay stations are all undone." Taresa's calm seemed unworldly. "The men and horses have all headed for their homes or joined the others in Narbonne."

"I'll leave with Galahad now." Orlando couldn't see another way, though he felt as frantic as when he'd heard hoofbeats on the Narbonne road. "Mme Marguerite, where are my boots?"

"I'll come with you." Taresa began to hand off to Mme Hélène the linen in her lap.

He didn't argue, but noticed Marguerite's startled expression. "We'll have to go overland, not down the Narbonne road. Is your little army still in the hills?"

"No," Taresa shook her head. "Our courier already sent them on to Narbonne."

"Go now," Hélène said. "I'll remain for a day to handle rumors."

"Will you be safe?" Taresa asked.

"Me? I'm the dowager marquesa of Beaurain. And I've been grievously betrayed," Hélène said. "My protégé eloped to Paris with a penniless fortune hunter."

"How can I help?" Marguerite watched only Orlando, who'd found his boots and sat on the bench by Taresa again to put them on.

"Keep the other boys safe," Orlando said. "Which you've been doing, heroically, madam. Be surprised that any boy is missing. And that I'm missing."

"Once more, Captain?" Marguerite's voice grew warm with emotion, which he recognized but likely the other women did not.

"We'll get a message to you as soon as we are safe," Taresa said. "It will take us a couple of days longer to get to Narbonne, since we'll be riding overland."

"We won't be in danger," Orlando said, "once we're in the hills. Simon won't be back until tomorrow. Do you ride well, Mme Taresa?"

"Made it home from Andalusia." Taresa was up and ready to follow him, though she still clutched that tapestry with his face embroidered into the picture, her hand on Marguerite's shoulder. "I promise to keep them safe, Marguerite. Keep Hélène here with you, so she can plead that she didn't know I'd left."

"Remain in a house with wild boys?" Hélène frowned.

"You are safe in my workroom," Marguerite said.

"Or," Taresa said, "go nurse your *bon amic* in the monks' infirmary. Help Badoyn survive until—"

"Until the angels of judgment appear?" Hélène brightened. "I'll return home to Arles once I hear you're safe."

When Orlando stood, Marguerite reached for him, and Orlando did not care how the other two women perceived it. He embraced her. Spoke into her hair. Which smelled of mint and lavender. "We two are joined in this. I can't say farewell, though I don't know how we'll meet again. But I'll find away, as soon as Galahad is safe."

"Just tell me where you are," Marguerite said. "I made it here from Paris by myself with far less to call me. I shall come to you."

"If you both live long enough, I'll make sure she travels to where you are." Hélène interrupted their farewell. "Run now, Captain."

"Deep in my heart," Marguerite said, "I believe that Galahad will be happier if you take Perseus, too."

■

Mme Marguerite stood under the portico, arms wrapped around herself as if the wind that stirred her veil and skirts was much colder. Mme Hélène remained beside her, an arm around the taller woman's waist as if offering her comfort, though it had never before seemed that Hélène had any to offer.

Taresa insisted they meet at Mme Agnes's villa, so she could dress to travel, also insisting that she'd bring the two boys to her villa while Orlando fetched horses.

He'd sent word ahead to the knights' stable, so when Orlando arrived, Master Ansel had Midnight and a sumpter mare saddled and ready.

Ansel said, "The way they carried you into the city this morning, I'm surprised the monks let you out of their infirmary."

"Just bruises and a headache," Orlando said. "It looked bad, but it was another knight's wounds that drenched me."

"And now you're out to inspect the massacre site, Captain?" Ansel grimaced, then he tilted his head. "Or do you plan to find the Catalan knights missing from your questing party?"

"We need Simon's knights to help search the countryside," Orlando said. "The rumors I heard on the way here? No one wants to go farther than the villages until Simon returns."

"Yes," Ansel nodded. "It was hard to gather a dozen guards willing to ride out last night when the horses returned without riders. What do you suppose became of those Catalan knights who rode with you?"

"They were rich enough to hold for ransom," Orlando said. "Any man with the sense of a goat knows it's foolish to kill a man of rank and lose a ransom. Which makes me wonder why my cousin didn't surrender instead of fighting."

"But you, Captain Orlando? You returned covered in blood. No surrender for you?"

"Not one soul in Christendom would ransom me."

Ansel laughed, slapping Orlando's shoulder. "So what chore are you off to?"

That offered Orlando the chance to tell the tale he wanted to circulate through the guards and then throughout the city.

"I intend to carry my condolences to my sergeant Umbert's widow. And I have another chore. Mme Agnes—do you know her? The martyr's widow who lives near the *petit* well? Her servants found a trio of orphans sleeping in her garden this morning. I'm taking them back to St-Marco village, where they belong."

"How—" Ansel's eyes widened in surprise.

"The guards did a poor job of counting the departures last night. Otherwise, there'd have been a search when the numbers didn't match those who came into the city for market day."

"*Aiieee!*" Ansel exclaimed. "But what can we expect? Seems like Simon sent the worst of his infantry here to hold this city. Then he expects these crumbling walls to protect us."

"He left only a handful of us to manage the *gardes du corps*. And now we're missing Louis. May the Holy Mother and all the saints guide his soul."

Ansel struck his fist to his chest, bowing his head. "A good man. I hope Simon lets his wife keep her house. She's widow of a martyr to God's work, too, like Mme Agnes."

"Will your wife visit her? I know Mme Marguerite expects to spend the afternoon with Louis's wife."

"Ah, that widow is a good woman, too. We take care of our own, don't we, Captain?"

Orlando nodded, then said adieu. *You're leaving that woman alone. Marguerite, who loves you. Who will take care of her?*

He wanted to sling all the defenses against demon-thoughts that he'd practiced the last few days. But it was his own thoughts, his own concerns about doing what was proper and honorable.

By the time he'd walked to the stable and then to Mme Agnes's villa, his confusion had turned to fury over being tricked, and then he turned to the most appropriate target for his fury: his own careless action, not realizing he'd carried away the wrong boy.

At Mme Agnes's house, Taresa appeared at the door when he knocked, and the noisy music of a tumult of boys rang behind her. She'd managed the removal of two boys from the academy by bringing all the boys to sweep this villa's attic, supervised by Mme Hélène's borrowed house-knights. A trio of servants loaded travel packs onto the two horses.

Just inside the foyer, Galahad and Perseus waited, Renard close by. The boys more closely resembled Robi, dressed in raggedy linsey-woolsey, which Taresa also wore. Perfect for the story Orlando told Ansel. Except for Perseus's boots. But Orlando only had to point, and Perseus went into the garden to smear them with dust.

When Taresa ran to fetch another blanket, Orlando folded his arms in a posture he knew intimidated delinquent boys, and asked about the previous evening's desertion. He needed to be stern, but he had to swallow his anger, knowing it had been his mistake, not a transgression by these boys.

"Thank you for joining us on this journey, *garçons.*" Then he addressed Perseus, since he felt uneasy about scolding a king, even though that particular little boy kept finding trouble. "How was it that Galahad came to remain in the city last night? We had a plan to carry him to safety."

"We also were seeking safety, Monsieur Captain." Perseus answered in French. "I overheard Umbert and Badoyn on the portico, after Galahad came home from his Quest. Badoyn claimed you were going to help seize—he called it 'the prize.' But I knew he meant Galahad."

"Why would you believe him? Didn't you already know my cousin is a scoundrel?"

"Umbert told Badoyn—" Perseus folded his arms, perhaps mimicking Orlando "—that you didn't want Simon to call you traitor. So you'd do whatever Badoyn told you."

"Umbert said that where you could hear?" Why ask? Orlando knew his cousin—and Umbert—to be fools, not cunning conspirators.

"Everyone else was in the refectory. But in truth, neither man possessed much mother wit, Captain."

"I see." His walk to and from the stable had given Orlando time to overcome confusion and fury. Now he began to feel awe, listening to Perseus's calm explanation.

Galahad said, "When Karles told me of the plan to leave Carcassona, I asked whether you'd come to Narbonne, and he said no."

"Because," Perseus said, "you're a Frankish knight, Captain. Not a sworn knight of Aragón."

Orlando wanted to cry out: Why didn't you ask me? But he quickly understood that, after they'd overheard Umbert, neither Galahad nor Perseus had any way to verify Orlando's loyalty.

"So we made a plan with Ajax," Galahad said, "who was my only friend in Fanjeau."

"I knew Taresa was going to follow you," Perseus said, no note of apology in his voice. Orlando finally saw that the boy was older than the eight years he'd guessed when they met. "So we intended to follow Taresa out of the city. We knew for certain that we'd be with Pedro's knights if we went with Taresa. But she left the city before we could find her."

Galahad exclaimed, "Then Perseus said we had to leave on our own." He looked to Perseus for agreement.

"Yes, Captain. Everyone who was supposed to protect Galahad left the city. Except Mme Marguerite. And she wouldn't be able to protect Galahad when Badoyn came back to the city. So we left."

"*Je suis desolé*, Captain. We thought your cousin had deceived you," Galahad said. "We should have trusted you."

"You spent the night outside the walls? But Mme Marguerite found you in the barracks at breakfast."

"We planned to shelter in a place Taresa showed me," Perseus answered.

"But then Renard found us and led us to Robi and Lop," Galahad said.

"So it was late when we came to find the shelter," Perseus said. "We'd already heard the horses coming back. Then we heard the guards riding out."

"And when we crawled into the shelter, we found you there, Captain."

"Was it you who saved me, *garçons?*"

"We could only drag you to the river. You're too big to take through…" Perseus trailed off, stopping short of the missing detail that Orlando hadn't yet heard: that they had a way in and out of the city besides through the Narbonnese gate. Too narrow for a tall knight, but adequate for boys, a greyhound, and a young woman with an invisible guardian angel. Orlando's thoughts darted to which rotten parts of the wall might contain a secret exit. The ruined river gate, or—

"Robi went to find people to take you back to the city," Galahad said.

Perseus said, "And then Robi said he'd spied Taresa at the shelter, looking for you. So we decided to go back to the city, that we'd be safe."

"I thank you for your service, *garçons*. But you put Ajax in peril." That was the hare-minded part he disliked, now that he understood why they'd run from the original plan.

"Ajax begged to serve our cause," Galahad said. "He's my true comrade, like you taught us. We learned from you to be faithful and help each other."

Except they hadn't trusted their captain. Orlando felt bruised around his newly repaired heart.

"Ajax intended to shout his real name if your cousin appeared." Perseus folded his arms, insistent that they'd made proper choices. "Or if you were—"

"—tricked into helping your cousin," Galahad said. "He's Ganelon, isn't he? Like in Roland's story?"

"Yes, *garçons*. He's a traitor. Are you ready to ride?"

The greyhound nuzzled Galahad, taking his attention from Orlando's inquiry. "Can Renard come, Captain?"

"If you will obey your captain this time," Orlando said.

"We obey!" the two boys shouted.

Orlando dropped to his knee, since the moment seemed like it needed more from him. "And I swear upon St-Denis and the Holy Mother of Our Lord that I shall protect you with my life."

He put the two raggedy "orphan" boys on the two horses. Orlando and Taresa held the reins, walking the horses to the Narbonnese gate.

"Going into the wilderness dressed as an orphan boy this time?" Orlando asked. "Not a magical knight?"

"Best way to get through the gate," she said. "I'll become Tarek again after we retrieve our cached armor."

"Then I didn't dream that? Or the story you told? Will you tell me what magic you used?" He'd grown used to having a whole body, *sans* pain, which left him inclined to accept that impossible things had happened.

"No magic. I was intent on keeping you awake, Captain."

"But they killed you." As he'd seen in his dark visions, like Louis and Mme Estela had died in the ways he envisioned. "Then you weren't dead. I don't know what to believe."

"Surely you believe what we did together, you and I?"

"We killed those men."

"So they wouldn't kill us. You've been on the wrong side since you left Troyes, Captain. Last night, you fought your way to the right side. And, lucky for you, I stopped Badoyn from killing you." Taresa smiled up at him. "Though perhaps I was only a servant to your mother's charm."

"*Merci.* Did you indeed carry me on your shoulders for a league? And put that sphynx creature on me to fix my wounds?" The magic of the past night's disordered world haunted him. "And you've listened to my thoughts since we met. Is that magic, too?"

"No, it's not magic. And I can't hear your thoughts. That's why I didn't know about Marguerite and you." She touched his hand.

"It's rude to spy on what's private." He shook off her hand. "If you did indeed lend me your magical companion—if I didn't dream that—can your companion also protect Galahad?"

He felt that he was in an upside-down world. Once before the world had felt all wrong—when catastrophe fell in Constantinople. It took months to accept it. This mirrored that upset, except this time he was well. He had to accept this change quickly, since this time the shook-up world had treated him reasonably well. Already, he felt more assured fleeing from Carcassona than he'd felt the day before.

"Oh. Uh, I didn't think…we didn't think…" She fell silent, perhaps talking to her magical companion.

At the Narbonnese gate, while the midafternoon nones bell rang, the guards were stopping everyone who sought to leave the city. Orlando felt confident that the guards had already heard from Ansel that Captain Orlando was on an errand to correct a mistake the guards had made the day before. But the line through the gate wasn't moving, and the guards were pressing people to move away from the gate.

"May we pass?" Orlando asked. The guard was one of the men he'd upbraided on Tuesday for transgressing on laundry women in the early-morning inspections, but the man either had no memory of the incident or bore no ill will.

"*Je suis désolé*, Captain. The road is closed while a large party rides up the trail to the city."

Taresa tugged Orlando's jerkin. "Who is it?"

The boys slipped off the horses, huddling near Orlando and Taresa. Perseus said, "*Aiieee*, it's Simon! We're too late!"

"Let's pray that it's not Simon," Orlando said. *S'il vous plait. Not Simon.* He strained to hear the answer to the questions the guards at the gate shouted up to the men atop the wall.

Then six guards found great joy, joining in pairs to grasp ends of lance poles to form make-do barricades and shove the small crowd at the gate back up into the streets. They stepped past Orlando, seemingly out of deference, but caught Perseus and Galahad, shoving them back among the laundrywomen and bakers' boys seeking to return home after work.

"*C'est Simon!*" A voice called from the watchtower. "I spy the vicomte's banner."

The faces of the boys Orlando swore to protect appeared and disappeared amid the three dozen women and children being herded away from the gate.

"*Arrêter! Arrêter! Arrêter!*" Orlando shouted, but he was as disregarded by Perseus and Galahad as he had been in the riot at St-Luc village.

Guards echoed the call along the tower, though any man with ears could hear the first call. Others on the wall argued. *C'est Simon! Ce n'est pas Simon! Non, bricon, c'est Simon!*

"*Aiieee!*" Taresa cried. "The boys! They're gone."

"We have to go—" What? He held the reins, jammed between the make-do barricade and the guards.

"I'll find them," she called to him in Catalan. Taresa ducked under the barricade, springing into the crowd. "Stay with the horses. Meet me at our armor cache."

"No. Wait, we shall..." Dropping the reins to the ground, he pushed at the barricade to follow her. The guards pushed back, then pushed against the crowd again.

Along the wall above the gate, another guard shouted, "It's not Simon, you fools."

A watchtower guard shouted, "I'm not blind, *bricon*. It's Simon."

No sign of any boy or Renard the French dog. Or Taresa. They'd already retreated into the city streets.

"It's a Church banner," a guard on the wall called. Then: "There's a herald riding up to the gate."

Outside the gate, a voice called out in heavily accented French.

"Pietro di Benevento bears a message for Simon de Montfort from the Most Holy Father, Pope Innocent. We request shelter in Carcassona while Monseigneur Pietro conducts the Holy Father's business."

God's bones! It was the prelate, the pope's lawyer, that Simon had complained about—and instructed Orlando and Louis to clean the neighborhood of rebels and heretics before this prelate arrived.

A cry rang around the wall from guard to guard.

Then another cry, just as Orlando bent to retrieve the reins of the two horses that stamped beside him, uneasy in the milling crowd.

"Orlando de Troyes! Captain!"

Startled, Orlando looked to the guards. "Why call my name?"

"The chancellor and his deputy left with Simon," one guard said.

"And Captain Louis got himself killed by heretics," said another.

"So you have to welcome this pope's man. We're opening the gates now, Captain, with your permission."

"*Bien,*" Orlando said. But it wasn't fine. "Send a messenger to tell the bishop we have guests." Though surely everyone at the St-Nazaire basilica heard the guards' shouts. He called up to the men on the wall over the gate. "Proclaim a welcome to Monseigneur Pietro di Benevento, a prelate from the Most Holy Father."

And shout it loud enough that Taresa and the boys can hear. It's not Simon!

Midnight nosed Orlando, shoving him forward. He reached to calm his horse while the guards opened the gates. Taresa must have heard the shouts. Since it wasn't Simon, perhaps she'd return as soon as she found the boys. Or were the three of them escaping, so he'd have to find a way out the gates as soon as possible to join them? And where was last night's magic? He needed some now.

30
Old Ashes

THE HERALD, WITH THREE RIDERS behind him, dismounted at the gate. The *gardes du corps* at the gates hung back, leaving Orlando to step forward to meet the man.

It's only a herald. You're a knight from the Pays de France.

As Orlando crossed to greet the herald, he relaxed into hearing his own thoughts instead of a spiteful imp's. However, once Taresa had touched his hand earlier and then left his side, he again limped a bit. It just didn't hurt much. Which must mean that she'd reclaimed her magical companion, so he had no help in this new predicament.

At least he didn't feel jittery about this encounter, because most every possible catastrophe had already happened. The prelate was Simon's problem, not his. Orlando's sole problem to be solved was to get himself and his horses on the other side of the city gates. And find Taresa and the boys.

The herald said, "Pietro di Benevento requests audience with the vicomte Simon de Montfort."

"Vicomte Simon is gone from the city until tomorrow," Orlando said. "I'm Orlando de Troyes, next in command here. And I'm happy to make your master welcome."

"Orlando de Troyes?" The herald spoke French with an odd accent. "You're Fabien's son? I knew your father at Acre. *Bonjour*, Captain! I'm called Matthew. I rode under William of Sicily. Though I'm sure your father has never mentioned me."

"I salute your service in the Outremer, monsieur. Regretfully, I lost my father before I was old enough to hear stories about his companions."

"May God rest his soul." Matthew the herald had his hand over his heart. "Fabien was an honorable man and a great warrior."

Such peaceful words, while Orlando's insides roiled and he longed to rush past the herald and escape the city.

"It is kind of you to say so." Orlando then offered formal welcome to the city. "We shall do what's needed for the comfort of the Monseigneur, your master, while waiting for Simon to return."

"I believe, for a certainty," the herald said, "that the prelate wants to begin his business today. Is His Holiness the bishop here in Carcassona? Can you call him to greet the Monseigneur?

"Rather than calling the bishop out into all this dust," Orlando spoke as if he knew what he was doing, "shall we congregate at the basilica, to discuss the prelate's business there?"

The affable herald agreed, and yet Orlando saw no fit time to say what mattered most: that anything the bishop or Simon said about heretics or lost tithes in the neighborhood would be wrong, misconceived. And last night's massacre—the bishop was bound to raise it—came about because of Simon's evil, not heretics, not bandits.

How could he express the truth to the herald or the prelate?

That the Peace of God would reign here if Simon would let it?

That the pope should worry about Simon grabbing power, not about innocent herb-women and addled old ladies and shepherds who kept saying that it will all be as it pleases the Good God?

Matthew the herald said, "I shall leave the proper welcome in your hands."

While the guests entered the gate and the quiet city bustled to receive them, Orlando continuously calculated how to slink out the gate with the horses. As moments passed, he came to believe that his companions had escaped through their secret passage—with no trail food, no blankets, no horses. How long until he could join Taresa and the boys? One of Ansel's squires appeared, sent to take charge of his horses. Orlando didn't have an excuse to stop him while surrounded by a dozen sergeants asking what they were supposed to do next to accommodate the visitors.

"The same as you would if it were Simon." Orlando snapped the answer, impatient.

But what he heard as a pair of sergeants walked away: "*Salaud arrogant.* Thinks he's better'n us."

Arrogant? No, desperate. *Quiet your heart.* If he retained any of the magic from the previous night, if Taresa hadn't carried it all away, it was the voice that insisted he calm his pounding heart, save his blood. But instead he had to be assiduously polite to the herald and the half-dozen sergeants from the prelate's party, who clung close by his side, each seeking instruction from him.

When a large party comes into any city, everyone is thrown into their grandest roles: The stablemasters shout abrupt commands to squires to help water, feed, and wipe down the horses, and then move them to paddocks; the chandler calls to servants to bring water, wine, and refreshments to the visitors, to be served in the proper order; sergeants of the *gardes du corps* show the traveling sergeants where to camp in the yard outside the chateau; duty-sergeants show visiting knights where they might bivouac in the chateau's inner courtyard or take up bunks in the bachelors' tower.

The ill-trained *gardes du corps* of Carcassona seemed struck dumb with the thrill of escorting and assisting these visitors, most of whom were Knights Templar, dressed in their finest surcoats, chainmail ringing softly as they moved, war sword buckled at each knight's side, battle helmet tucked under each knight's left arm.

The *gardes du corps* stumbled about, overawed. Orlando—who cared only about joining Taresa and the boys—had encountered bands of Knights Templar frequently. First, in the crusade that ended up invading Constantinople. Then at the siege of Minerve, though they didn't appear until the final days, since this expedition of peace in the south did not seem to interest the Templars, except for how the chaos disrupted their supply lines in support of other missions. And then he'd encountered them in the city as travelers, using Carcassona as a resting stop on their way to other Templar holdings. On this day, Orlando observed the awe with which the wretched *gardes du corps* treated the visiting Templars, without feeling that awe himself. He'd talked with men like these, understood how faith was coupled with honor to drive them to be the best warriors they could be. All of them, like him, *hommes célibataire*.

But for Orlando, it was pursuit of his own honor as a knight that drove him. Not faith. And not because that evil imp had kept him from performing more than beseeching prayers. Just as the last visiting knights arrived, Orlando determined he was like Tomás and Chrétien. He was a knight solely for the sake of honor. And now that he knew, he'd live up to his father's honor. That idea felt invigorating, as if he'd woken to find new blood flowed in his veins.

The last riders came through the gate, and Orlando found himself finally away from that herald's side, so he moved through the crowds as if with purpose, though his purpose was to retrieve his horses and get through the Narbonnese gate.

At the knights' stable, a commotion drew the squires away— just the kind of magic he needed! But before he entered the stable, the color and emblems on the surcoats of the dismounting French knights caught his eye.

The slate-blue and snow-white colors of the marquis de Beaurain.

When Orlando lay in the hospital tent outside Minerve, the day they burned the heretics, that was when he last saw the exiled knight that he and Badoyn had betrayed in Constantinople. The French knight was that day's hero, having convinced Minerve to surrender. The next day, the day when Orlando's knights deserted him and stole his horses and armor, Hugues de Beaurain died. That formerly exiled knight was named the new marquis de Beaurain.

Here in Carcassona, Jean-Luc de Chartrain, the new marquis de Beaurain, dismounted from a beautiful black war horse, shook dust from his slate-blue surcoat. He was, as Orlando had seen him five years earlier, a powerfully built, giant of a man. Jean-Luc pushed back his coif, revealing dark, luxuriant hair, proving to be, as his grandmother used to say, more handsome than should be good for a man. The marquis paused to speak with a white-haired, black-clad man who'd also dismounted. They shook hands, agreeing on something before the white-haired fellow walked off with a coterie of knights. The marquis glanced about, then advanced toward Orlando, who felt he might catch fire, burn, and turn to ash. Jean-Luc held out his hand in formal greeting, like one French knight to an equal. Orlando shook the hand of the French knight whose life he'd helped to ruin in Constantinople.

The marquis smiled. "They say you are Orlando of Troyes. My father fought with yours at Acre. He always spoke of Fabien as the most honorable man. *Bonjour*, Captain!"

.

Just outside the great oak doors of the St-Nazaire basilica, where the Templar knights and others piled their weapons in the traditional sign of peace, Orlando stood trapped beside the marquis de Beaurain. He forced himself to attend only to the papal legate who'd come to Carcassona, who was being flattered and praised by the bishop to such an embarrassing degree that most of the men in the legate's party shuffled, uneasy. Except Jean-Luc, who kept the stoic calm that French knights of honor learned from the cradle to present in exalted company.

The legate, a small, slim man, resembled Renard the greyhound: lithe, bred for performance. Exotically handsome, dark, with a tidily trimmed mustache and goatee. He wore his riding clothes, which were garnet-colored leathers and a surcoat lined with lambswool, but no chainmail. The leathers fit him so tightly, you might guess they'd been stitched on him, and his tall leather boots had been shined and oiled, so that he gleamed, in spite of riding in the southern dust.

Although a small man, when the legate Pietro spoke, the words came out as if he were singing, his accented French a rich kind of music. Which contrasted with the bishop's screechy but perfectly pronounced French. The bishop had sufficient warning from messengers, so he had chairs in the basilica's portico for himself and his guest, with a small table between them to hold refreshments. The marquis, Orlando, and everyone else stood in the sun at the edge of the portico, the knights and clerks at rest while the bishop offered almond cakes and wine.

And then the bishop went on to embarrass himself, to Orlando's way of thinking, with excessive flattery. "It is with God's blessing that we have the gift of your visit. Monseigneur Arnaud, the archbishop at Narbonne, shared your *Compilatio tertia*. A remarkable treatise!

This is a lifetime wish, that we could consult with a canon lawyer who has earned the esteem of all of Christendom."

Please, let the fool keep talking. Talk until the vesper bell. Orlando watched this exchange, praying that the flattery and formal language would draw out for long moments, while Taresa moved the boys to safety. Away from Simon's reach. But without food, blankets, or horses. His heart beat like it had in battle the night before, yet he could neither flee nor fight. *Calm your heart.* He'd find a way to join them.

The legate smiled, modestly declined the bishop's tributes, and let the bishop natter on until he ran out of words. Then Pietro took command of the conversation.

"His Holiness Innocent, the third of that name, has instructed me to adjudicate for the people who have come to him for aid."

"Excellent!" the bishop squeaked. "What better resolution than that those most interested in the Peace of God in Christendom shall protect God's appointed rulers."

Pietro set down the wine cup, from which he had never once sipped, and folded his arms. "Indeed. We shall work together to resolve the question of who shall hold the son of Pedro d'Aragón until he is of age to rule."

God's bones! This was the boy-king's rescuer, sent by the Church. Except the boy was likely out roaming the Pays d'Òc countryside.

"Monseigneur!" The bishop seemed surprised.

"While we debate the question," Pietro said, "the Holy Father requests that I hold the safekeeping of the boy-king."

"A truly fine idea!" The bishop clapped his hands, and began a soliloquy about how the Church was God's best shepherd on earth for how men were to be led to righteousness by priests and kings.

Every fiber in his body wanted to run, to find Taresa and retrieve the boys. But honor demanded that Orlando stand waiting for a calamity, stiff as the best of soldiers, beside the marquis and a phalanx of Knights Templar. Among the worst of those long moments, the marquis caught Orlando glancing over his shoulder to search the basilica courtyard and the nearby wall and towers with hopes that Taresa might reappear.

"Pietro should be asking you." The marquis whispered to Orlando as if they were conspirators. "But let the bishop have his charade."

The shiver up Orlando's backbone was like nothing he'd endured when tortured by that evil ghost-imp. That whisper buzzed in his ears, so he couldn't hear the bishop's blandishments and accolades. Pietro, the prelate, held up his hand, and it felt like the signal from a general to launch an attack.

"I should like to meet the king of Aragón." Pietro's musical voice surged with command. "Bring the boy."

"We don't have him here." The bishop spoke calmly.

"Truly?" Pietro managed to seem friendly while challenging at the same moment. Was it a trick canon lawyers knew? "We came from Fanjeau, where they assured us that Simon brought the boy to Carcassona a few days ago."

Nudging Orlando, Jean-Luc nodded in a way that might have been meant to be reassuring. Orlando shook his head.

Jean-Luc disregarded Orlando's refusal. "Monseigneur, I believe Captain Orlando de Troyes guards the boy."

"Is that true?" Pietro asked, his eyes fixed on Orlando, whom he'd scarcely acknowledged when introduced upon arriving in the city. His eyes now sought to peer into Orlando's soul.

"*Oui*, Monseigneur," Orlando said. "Jaume of Aragón was put in my charge on Tuesday. He has been kept safe in my school for *juvenes*...for pages." He took a breath to admit that he'd only lost the boy since the nones bell, that he had a strong belief about how to find him again.

"Will you please bring the boy to me, Captain?"

"*Salut! Salut!*"

The guards atop the wall again set up a cry: More travelers approached the city. Calls for identifying the new arrivals echoed to the watchtower, where the guards had a view of the entire countryside. Before Orlando could answer the legate, another cry went out from the tower.

"It's the vicomte! Simon is returning to the city!"

A subdued voice from the tower added, "*Je te l'avais dit!*"

I told you so. With Simon's arrival proclaimed across the neighborhood, neither Taresa nor the boys would return to the city or come out from where they might be hiding.

Orlando had spent four years pondering how to leave Carcassona for a better life, how to be treated as a bannered knight once more. Now, he likely wouldn't live through even one more tolling of the bell in the basilica tower if he didn't produce Galahad immediately—and then find a way out of the city. *Traitor! That's what Simon will call you.*

31
Livre le Roi!

"WE DON'T NEED TO WAIT for Simon. Don't you agree, Monseigneur, my dear friend? Let us meet the king of Aragón, if you please."

The prelate's barbed pleasantries were intended for the bishop, who didn't seem perturbed. It was only Orlando, hemmed in between Jean-Luc and a dozen Knights Templar, who needed to flee, both to find the lost boy and to avoid Simon's certain censure of his failures.

"If you will allow me, I shall fetch him," Orlando said, all the while calculating. Get a horse. Ride out the gate. Find the trio on the Narbonne road. Ride back. Before the vesper bell.

A monk stepped onto the portico, standing beside the bishop. "That man," the monk pointed to Orlando, "is a traitor to his oath. Do not allow him to leave the city."

"This man," Jean-Luc said, "is a French knight of honor."

God's bones! Was there a less likely person in Christendom to assert Orlando's honor?

"What are you saying?" The prelate looked between the bishop and Jean-Luc. Because the world had turned upside down, Orlando clung to the hope that Pietro paid more credence to Jean-Luc than to the bishop.

The monk didn't hesitate. "I tended a knight who survived an attack of insurgent rebels last night. He says this captain gave the boy-king to Catalan mercenaries and then participated in the massacre of half a dozen *gardes du corps.*"

"As God is my Savior, that is false," Orlando said, though it was only partly false: They were loyal knights of Aragón, not mercenaries. And it wasn't Jaume d'Aragón that they took from Carcassona. "As you shall see today—"

"What are *they* doing here?" Jean-Luc hissed beside him.

Orlando followed where Jean-Luc stared.

Tomás and Chrétien crossed the yard to the basilica, parting the crowd of Templars, hellfire burning in Tomás's dark eyes, soul-freezing ice in Chrétien's. Karles, the stoic Aragón knight, followed with Ajax on his shoulders.

"Praise be to God," Jean-Luc said. "Here is the king."

"No," Chrétien said, stopping a few steps from the portico. "This is Ajax, who is also called Francois de St-Severin. His father is a bannered knight from Orleans now living in Fanjeau. For a boy so young, he is an excellent rider. But he's no king."

Jean-Luc held his hand out to the prelate. "Monseigneur, may I present these knights of Pedro d'Aragón. Don Tomás de Morella. Chrétien of Cyprus and Toulouse. Karles of Barcelona. They are sworn to protect Pedro's son." He turned to the three knights. "His holiness, the cardinal Pietro di Benevento has been sent—"

Tomás interrupted, arms crossed. "With all respect, Monsenyor, it's about time! It certainly took long enough."

The prelate took quiet pains to describe the cardinals' discussions and the pope's decisions, and how long it took him to travel. Orlando shifted, wracked with nervous anxiety. Then a commotion atop the wall grabbed his attention. A blond thatch of hair caught the afternoon sun. A boy ran along the top the wall. Another figure followed, a red scarf waving behind. When they reached the Church mill tower, two dogs leapt, pulling down a guard who'd turned to see the commotion. A clutch of boys ran out the other side of the tower, a smaller boy riding on the tallest figure's shoulders. The tall one must be Taresa, carrying Galahad. The blond head was Perseus. Given that there were two dogs, the other boy must be Robi

"*Par tous les Saints dans le ciel!*" Jean-Luc sighed.

Mme Hélène stalked across the basilica yard, headed for the Church mill tower, her crimson skirts tossed by the mistral. Just ahead of her, risen from what they said was his deathbed, Badoyn pulled open the heavy oak door and entered the tower.

Forgetting about fleeing the city, Orlando jumped from the line of knights standing outside the basilica. He grabbed a sword from the pile of arms that knights had deposited outside the basilica. He sprinted for the city wall, but not for where he'd seen the boys or for where Badoyn was climbing a tower, pursued by Hélène. He ran instead for the ruined Roman tower, certain that was where the boys and Taresa were headed. That half-decayed tower must lead to their secret escape from the city.

He scrambled over fallen stones and broken steps, the passage-way up the ruined tower increasingly difficult once he passed the first floor, where guards gambled after curfew. He wanted to believe what he'd seen, that Taresa had Galahad on her shoulders. *She's sharing her companion's protection against steel.*

Hoping her magic worked, Orlando reached the top of the tower and stepped from the ruins onto the wall. Taresa appeared, holding Galahad on her shoulders. Perseus and Robi stood in front of her, the two dogs barking furiously when Badoyn approached them.

Two guards had followed the boys, but when Orlando emerged from the ruined tower, he waved them away. "I'll handle it!" he called. The guards didn't care for the dogs, and so readily turned and tramped back to their posts in the Church mill tower.

"Henri!" Taresa called to Perseus. "Take the dagger from my boot!" While Perseus complied, arming himself, Robi snatched up gravel from the rubble strewn near the tower, pelting Badoyn with his slingshot.

"*Arrête!*" Badoyn call for them to stop. He held out his hands as if pleading. "I only want to help you."

While the dogs barked madly, the boys shouted the worst names they knew, in three languages. Perseus and Robi knew some that Orlando had never heard.

"Cousin!" Orlando hoped his voice was greater than the others' shouts and barks. "It's too late! A prelate is here. Simon has returned. Give up your evil designs!"

He pushed through the boys, facing Badoyn with a sword, poised like a knight in a fable. Prepared to protect a king with his life, like his father.

"No one needs to be hurt or unhappy here," Badoyn said, in his familiar oily purr. "It's still our chance, Balthazar, to seize glory."

"I won't allow you to hurt this boy."

"Hurt? No, it's time to rescue the child. To deliver him to the Church." Badoyn motioned, as if Orlando should come join him. "This is your chance, O righteous knight! Blow your horn like Roland, to warn kings. We shall be heroes."

Orlando blinked, confused about what Badoyn meant.

"*Doutz Jhezu!*" Hélène swore softly, speaking in the local tongue. "You'd sweet-talk your own mother into believing you weren't sired by the Dark God's evil angel."

"Hélène, *ma chère dame amour*. I love you. I think and plan and hope only for you and your happiness."

The small woman tipped her head back as she laughed, a shriek caught on the wind and lifted to heaven, like the mistral lifted her veil high overhead.

While Orlando stood at the ruined tower door, Taresa had forced Badoyn into a niche on the city-side of the wall, where the wall was too high for the crowd in the courtyard of St-Nazaire to see this meeting. Tall as he was, Orlando could see only the sea of Templars and other knights in the courtyard, not the prelate or bishop. Or his new champion, Jean-Luc.

Then Taresa rushed to Orlando, thrusting Galahad on him, so that he dropped his sword to catch the boy. She snatched her dagger back from Perseus and charged Badoyn. The dogs followed at her heels, barking furiously, wanting to get past her to attack.

Her charge toward Badoyn surprised the man, so he delayed defense for a heartbeat, only holding his sword in front of him. When it seemed as if Taresa might impale herself on that sword, she turned, so his blade sliced through her tunic. Blood splashed.

Robi was again slinging pebbles at Badoyn, standing atop the outer wall so that he could aim past Taresa. Badoyn flinched.

"Get down, Robi," Orlando commanded. "Before you fall."

"*Òc, lo mieu capitani!*" He let loose one final pebble, which hit Badoyn in the temple.

Taresa knocked the sword from Badoyn's hands so that it clattered to the wood-and-stone walkway outside the tower. She picked him up as if he were no more a burden than Galahad had been, and balanced him atop the crumbling stone wall.

"An innocent!" Taresa hissed in Catalan. She had her dagger at Badoyn's throat. "You seek to harm an innocent child! And I saw you kill Louis. A cold-blooded murder!"

"My love!" Badoyn turned to Hélène as if she were his savior. "Call away these beasts! Tell them it's—"

"Tell them that you're a scion of that serpent Giles? Using me to hurt my friends?"

"*Arrête!*" Orlando shouted. "We shall take him to justice. We aren't murderers like he is."

"We saw him kill Louis, but who shall believe us?" Taresa said. "He's Simon's mardi gras puppet."

"Who just now declared himself willing to betray Simon to the Church," Orlando said. "For the sake of honor, we want justice, not revenge."

"*Aiieee!*" Badoyn cried. "We can explain the confusion together, cousin. You are the good and noble knight, Balthazar. Whom I have loved and protected."

Hélène walked languidly toward where Taresa had cornered Badoyn along the wall. She held that dagger she's begged for at the Thursday market. "Step aside, Taresa. You promised he'd be mine."

Recognizing what Hélène intended, Orlando called, "No, we must take him to judgment!" He tugged at Perseus and Robi, wanting them inside the tower, away from the scene on the wall. He set Galahad down and motioned all three boys back, then he braced in the arch of the tower door, preventing their view out of the tower.

"Judgment? Before the bishop and vicomte, who both knew what Simon hoped for?" Hélène stood beside Taresa. "They sanctioned it. What justice is possible?"

"I never hurt you," Badoyn pleaded. "Or your friends."

"You," Hélène tapped his jerkin, "and Giles destroyed the life of my own true love. And you bragged to me about it."

"You murdered Louis. I saw you." Taresa repeated what she'd seen on the road to Narbonne.

"Will you let these women stop you from doing the right thing by your family?" Badoyn stared past Hélène to Orlando, his face white with fear. "Do your duty, Balthazar, like the honorable knights of old."

"Do your duty, Orlando," Taresa said, "and protect those boys."

Badoyn still called to Orlando, half sobbing in dismay, cornered by two women and unarmed. If Badoyn rushed past the women, the two dogs would tear him down. "Cousin, let us still be heroes together and carry the child to his saviors. Call your higher angels of righteousness."

"We are the higher angels." Hélène stepped closer. "I am your own angel. But of retribution. Not righteousness."

The marquesa was small, and Taresa not much larger, but they'd trapped Badoyn on the wall's edge, Taresa holding him in place. The two dogs pranced behind the women, barking, as furious as the women. Taresa stepped aside.

Hélène seized a handful of Badoyn's breeches along his inner thigh, that little dagger from the market in her other hand. Badoyn leaned away from her dagger. She stepped close. He leaned back, and she pushed, her whole body a bundle of fury.

Badoyn shrieked as he went over the wall. Doves flew up from the basilica roof.

A cry rose from the crowded courtyard, as if the knights were all a single body. Then shouts and the crunch of gravel as boots thudded across the courtyard.

The dogs ceased barking, trotting back to sit beside Orlando.

"May I borrow your shawl?" Taresa asked Hélène, who still trembled with fury. Or maybe it was the wind. "I'd like to cover this tear in my tunic when we greet people below."

Orlando's heart thumped hard enough for all of them, while these two women stood calm and cold as the mistral after dashing a man to his death. Taresa carefully folded the edges of her slashed and splashed tunic, pinning the shawl Hélène handed her so it covered the bloodied rip. Otherwise, she showed no shock for harm, given the slice she'd taken from Badoyn.

Hélène studied the wall, found a step that allowed her to peer over the wall and see the scene below. "You know, *ma chère fille*, I've decided that you are right. It's evil to use one's…private personal powers…to defeat a man. I swear to never do it again. But we did keep him from murdering a king."

Taresa stood on tiptoes, barely able to see over the wall to observe what Hélène saw. Orlando came away from the tower door to stand beside her. Below, a few Templars were examining the fallen and crushed Badoyn.

"Oh look, *ma chère*." Hélène resumed her languor. "Your uncle Jean-Luc is here. And Simon has arrived. Perhaps neither Jean-Luc nor Simon needs to hear details from any of us."

Taresa's uncle? Orlando stared down where the three tall knights, Jean-Luc and Chrétien and Karles, stood near Tomás of Morella. Hearing Jean-Luc's name revived all the trepidation he'd felt standing by the marquis outside the basilica.

"You don't want Jean-Luc to know what you did for his sake, *ma dòmna?*" Taresa peered over the wall.

"He swears that Constantinople is behind him," Hélène said. The word *Constantinople* sent all that trepidation rampaging through Orlando's heart. "Just like our old affair is behind him. A fire burned in my own heart, seeking to take revenge for his sake. We should let Jean-Luc continue to forget."

The boys shoved at Orlando, wanting past him to see, and thrusting him into Hélène's way. She pulled her veil close, preparing to turn back to the other tower.

"And me?" Orlando called to Hélène. The boys were scrambling around him, then trying to find stone toeholds to boost themselves up, to see over the wall near Taresa. "I was with Giles and Badoyn in Constantinople."

"*Òc, mon ami.*" Hélène nodded, merely agreeing. "Where Giles de Nully promised you a place with knights who swore to act as brothers. May St-Jordi and the Good God find you better brothers than Badoyn and Giles." She passed him, seeking which way to go to leave the wall.

Taresa still peered over the wall. "Tomás and Chrétien are here, too. Chrétien had better produce that sword he owes me."

.

They carried the boys down from the tower, Perseus on Orlando's back, Galahad on Taresa's. Robi and the dogs followed. Hélène took more time, coming after them slowly. They set the boys down before walking out of the ruined tower.

"*Garçons*, wait a moment, *s'il vous plait*." Orlando said. "Come when I call you."

Perseus prepared to protest. "But we—"

"For a few moments more, *garçon*, I am your captain. All *juvenes* do as their captain commands. And so?"

"We obey!" the boys shouted.

When Orlando and Taresa emerged from the tower, several people remained around Badoyn's crumpled body. A monk leaning over him straightened and then finished a blessing. Simon de Montfort stood nearby, his hand on the bishop's shoulder. Simon knelt beside Badoyn's body, bringing the bishop down to kneel with him. First, he folded his hands in prayer, and then laid a hand on Badoyn's breast, over his heart.

"A good and faithful man," Simon said. "Gone to God too soon. Pray for him, Monseigneur."

Likely, not gone to God. But then, what Orlando observed seemed beyond the reach of the bishop's prayer. That sphinx-like creature (what did Taresa call her companion with the beautiful face? Amastri?) crouched on Badoyn's battered torso, then crawled up onto Simon's shoulder. Slithered down his front, reaching a paw inside Simon's jerkin. Deeper than that, as if reaching inside Simon. Then it—she—the spirit was gone.

Close beside Orlando, Taresa drew a breath. And whispered. "I thought she gave your zaar to a wild cat."

Hélène came up beside them. "He jumped." She had a kerchief to her face, weeping into Marguerite's embroidery. "He cried in despair. Said he couldn't live with what he'd done to the baby king."

Simon looked up, startled, began to stand, then grabbed his belly as if in pain. "What are you saying, madam?"

"Badoyn was—he was—a sad and sinful man." Hélène wept. Taresa slipped her arm around Hélène's waist, patted her head, put her own head on Hélène's shoulder for comfort. "He believed that he'd killed the boy-king last night. That mistake was more than his soul could bear."

Behind Simon, Jean-Luc watched the two women. When Orlando caught him staring, the marquis rolled his eyes and folded his arms, not believing a word Hélène said.

Matthew the herald parted people, waving them away, until the prelate Pietro joined the ring around the fallen body of Badoyn of Troyes.

"Gentlemen, it is a tragic moment. But we have important business to complete for the Most Holy Father. I would like to see the boy you are holding, Monsieur Vicomte."

Simon straightened, and pointed at Orlando, his finger wavering. "Captain Orlando has the boy. That is, he's supposed to have the boy, if he and his cousin haven't murdered him."

Orlando stepped away from the tower's crumbling door. He found himself standing beside Jean-Luc, so he needed to take a breath, to reclaim his courage.

"Perseus? Galahad? *Viens à moi.*"

Perseus came out from the tower, standing beside Orlando. Robi came to stand at Orlando's other side.

"I am Henri of Montcava, a seigneur of the Counts of Toulouse and Barcelona." Perseus spoke in the local tongue, not French. He took a breath, glancing back to the tower door. "Monsenyor, please allow me to introduce—"

Perseus looked to Orlando for guidance, who said in French, "Follow the proper order, *garçon*. You introduce this man to the king. He's called Monseigneur Pietro di Benevento, in service to the Most Holy Father, Pope Innocent."

Perseus nodded and repeated the proper form. Then he spoke, again in the local tongue. "We serve Jaume, king by the Grace of God of Aragón, Count of Barcelona and Roussillon, and Lord of Montpelhièr, son of Marie of Montpelhièr and Pedro the Second of Aragón and Barcelona and, as you know, anointed vassal to Innocent the Third of that name of the Holy Roman Church."

Perseus stepped aside, and Galahad came from behind him to stand by Orlando.

"You may also call me Jaime, your Holiness." Galahad looked up to Orlando. "Is that the proper form of address, Captain?"

Galahad's black eye from predawn Wednesday had faded to sick-green and saffron-yellow, more noticeable because the boy's hair had been shaved to a nub. He wore linsey-woolsey rags, too large for him and covered with stone dust and dog hair. Renard the grey-hound stayed by his side, ready to challenge anyone who came closer than he liked.

Robi cried out and fell to his knees.

"Monsenyor? Jaume d'Aragón? Our king?" He tugged at his wolf-collared dog. "Lop, you must bow."

Beside Orlando, towering over where Robi kneeled, Jean-Luc muttered, "Marguerite said to trust you. Please tell me the true story when we're alone."

32
Une Affaire du Coeur

Pietro di Benevento, for being the smallest man among the leaders in the basilica courtyard, was enormously commanding. Simon, the bishop, and Jaume d'Aragón accompanied him to the chateau for conference, surrounded by a dozen Knights Templar who seemed to form the prelate's own guard.

"You did it!" Jean-Luc, the marquis de Beaurain, embraced Taresa, then kissed her hand. "You are the hero you wanted to be."

Beyond their coterie, the young king of Aragón twice looked back at his friends, the prelate at one side, Simon on the other.

"*Merci*, uncle. But it took many people working together."

"Some of whom," Tomás joined them, with Chrétien beside him, "cheated."

"We didn't know about Ajax." Taresa pointed to Orlando, then herself. "You likely knew before we did."

Tomás folded his arms. "But you claimed to possess the grand rescue plan."

"And you didn't have to fight off Badoyn and his knights and guards. And you had use of the relay stations I set up." Taresa mirrored his stance, her arms folded.

"How—" Chrétien began. "No, what we must do next is to protect our *petit frère* Orlando from Simon's revenge."

"I invited him to join the Valerós domus," Taresa said.

"And I invited him to my household in Arles." Hélène had remained back, trading glances with Jean-Luc that Orlando couldn't interpret.

"You are kind," Orlando said. "I am grateful, but—"

"No," Jean-Luc said. "A dowager's house is not an appropriate choice for the son of Fabien of Troyes. He's a bannered knight."

"*Cossí vos disètz, senhór.*" Hélène answered his denouncement in the local tongue. She turned her attention—literally turning her back on the marquis—to Henri and Robi, who'd waited patiently, petting the two dogs. "You have no need to go to school now, Henri. I'll take you back to Toulouse on the way home."

Henri's eyes darted to Tomás and Chrétien. "*Merci,* madam. I'd appreciate that. I prefer a more civilized city than—" He swept a hand, encompassing the ruined walls behind the basilica.

"Let's see what Mme Agnes's cook has for dinner." Hélène tapped Henri's shoulder, so he'd follow her, then glimpsed Robi. "I suppose you can bring your friend."

Robi bowed low, his approximation of what a lady might be due. "*Mercés, ma dòmna.* But Lop wants to return to his sheep."

Robi walked away with Henri, in the direction of the *petit* well, and apparently then on to the city gate. Hélène said adieu and followed the boys, carelessly waving over her shoulder.

"Don't decide now," Jean-Luc said. "If you'll permit, Captain, I'll claim your oath until you know—"

"*Jhezu del tron!*" Taresa exclaimed. She burst past Tomás and Jean-Luc, bumping into Chrétien, then scrambling past him to dash into the shifting crowd of Templars and French knights leaving the basilica courtyard to tend to what Carcassona offered for their doss and refectory needs. She bashed into Templars and French knights in chainmail, who mistook her for a boy and shouted deprecations.

"*Bon sang, mon garçon!*"

"*Attention, sale chien!*"

Minor chaos followed Taresa, then parted to swarm around her when she flung herself on a tall, red-haired knight.

The captain of the Catalan army that Orlando had met in the hills beyond Mas-de-Cours.

"Is that Sebastián?" Jean-Luc was asking Tomás.

"*Òc.* He went to Rome with the Aragón ambassadors. I'm surprised he wasn't with you and the prelate."

"I joined the prelate in Montpelhièr," Jean-Luc said. "He has only a couple of the ambassadors in his entourage now." He paused. "The boy is tall for a grandson of Pèire Leteric."

"Plenty tall for a scion of those Beaurain bastards who—"

Jean-Luc waved Tomás for silence, a curt gesture. Orlando, confused, attempted to guess who Tomás meant. But Jean-Luc said, "All that's over, isn't it? Aren't the last of them in God's hands now?"

"If God has time to waste," Tomás said. He glanced around. "We need sleep, and we'd better reclaim our beds in the chateau before a pack of Templars usurps our doss."

"I should like to entertain you," Jean-Luc said, "to toast everyone's success. But this isn't my city. And I'm leaving for home in the morning."

"Stop in Toulouse, *bonfraire?*" Chrétien said. "We'll treat you. We expect to leave in the morning, too."

Tomás and Chrétien ambled off to the chateau. Karles had joined a knot of Aragón and Catalan knights, all drifting toward the knights' camp near the grand well. Taresa and her red-haired Catalan knight had disappeared, and Hélène and the boys had departed for Mme Agnes's villa. Jean-Luc had been trapped into a conversation with a knight who wore the Beaurain colors.

That would be the moment to drift away, find Midnight, and depart. But Jean-Luc laid a hand on his shoulder.

"I must thank Mme Marguerite for her brave help. Can you show me to her house?"

·

"What happened up on that wall?"

Jean-Luc sought to satisfy his curiosity as soon as he and Orlando were four paces from the crowd of French knights and Templars.

"Mme Hélène wanted revenge. Mme Taresa let her have an opportunity."

"Revenge? Because your cousin Badoyn was a toady of that pretentious fool, Giles de Nully?"

"No." Orlando had ten years to prepare for this moment, and hoped to manage it with something like courage. "Badoyn bragged to Hélène that he'd betrayed you in Constantinople. She wanted revenge for your sake."

"But all that is in the past. Does she intend—"

"Monsieur, she didn't want you to know what she did."

"I meant, does she intend revenge on you also?"

"Monsieur, I—"

"Your tattoo, Captain." Jean-Luc touched the place just above Orlando's ear. The Wheel and Serpent tattoo, the sign of evil that he continuously forgot he carried.

"Monsieur, I cannot describe the shame and guilt I've carried since that day. I cannot beg your forgiveness for—"

"For being betrayed and fooled by your own comrades?" Jean-Luc had a hand on Orlando's shoulder again. "It's in the past. And my comrades claim you as their little brother. And Mme Marguerite writes that you are the worthiest knight in city."

"Which isn't saying much." Orlando's voice sounded like the crunch of gravel as they walked through the city streets. He couldn't let go yet, of all the guilt that had choked him for so long.

"But you helped save the king of Aragón, Captain. What are you choosing for the future?"

"I'm not sure. Five years ago, my knights deserted me and stole my horses. And I've learned this week that my grandfather stole my father's honor and his wealth. Until now, my sole wishes have been to leave this place. And to be a bannered knight again."

"And now?"

"Right now, I have to be gone from the city, since the first time Simon sees me when he has a free moment, he'll hang me."

Jean-Luc said, "Come north with me. We'll ask Philippe to restore your place—and to reward you for what you've done for Pedro's heir."

"I washed the boy's cuts and bruises. Taught him to curry a horse. Let him keep a dog against all the city rules. I'm not a hero."

"That's far more than nothing. It's what your father did for my brother and me, when we were runts in the Outremer. It's how we knew Fabien was a hero."

·

The Noble King pressed his fingers in prayer.
'You risked all for your lord and comrades.
I name you Knight of the Realm
With lands, knights, and a banner.
May the great martyr, St-Denis,
bless all your doings, Sir Balthazar.'

"Monsieur, wake up. Your comrades are here, calling for you."

A sweet voice disturbed his dreams. Marguerite. He rubbed at his eyes. She'd fed them the night before at her private table—Orlando, Jean-Luc, and his white-haired friend Nunó. He and Marguerite had recounted the week's adventure and answered questions about life in Carcassona, while Jean-Luc and Nunó described meeting the prelate in Montpelhièr and traveling with his entourage. Jean-Luc told a long, long story about his years after Constantinople. There was a fire to defeat the chill of the mistral. There was wine. And long rounds of cheeses and sweets. When the compline bell rang, Orlando found that the energy he'd enjoyed in the morning, with evil scrubbed from his body, had gradually ebbed away. Jean-Luc and Nunó said goodbye, to claim their beds at the chateau, and Marguerite once more gave him the bench in her workroom as a bed.

"Orlando?"

When she called his name to wake him, he remembered why he wasn't in his bunk in the bachelors' tower. He remembered, too, that he was avoiding Simon. So as soon as he woke, he went looking for his boots, knowing he needed to leave the city before the prime bell.

But the bell that tolled when Marguerite called his name was the sext bell.

Already midmorning.

"Hola, little brother." Tomás sat on the bench where Orlando was pulling on his boots, shoving him over. But Chrétien sat on his other side, squeezing Orlando in the middle.

Jean-Luc settled into Marguerite's sewing chair, the leather creaking under his weight.

"Weren't you leaving for Toulouse this morning?" Orlando asked.

"We were delayed," Jean-Luc said. "Nunó called me into breakfast with the prelate and the vicomte."

"And we couldn't get the chandler's attention to give us trail provisions." You'd think Tomás would be complaining, but he seemed in a high, humorous mood.

"Did your fingers tingle, Captain?" Chrétien asked. "Isn't that what happens when people are talking about you?"

"Me? God's bones. Simon wants my hide."

"That may be," Jean-Luc said, "but the prelate wants your service for the next part of his journey."

"He has Templars and—"

"And a little boy king," Tomás said. "The prelate asked Jaume what he desired for the journey to Montpelhièr."

"And the boy asked for me?" Orlando felt an unexpected warmth, that Galahad would think of him. Meanwhile, Chrétien had gotten busy, lighting the charcoal in the brazier that had warmed the room the night before.

"He asked for you," Jean-Luc said, "after he first asked for his dog and his friend Perseus to come along."

"So I'm to go with the prelate? To care for two boys?" His first thought: poor Midnight. A long journey for an old horse.

"More than that," Jean-Luc said. "Pietro doubled down on who must travel with Jaume.

Tomás explained the source of his glee. "The prelate declared that all the boys from Fanjeau are going to Montpelhièr with Jaume. He wants their fathers to come explain why they collaborated in keeping the king of Aragón from his people."

"They need more than Karles to herd them, the way he did when he guarded the boys on the way here from Fanjeau. And Jaume wants his fight-master."

The hole that had drained his life for so long, gone now, seemed to be replaced by a pleasant, warm fire.

"So, if you're to be Jaume's guide and teacher," Chrétien said, "we want you to be our true brother, our *bonfraire*."

"If you agree," Jean-Luc said, "we shall remove any final traces of your former compromising comrades." He pointed again at the incriminating tattoo, the Wheel and Serpent, above Orlando's ear.

"Indeed," Chrétien said. "But I recommend growing out your hair again."

Orlando had gotten used to the sensation of being lost in every conversation with the two Catalan knights, and found himself lost again. Jean-Luc noticed his bewilderment and seemed to want to relieve him—before either Tomás or Chrétien could tease again.

"Our fathers and yours created a brotherhood of knights when they served in the Outremer. *La Confraria de la Crotz.* Tomás's father led it for a long time, but we are now mostly scattered to the wind."

"We call each other *bonfraires.* We want you with us, Orlando," Chrétien said. "You only have to swear what you already believe in. That is, I assume you aren't a heretic goodman who can't say an oath. Do you pray?"

"At every bell for the daily offices." As Orlando answered, he saw that he'd missed several bells and many prayers since Taresa had removed that evil spirit. But it wasn't loss of faith, just no time while striving to stay alive.

"Then place your hands on this cross," Tomás said, holding out his sword, "and repeat these words." As soon as Orlando touched the crosspiece of his sword, Tomás mixed Latin and Catalan, saying, "*Sodalitas, fidelitas, virtus.* Upon my honor, I swear absolute loyalty to my brothers when called to arms."

Orlando repeated the Latin and said the other words in French.

"There's more," Jean-Luc said. "Whoever might be your favored saint, swear on the name of Our Savior and the saint who guides you to stand by your lord and king. Swear to stand ready to serve as a defender of the poor and of all who love God."

Orlando repeated the words.

"And there's this." Chrétien grasped Orlando's right hand, pulling it away from Tomás's sword. He turned it over and—Orlando didn't see it coming—snatched an iron brand from the brazier and burned the back of his hand.

Orlando sucked air through his teeth. "I've felt worse, but—"

"That burned out any last hold the Wheel and Serpent might have on you," Tomás said.

"It burned out long ago." Orlando studied the burn: a perfect square. The brand Chrétien held was a crossbow bolt. All three men turned their wrists, showing that they shared a similar scar. Where had he seen it before? "Taresa." Orlando murmured her name. "She's one of you."

Jean-Luc grimaced. "It happens. I have a mother-in-law who calls herself a *bonfraire*. Our fathers initiated her in the Outremer."

"Have any of you changed your plans," Orlando asked, the smell of burning flesh still in the air, "and might instead be going to Montpelhièr with the prelate?"

All three men—his *bonfraires*—shook their heads.

Jean-Luc said, "You'll ride under Nunó, who is Jaume's closest relation and has good claim to be guardian, if not regent."

"Nunó, the man we drank with last night?"

"*Òc*," Tomás said, "the count of Roussillon."

Orlando had missed hearing Nunó's title in the introductions the night before.

Jean-Luc said, "I'm leaving four bachelor-knights with you. They're Pedro's men, marooned after the battle at Muret. They joined with me only to pursue justice for Pedro and Aragón. They're a band of *amis*, who understand how good companions form a *compagnie*. They have armor and horses, and a year's pay. And I'll leave you three horses. Do you need armor, too?"

"Monsieur, I cannot—"

"You cannot say no, little brother," Tomás said. He thumped Jean-Luc's knee. "And this *bonfraire* has more gold than he has worthy knights to spend it on."

"Besides," Chrétien said, "you earned it."

"When we see each other next season," Jean-Luc said, "after I've met with Philippe, we might discover that your father left all you need to support four knights under your banner."

"The prelate intends to leave on Monday morning," Tomás said. "He's only lingering long enough to rest horses and men."

"And to say Pentecost prayers in the basilica," Chrétien added.

"Can you be ready to depart by Monday?" Jean-Luc asked.

■

Because he once more needed to say goodbye—though this time he knew his destination—Orlando went to find Marguerite, who was seated on the portico, watching the boys run relays in the courtyard.

When Orlando appeared, the boys stopped running as if they'd heard a secret signal.

"*Hourra!*"

"*Vive notre capitaine!*"

"*A votre santé!*"

They lined up—whatever order they'd decided for themselves, but that seemed to give the oldest boys precedence—to take turns to shake his hand and briefly drop to one knee. The way that he'd taught them that *juvenes* must greet their bannered knight after a trial in the lists or at the end of battle.

When it was over, Orlando sat beside Marguerite on the portico.

"It's enough to make a grown man weep."

"They've been well-behaved all day," she said, "though impatient, with your sergeant gone, and Karles too. And you."

"Madam, I'm invited to leave on Monday, to accompany Galahad to Montpelhièr. It feels like—"

The bench shook. She had her hands over her eyes. "Karles told me. I am so happy for you," she said. "I shall be leaving Carcassona too. Jean-Luc asked me to go north with him."

"But—"

"When I heard what the prelate intends, I hoped that I'd be allowed to travel with the boys. But Karles says the Templars forbid unmarried women, even though I'm a widow who only seeks to care for those children."

"Madam? *Aiieee!*" Orlando jumped up. One of the boys missed his stop in the relay and skidded across the gravel courtyard. Orlando had him in hand, catching the boy before he slid farther, but not before a great deal of skin had been peeled from the boy's forearms.

Marguerite was there nearly as fast, and they quickly had the boy on the bench, where Marguerite washed the boy's scratches and applied an ointment. Orlando wrapped the wounds with strips of linen from her sewing basket, asking the boys to observe, to make sure they saw how to bind wounds properly. Then he set the injured boy to judge the relay while the others began sprinting between posts again.

He settled on the bench beside Marguerite, while at the same time feeling that he was diving in to deep water.

"Marry me, madam. Come along, so you and I can continue to work together, for the boys' sake. Even if you don't want—"

"Come along?" She brushed a stray lock from her forehead.

"As you said, you can't stay here. And the boys need you. And I…" He had no idea how to do this. "You're the handsomest woman I know. The kindest. You make peace where others provoke. You…"

Marguerite waited for Orlando to finish his thought, twisting a corner of that towel. She whispered, "I do want to come along, to restore the boy to Aragón. But there are so many years between us, monsieur. You should always be free to do as you wish. I don't want to trap you." After that torrent of words, Marguerite stopped, flushing red, embarrassed in a way he'd never seen her.

"Trapped? No, madam. I—" What had Louis said? *Un béguin. She's more than fond of you.* "We need to do the work that lies before us. We trust each other. And—" Was this how it was done? "And I love you."

"They will say the old woman bewitched the young knight."

"And I shall say," he kissed her, brushing his lips on the soft skin at the edge of her veil, "*C'est une affaire du coeur.*"

The way ahead had never seemed so clear to him before. Orlando wrapped both arms around her waist. He kissed her again.

"Monsieur. Captain."

"Orlando. Call me by my name, Marguerite."

She softened in his arms, like he'd never experienced with a woman. And she kissed him.

She tasted of spiced wine, her lips as warm as a Pays d'Òc summer's day, as soft as—nothing an impoverished knight was ever allowed to touch.

> *Mme Marguerite galloped astride an Arabian pony, her unbound hair streaming down her tapestry cloak, riding in the heat of day alongside a bannered knight. Like a scene from Arabian tales or from the poet of Troyes. Her face triumphant, like a queen.*

Not a vision of death. Marguerite was alive, at his side. The mistral had paused, so the only sound was her breath soft in his ear.

Also, the boys had stopped running and stood in a silent semi-circle at the edge of the portico, their faces bright. And curious.

33
Après le Mistral

SEBASTIÁN WOKE. THE SUN HIT his face, but something else had stirred him from sleep.

That infernal wind had stopped. The mistral.

It was past sunrise. There was dew, but it was drying rapidly because the sunshine was finally warm. There wasn't even the slightest breeze to dry sweat that came from earnest and prolonged effort.

He lay still, pinned in place by his wife, who'd thrown her thigh over his, moments before they both fell asleep, moments after the matins bell rang. The chanted psalms followed them into dreams.

Taresa smelled of spice, scents he hadn't known for—how long? Ten months? Cinnamon. Something like hay, but not like in a stable. It must be saffron, the flavor and color that he imagined when he lay in his bedroll at night, thinking of her before he drifted into dreams, missing her. Months of living as if his soul had been split in two and he couldn't find the other half.

They'd dragged a feather bed up into the old woman's attic where Taresa was living, so they could sleep under the stars—since the roof remained destroyed from when the French first came to Carcassona. With the mistral finally gone, what he smelled (besides his wife) was the city: too many horses, too many men. With so many visitors, the night-soil workers couldn't keep up. He schemed: how soon could they leave? To be on the trail to Valerós? Today? Or were they stuck in an overcrowded city until Monday?

Through the hole in the roof, now that the stars were gone, he caught the white flash of doves flying over. The cawk of a single crow with no friend answering.

The spiced and freckled goddess beside him stirred. She drew him closer with her crossed-over thigh.

"Sebastián? Are you real? I dream every night—"

Her breath poured over his neck, a balm like men of ancient times stole from the gods. Her hand on his jaw, she held his face and devoured him with kisses.

He couldn't ask, he couldn't say a word until she'd once more had her way with him. That's what she called it. Having her way.

When the sext bell rang, she released him.

"Hungry?" she said. She rose and groped for her clothes, which were the same filthy boy's rags he'd found her in. He had high hopes that he'd see her in better raiment before the day grew long. "I'm starving."

"I want to hear your story, Serena Taresa." He tugged her down beside him again. This time, he pinned her. He had a provoking wife. When she smiles upon you, a spirit rises within, to kneel before fire and beauty. To beg to serve. But then she's already turned away, saddling her own horse, carrying her own baggage, shifting barriers out of her own path—however much you might long to be her hero.

"Tell yours first, Sebastián. Why didn't you arrive with the prelate?"

"I left him at Montpelhièr, and went to our villa in Toulouse. There I learned that you'd left with the Valerós knights and were camping in the western hills, so I joined them, thinking I'd find you. When your message sent my knights to Narbonne yesterday, I came to Carcassona to find you. Now," he wrapped his arms around her, rolled them both over, "your story, cor dolç."

"There's all the time in the world, Sebastián. Especially if we're riding to Valerós. We can talk along the way."

He pressed her shoulders into the feather bed, nestled his leg between her thighs. "Before breakfast, you have to tell me one thing." He rubbed his cheek along hers, enjoying the sensation of softer flesh than he'd felt since leaving this world to live with celibate knights and randy ambassadors obsessed with their exotic mistresses.

"Fine. Only one thing. If I don't see an egg and toast soon, I'll dry up and blow away with the mistral."

"The mistral stopped. Can't you hear the silence, *kalila?*"

"Is that the one thing you want to ask before breakfast?"

"No."

Sebastián settled between her thighs. He was taller; she was only an average-sized southern woman. She was sturdy, and had magnificently soft breasts. His shoulders were broad, broader than when she'd last seen him—in fact, he needed new chainmail. The training he'd undertaken while traveling stretched him, and his mail was unforgiving.

"I want to know," he stroked her earlobe in the way he'd learned she loved, not long after they first met, "how it is," he traced her lips with his finger, finding that the calluses still made her shiver deliciously under him, "that you, *cor dolç,*" he called her sweetheart and folded his fingers with hers, as if in unholy prayer, noticing again the *bonfraire* burn on her wrist, "can pick me up and hold me over you, while I'm engaged in—"

She did it again, this time dropping him flat on his ass. On purpose.

Then she folded up to sit, leaning against his bare belly. She reached to stroke his face, then to twine her fingers in his hair.

"It's quite a long story," she said. "And it's all your fault, for sending me off to hunt snipe and cuckoos with your brother while you pranced off to Rome."

"You're about to demand breakfast before you'll tell me, aren't you?" He felt her head nod against his belly. "Will you at least give me a hint?"

"*Òc.* Did you ever hear of the fraternal order of the Wheel and Serpent?"

END

From Jean-Luc's Stories

An excerpt: *Bone-mend and Salt,*
Book 1 in the Accidental Heretics Series

"It's the Wild Man of the Wood"

"IT'S JACQUES THE GIANT!"

The children in the village outside Castell-de-Valerós called the man names, threw clods, and then ran away to hide, dodging behind trees. The huge, bearded man ignored their taunts and set up camp by a stream. The children crept back for another look.

He wasn't a real giant, just tall and strong, with ice-blue eyes like slices of the sky shining amid his stork's nest of beard and wild hair, both dark as charcoal from road dirt.

"Bon día, mon amics." The giant greeted them in the common tongue of the south, except he talked through his big broken nose.

He trapped a rabbit faster than any of their fathers could, and then he showed the boys how to tie knots for a trap like his and how to set the bait. He laid twigs to start his campfire in a peculiar way, but it flamed up instantly at his touch. He set his portable forge in the fire and used it to bake bread from dough that he'd set to rise in his pack.

A brave boy whose father was a bordonier, a freeholder who fought in the last crusade, asked, "Do you know magic, senhór?"

"I'm just a smith," he replied, shaking his big head. "But the fire-spirits and I have a special understanding."

The fire-spirits must not be kind, the boys decided, because an angry burn crawled up the giant's right arm. He shared his bread-cakes and told the boys about the Outremer, where Saracen servants fanned Frankish lords and served glorious food that Christians on this side of the Great Sea never dreamed of. While the rabbit crackled, roasting over the fire, the smith told bloody stories about the siege of Jaffa, when the Angevine King Richard and the Franks' King Philippe strove to reclaim Jerusalem.

The boys forgot their chores, so the girls tattled on them. Consequently, the Valerós marshal and parish priest came to greet the giant camped by the stream.

"I'm Father Anselm and this is Marshal Guillem. Valerós welcomes former crusaders needing work and shelter."

"I'm no crusader," said the giant. "My name is Jehan of Breton. I'm a smith who's lost his master."

The marshal frowned, his great moustaches twitching as if he smelled a falsehood.

"Our smith fell ill this past fortnight," the priest said. "You might be the answer to our prayers." The marshal stroked his moustache, seeming to think as the smith did: the big man had never been the answer to anyone's prayers.

·

On Easter Monday, the man who claimed to be Jehan of Breton crawled up to the loft over the castle's smithy forge, dragging the new blanket and clean straw ticking the marshal had given him.

However, once alone, he was the spy Jean-Luc who served Viscount Gerard de Chartrain from the Pays de France. He probed the corners of the loft, which smelled of mice. He tried to open the hatch under the eaves. Nothing could get in without coming up the loft ladder, so he lay down, too tired to sweep out the corners.

This high in the Pyrenees foothills, the nights were still bone-freezing cold and heat from the forge dissipated quickly. Jean-Luc felt grateful for vermin-free straw and a wool blanket, because old injuries pained him. Each time he rubbed the gnarled tissue on his arm and the long scar on his thigh, a host of memories sprang free. He fingered the boar's-tooth charm on the string around his neck and stared up at the rafters, because if he closed his eyes, he'd once more see that church in Constantinople, where an icon of a sad-eyed Madonna fell into his lap from the hands of a dead man. His night terrors started there, back when he'd been a knight of the Cross with a real name. When he was a soldier, not an itinerant smith who spied for a French lord, to learn how things stood with certain seigneurs amid the chaos in the Languedoc.

At dawn, he stoked the forge fire so it would blaze hot when he returned from matins. Then, as Jehan the smith, he knelt in the chilly stone chapel to pray amid strangers. He prayed that he might finish his business here by Pentecost, as his lord required, and then that he might resume searching for a man—any man—who would swear to the truth and redeem Jean-Luc's name and honor.

The marshal knelt beside him, his elbow prodding the smith when he folded his hands. The nudge left Jean-Luc aware that this castle housed an inordinate number of battle-tested crusaders, and likely each of them lay awake at night nursing wounds and regrets and betrayals.

Pray for us, O Holy Mother of God, that we may be made worthy.

END PREVIEW • ACCIDENTAL HERETICS

Read all the tales of Jean-Luc's and Tomás's adventures.

Accidental Heretics Series: Lost in the Languedoc Crusade
Book 1: *Bone-mend and Salt*
Book 2: *Trebuchets in the Garden*
Book 3: *Crux Lunata*
Book 4: *Song of Valerós*
The Mad Woman of La Catalane: A Novella
www.eastewartauthor.com

Carcassona, 1214 — A Map

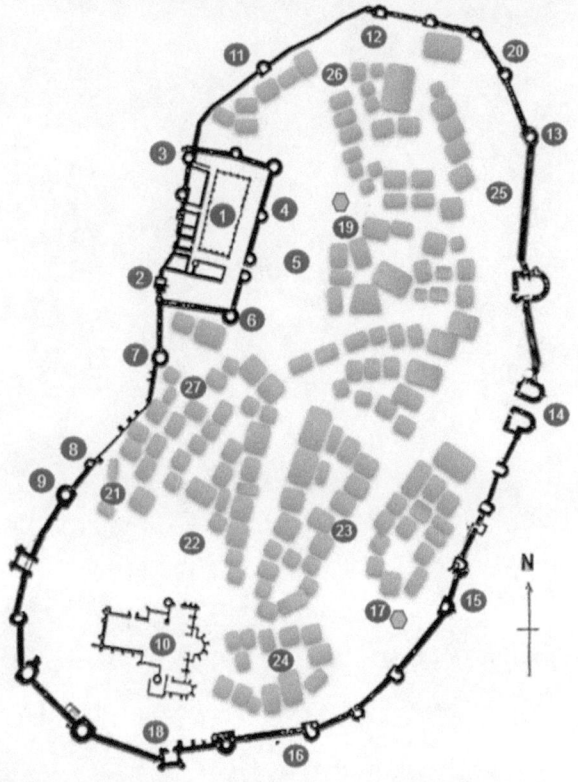

1. Vicomte's chateau
2. Watchtower
3. Chapel tower
4. Barracks
5. Courtyard (barbican: ~1240)
6. St-Paul's tower
7. River gate (Aude gate)
8. Roman tower (Visigoth tower)
9. Young squires' school
   (later, Inquisitors' tower)
10. Basilica St-Nazaire
11. Carpenters' tower
12. Vicomte's mill tower
13. City mill tower

14. Narbonne gate
15. Battered tower
16. Prison tower
17. *Petit* well
18. Church mill tower
19. Grand well
20. Smithy
21. Louis's villa
22. Orlando's school
23. Mme Agnes's villa
24. Church ovens
25. City ovens
26. Visitor hostel
27. Common stables

Place Names

Valerós and Montcava exist within the world of the Accidental Heretics and in these Legends, but nowhere else.

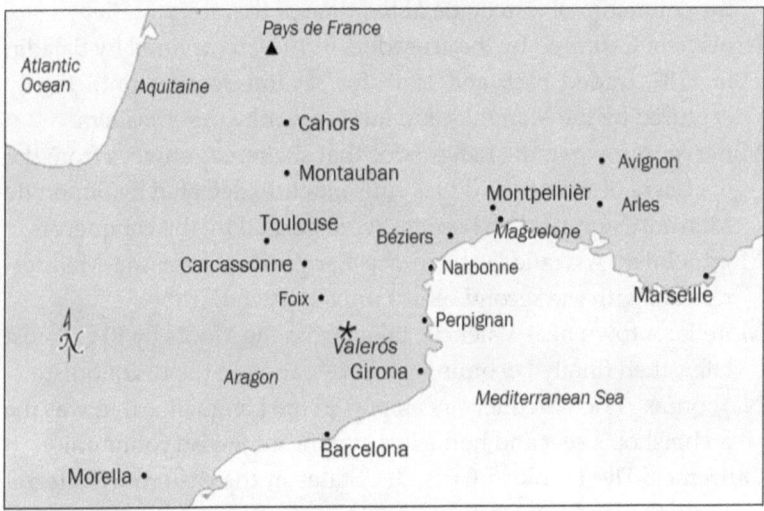

Acre: A city on Haifa Bay in the Outremer, now part of Israel. At the time of this story, it served as the capital of what was left of the Kingdom of Jerusalem.

Aragón: A union of the Kingdom of Aragón and the County of Barcelona, which established the dynastic Crown of Aragón under Jaume I, *El Conqueridor*, with tributaries across the Languedoc.

Barcelona: A territory on the Mediterranean, now approximately the political entity of Catalonia, for which Pedro II held the title Count of Barcelona.

Cahors: A town in the Occitanie region, north of Toulouse and on the connecting route to Paris.

Carcassona: A fortified city in the Languedoc, which surrendered to the French crusaders in 1209.

Constantinople: Capital of the Eastern Roman Empire, sacked in the Fourth Crusade, becoming the seat of Norman rulers for the next fifty years.

Cyprus: An island in the Mediterranean, south of Turkey and north of Cairo. During the Third Crusade, its Muslim rulers were conquered by Richard Lionheart who sold it to the Knights Templar, who in turn sold it to Guy de Lusignan.

Girona: An ancient city in the northeast corner of Catalunya; part of the countship of Barcelona at the time of this story.

Jerusalem: Captured by the crusaders in 1099, recaptured by Saladin in 1187, traded back and forth for several decades until finally captured by the Mamluks and lost forever by the crusaders.

Minerve: A town in the Languedoc that sheltered refugees from the massacre of Béziers and was subsequently defeated by Simon de Montfort, and its own heretics were burned by the conquerors.

Montpelhièr: A walled city in the Languedoc, near the Mediterranean, with the second oldest university in Europe.

Morella: A town near Valencia, taken from the Moors by El Cid, lost later, then finally becoming part of Aragón in the Reconquista.

Narbonne: A rich Mediterranean port in the Languedoc that was the archbishop's seat and home to a significant Jewish community.

Outremer: The Frankish Crusader States in the eastern Mediterranean; the land overseas.

Pays de France: The original royal demesne of the Capetian kings, adjacent to Paris. A larger area was designated the Île-de-France in the Renaissance.

Pays d'Òc: The Languedoc.

Provence: A county on the Mediterranean, ruled by the counts of Barcelona; governed by Pedro's brother Alfonso at this time.

Roussillon: A region in the southeastern Pyrenees and foothills.

Toulouse: A county in the Languedoc, whose count owed allegiance to the king of France at the time of this story. The city, on a major trade route between the Mediterranean and central France, was a bishop's seat.

Troyes: The capital of the counts of Champagne and an important trading town on the Seine river, southeast of Paris.

Urgell: A county in Catalan-speaking lands between the Pyrenees and Lleida.

Glossary

A – C

Angevines: The Plantagenet dynasty that ruled from Ireland to the Pyrenees. The Angevine empire grew through the marriage of Henry II and Eleanor of Aquitaine.

armiger: A servant who manages a knight's armor.

arrèsta; arrête: Stop.

avec moi: With me.

aventail: A chainmail curtain to cover the neck and shoulders.

baquelar: Villainous rogue.

Beau, fidèle et intrépide: Beautiful, loyal and fearless.

béguin: A crush.

beneeixi: A blessing.

bon amic: Good friend, or boyfriend.

bon dia: Good day.

bonfraires: A brotherhood.

bonhommes: The so-called Cathar community's term for itself; Good Christians.

bon sang: Damn it.

booty: Treasure; during the crusades, the primary way crusaders financed their armies or to pay their mercenaries. That is, rather than "looting" as we now think of booty, these cultures considered booty as legitimate plunder. ("To the victor go the spoils.")

bouge, fils de pute! Move, you son of a bitch.

bricon: Scoundrel.

bruixa; bruja: Witch.

capitani mèstre: Master captain.

Catalan: In the Middle Ages, a language, not a political entity.

ça va faire! It will do.

cavaller: Cavalier, knight.

c'est quoi ça: What's that?

chère fille: Dear girl.

comment ça va: How is it going?

cossí vos disètz: If you say so.

D – L

denier: A medieval coin; a silver penny in English.

Devoir! Dieu! Fidélité! Duty, God, fidelity.

domus: Household, meaning the larger economic household of a titled landholder in the Pays d'Òc.

don: A courtesy title for a gentleman from the landed classes.

donzel: A young gentleman, in training for knighthood.

doux cheval: Sweet horse.

estàs bé: How are you?

fadrin: A lad, a term of endearment.

fiefs *d'argent:* Money fiefs.

fraire pichon: Little brother.

Franks: At the time of this story, a reference to western European people.

fustian: A heavy cotton fabric.

gardes du corps: In this story, the city's guards (not knights).

goodmen, goodwomen: A reference to the people whom the Church called heretics; now commonly called Cathars.

gojat: Boy.

gos: Dog.

gràcies: Thank you.

holá: Hello.

homme célibataire: A celibate man.

hourra: Hooray!

Je suis désolé: I'm sorry.

jeune homme: Young man.

Jhezu del tron: Jesus in heaven.

jongleurs: Medieval minstrels who sang the troubadours' songs.

juvenes: Young knights in service; Orlando's complimentary term for his students.

Knights Templar: A monastic crusader military order, the most elite of the crusader armies.

lo mieu aimat capitani: My dear captain.

M – R

ma dòmna: My lady.

mains froides, coeur chaud: Cold hands, warm heart.

marquis, marquesa: A lord (and his wife) whose land is on a frontier border, and so must be a capable defender.

maudit chien: Damn dog.

mercé, mercés, merci: Thank you.

misericòrdia: Mercy.

mon amics: My friends.

Monsenyor: An honorific, such as for a king or a bishop.

Moors: People from northern Africa who settled on the Iberian peninsula under Muslim leadership. Colloquially at the time of this story, a person of mixed heritage or dark complexion.

Normans: Descendants of the Viking Northmen who settled Normandy, and later invaded Britain and also conquered the Muslims in Sicily in the eleventh century.

òc: Yes.

Outremer: The lands across the Great Sea, where the Crusader States were founded and other territory seized by Christian invaders.

papillon: Butterfly.

paratge: A world view from the time of the troubadours, with multiple connotations about honor, civility, nobility, grace, and tolerance, defining a culture's view of "right living."

Par tous les Saints dans le ciel! By all the saints in heaven.

paysans: Peasants.

peccador: Sinner.

pell: A wooden practice sword.

petit déjeuner: Breakfast.

poulain: A foal; colloquially, the offspring of a crusader and a local in the Outremer.

punxor: Prick.

pute: Prostitute.

que dieu vous bénisse: God bless you (a response to a sneeze).

qu'elles durent toujours: And all your lovers (a conclusion to blessing a series of sneezes).

qu'est-ce que c'est: What is it?

qui est un bon garçon: Who's a good boy?

qui s'ho creu: Who knew?

S – Z

salaud arrogant.: Arrogant bastard.

Saracen: Colloquial term used in Europe for Muslims.

se vos plai; si us plau; s'il vous plaît: If you please.

seigneur: A man of rank who rules lands and a household.

senhór, senhóra: Titles of respect, equivalent to señor, señora.

Sodalitas, fidelitas, virtus: Latin motto of the *bonfraires*: fraternity, fidelity, virtue.

sommetier: Sumpter; a pack animal.

sou: A French coin.

squire: In the Pays d'Òc, a fighter of rank between knights and foot soldiers, for his lifetime. In the French system, squires rose to become knights.

surcoat: A long coat worn over other clothes or armor.

tor de l'escòla: School tower.

trouvère: A singer; compare *jongleur*.

vés amb compte: Be careful.

vicomte; viscount: A European noble rank, above a baron, below a marquis.

viens, mon chien! Come, dog.

woad: A plant used to create a blue dye similar to New World indigo; grown as a cash crop around Toulouse.

About the Author

E.A. STEWART is an American writer whose *Legends of Valeros* and *Accidental Heretics* series explore intrigues in France and Spain in the early thirteenth century.

Ms. Stewart lives and writes in Seattle.

To learn more about
the Accidental Heretics series, visit:
www.eastewartauthor.com

Acknowledgments

Thanks to Ajax Bell, Elizabeth Bjorkman, Jacyn Stewart, Susan Urban, and Laurie Cropp for critical and editorial reading. And thanks to Waverly Fitzgerald for Mondays and Thursdays at Liberty Bar on Fifteenth Avenue East.

Notes from the Author: A few named characters in this story can be found in historic chronicles. The prelate Pietro di Benevento did come to the Languedoc in May or June of 1214 and took possession of the boy who came to be known as James I the Conqueror, king of Aragón. In September 1213, Pedro II of Aragón did die in battle at Muret, near Toulouse. Simon de Montfort, the viscount of Carcassonne, did hold the young king of Aragón until the prelate arrived, but there isn't a historic record that indicated he perpetrated a conspiracy like the one described in this story.

Now, my other notes rise from questions asked by the critical readers described above. First: Renard's black snout. My research found medieval illustrations of greyhounds described as "red fallow with a black muzzle." Bones found (in Scotland) seem to show skulls larger than modern greyhounds, and other texts describe a range in size of greyhounds, up to the size of an Irish wolfhound. Other notes indicate that in what we now call France, a greyhound might be worth more than a serf.

The map that sketches Carcassonne is loosely derived from a drawing from *The City of Carcassonne* by Eugène Viollet-le-Duc, who "renovated Carcassonne in the nineteenth century. In 1214, however, the second curtain wall did not exist, and the other thirteenth century repairs and additions had not yet begun. Items numbers 20–27 on the map in this book are invention and conjecture.

The descriptions of how the French conquerors interacted with the former residents are purely my invention.

The songs Orlando uses to teach boys and console himself area free-range transliterations of medieval songs. If you'd like to sample some of Chrétien of Troyes Arthurian romances, in reasonable translation, see The Project Gutenberg eBook of Four Arthurian Romances at https://www.gutenberg.org/files/831/831-h/831-h.htm.

Learn more about the Languedoc crusade at:

http://eastewartauthor.com/heretics-notes

From Jugum Press

HISTORICAL AND CONTEMPORARY FICTION

Nzinga, African Warrior Queen by Moses L. Howard

Nzinga is a brilliant leader during a time of violent upheaval. This fictional biography brings to life the 17th century flourishing African kingdom, now lost, where early explorers' maps of West Africa call out: "Here reigned the celebrated Queen Nzinga!"

No One Dies by Annie Pearson

Near Cambridge, 1685, the once noble Foxe family undertakes genteel highway robbery to survive. They observe strict principles and take only from cheats and thieves who robbed their villages. A risky heist might save them—if they can hold to their #1 rule: No One Dies. Book 1 of the Restoration Rules series.

This Charming Man by Ajax Bell

A chance encounter with an intriguing older man inspires Steven Frazier with visions of a more rewarding life. A vibrant snapshot of Seattle in the early 1990s, this story captures the drama of coming into one's own as an adult.

A Summer in Peach Creek by Michele Malo

Teenaged Faith travels to Peach Creek, West Virginia for a visit with relatives in 1932. When a scandalous murder occurs, Faith discovers the corrupt underbelly of Logan County. As summer progresses and peaches grow, Faith finds her own moral center.

PERSONAL VOICES IN HISTORY SERIES

Journey into Gold Country: Memories of a Forty-Niner
by Ralph Buckingham; foreword by Charles Barker

The California Gold Rush, remembered sixty years later by a New England younger son who went to seek his fortune.

We Were Walimu Once and Young, edited by Brooks E. Goddard

True stories from the Teachers for East Africa and Teacher Education for East Africa experience in the 1960s.

Find print and ebook editions:
www.jugumpress.net

* 9 7 8 1 9 3 9 4 2 3 8 9 4 *